MARGARET BALL
FLAMEWEAVER

BAEN
FANTASY

FLAMEWEAVER

Copyright © 1991 by Margaret Ball

A Baen Books Original.
Baen Publishing Enterprises
P.O. Box 1403
Riverdale, N.Y. 10471

ISBN: 0-671-72095-3

Cover art by Stephen Hickman

First printing, December 1991

Distributed by
SIMON & SCHUSTER
1230 Avenue of the Americas
New York, N.Y. 10020

Printed in the United States of America

BEGINNER'S GENIUS

The air seemed to quiver around me and I stopped with my mouth open, on a rising note that had nowhere to go. Tamai had always stopped me before I reached the end of this section, and she had never taught me the next verses. Now she prompted me, one word at a time, lips moving in unison with mine.

It was the chant Nirmali had used to shape the overworld, repeated and magnified in my voice and the myriad voices of the spirits she called, and as the words echoed around me the toy soldier on Gordon's desk seemed to quiver and break apart into many thousands of pieces. Each of those tiny red or blue painted pieces took into itself one singing voice and grew again to the size of the original toy, then taller, larger, until an army of six-foot soldiers in the red coats of the Royal Lancasters marched across Gordon's desk and vanished through the walls of his study.

I came, unprompted, to the last dying lines of the chant and let my voice fall to a whisper as the soldiers disappeared from view. Tamai had no need to tell me the words now; there was only one way for the song to end, unraveling the shapes of illusion that had been woven together in the opening lines.

Tamai's eyes shone with unshed tears, and I had no need to ask if she had shared my vision.

"You will be greater than I," she whispered. "You will take my knowledge and weave your own vision of the world. I hope—oh, I hope I have done right!"

So do I. This new power, even if it is only the gift to raise illusions, confuses and frightens me.

Tomorrow I will try it again.

CHAPTER ONE

Three of the walls were of cedar, as were the four pillars that surrounded her. The rafters were piled high with fresh-cut branches, and a small fire of cedar bark burned behind her. On either side of the fire, where she could not see their faces, stood the pillars dedicated to Kshumai of the herds and Lunang of the running waters. To right and left, Dizane of the wheat field and Nirmali of women in childbirth smiled down at her from their carved pillars studded with raw turquoise and banded with gold wires. Tamai did not expect any aid from Nirmali, but she did look at Dizane's pillar. The patterns incised in the dark wood symbolized the circle of the year. The leaning spikes for the time of field-in-grain flowed into the broken lines of sickles-reaping, crumbled to emptiness for the cold time of ashes-sitting, then rose again in regular curves of field-in-seed and straightened to become field-in-grain again, line upon line without end. Her eyes rested in the endless circle and she drew strength from Dizane's goodness, and the walnut shell that was her present task lay forgotten before her.

"Attention, Tamai." A husky voice broke the flow of the circle and reminded Tamai of the task she had been given. It was the Dhi Lawan, head of the Council. She

1

sat with five other Council members by the smoky cedar
fire at the back of the room. Tamai could feel their eyes
on her, some curious, some openly hostile. Kazhirbri, she
knew, was against her; Sunik, who alone had spoken for
Tamai's right to a formal test, would be praying now for
her friend's success; the other three wisewomen would
be neutral at best. And the Dhi Lawan? Tamai could
envision her face without turning: ancient skin weathered
by season after season of breathing cedar smoke for
visions, eyes like chips of the dark jade called night-
without-moon, bright and impenetrable. The Dhi Lawan
had cast her vote with Sunik's for a formal test, but it
might be she only wished to settle the question of
Tamai's supposed power. She had said more than once
that it was difficult to have one in the city who carried
so much potential power and yet had so little chance of
using it. If Tamai failed this test, would she be exiled?
Tamai's stomach contracted into a cold, hard knot at the
thought of life outside Gandhara.

"She can't do it," whispered an ancient, dry voice
behind her. "I told my sisters this was folly. Why must
we—"

The malicious rustling whisper broke off suddenly, and
Tamai smiled to herself at the thought of Dhi Lawan
turning those bright, dark eyes to silence a wisewoman
of Council like a giggling schoolgirl. With the moment's
amusement, the cold knot of fear that held her thawed
somewhat, and she was able to send her spirit forward
from her kneeling body, searching for the tendrils of life
that would enable her to weave a green growing tree
from an empty walnut shell.

She felt nothing—nothing. It might have been a rock
or a clod of earth that lay on the cedar floor before her.
The blue smoke of the fire eddied and swirled round her
head and the chattering of mountain sprites filled her
ears. Tamai shook her head to still the sprites' voices.

"Do you resign?" That, Tamai knew, was Kazhirbri,
her own great-aunt, and the one member of Council who
had most strongly opposed this test.

"I do not," she replied without looking round.

"Then don't move! Is this the dancing floor?"

Tamai swallowed the words of defense that rose to her lips. Most likely Kazhirbri would not believe Tamai had heard sprites whose voices were inaudible to a wise-woman. And in any case, a mistress of the Disciplines was expected to be able to put aside minor distractions. The voices of the sprites were no excuse for failing the simple little test that had been set before her.

But for all that, Tamai thought as she sought in vain for a seeming of life within the withered shell, it was not a fair test. The young mothers who were being trained in the Disciplines might make illusions of walnut trees heavy with nuts to tempt those without power into picking the nuts and breaking the harvest laws, but they played that game in the fall, with a fresh ripe nut to work from, and they raised images of things in their season. Now it was the time of field-in-seed, and the shell before her had forgotten its nature in the long months of winter, and in any case it would resist being shaped into a harvest-ripe tree out of its proper season.

Her knees ached with kneeling so long in one position on the hard floor, and the back of her neck ached with tension. She dared not look at Dizane's pillar again for fear of being caught in the eternal circle, and she had been warned against looking out the open side of the house where the cliffs fell away and offered a vista of infinite space. When a wisewoman sent her spirit outside the body, it was important to keep the eyes of the body firmly fixed on the place where she worked her magic; otherwise the spirit might become confused and wander forever in the empty air. The open side of the testing house was a deliberate temptation that candidates were supposed to overcome. Tamai in particular, lacking the bonds to earth that gave most wisewomen their full power, was supposed to be especially at risk of losing herself in that bright emptiness.

Small chance of that, Tamai thought, *when I can't even send my spirit two handspans away to raise up this dead seed!* She raised her head and stared out into space, sky and clouds and the distant hint of snow-covered peaks, and for a moment imagined that she could taste the freedom of a bird in flight.

"She looked up!" Kazhirbri announced. Too late Tamai recognized that by looking away from the walnut shell for a third time she had admitted her inability to animate it.

"Child, do you resign?" Dhi Lawan sounded weary and very, very old.

"Yes—no—I *can* do it," Tamai said desperately. "Let me try once more. . . ." She could feel the power within her, heavy as a damned-up lake with no outlet, craving to be released on some object. She had the power. She had been taught the forms of the Disciplines. But at twenty-six, with half her life behind her, she still could not control her magic in the strict forms required by the Council. Tamai sat back on her heels and let out a brief frustrated sigh. For all her sense of power unused and frustrated, her lifetime of flashes and glimpses of things hovering just out of control, she could not do this one simple task to order. She was just an oddity, a barren woman surrounded by flashes of fire and the chattering of mountain sprites and the sense of flight and a dozen other petty, useless gifts that came and went without her conscious control. Join the Council? She would be lucky if they allowed her to remain in the City.

Again the cold knot of fear clenched in her stomach, this time to be dispelled by anger as, in a scornful parting gesture, one of the wisewomen behind her turned the floor and the walls and the carved pillars of the goddesses into a living grove of cedar trees. Tamai knelt on the intertwined roots of the trees, saw the walls of the testing house as a receding vista of dark trunks, felt the breeze overhead moving through layers of green needles. Nirmali's pillar was a tree ripe with tart blue-green berries; Dizane's, a slender fan of branches swaying in the illusory breeze. Everything was real, save that no sunlight came through the branches overhead. The clearing glowed with the pale clear light of magic, without source, casting no shadow.

No sun, Tamai thought. *Then this is Kazhirbri's work. She never could lightweave. That's why she will never be the Dhi Lawan.* The head of Council gave up her birth name and her coming-of-age name when she assumed the leadership of the City, and henceforth was known only as Dhi Lawan—Daughter of Light—in token of her supposed closeness to Nirmali the Maker, who rode the sky with the sun in one hand and the moon in the other. Before all else, the Dhi Lawan had to be a mistress of lightweaving, the last and most difficult of the Disciplines. There had been a time when everyone predicted that Tamai's inborn power would make her a Dhi Lawan some day. Before—

Tamai shook her head to cast out memory, and with the gesture, the illusory grove melted. The testing house was as it had been, an empty room of red cedar and blue smoke and carved pillars, looking out onto infinite space. The wisewomen were folding their cloaks of power and preparing to climb down the ladder at the back of the room. Kazhirbri was complaining, just audibly, that Tamai's untrained, unusable power was a danger to them all—"Did you see how she made my cedar grove vanish? Spoilt in herself, she spoils others' work as well."

Tamai blinked back tears and stayed where she was, staring out into the space that overhung the cliffs, while the wisewomen made their way down to the path. They all knew she had failed; there was no point in joining them now only to hear the words. Kazhirbri's triumph at being proved right would be hard to face, but worse would be gentle Sunik's disappointment. Sunik had been like an elder sister in the years after Tamai's own family was lost in the KamKhel raid, a sister and a beloved friend who did not forget Tamai even after three children and Council duties filled her days. Sunik had wished so greatly for Tamai to prove her right to full Gandharan citizenship, so that they could be together now as they had been in childhood. They would have done better to leave the matter untested. Her best hope now was that if she stayed out of the Council's way for a while they would forget to exile her, or would decide that her little untrained power was not such a problem for the City as Kazhirbri insisted. She would be quiet and inconspicuous—and she would definitely *not* allow her spirit to go wandering again, listening to the mountain sprites and playing with stray beams of light and otherwise making trouble for her!

Tamai scowled at the empty walnut shell as she made this last vow. The shell promptly burst into flame.

Mirjan sighed in relief as the Dhi Lawan set her feet on the ladder. The testing must be over. He wouldn't have to interrupt the wisewomen at their work.

"Dhi Lawan. Councilwomen." He began speaking before the Dhi Lawan had reached the ground, while the others were still on the ladder. As they came down to the narrow path, he had to back up while he was talking; there wasn't room between cliff face and sheer drop for two people to stand side by side. "There's a foreigner coming up through the river valley."

"South? Through the KamKhel tribal lands?"

Mirjan nodded, accepting the Dhi Lawan's surprise, but sure of what he had observed. Few came that way to trouble the boundaries of Gandhara; if the Chitrali slave traders didn't stop them, the KamKhels and the other hill tribes with their perpetual small wars were enough of a deterrent to casual travellers. Most of their troubles came from the north—especially lately. But Mirjan could report that he had seen the man himself—no KamKhel, and certainly not a Gandharan—making his way from boulder to boulder across the river, stopping from time to time to scratch charms on a piece of white bark or to consult a small glittering demon that he kept in the folds of his clothes.

"So I thought—since I knew you were testing Tamai today, and it might take too long to bring anybody from the City—" Mirjan stopped and cursed his unlucky tongue as Tamai slowly came down the ladder from the testing house. One didn't have to be a wisewoman to see that she had failed. Her shoulders slumped under her wide tunic. Even the ends of her long black braids and the embroidered fringe of her sash seemed to sag in defeat. Mirjan hated to see her like this, and she would hate to see him at this time. Even more, when she heard his other news. Well, perhaps that could be delayed until she had returned to the City.

"You did well," the Dhi Lawan commended him. "My sisters and I will see to this matter at once. Mirjan, you and Tamai will guard us while we work."

So much for avoiding Tamai. Mirjan leaned into the cliff face to let the wisewomen pass, then fell into line behind them. "I'm sorry," he murmured over his shoulder to Tamai.

"You didn't even ask how I did," Tamai observed. "Were you so sure I would fail?"

Actually, he had been. He hadn't lived five years with Tamai without knowing the bounds and the frustration of her untamed power. But this didn't seem like a good time to say so.

"Never mind." Tamai sounded more resigned than bitter. "You were right to leave me, Mirjan. I'll never pass the tests and take my mother's place in Council. The KamKhels saw to that, even if they didn't know what they were doing."

"I didn't leave because you were barren, Tamai. That is not important to me. I do not require a wife who will become a wisewoman. All I wanted was a little peace in our house." It hadn't been the fires so much, or the things flying from high poles and breaking, or the fact that half the time Tamai seemed to be listening to voices no one else could hear. It had been her bitterness that drove him away—the anger and self-hatred that colored everything she said or did.

"Mirjan," Kazhirbri called back to him, "what of your woman?"

And so much for putting off the telling of that news.

One did not lie to or evade a wisewoman's direct question.

"The Lady of sun and moon smiles on us," Mirjan replied. "Chakani is with child."

"How fortunate," said Tamai behind him, "that even you, who do not require a wisewoman to wife, shall be blessed with one anyway."

After that, it was rather a relief to reach the rocky part of the trail where both Mirjan and Tamai had to use all their strength to help the older wisewomen up the last ridge that marked the southern boundary of Gandhara.

The foreigner was still there, resting on the near side of the river. Bareheaded, dressed in strange clinging garments, weighted down by a heavy pack, he seemed a small enough threat. But it was enough, and more than enough, that he had crossed the river. Even the Kam-Khels did not venture so close.

"He *could* be a peddler," Mirjan said doubtfully.

"With that hair?" Tamai scoffed. The foreigner's head shone like polished brass. "He looks like those men of the north who keep sneaking around our pasturelands. Probably he is one of them, only he thought to be very clever and surprise us by coming around this way. Dhi Lawan, Mirjan had no need to trouble you for this small matter. I can put an arrow through him from here."

"Child, we do not kill needlessly," the Dhi Lawan reproved her. "Wait till he rises to resume his journey. We can deal with him then."

"No true wisewomen would speak so lightly of killing," Kazhirbri remarked to the open sky.

"I didn't say I would put an arrow through anything important—I just wanted to discourage him," Tamai argued halfheartedly.

Mirjan thought he understood how she felt. Having just failed in her first formal test of the Disciplines, she wanted to show that she could do something well. And she could. She was a better shot with bow or jezail than any man in her age group, she could outdance any of them in the chakri circle, she could hunt as quietly as the shadows from which she took her name. And none of this would help her if she picked a fight with the Dhi Lawan and five Council members at once. *Tamai, dear Tamai,* he thought, *can't you see that now is not the time for this argument?* He felt angry and frustrated and sorry for her all at once—just as he'd felt during the five years of their fruitless marriage. Which was, after all, why he'd left her.

"Hush!" The foreigner was standing. Mirjan averted his eyes as the wisewomen covered themselves with their black ceremonial cloaks. He stared out across the river so that he wouldn't accidentally see the bright embroidered patterns that covered the secret undersides of the cloaks; a casual glimpse might do no harm, but there was no point in taking the risk of offending Nirmali or Dizane by looking too closely at women's secrets.

He saw a faint hint of movement, a trembling of green leaves among the bushes on the far side of the river. The KamKhels must have tracked the man this far; he was lucky to have got across the river, where they dared not follow. But it made his very presence there a greater threat than ever, regardless of what the man himself meant. If the KamKhels saw that a foreigner could cross the river with impunity, they would soon test the boundaries of Gandhara for themselves, raiding and stealing children as they'd done before the last Dhi Lawan gave her life to burn them back to their tribal lands.

Beside him, Tamai was all tense impatience, fingers on her quiver, taut as a stretched bowstring. The wisewomen sat perfectly still while they sent their spirits ahead to confuse the intruder. Far below, the air of the valley shimmered with power, danced and stretched and sent the sunlight gliding at sharp impossible angles around the foreigner's head. Mirjan himself felt ill, looking down at a valley that was suddenly distorted as if by the glare of bright sun, with rocks and earth and clouds tilting awry.

If the sight of the Veil working at a distance did this to him, what must it be doing to the intruder? Mirjan imagined a world where the vertical cliff of sheared rock looked like level ground under his feet, where the true ground felt as if it were twisting to throw him off into emptiness. And he knew what caused these changes, knew them for illusion. This foreigner should be confused now, unable to see the way that had been so clear before him a moment ago.

Mirjan saw the foreigner's shining yellow head dimly, through a maze of tortured air and distorted light. The man stopped, turned, shook his head, and pulled out the small glittering demon he had consulted before. He stared at it and then, incredibly, moved forward into Gandharan land again. Mirjan drew in his breath with a sharp gasp of surprise.

A rustling sigh passed through the wisewomen as though they were one body taking one breath. If they had been still before, they were stones now. Ice formed on the slopes beneath the foreigner's feet, and a wind came shrieking out of the hills and howled around his ears. He slipped, dropped his demon, stumbled a few paces in a half-circle. Mirjan could only imagine what he must be feeling: the dizzy sense that the flat river bank had turned into a cliff to throw him out, the fear that the wheeling land would open up and crush him, the ice crystals sparkling in a cloud before his eyes to shut out the sun—all his senses battering at him together, until all he could want was to escape the place where such things happened to him.

Now he had stumbled into the river, and the wise-woman let their spells recede a little—just enough to let him glimpse the far shore, where the KamKhels waited behind the bushes. On that side of the river all was peace and sanity; on this side, the mists and the sparkling snow and the tilting, whirling, opening land all assaulted the man's senses. He moved as if drunk or demon-ridden, stumbling through the shallow water; he wanted to get

away now, but he was too confused to make a straight
path through the river.

It seemed to Mirjan that the foreigner's staggering
flight away from the Veil of Gandhara lasted for an eternity of splashing and staggering through the river ford.
He was almost at the far shore when he slipped on a wet
stone and went down heavily, with no effort to save himself, and knocked his head on another stone. He fell
limply half in and half out of the water. Mirjan strained
to see if the stranger's mouth was out of the water, but
he didn't have time to tell. The KamKhels slipped out
of the bushes, lithe dark men in dirty woolen robes. They
clustered around the foreigner, blocking Mirjan's view.
Knives flashed; the shallow river water took on a red
tinge.

"A wisewoman does not speak lightly of killing," Tamai
quoted under her breath.

"We did not kill him." Kazhirbri sounded righteous as
ever. She stood slowly and turned away from the ugly
scene below them, where the tribesmen were still gathered about their victim.

"No. We weren't that honest. We let the KamKhels
be our butchers."

"*Shut up,*" Mirjan hissed at Tamai, grinding his foot
down on hers for good measure, and to his astonishment
she obeyed him as she'd never done when they were
married.

Most of the ledge on the south face of the mountain
was too narrow for comfort, but Tamai had found a niche
halfway along the ledge where one slim woman could sit
crosslegged, with support for her back and enough space
before her to set a small thing—a walnut, for example.

This was not the empty shell used in her formal test,
but an ancient whole walnut from last year's stores. Perhaps that would make a difference. She couldn't be sure.
What made more of a difference, to her mind, was that
she had good solid rock at her back instead of a cluster
of wisewomen waiting for her to fail.

Tamai took three slow, deep breaths and concentrated her will on the nut. *Grow!* she commanded silently. *Be as you were, be tree, be living, be life.*

A fat white worm crawled out of the walnut. Tamai said something impolite about Nirmali the Maker and her sense of humor, brushed the maggotty nut off the ledge, and took a replacement from the deep pocket in her sash.

The world narrowed until she was no longer conscious of the white space of air around her or the cliffs at her back. A faint green haze hovered about the walnut shell. Tamai sank into that promise of life and the rocks were no more, the mountains were no more, Tamai was no more: there was only the tentative upward thrust of a fresh growing shoot, the spreading of branches and the unfurling of tender leaves. Tamai's spirit sang in triumph through the new young stem, and she became the leaves and the green light, a dance of light and rainbows and crystal song where the branches of the tree should have been. That was wrong; something within her knew it, but she could not stop. Why should she stop? Was it not better to be this wonder of light than to return into that tense dark woman crouched on the cliff? She was so much more than that shell of a body; she was light, was rainbow, was light shattered, was the dance. . . .

A kite plummeted through the illusory tree of light and shrieked in protest at finding nowhere to set its feet. The vision of light dissolved and Tamai slumped to one side, shuddering with the release of effort. Her pulse was hammering and her tunic was soaked with sweat. What a fool she'd been! She'd been warned and warned that the Disciplines were too dangerous for a woman without children to attempt. Power drew you to the sky, but the power a woman invested in her children kept her in touch with earth. Power had to flow continuously between earth and sky; otherwise the spirit had no way to return and the body could literally burn itself up in the unchecked flow. If Tamai had any sense, she would never practice the Disciplines away from a group of wisewomen who could break her trance for her when she failed to do it for herself.

If she had any sense, she wouldn't have been here in the first place. So why give up now? She just had to exercise a little more control.

The next three walnuts burst into flames: one hot red flame that singed her fingers when she beat it out, one cold blue flame that made her hand feel as if she'd left it in a snowbank overnight, and one weak creeping green firetongue smelling like meat that had gone very, very bad in a sudden thaw.

"At least I achieve variety," Tamai said aloud.

"That's something to relieve winter's boredom, then," said a voice from the path above her. "But it's spring now, cousin, and I've got better sport for you than burning last year's walnuts."

"Paluk!" Tamai sprang to her feet, heedless of her danger on the narrow ledge. She leaned her elbows on the path at his feet and looked up into the laughing face of her nearest and best beloved cousin. "You were spying on me."

"Say rather, keeping others from doing so."

"Who?"

Paluk spread his palms out and shrugged. "Well, if anybody *had* come along this way, I would've stopped them."

Tamai smiled reluctantly. Any other who'd spied upon her failures would have been risking his life. But it was impossible to be angry for long with Paluk—and he took full advantage of this fact.

"Now," her cousin said, "if you're quite through playing with fire, how about being some use to the world for a change?"

"When you say that," Tamai commented, "you generally mean that you want me to be some use to Paluk. What do you need?"

Paluk looked sheepish. "Well. The planting is finished—a little detail you may not have noticed in your absorption with your studies—and Dizane's festival is tonight. And I did promise to bring back some meat for the feast . . . and since you're a *much* better shot than I am, I just thought you might want to come along. . . ."

"All right," Tamai said abruptly. She did not relish the thought of going back through the City to get her weapons from the narrow house she had once shared with Mirjan. But she would have to face her neighbors some time; no good putting it off. And it would be good to exercise her real skills in stalking and shooting. That might help her to forget the day's failures. Paluk had been right, she would feel better for an afternoon on the mountain, and the fact that he stood to benefit from her services was—well, that was just the way Paluk did things.

"Thought you would come," Paluk said complacently. "I brought your jezail, so we don't have to waste time going through the City."

And so she wouldn't have to face the pitying or curious glances of her neighbors. But Paluk was too tactful to mention that. Tamai set her foot in a crevice on the cliff face and leapt up to the path in one smooth motion. "I'm surprised Dushmuni let you take it."

"I brought Dushmuni, too," Paluk said. He waved one arm in wide circles. The golden eagle plunged out of the sky and plummeted between them as if she spotted a fat rabbit between their feet, stopping at the last minute with a frantic beating of her seven-foot wings that raised a storm of miniature dustdevils around them. Tamai bound the hunting leather that Paluk offered around her arm from fist to shoulder. She held out her closed fist to Dushmuni; the eagle fluttered up and landed with a bone-jarring weight. Tamai's fist dropped and Dushmuni walked up the slope of her arm to perch on the leather-guarded shoulder.

Paluk ostentatiously shivered. "I did not choose to carry her that way, you'll notice. Has it ever occurred to you that she could rip your face off with one move?" The golden eagle's eight black talons curved completely over Tamai's slender shoulder, strong enough to paralyze a wolf with their grip while the beak tore out chunks of living flesh. On Tamai's shoulder she sat as lightly and gently as a mother covering her new-hatched chicks. All the same, the leather shoulder guard was necessary for both of them. Dushmuni would not have been able to stand securely on loose unprotected human flesh, and the slightest involuntary contraction of her talons could have ripped Tamai to the bone.

A head covered with golden feathers butted against Tamai's cheek and a sense of warmth and welcome flowed through her, loosening muscles she had not known were taut, reducing the little problem of a dead walnut in a shell to its proper trivial place in life. What did the Disciplines matter, against the wordless communion she had shared with Dushmuni since the eagle's nestling days?

"It was very brave of you to bring her at all," Tamai acknowledged with a smile.

"Actually, I did not have much choice. I think," Paluk said, "she was worried about you. . . . At any rate, it was perfectly clear even to me that she wanted to join us, and I think I made it clear to her that you would be glad to see me. You may express astonishment and admiration if you like," he added graciously. "I may be only a man, I may not be able to farspeak your eagle, but I *have* been hunting all my adult life and I *do* have some slight understanding of the creatures."

It was much, much easier to enter the City at dusk, with the body of a mountain goat slung on a pole between her and Paluk as their contribution to the feast and an explanation for her absence. In the half-darkness Tamai didn't have to worry about meeting the eyes of her friends and neighbors; she was pleasantly tired from the afternoon of climbing, the sharp mountain air had given an edge to her appetite, and she had—almost— forgotten her fear of being exiled from the City. In any case, that was not something to think about now, during Dizane's festival.

The City was more lovely than ever in the dusk, with the last rays of the sun striking golden lights from the glazed roof tiles of the highest towers, with the first torches of Festival echoing those lights in the narrow stone-paved streets. Tamai left Paluk and "his" kill at the door of his family's tall house and trotted happily through the streets to her own home, two rooms one on top of the other squeezed between the west tower and the out-flung curve of the City wall. For once she didn't think about coming home to darkness and emptiness, or about the days when she and Mirjan had hoped to need more room for the seven sons and daughters Tamai would need to carry power as strong as hers into the next gener-ation. It was enough to be alive in the crisp cool air of a spring night, to feel Dushmuni's talons gripping her shoulder through the leather band, to wash quickly in cold water and dress as quickly in her fine festival tunic and trousers of shimmering green Chin brocade embroi-dered with moonsilver. Tamai flipped her dark braid up and around her head and skewered it in place with a long pin of carved sweetwood, settled Dushmuni on her perch and was ready to go.

By the time she reached the dancing ground her legs had recovered from the long steep downhill trudge to the city and she revised her plans for the evening. The drums were beating out the soft compelling rhythm of the Dunni, the old music master raised his clarinet of apricot wood and added a lingering sweet air to the dou-ble drumbeat, and the young men who stood with arms linked around the edge of the dancing ground began to sing the ballad of Suri Khazara and her death in battle against the White Huns.

Dancing, Tamai thought happily, was *important*. As was hunting. She could wait until later to fill her belly with the crisp fried sweetmeats and spicy stews tradi-tional for Dizane's Night—maybe until Paluk had roasted the goat and brought that to share with the dancers. She leapt up onto the dancing platform and balanced lightly on the balls of her feet, surveying the women already circling there and judging where best to break into the line. None were close friends—but then, that was hardly likely; Tamai hadn't let many people get close to her since Mirjan left. She had been counting on finding Sunik there, though; even after three babies in four years, Sunik never missed a dancing night. And this would be a good way to meet her friend again; they could dance and feel Dizane's grace entering them and there would be no need to speak of Tamai's failure that morning.

One of Mirjan's many little sisters saw Tamai and broke the line to let her in. Tamai joined in on the last lines of the chorus and caught the rhythm at once, the double stamp and four quick light steps to the left that made you feel as if you were flying. "Where's Sunik?" she asked during the pause between verses.

"Up to the north pasture with Kazhirbri and some others. That new tribe from the north is trying to come over the pass."

"What, again?" It seemed those strange fair-skinned northerners had been edging towards their boundaries all this spring. Tamai couldn't understand why they didn't give up and go away as any intelligent hillfolk would. After a few experiences of vertigo and unseasonable snowstorms and inexplicable cravings to go away, most of the neighboring tribes had sensibly concluded that the mountains bordering Gandara weren't worth bothering with and that there probably weren't any passes through the mountains right there anyway and that furthermore they had never really wanted to explore in that particular direction.

"And on Dizane's Night, too!" Mirjan's sister said with a toss of her shining copper-colored braids. Little copper bells, braided into her hair with silk threads, tinkled when she moved, as did the long silver chains hanging from the triangular charm on her breast. "Sunik will miss the best dancing of the year. Have they no sense of what's right and proper?"

Tamai suppressed a grin. She *knew* Mirjan's sisters weren't terribly bright; it didn't really matter, since none of them, mothers or childless, had enough power to kindle a light at midday in the season of grain-ripening. Even she, who'd never left the valley of Gandhara willingly, had spoken with enough traders from the yearly caravans to know that other tribes had their own gods and their own festivals, that Nirmali and Dizane did not rule everywhere. Some of these outland tribes not only didn't know the gods, but didn't even have a proper Council of wisewomen, letting the men's council or a king speak for the whole tribe; what sense or decency could you expect from people like that?

"Oh, well, I expect she'll be back soon enough," she said, and lifted her voice in the next verse of the song. *Suri Khazara, dawn is breaking, Suri Khazara, the enemy rides! Suri Khazara, bring your sword, your silver-mounted axe and your spear . . .*

The sun was gone now, but the festival torches were like many little suns flaring around the dancing platform. As she stamped and swung about the circle, Tamai glimpsed all the faces of Gandhara, some covered with festival masks, others bare to the golden torchlight and the black shadows. Dizane's Night gathered all together to give thanks for the planted fields and to pray for the growth of the grain: the wisewomen with their bright unreadable eyes, the young mothers suckling infants and feeling the new release of power flowing through their bodies with the milk, the hunters and the men who worked the fields and the smooth-cheeked boys swaying together with the song. Tamai worshipped Dizane with her body, with the dance that quickened tired legs and made her forget hunger, and she felt at one with all her people and her city.

The double beat of the Dunni gave way to the quick-stamp of the Sarikoli dance, and the music of flutes and trumpets was added to the voice of the solitary clarinet. That lively dance ended in its turn and the drums and trumpets fell silent, leaving a single flute to carry the smooth gliding tune of the slow Tajwer steps. "As the hours of the night festival passed, the moon rose over the blue walls of the City, and the silver light seemed to dance to the music, meeting and retreating from the golden circles of torchlight. Dizane's grace entered the dancers as they moved through the slow deliberate steps of the Tajwer, and Tamai felt as if the music lifted her bodily from the dancing floor to float upon the night air, suspended between two worlds."

A long, high-pitched cry interrupted the sweet wailing tune of the flute, and the dancers stumbled, almost losing the trance of movement. Again the cry came, and a third time, and the line was in disarray. *Dizane will not be pleased,* Tamai thought. *A bad omen for her Night.*

But it was more than an omen. One of the oldest of the wisewomen had cried out; now she was babbling unintelligible phrases to the circle that surrounded her. Tamai caught a few words and a prickle of uneasiness lifted the short hairs that had come free of her braid. "What is it? What's happened?" She pushed her way towards the front of the circle, but before she got there another of the wisewomen had fallen to her knees with a cry of despair, and then another. The babies in their mothers' arms picked up the general sorrow and began wailing. It was impossible to know what was going on. The wisewomen were all pointing towards the north; Tamai went towards the north gate, along with half the population of Gandhara. A stream of revelers in festival clothes and masks carried her along; a smiling Dizane of turquoise and silver winked at her in the torchlight, a red-striped mask of a beast's head lifted to show a man's worried face beneath it, the jingling of little bells and silver chains played a merry counterpoint to the worried questions that everyone asked and no one could answer. There had been some disaster to the north, something that stabbed the wisewomen like a knife in the dark, but what? *Something to do with the northmen,* the whisper ran through the crowd. *Have they crossed into Gandhara? Didn't we send wisewomen to stop them? There's been a death. They were crying out about a death. What could kill a wisewoman?*

The news had not been farspoken from the high range where it happened; few, if any, had the power to farspeak from a distance so great, or to somebody they couldn't actually see. The wisewomen in the City had picked up the sense of grief and disaster from the women returning to the City when they were already quite close to the gates. By the time Tamai had fought her way to the front of the crowd, one of Paluk's aunts had recovered herself enough to make light. The clear, shadowless, passionless white light that had illumined the illusion of the cedar grove now shone on the three women returning to the north gate, and on the burden two of them carried upon an improvised litter of cedar poles and somebody's cloak. The third stumbled before them, tugging her braids loose over her face and wailing aloud.

It was Kazhirbri. And as she drew close, Tamai understood her words. The northmen had broken through all their defenses, because there were too many of them to hold with illusion, and because when one fell back their chiefs sent two others to take his place. They were camped at the top of the pass. But that was not the worst. They had jezails that could fire from a great distance, too far away for the wisewomen to distort the marksmen's aim as they did with the local tribal wars. One of these foreign marksmen had fired right into the grove where the wisewomen sat, held quite still in the working of their magic, unable to move even had they known what was happening. That was what had disrupted their efforts, Kazhirbri insisted. They had not expected to be fired upon. They had not been ready. Tomorrow they would go back and drive these intruders from the land. . . .

Tamai stopped listening. The two wisewomen behind Kazhirbri were close enough to be recognized now, but their heads were bowed and their shoulders slumped in defeat. She couldn't tell which one was Sunik. . . . One of them *had* to be Sunik. . . .

The cloak covering the litter slipped to the ground, and the cold pure light of magic that shone about the wisewomen showed Tamai where Sunik lay, quite peaceful except for the small, round hole in her forehead.

CHAPTER TWO

Kazhirbri was out of breath by the time she reached the last ridge overlooking the northeastern pass that she had been sent to watch. She hated her own weakness even while acknowledging that it was reasonable enough. Who had ever heard of sending a grandmother in her fifties to scramble over the rocky cliffs of this barren valley? But in this hot month of field-in-grain about to give way to sickles-reaping, after a long summer of war, there were simply not enough hands and eyes to watch all the border points of Gandhara. The high green pastures where the herdbeasts should have grazed this summer were already lost to the enemy, as was the northwestern valley with its sweet running stream of clear, snow-cooled water. Week after week the northmen pressed upon them, killing from afar with their foreign-made jezails, taking control of a ridge, a wooded slope, a crag overlooking a pasture. The bounds of Gandhara were much contracted now, but even so there were not enough wisewomen to keep strong nets of illusion about what remained.

And Shushibai, whom she had been sent to relieve, was even less fit for guard duty. She'd had a hard birthing just two weeks previously; she should have been resting and learning to apply the Disciplines over which motherhood had given her control, but she had insisted on taking her turn on the borders as soon as she was walking again. She looked glad enough to see Kazhirbri coming now; no doubt her breasts were aching with milk for the baby.

"Time to go down now, my love," Kazhirbri said cheerfully. "My great-grandson will be howling for his meal!" She was dismayed, though she tried not to show it, by the lines of pain and fatigue that showed in Shushibai's thin young face. The girl should have been chubby from her pregnancy, but it seemed that all her strength and all the scanty rations she'd eaten that summer had gone into making the baby. Her full breasts hung incongruously on a thin body; her cheeks were narrow and there were dark shadows under her eyes. Kazhirbri knew that she herself looked little better, but after all, she was a grandmother—a great-grandmother now, thanks to Shushibai—and she could hardly expect to appear as bright and lively as this child in her teens should have looked.

"No trouble during your watch?" she questioned the girl.

Shushibai shook her head. "I thought I saw something moving behind the trees there, but it must have been a wild goat."

"Or a wild northman," said Kazhirbri dryly. "Get behind the rocks, child." They had all learned something about not exposing themselves to the northerners' weapons; all those who survived, anyway. Kazhirbri shaded her eyes with her hand and leaned forward now, uneasy. Something had flickered where there should have been no light. Sun on a bright rock? No, not in the deep shadows of that tree-covered slope. There it was again—and again. Recognition flashed in her mind and she moved instinctively to block Shushibai's view of the slope. "Go on back to the City, child," she said, very calmly, "and when you are close enough, farspeak the Council. Let them send any rainweavers who may be free—or any other wisewomen—"

"What is it?"

"Just do as I tell you!"

"Not until I know." Shushibai planted her feet stubbornly beside Kazhirbri.

"It seems the northerners have thought of another weapon that can kill from a distance," Kazhirbri said calmly. "Fire. You are too new in the Disciplines to help me, child; if you stay, I'll only have to protect you when I should be in trance." And if she was to die here on this ridge, facing the northmen's fire, she wanted to know that her granddaughter was safe to raise more children for Nirmali. "Now—will—you—*go*?"

Sixteen years old and just two weeks a wisewoman, Shushibai was no match for a matriarch who'd spent a lifetime with the Disciplines; she was running across the meadow before she had consciously decided to obey.

She never heard the shot that brought her down among the summer flowers, the lucky shot of a marksman posted high in the cliffs to watch the progress of the fire that his comrades had set.

His next shot took Kazhirbri, but he had aimed too low. Through her trance she felt the snap of a breaking bone. Her body settled into a puddle of rusty black skirts, taking the weight from her broken leg and incidentally removing her from the marksman's line of sight. The pain in her leg was trivial compared with the heat of the flames into which she had already sent her questing spirit. The knowledge that she could not run from the fire now was less trivial, but she could not afford to let herself be distracted by fear. All that could save her now was the chance of drawing the scattered clouds overhead into a rainweaving before the flames reached this ridge.

Tamai's sleeping body twisted and turned while her spirit fought the shapes of men and demons in the underworld. Disconnected images seized her mind and shook her. She was exiled from the City, a lonely, black dot toiling across the expanse of the winter snowfields. She was trapped in a glittering reflection of ice and cold and her spirit flew from side to side, breaking itself on the mirrors, while a demon laughed at her from somewhere outside her prison of ice. The demon shrank and split into many small parts, each of them a laughing man holding her down, and she was a child again and unable to fight the KamKhels who thought they knew how to break a Gandharan witch's powers. And this time the Dhi Lawan would not save her, there would be no help from the City, she was alone, alone, and the flames were coming closer.

She woke with a painful start, sweating and disoriented, and banged her elbow on the wooden sill of the window by her pallet as she wrestled her way out of a tangle of embroidered felt coverlets and soft furs. Dushmuni woke on her perch and let out a cry that felt like a jagged blade slicing through Tamai's head.

"Hush, will you!" she snarled at the eagle. "I had a bad dream, that's all. Nothing for you to get so excited about. Happens often enough, Nirmali knows." She did not sleep well these days; none of them did. Hunger was one of the problems. With the herdbeasts penned up beside the City walls all summer, grazing the nearby pastures bare and having to be fed on last year's grain, they had all been on short rations until the harvest should be brought in—any day now, Dizane bless! And lately Tamai had been on night patrol, stalking the new, close bounds of Gandhara with Dushmuni on her shoulder, guarding the wisewomen who kept watch on the northmen during the night. It was an honor to be chosen for such a duty, but it also meant that every night Tamai was reminded of how little she could really do for the City. While her age-mates wore themselves to a thread using all the Disciplines to trick and slow down the relentless advance of the northmen, all she could do—she who should one day have become the Dhi Lawan—was to keep watch over their heads in the hope of shooting a single careless northerner. And during the day, when she should have slept, the bright sun of a rainless harvest month kept her turning restlessly in broken half-slumber.

Small wonder, under the circumstances, that her

dreams should jumble together all her worries at once, from the fear of exile to the memory of the KamKhel raid that had left her bleeding and broken and unable to bear the children who might let her fulfill her promise of power.

But none of those worries were immediate, and the sense of fear and urgency the dream had imparted should have dissipated in the bright light of day instead of hanging over Tamai like a cloud. No one spoke of exiling her these days; she had more than proved her worth to the City since this war began. She might never be a wisewoman herself, but her sharp eye and superbly made outlander jezail had brought down more than one northern marksman before he could kill a wisewoman who guarded the City's boundaries.

As for the other matter, it was ancient history. Tamai had no intention of allowing her waking hours to be dominated by the memory of something that had happened eighteen years before. If any man of the KamKhel tribe ever laid a finger on her again, she would consider that a good enough reason to kill the one who touched her. And there was nothing more to be said about it—waking or sleeping.

Tamai stabbed a long, carved pin through her knotted braids and glowered at Dushmuni, who was still shifting from one taloned foot to the other and half raising her wings as if she sensed danger nearby. "I can't sleep," she told Dushmuni. "I'm going out. *You* sleep. One of us should be alert tonight." *No worry, all fine now, warm sun sleep peace,* she subvocalized beneath the spoken words. She had never been sure exactly what Dushmuni understood of words or thoughts; the bond between them was something more intense and less verbal than the farspeaking customarily practiced by the wisewomen who kept birds for hunting.

Instead of settling on her perch as she should have done, Dushmuni raised both her wings and screeched aloud. The white carpal patches on her wings flickered like leaping flames, and the fire of the eagle's cry ran through Tamai's head and scorched her thoughts. *Alone fire help burning burning.* . . .

Tamai swallowed. It wasn't a dream. Something real was coming to her from too far away to be heard clearly. Dushmuni felt it, too, perhaps more strongly than Tamai herself; the images of burning fields and distant mountains in her mind were from Dushmuni, not remnants of her dream. Did the Council feel it? Did the wisewomen know what to do about this cry for help?

Tamai ran down the narrow street, still wrapping her wide embroidered sash about her waist. Dushmuni circled above her head and swooped from rooftop to rooftop, her golden hackles turned to fire in the morning sun. Tamai slipped on smooth, rounded stones that had been set in place when the White Huns were still ravaging the southern plains, banged her knee on a post carved to Dizane before the first roofs had been set on the houses of Gandhara and fell against the great wooden doors of the Council house in an untidy heap. Even as she reached the house, she heard a cry from within, and the desperate voice calling in her head rose to a peak of anguish that made her moan and squeeze her forehead with both hands. Dushmuni folded her wings and stooped like a stone falling from the sky. Before the eagle landed, the pain and desperation were gone as utterly as if they had never been. The doors of the Council house swung open and Tamai saw three wisewomen clutching their heads.

"I felt it, too," she said quickly, before she could lose courage before the wisewomen. "Need, farspoken—and fire—"

"Where?" one of the wisewomen questioned her. "I felt nothing but the fire."

"I, too," said another. "Too far for clear images—"

"Could be any place along the borders—"

"You think it was a border attack, then?"

They were all speaking at once. Tamai searched her

own memory for some image that would help them iden-
tify the place. Dushmuni settled on her shoulder and
leaned a feathered head against Tamai's braid, and a
picture grew clear in her mind: heavy ripe heads of wheat
bending the golden stalks, and their pale gold put to
shame by the blaze of open flames advancing on the
field. And above the smoke, the peaks of Twin Markhor
Mountain, with the high green summer pastures that had
long since been lost to the northmen.

"Not the borders," she said. "It's past there by now.
The east fields." Ripe and ready for harvest, dry with the
long, hot, cloudless month of field-in-grain: could there
have been a worse time for fire to break out?

"Shushibai was watching the northeast pass from Twin
Markhor," one of the wisewomen said slowly.

Another shook her head. "No. Kazhirbri went to
relieve her. Shushibai should be back by now—she is
never late to feed this small one." She looked at a leather
cradle on the floor. The sleeping baby screwed up his
face and snuffled uneasily.

While they spoke, the wisewomen were gathering up
their cloaks and bags. Tamai averted her eyes. For a man
to see the tools of the wisewomen's magic would bring
bad luck on the city. It might be even worse for her, a
barren woman without Nirmali's favor, to look on these
things; even though, from her fruitless training in the
Disciplines, she already knew what the soft leather bags
must contain. The wisewomen would bring to their work
incised bones and twigs of cedar for divination, pinches
of sleep-no-more and tranceweed for strength during
visions, the crystal Tears of Lunang set in silver for powers of water and the turquoise Nirmali's Eye in a wrapping of fine gold wires for women brought to bed. They
would work under cloaks of fine black wool that anyone
might look at, but the undersides of the cloaks would be
bright with an intricate dance of woven and embroidered
patterns, each representing a Discipline mastered or an
important episode in the wisewoman's history. The cloaks

of the older wisewomen were solid masses of embroidery.
Sunik's cloak had borne only three bright bands; Tamai
had seen them when her friend's body was carried back
to the City, the cloak fallen open over the improvised
litter. She supposed it did not matter, when a wisewoman
was dead, if the uninitiated got more than a casual
glimpse of the glory that had been her life in the
Disciplines.

Shushibai's cloak would bear no more than a thin red
strand of embroidered flowers, for the birth of her first
child. Tamai hoped desperately that she was not about
to be permitted a sight of those flowers; let them be
secret still, let Shushibai come back safe, let it all be a
mistake!

Before they reached the eastern wheat fields, runners
had brought word of fresh fires to the west and south-
west. The border guards on those sides of the city lived,
but had been distracted from their tasks for precious
moments—one by the winking eye of a demon on the
western horizon, another by something that sounded like
a crying child.

Through a cloudless afternoon the people of Gandhara worked shoulder to shoulder, old men and hunters,
maidens and wisewomen, to put out the fires that took
their harvest and their hopes. At each set of narrow terraced fields a knot of wisewomen gathered together their
Tears of Lunang, trying to call clouds and rain that might
save the grain, trying to beat back the real leaping flames
with the illusion of Lunang's running waters. Tamai was
in a line of men and children beating at the flames with
wet cloths, her hands scorched and her throat raw with
smoke and hot air, when one of the wisewomen from
the Council house touched her shoulder.

"Come away from there—we need you elsewhere,"
she said tensely. "We have moved four times, but each
time we settle in trance the northmen shoot at us. If we
retreat out of sight of the fields—"

Tamai nodded. It had never seemed a weakness that most of the Disciplines must be practiced within sight of their object. Now, though, the northmen with their deadly long-range weapons were turning that weakness into Gandhara's death-wound.

"Paluk says that if anyone can drive away the northern marksmen, you can," the wisewoman said reluctantly. "Because your jezail is the best—"

And because I am the best shot in the City. Were they reluctant to grant her even that much honor? Did it all have to be due to the southern-made jezail for which she'd traded all her mother's store of raw turquoise?

Tamai shrugged off the question and ran for her jezail. Paluk met her halfway to the City gates, carrying the weapon and her ammunition. Tamai ran back to the fires without speech. There was no need; Paluk understood.

So did Dushmuni. The golden eagle soared and hovered in a sky that shimmered with heat, pointing out the positions of the hidden marksmen to Tamai. She aimed and fired, took her new range from Dushmuni and fired again, seemingly without pause. Her shoulder ached with the repeated recoil of the jezail and her arms shook with the endless effort of loading, lifting the long-barrelled weapon, aiming and firing. Once Dushmuni swooped through tongues of flame, screeching and flapping her wings in Tamai's face, and she realized that the fire had come around her on three sides. She ran across the hillside and heard the whine of the northmen's missiles passing her head; they knew the source of their opposition, and she was as much a target as the wisewomen. She fell behind an outcropping of rock and motioned Dushmuni to settle beside her. *Danger enemy hide* she subvocalized, and Dushmuni laughed in her head with pure joy of battle and rose into the air again.

Fire, duck, reload, pray for Dushmuni, aim . . . Tamai lost all sense of time in the endless battle. Something squirmed beside her, touched her shoulder; she swung with a snarl, lips drawn back, and just stopped herself from knocking the long barrel of her jezail into Mirjan's head.

"The wisewomen say stop," he told her. "This field is gone. Maybe on the west side you can be some use."

But when they reached the other terraced slopes, there was nothing but ashes where that morning the hillside had been golden with ripening wheat, the promise of food and plenty through the winter. There were no northmen here to kill; they had withdrawn as soon as they saw that their object was accomplished.

In the morning, when the burned-over slopes were cooling, the wisewomen of the Council went out and found Sushibai and Kazhirbri where they had fallen in defense of the City. Shushibai's skull had been shattered by a northern missile, presumably before the fire took her.

Kazhirbri was still alive, but only just. The clouds she had sought to call had become a shell of moisture, perpetually burned off by the fire and renewed by her will; but the price of that will had been a trance so deep that she could not be reached by any outside call. She lay in the contorted posture in which she had fallen, marked by smears of black ash where her clothing had burned down to the skin.

"Those who go so far never return," the wisewomen whispered among themselves.

"Kazhirbri will return," the Dhi Lawan said. "We cannot spare her now. And when she comes back from this deep trance, she will be one of the wisest of us all."

But the younger wisewomen did not have the Dhi Lawan's serene certainty that her will must prevail.

"Perhaps her kin will call her back," one suggested.

But Kazhirbri's daughter and granddaughter were both dead. Her last living descendant was Shushibai's baby. And he shrieked for four days and refused the thin goat's milk that he was offered in a rag, refused the breast of a young mother who had been worn thin already nursing the twins born to her three months earlier, and then died with his face contorted in an angry howl.

"He may have been lucky," Tamai said somberly as she walked away from the small grave where the unnamed baby had been laid beside his mother's charred bones. "He'll not be the last child to die this winter."

"We still have some grain stores," Paluk said quickly, "and it's almost time for the fall caravans."

Tamai looked at a gray sky, dark with the rain clouds that could have saved the City if they had but come four days earlier. She wanted to walk farther than the short way to her house, to come to terms with the decision she'd made. But there was nowhere to walk. The Council had decreed that the boundaries of Gandhara were now the City walls themselves; no outlying territory could be defended. They were closed in here, and Tamai, who had never wanted to leave the valley, now felt the walls of the city and the low clouds overhead like the sides and lid of a box that pressed the life out of her. Perhaps, after all, it would not be so hard to do what she must.

"Do you really think," she said, "that the caravans from Chin will come through the war to lay down their silks for us? If they trade with anybody this year, it will be with the northmen. Perhaps that is what this war has been about. And if they do not come, what will we have to offer the Chitralis to the south?"

"Turquoise and gold, silver and night-without-moon jade, Lunang's Tears from the river bed . . ."

Tamai nodded somberly. "Yes. We can sell off the wealth of Gandhara and buy food enough—perhaps—to last through this winter. If the Mehtar of Chitral does not guess how desperate we are, if we pretend it's only a greed to build up our own grain stores, he will take his profit from us. This year. And next?"

"Next year," said Paluk, "is another story. In the spring we'll plant early, if the rains permit, and fatten up the herds again. You see, Tamai, things aren't so bad as you think. We can survive a bad year."

"One. Yes." Tamai spoke slowly, as if she were reasoning it all out again, but she couldn't make herself come to any new conclusion. She'd been through all the arguments already in the nights since the fields burned, arguing against herself with no company but Dushmuni silent and watchful on her perch. "And if the northmen are still there in the spring, Paluk? If they don't let us plant our fields, if they still camp in the high pastures where we fatten the herds?"

"Why should they return?" Paluk argued back. "What tribe can afford to keep all its men at war through the planting season? All right, they've been raiding at our bounds longer than most, and they've been more destructive than a few half-naked KamKhels looking for enemy heads—oh, sorry—"

"It's all right, Paluk," Tamai said. "I don't have screaming nightmares every time somebody mentions the KamKhels." *Only every third or fourth time. And mostly I dream of killing them.* "But—I do not know where these northmen come from, but they are not a tribe like those around us. They must have a kingdom as big as Chitral, somewhere in the north where we've never been. Look how quickly they conquered the Kirghiz, before we even knew there was a war on the steppes! I don't think winter will drive them away, Paluk, and I don't think they will go home in the spring to plant their own fields. And if we couldn't keep our own boundaries safe this year, we will surely not be able to drive them back in the spring. There are too many of them for our wisewomen to send away, and they seem to have demons that tell them where they are going even when we try to confuse them—and their jezails can kill at a distance too great for the wisewomen to work well."

"You would have it that we can do nothing." Paluk's face was sullen; he didn't like being argued down. "What good is it to sit in the City and bemoan our doom, then?"

"None at all. And I don't mean to do so," Tamai said calmly. "Maybe the wisewomen can't stop these northmen, maybe they have demons helping them, but they themselves are as vulnerable to a jezail as any other mortal men. Half their strength comes from the fact that they're better armed than we are. What if every hunter in Gandhara had a jezail like mine?"

"But they don't."

"Not yet."

"And we don't even know where yours *came* from. All you know is that pack of lies the trader told us. . . ."

"Maybe not lies," Tamai said. "I have been trying to remember exactly what he said. He claimed there was a great kingdom now in the plain of Takshasila where the first Gandhara stood, a kingdom far more powerful than Chitral or Badakhshan, with tens of thousands more tribesmen—" She broke off laughing at the long, twisted face Paluk made to this story. "Well, all right. Clearly he was exaggerating; that's his business, after all, to make a good story about his trade goods. But this jezail had to come from *somewhere*, didn't it? And it wasn't made by any of the tribes we normally deal with—so why not from some southern tribe, too far away for us to know of them or to see much of their wares? No one can count the generations since we fled into the hills to escape the White Huns; perhaps new tribes have made their home in the ruins of the first Gandhara, and perhaps they have grown rich making and selling things like my jezail.

"Dushmuni and I are going to look for them, Paluk. The Council does not approve, but the Dhi Lawan spoke to me secretly this morning. She has promised to give me turquoise and silks of Chin to take as trade goods. She agrees that we had best barter our wealth for weapons, rather than spending it all on food for this winter with no plan for next season.

"If they are there, I shall find them, this tribe called the Angrez. And I shall buy at least fifty of their fine jezails for us. I can even remember the name of the maker," Tamai said with pride. Her fingers brushed the angular charms embossed on the stock of the jezail and she repeated the strange sounds that the trader had spoken when she first looked at the marks. "*MartiniHenry rifles*. That's what we need, Paluk, since charms and spells have done us no good against the northmen. Fifty or a hundred Martini-Henry rifles."

CHAPTER THREE

[Excerpts from the journal of Louisa Westbrook]

15 May 1884:

Despite the servants in every corner, the house seems so quiet and empty today that I can hardly bear it. I had promised myself that I would not grieve excessively in front of Gordon, but in his absence I do not know if I can restrain myself. I had hardly imagined that I would return only to find that he too had departed, on a wild and surely fruitless search for this hill-kingdom of Gandhara that has been his obsession of late—

I can almost hear his voice reproving me now. *Order, order, my dear Louisa! Must you always begin a story in the middle?* Not that it can possibly matter, here in the privacy of my own journal, but I suppose Gordon is right. We should strive to be disciplined and controlled in private as we appear in public, to set as good an example before God and our consciences as we do before the natives. And so I begin again, this time taking care to set down all the facts exactly as they occurred, without digressions or emotional interruptions.

I returned from Bombay late last night. The journey had been a long one and I was fatigued, not only from the jolting of the tonga in which I rode the last stages

36

but also from the sleepless nights I have endured ever since seeing Alice and my little Harry off at Bombay. To be sure, dear Mrs. Johnson has promised to look after them with her own brood until they arrive in England, and I must trust that the family Gordon has chosen for them to live with will treat them well in a spirit of Christian duty—Gordon would never, surely, choose guardians for his children who did not understand the concept of Christian duty—but it is *such* a long way, and they *are* so young! I think I will never forget the sight of their little faces as they stood on the deck of the ship, leaning over the rail to catch a last glimpse of their Mama as she waved farewell. May they never know that Mama was so weak as to sob into her handkerchief the moment they were out of sight! Even now, I cannot bear to relive that moment of parting.

Nor ought I to do so. Gordon would say, and quite rightly, too, that I am indulging myself in an orgy of useless sentiment; that I ought to forget the children and get on with the task before me. And so I shall.

As I was saying, I arrived late last night, only to find our bungalow dark and the servants apparently all asleep. This in itself surprised me not a little, as Gordon is in the habit of sitting up until all hours while he works on his Dictionary, and he would never consent that his personal servants go to sleep while he might still need them. But the *khansamah*, who came himself to take my baggage and pay the tonga-wallah, gave me an explanation that was an even greater surprise—not all at once, I might add; I had to drag it out of him, a sentence at a time, as is so common with these people.

"Where is Sahib?"

"Master Sahib go hills."

"Why?"

"Last week very bad carriage accident in bazaar."

"Was Sahib hurt?"

"No, Memsahib. Sahib not there."

"Then what has the carriage accident to do with anything?"

And so on. To save space—for it sometimes seems to me that the recording of even one native conversation could use up all the pages of this journal—I shall summarize his story. It seems that last week a runaway carriage grazed the edge of a fruit stall in the bazaar. This would have been no great matter, save that the driver of the carriage was a Musselman, and the proprietor of the fruit stall was a Hindu who had just been decorating his stall in honor of some one or other of the multifarious heathen festivals celebrated by these benighted people. Naturally the Hindu took the accident as a deliberate insult to his religion, and the Musselman replied in kind, and there was a small riot, and several unfortunate natives were trampled under and badly injured, and two of them killed outright. One of these was poor Bilizhe, the hillman who had been teaching Gordon words of the Gandharan speech in return for money for opium. Gordon had paid him well only the day before, and it is to be presumed the unhappy man was too drowsy with the effects of the drug to get out of the way of the rioters.

Gordon was most distressed when he heard of the accident, because he had been making plans to publish his Dictionary, along with his suppositions about the Gandharans being the last remnants of the noble armies of Alexander, in the next volume of the Proceedings of the Royal Geographic Society. Apparently he felt that the work was still too incomplete for publication; and since Bilizhe was the only man of this tribe whom Gordon had ever found, he was desperate to acquire a new informant. He inquired in the bazaar for two days without result, and then applied to Colonel Vaughan for leave. The colonel granted him leave immediately, supposing that he meant to travel down to Bombay to offer me his support on the journey back up-country—and that is all that anyone knows, for Gordon disappeared the next day. The *khansamah* and the other servants are convinced that he went up through the Malakand Pass into the territory of the Mehtar of Chitral, for it was his theory—based on Bilizhe's vague and opium-distorted ramblings—that the tribe of Gandhara must be found somewhere in the unexplored mountains north of Chitral.

That he has gone in such a direction seems very likely to me, for the discovery of a friendly tribe in this area would be a great accomplishment, one that might change the face of civilisation as we know it. Like most of those who serve the Raj, Gordon has long been indignant over the accident of geography that channels the bulk of the lucrative trade from the Hidden Empire into Russian hands. Britain rules the seas, but we shall never force the Emperor of Chin to open his doors to us by sea power; that has long been accepted. Our scientists have never been able to explain the mysterious storms that enshroud the coasts of Chin, bringing all foreign vessels to shipwreck, but their *existence* is a certainty. The common seamen who have returned from our few disastrous voyages towards Chin even whisper of storm-demons and wind-devils, so impressed are they by those calamitous seas.

And so it is by land that we must attempt to make our trade with Chin. By land, and by the treacherous routes that lead across the Taklamakan Desert, through which too few caravans each day wend their way. One can hardly blame the masters of those caravans, having braved the salt wastes of Lop Nor and the burning sands of Taklamakan, if they choose after Kashgar to turn north into the comparative peace of the Rus Empire, rather than risking their goods among the hostile tribes of the Hindu Kush. One cannot blame them, but it is a great pity. The ladies of the Tsar's court, they say, wear silk as we wear our Indian muslins, and the little silk that reaches English traders bleeds our country of gold that goes to pay for the Tsar's guns.

But I am rambling again, for these matters of trade and geography and high strategy, as Gordon has often told me, are quite beyond a female's feeble understanding. I do but seek to reassure myself that my husband's quest has a wholly worthy goal. He is not solely, selfishly concerned with establishing his own fame as the scholar who linked Gandhara with the armies of Alexander; if he is risking his life among the hostile tribes and fierce mountains of the Hindu Kush, it is for the good of his country, which so desperately needs a trading outpost near Kashgar and a series of safe roads south to India from there.

So I must believe. And I must not allow the dark prediction of the servants to infect me; for they are convinced that he will never return from this quixotic expedition.

Naturally I have done my best to scotch this superstitious fatalism in them, but I can hardly control what they whisper among themselves when my back is turned. Gordon will be most annoyed with me if he comes back to find the bazaar full of foolish rumours about his journey, but there is very little I can do about that. I have therefore turned my attention to another matter which might also cause him some annoyance if I cannot remedy it quickly.

As soon as Gordon had left Peshawar, the *khansamah* and the head bearer combined to have his study cleaned, a task which he never permitted them to order when he was at home. They proudly showed me the results and I near fainted with dismay; fortunately I was able to recover myself in time to assure them that I was fainting with amazement at their wonderful work, for it would never do to let them lose face before the lesser servants. But, oh dear! If Gordon were to see his study now! All the little scraps of paper on which he had jotted down words and phrases, disposed in piles about the room under bricks to prevent the breeze from the punkah blowing them out of order—all these bits of paper had been neatly stacked in a single mountainous pile atop his desk so that the head bearer could direct his underlings to scrub the floorboards and corners and shelves. Whatever system Gordon had devised to organize his thoughts and writings, it is completely gone now, and I dare not think of the consequences should he return in time to discover this.

I have therefore resolved to do what I can, myself, to restore order. There is no hope of my replacing everything as it was, for Gordon never admitted me to the intricacies of his system, but if I can fair-copy his notes and place the words for his Dictionary in alphabetical order, perhaps he will not be so *very* angry that everything has been changed around.

And the task should prevent my having leisure to fall into those emotional fits of which he disapproves so much, for his handwriting is very bad and the collection of Gandharan words and phrases is quite extensive.

20 June 1884:

It has been six weeks since I parted from my darlings at Bombay, and as many weeks again must pass before I can hope to hear word of their safe arrival in England! Gordon is not returned from his expedition, so there is no one to remind me of the folly of grieving over what cannot be helped, although Mrs. Colonel Vaughan has this morning done her best to reconcile me to this stern necessity.

She called at nine and found me *en deshabille*, going over Gordon's notes for his Dictionary, in which I have made not a little progress since I last wrote in this journal. I had the feeling that she disapproved of this occupation; indeed, she hinted very strongly that I might have been more suitably employed in making fancywork articles for the Christmas bazaar at the church.

"Christmas is still some time away, Mrs. Vaughan," I said, "and I assure you I shall not neglect the church sale. At present I feel it is more important to go on with my husband's Great Work, that he may find all as he would have wished it upon his return."

"Prolonged study has been shown to be damaging to the female brain," Mrs. Vaughan informed me.

"I do not find it so," I replied, with, alas, somewhat more spirit than the wife of a mere captain ought to show to the colonel's lady. "Indeed, I find that the concentration required to complete Captain Westbrook's

Dictionary is most beneficial to me, as it distracts me from lowering reflections and helps me to keep up my spirits."

Mrs. Vaughan sniffed. "I suppose that means you are still crying your eyes out over the necessity of sending your children home? I am sorry indeed to see you so poor-spirited. We have all parted with children when the time came, Louisa. You would not wish to see them growing up like dirty little natives burned black by the sun and speaking Hindustani better than English."

"At least," I could not help saying, "then I should *see* them."

"Separation from one's offspring is inevitable for those of us who have the honor to serve in India," Mrs. Colonel Vaughan pronounced, "and it is your duty to reconcile yourself to God's will in this. I am disappointed in you, Louisa, but at least I am glad to see that you have remained here, by your husband's side, as is proper for a wife and helpmeet. I believe it is a mistake for young couples to be separated just because the wife is too tender to allow others to rear her children, and I should have thought less of Captain Westbrook if he had permitted you to escort the children to England."

At least this threw some light on Gordon's refusal to let me go to England with Alice and Harry, for everyone knows that Mrs. Colonel Vaughan has great influence over the colonel, and her disapproval might have been prejudicial to Gordon's career. But I digress—

"Now, Louisa," Mrs. Vaughan continued, "next time I call I hope to find you properly dressed and going about your duties in a Christian spirit of resignation. If you would apply yourself to some useful task, like making beaded silk purses for the bazaar, you would not have time for such follies as weeping over your babies, or playing with your husband's papers, or going down into the native town."

Aha, I thought, now I know the real purpose of this visit. She has heard about my visits to Meeta.

"We are commanded to feed the hungry and clothe

the naked," I said demurely, "and I feel it is no more than my Christian duty to see to the well-being of a servant in need. Meeta's husband is crippled, you know, and she has all those children to feed—"

"Then let her find other work," Mrs. Vaughan replied. "The woman is no longer your servant, Louisa, nor is she your responsibility. Will you feed every stranger in the bazaar, all the teeming millions of India, out of Captain Westbrook's pocket?"

I felt this was hardly a fair statement of the case, as Meeta could hardly be considered a stranger. She had served us faithfully as the children's ayah since Alice's birth seven years ago. Indeed, I was somewhat dismayed when I returned from Bombay to find Gordon had dismissed her as soon as the children and I had departed. We employ so many servants, surely some other position could have been found for her! Naturally I could not override his decision, but I thought there could be no objection to my helping her family with a little food and money to tide them over until Meeta did find other work.

But it would certainly do Gordon's career no good for me to argue the point with the colonel's wife, so I changed the subject and we spent a quarter of an hour engaged in harmless gossip about the doings of the station before she took her leave. Even then, I fear, she was somewhat annoyed with me, for she managed to make one last barbed comment even as she stood at the door.

"I hear that Major Phelps has dropped the Scully girl," she said. "It seems that after determinedly pursuing her all spring, and making her conspicuous by dancing three times or more with her at every ball, he has learned that her father's reputed fortune is all a sham—and so he leaves the poor girl to her own devices, just when she was in hourly expectation of his making an offer! Do you not think it shameful?"

"I think she is well off," I said, for I quite like Barbara Scully and I have always been slightly repulsed by Major Phelps's manner. He is one of those men who garbs innuendo, flirtation, and all manner of overly personal comments in the guise of a joke, so that his conversation is always unpleasant and yet there is very little one can do to stop it. "A man who would marry her only for the sake of a fortune could never be a truly loving husband to her; such a marriage would be worse than none at all."

"Ah," said Mrs. Colonel Vaughan, and I could see from the gleam in her eyes that she thought she had trapped me roundly, "you say so now, Louisa, but is that what you thought eight years ago? Or do you speak from the benefit of experience?"

With that parting shot, she sailed out the door in a positive tempest of rustling silk petticoats and unnecessary flounces, and I put my head down on Gordon's desk and had a good cry. I don't particularly mind her insinuating that Gordon married me only for my inheritance, for I realized long ago that he was not in love with me; indeed, he would have felt it unbecoming to pretend such a thing. But our earlier discussion had rather unsettled me. All her exhortations to accept the children's departure as part of my duty only brought Harry and Alice to my mind as clearly as if I had only kissed them good-bye yesterday. It will be weeks yet before I can hope to receive letters from them—and I cannot, I *cannot* reconcile myself to my duty and trust in Providence as I ought!

I wonder how Gordon is getting on in his search for Gandhara? I should have thought he'd have returned by now; his leave is nearly up.

28 July 1884:

This afternoon I had a most unexpected caller. Hearing some noise outside, I peeped out between the blinds and saw the colonel's carriage, and congratulated myself that I was, for once, busy at a task Mrs. Colonel Vaughan could not but approve—perhaps not beading silk purses for the Christmas bazaar, but at least I was sewing like a lady instead of poring over Gordon's notes for the Dictionary like a bluestocking. Unfortunately, it was the colonel himself who called, and not Mrs. Vaughan, so my display of ladylike industriousness went for naught.

"I have come to see how you are doing in your husband's absence, Mrs. Westbrook," he said, but I felt that he had some other object in mind, for he seemed strangely ill at ease. At the time I thought only that he was hinting that Gordon's leave had been unduly prolonged—and I, of course, had nothing to say to that, as I hastened to make clear to him.

"Thank you, Colonel Vaughan," I said. "I have nothing to complain of. But if you wish to know when Captain Westbrook may be returning, I am afraid I cannot enlighten you. I have heard nothing from him. Will you take a cup of tea?"

I clapped my hands and sent the bearer for tea and cakes. Unfortunately he brought the good silver teapot, in honour I suppose of the colonel's visit, and I was so awkward in pouring, that tea splashed all over his saucer. I was so distraught that I had not even begged him to forgive me for the accident when he spoke.

"I see that arm is still troubling you, Mrs. Westbrook. Has not the break healed yet?"

"Indeed it has," I said, "but Dr. Scully warned me that I ought not to lift anything heavy for some time, and I must confess I had forgotten how much this teapot weighed."

Colonel Vaughan looked at me narrowly, and I remembered that he himself had been a medical man before going into the military. "Yes, perhaps it is too soon for you to have recovered the full strength of that arm. It happened in April, did it not? You fell down the stairs from the verandah?

"You remember correctly," I said, somewhat shortly. It was not an event on which I chose to dwell.

"And before that you had a fall from your horse, as I recall, last January, which left you bruised about the face and shoulders? You really must be more careful, Mrs. Westbrook."

"I fear I am shockingly clumsy," I agreed, for what else could I say?

"But you have suffered no accidents this summer."

"No." I smiled at him, though I felt very little like doing so. "Perhaps I am outgrowing my tendency to stumble."

There seemed very little more to say on that subject, and I was relieved—for a moment—when the colonel reached into his breast pocket for a paper which he studied for a minute before engaging me in conversation again.

"I have had," he said, slowly and somewhat heavily, "a communication from the Mehtar of Chitral."

"Oh?" He had finished his tea during the pause; I poured out a fresh cup for him, and was pleased to see that this time my hand shook hardly at all.

"A somewhat disturbing communication."

I waited for him to go on, since I could think of no polite social comment to make to this information.

"He tells me that Captain Westbrook passed through his state in mid-May, at a time when Chitral had suffered serious depredations from the Kanjuti raiding tribes in the mountains to the north and east. Given the unsettled state of the country, the Mehtar felt it his duty to refuse Captain Westbrook permission to travel on. However, the captain apparently departed by night and crossed the borders of the Mehtar's domain against orders."

Colonel Vaughan put his piece of paper down and studied my face carefully. Somewhat unnerved by this prolonged scrutiny, I took up my sewing and endeavored to resume my work, but my hands were trembling so that I had difficulty in making the stitches.

"The Mehtar seems rather embarrassed at the failure of his guards," he remarked. "It seems they had been commanded to keep Captain Westbrook within the border fort for his own safety. This may explain why he delayed so long in sending this message. He says that he waited because he had hoped to be able to report Cap-

tain Westbrook's return or to have some news of his
further travels, however slight."

He paused again, as though waiting for me to comment, but what could I say? I know nothing of the wild
mountains beyond English territory, nor could I specu-
late as to what had delayed Gordon so long past the time
of his leave.

"He has heard nothing," the colonel went on, "and,
worse than that—the men whom he sent to make enquir-
ies in Kanjuti villages were told unequivocally that no
foreigner had passed that way. This must have been a
lie, for Captain Westbrook had announced publicly that
he intended to go through Bashgul and KamKhel territory in his search for Gandhara. The Mehtar feels—and,
my dear Louisa, I agree with him—that Captain Westbrook must have met his death at the hands of these
savage tribesmen, and that they are lying for fear of
punishment."

I stabbed my needle downwards through the fabric
and pierced my thumb. For a moment I felt no pain,
only a mild surprise at seeing the growing spot of red on
the white muslin I held. "Y-you see, Colonel," I said,
holding out the cloth for him to inspect, "I have not
quite outgrown my clumsiness after all."

"Louisa, have you understood what I am telling you?"
he demanded. He must have been severely agitated, otherwise he would never have committed the impropriety
of addressing me in such a fashion.

"I understand perfectly," I told him. "You, and the
Mehtar of Chitral, and any number of other gentlemen,
believe that my husband must be dead."

"My dear Louisa," the colonel said, "I am so very sorry
to be the bearer of such distressing news."

I remained silent for a moment, marshalling my
thoughts, and Colonel Vaughan averted his face.
Doubtless he expected me to weep for Gordon. It
seemed to me that such a display of emotion would be
decidedly premature.

"Colonel Vaughan," I said at last, "I am not prepared

to go into mourning for my husband on such scanty evidence as you set before me. You speak of rumour and supposition and probabilities; I look for certainties. Who has seen Captain Westbrook's body? Who has spoken with his murderers? A man goes exploring in unknown territory, and he does not return as soon as expected—is that reason to presume him dead?"

The colonel seemed taken aback at my refusal to join him in his reading of events. "But, Louisa—Mrs. Westbrook," he corrected himself, "surely Captain Westbrook would not absent himself for so long without sending some word to you?"

"Colonel," I said, "if he has made a new ethnological discovery worthy of publication in a scientific journal, Captain Westbrook is entirely capable of forgetting that he even *has* a wife. No, Colonel Vaughan. I cannot, I *dare* not assume that my husband is dead. I thank you for your kind concern, but until I see proof positive of his death, I shall continue to anticipate his imminent return."

The colonel sighed. "Your devotion to Captain Westbrook does you credit, Mrs. Westbrook. And I would it were possible to satisfy your anxiety as to his fate, but at present I can hardly send anyone to inquire after him. Travel in these mountains is difficult at the best of times; in summer, with the melting snows flooding the river valleys, it is all but impossible."

"There, you see," I said. "Captain Westbrook may have been delayed in the hills for that very reason." But I felt no sense of triumph in pointing this out; rather the reverse.

"True," Colonel Vaughan agreed. "After all, we know very little of the topography of these mountains. Perhaps—" He broke off rather suddenly; his eyes gleamed, and I felt a sudden unease. The men who have served under Colonel Vaughan praise his subtle mind and his ability to turn any situation, no matter how minor, into a tactical advantage. Why did I feel that my very existence had just become one of those situations? "Mrs.

Westbrook, you are absolutely right. It would ill become our regiment to allow one of our own to be lost without further enquiry. As soon as the floods go down, I shall send one of my men through Chitral to find out more about Captain Westbrook's expedition. Major Phelps, perhaps, or—"

I could not restrain a violent gesture of negation.

"You are right," the colonel said sadly, though I had spoken not a word. "Major Phelps has, perhaps, not quite the tact one would desire in such a delicate mission, although his surveying skills are first-rate."

As if that had anything to do with the matter! Men!

"It will have to be young McAusland," Colonel Vaughan concluded, "and he will not be happy about being taken away from his work with the Pathan tribes on the western border. But you are absolutely right, Mrs. Westbrook. I—ha! I commend your devotion. We must investigate this matter of Captain Westbrook's disappearance quite carefully."

He was almost whistling when he took his leave, and his jaunty air seemed quite inappropriate in one who had come, as he thought, bearing tragic news. Since I could not for a moment believe he shared either my reluctance to believe Gordon dead or my personal reasons for that reluctance, I was at a loss to understand his abrupt change of mood.

15 September 1884:

It seems as though this hot season would never end. Was there ever a time when we walked abroad in the daytime or slept through the night without panting for breath and waking soaked in perspiration? The servants soak the *kus-kus* screens almost hourly, and I have hired two assistant bearers to help the punkah-wallah work through the night, but neither the evaporation of the water nor the constant movement of the heavy, sullen air brings more than a breath of relief. It should be some consolation to know that the children are spared the rigors of the hot season; I am sure I *would* find comfort in that, if I could but hear from them. But now I wake two or three times nightly from confused dreams of them and of Gordon. At one time I fancy my babies are little again and I can rock them in my arms; at another I imagine that Gordon has returned in the night and is lying beside me under the swathes of mosquito netting. And always I wake in tears.

And now there is another worry to add to my list. Lieutenant McAusland left Peshawar before the season of floods was quite over, intending to make his way north to Chitral and thence into the mountainous reaches held by savage tribes. I had thought he would wait until now, when he might have joined one of the caravans going up from the plains to buy silks and tea from Chitral, but he insisted that he could travel more freely and find out more if he went alone; and to my surprise, Colonel Vaughan agreed with him in this. Naturally I had no say in the decision, but I felt it keenly that this brave young man should be setting off into danger just because I could not accept the reports of Gordon's death without having seen his body. Now we hear that the traders do not mean to go up into the mountains at all this year, for there are tales of some tribal war there that will, they say, block the trade route to Chin from which the Mehtar of Chitral receives his silks. I cannot but suspect they fear being caught up in the fringes of the fighting; and if these men, who travel in large groups and well armed, have reason to fear, how much more should we be concerned for Lieutenant McAusland! I pray for him too now, as well as for Alice and Harry. The young man might not be best pleased to know that he has been lumped in with my babes as a subject for a mother's fears, but then, he is hardly likely to know or care about my petitions to the Almighty.

CHAPTER FOUR

Lieutenant James Robertson McAusland, lately a political officer in charge of a sizable group of Pathan tribes, now on detached duty somewhere to the north of the kingdom of Chitral, had no way of knowing that Louisa Westbrook was praying for him. Had he known, he would doubtless have been deeply sensible of the honor done him and most appreciative of her kindness. It was his opinion that somebody had better start praying for his health and well-being, and soon—preferably somebody who had led a less checkered life than James Robertson McAusland.

That life now seemed likely to be cut short before nightfall, rendering any promises of future reform valueless. All day, as he traversed the stony valley between the territory of the Bashguli Kanjutis and the KamKhel Kanjutis, he had been aware of a growing tension among his guides.

The trouble had started in the last Bashgul village. The headman there had first admired his rifle, then hinted that it would be an acceptable gift in return for hospitality. When that hint got no response, he had openly demanded that the "headman of the Angrez" give his people a quantity of new Martini-Henry rifles as a token of friendship. McAusland had explained to the best of his limited ability that the Queen whom he served would on no account allow him to sell British rifles to a tribe dwelling so far beyond her borders.

The men stared and muttered among themselves, and for a while he deeply regretted his limited command of their dialect. If only he'd been among "his" people, the Yusufzais and Afridis of the Pathan frontier, he could have dispelled the tension with a proverb and a jest. But here, among these isolated tribes where every village spoke a different dialect, he was limited to signs and gestures and a handful of basic words for most of his communication. Anything more complicated had to go through Mohsun Khan, the one Kanjuti tribesman with some command of Urdu, and he was not at all sure that Mohsun Khan translated his words accurately.

He had been looking forward to escaping the company of the Bashguli Kanjutis and to a day or two of marching, using the compass to guide him and making notes of the terrain through which he passed. He was not at all pleased when the Bashguli headman informed him that a group of warriors would "guide" him to Kamdesh, the first village in KamKhel territory, and that Mohsun Khan would accompany him as translator. A troublemaker and a group of armed escorts who were just as likely to consider him a prisoner as a guest—that was an inauspicious start for his mission. Not to mention that he'd be unable to take any notes while so escorted; the Kanjutis would certainly report such activity to their ruler, the Thum of Hunza. He in turn would tell the Mehtar of Chitral, who was absurdly sensitive about foreigners surveying the mountains that surrounded his state.

But the Bashguli headman had admitted to seeing another "Angrezi" pass through his territory, heading for Kamdesh, some months previously. "Not like this one, though," he'd told Mohsun Khan, with a contemptuous glance at McAusland that needed no translating. "Tall like a giant, with golden hair, and fair as a Moslem virgin. Are you *sure* this little black-haired man is of the same tribe?"

There was nothing for it, then, but to go on to Kamdesh: otherwise the Kanjutis would decide that he was not really searching for Captain Westbrook but was in their lands for some sinister reasons of his own. Besides, he did owe it to Louisa Westbrook to find out as much as he could about what had happened to her husband.

From the Bashgul village to Kamdesh would have been, McAusland later estimated, about two hours' walk over any reasonable terrain; the actual distance must have been something less than five miles. It took most of the day to get there by foot, toiling alongside a river gorge, then descending into the gorge by a series of shallow niches chipped in the stone, then crossing and recrossing the river at the bottom countless times before it was possible to ascend again. Encrustations of mud and dried branches on the cliffs marked the river's recent high level during the summer when melting snows from the mountains brought floods and mud slides through the gorge. At one point, teetering precariously on a slippery, rounded stone in the middle of the icy rushing water, McAusland looked up and estimated that the lowest such mark was not less than twenty feet above his head. Some seventy feet above that, a narrow cable of plaited twigs dangled from one side of the sheer cliffs.

Mohsun Khan followed the direction of McAusland's gaze and said, "Bridge! Broken now."

"That's why we have to wade the river?"

Mohsun Khan laughed merrily and mimed the disaster: the overladen man mincing along the cable that served as a bridge, the slow breaking of the twigs, the man's desperate clutching at the cable as it whipped loose and flung him into the foaming torrent of the snow-flooded river. The pantomime aroused general merriment among the rest of McAusland's Bashguli escort.

"Er—you saw it yourself?" McAusland inquired for lack of anything better to say.

Mohsun Khan shook his head vigorously and said, "Same like always, every year one bridge, two bridge break."

The discussion did not increase McAusland's confidence when at length they clambered up the side of the cliff, a mile or two farther on, and crossed the gorge by a very similar bridge of twisted twigs to reach the village of Kamdesh. However, it was true, as Mohsun Khan cheerfully pointed out, that this bridge consisted of *two* cables of twigs and bark, one for a footrest and one for a handhold, and was therefore twice as good as the broken one.

Kamdesh village consisted of a cluster of wooden houses perched on the sloping side of a gigantic rock, piled one on top of another in a dizzying array of rough walls and galleries and pillars and flat, mud-caulked roofs. The KamKhels had been watching the strangers as they climbed up the path from the bridge. They did not come forward with any cheerful greetings, but they did not shoot at them either. McAusland reckoned that for a people whose standard greetings, as recorded by Dr. Leitner, included such phrases as "Beat him now, kill him later," failure to shoot on sight actually amounted to a warm welcome in Kanjuti terms.

"His" Bashgulis paused at the foot of the narrow, steep pathway that led up the rock between the houses and began discussing their pay for the journey. McAusland had already agreed to pay each man what he considered a reasonable sum for a day's labor and a wholly extortionate sum for an undesired guide. Now the Bashgulis, led by Mohsun Khan, suggested that McAusland should triple their pay. When he refused the suggestion, Mohsun Khan leapt upon a wall projecting from the lowest house and began haranguing both his own Bashgulis and the curious KamKhels with long, sweeping gestures that invariably ended with an arm pointed straight at the Englishman. McAusland began to be grateful that he understood so little of the Kanjuti dialects; he thought he might have been tempted to take offense if he'd been entirely sure what Mohsun Khan was saying. As the Kanjuti's oratory rose to a peak, McAusland shrugged his shoulders and walked into the first house, turning his back on the crowd. Before they could come after him, pinning him down in the narrow room, he came out again with a three-legged stool in one hand. He seated himself under a tree, took out a book and began reading with the appearance of great interest.

The crowd of Kanjutis burst into laughter. McAusland peeped over the edges of his book and saw that their jeers were directed at Mohsun Khan. Good—perhaps he had defused the situation. He studied the narrow lines of print again. The valley was in shadow now and there was not enough light for reading, but that hardly mattered. He had no hope of really concentrating on a pocket volume of Tacitus while Mohsun Khan invited his neighbors to join in killing the tight-fisted Englishman and robbing him of the gold that they assumed he must carry.

Before long the novelty of this first joke had worn off, and the Kanjutis came crowding round him, jostling him and demanding his attention like tiresome children. Mohsun Khan jerked the book out of his hand.

"Terribly sorry, old chap," McAusland drawled in English, "but I'm afraid you lack the educational background to appreciate Tacitus."

If the meaning of the exact words was not clear to the crowd, the tone of contempt was. Mohsun Khan shouted something to the effect that McAusland should scuttle home to his English army for protection, or he would— He made a sign with his hand of plunging a dagger into his stomach.

McAusland's own stomach contracted involuntarily, but he forced himself to smile pleasantly. "Tummy ache, old fellow? Better go to Gokal Chand for medicine."

The itinerant Hindu medicine-seller traversed the Kanjuti villages twice yearly. His name was known throughout the mountains and that was enough to make McAusland's joke clear to the crowd. While they were still laughing, McAusland announced in very basic words of the Bashguli dialect, "Tired now. Sleep here tonight, march tomorrow." He turned on his heel and strolled with an appearance of unconcern into the house he had first entered, praying that his pretense of having everything under control would calm the Kanjutis.

For a few tense moments he heard the crowd shouting and laughing outside the door; then the noises died down and it sounded as if most of the Kanjutis were moving away to seek entertainment elsewhere. McAusland looked around the house he had commandeered and sighed. No Kanjuti house was comfortable or spacious, but most of them at least had two or three rooms, usually built one on top of another to make the most of the tiny patches of level land among the cliffs. Animals would be kept in the bottom room, the middle room would be a storehouse, and the highest room would be reserved for a sleeping place.

This house evidently belonged to one of the poorest among the poverty-stricken Kanjutis, for it consisted of one room only, with no wooden ladder leading to the next level. At this time of year, thank goodness, the goats were still grazing in a summer pasture and would not expect to share the room; but the floor littered with bones and feathers and anonymous dark lumps left McAusland fearing the worst about his night's accommodations. He might not be robbed or murdered tonight— if he had succeeded in facing down Mohsun Khan and turning the laugh on him—but he would certainly be dinner for a variety of insect forms.

"Angrez?"

McAusland whirled, narrowly escaping knocking his head on one of the low beams that held up the roof, and saw one of the KamKhel Kanjutis at the door.

"Is this your house, Grandfather?"

The old man shook his head and launched into a speech of which McAusland understood perhaps one word in ten. The gist of the speech seemed to be that this house was not a fitting residence for an honored foreign guest and that McAusland should follow the old man to a house higher up on the mountainside, where he might bestow his packs before joining the KamKhel Kanjutis in a feast of welcome.

Such generosity to a stranger had not been McAusland's experience among the Bashgul Kanjutis. He wondered cynically whether the KamKhels hoped to steal his pistol and rifle while he left them unguarded, or whether the feast was a prelude to another demand for British arms such as the Bashgulis had made. However, he could not refuse the invitation without insulting the village; and in any case, the feast would give him an opportunity to make the expected inquiries about Gordon Westbrook.

He followed his guide up a steep path on the east face of a great slab of rock. Houses rose in terraces to his right, one crowded atop another like Manchester tenements, but supported by a crazy network of wooden posts and smooth water-worn stones and burdened by overhanging wooden verandahs. Children wrapped in greasy rags tumbled about the porches and rooftops, unsupervised and seemingly in constant danger of breaking their necks. Kanjuti women, ornamented with clusters of silver and coral and dark with the smoke of their own cooking fires, leaned over the verandahs and called out shrill comments about the foreigner. McAusland understood somewhat less of the women's remarks than he had of his guide's speech, but still the back of his neck grew uncomfortably warm and he had a suspicion that his ears were turning red. He thought regretfully of the Pathan tribesmen with whom he normally worked, men who kept their women under lock and key and avenged any insult to family honor with gun or knife. These women were allowed an indecent degree of freedom, and look where that led! Unveiled, unrestrained in their speech, and doubtless unchaste as well, they were, in McAusland's opinion, a disgrace to their sex.

The house allotted to him consisted of the usual three rooms. The top room was furnished with a long, wide plank that ran all along the back wall, some six inches from the floor, to serve as bed and chair in one. Above the plank hung two round leather shields. Following the instructions and gestures of his guide, McAusland deposited his pack and weapons on the plank with some reluctance. He did what he could to secure the room by drawing up the "ladder"—a notched log—that gave access from the doorway to the roof of the room immediately below. A second ladder in the center of the room led upwards through a smoke-grimed aperture in the roof; McAusland followed his guide up this ladder and found himself on a rooftop terrace, beside and about three feet below the dancing platform where his feast of welcome was to be held. Both rooftop and platform consisted of wide, somewhat irregularly shaped wooden planks with a quantity of dirt trodden down into the cracks. A few dirty children were playing on the edge of the platform, courting broken necks as usual, and completely ignored by the adults, also as usual.

The Bashgulis who had escorted McAusland this far were seated on the floor of the dancing platform, whispering to one another and looking enviously at their KamKhel hosts who had donned their festival finery for this great occasion. The usual skimpy garments of tattered black wool had been set aside for long, flowing robes of Chin brocade with embroidered sleeves. The robes were so long that they had to be tucked up with sashes to prevent the skirts trailing on the ground, and the Kanjuti delight in color and ornament ran wild with these sashes; McAusland saw one man wearing an iron-studded leather belt, a woven sash covered with cowrie shells, and a strip cut from a Kashmir shawl, one atop the other until his torso was almost completely covered with the layers of belts. Above the ornamented sashes and silk robes, the Kanjutis' heads were decorated with brilliantly colored turbans and nodding feathers. The total effect was very nearly as gaudy as a viceregal ball at Government House.

The old man who had greeted McAusland, seeing his interest in the costumes, squatted beside him and proffered an interpretation of the different ornaments. "Red turban, man of family, on council. Striped turban—bah!

Young man, no kills, nobody important. Falcon feather in headdress, *mur-patay*. Peacock feather, *pot-mur-patay*. Gold band, *kaca-mur-patay*."

"Meaning?" McAusland asked. Not that he cared much about the organization of Kanjuti tribal life, but since his host was bothering to interlace his Kanjuti words with enough Urdu to be intelligible, it seemed only courteous to try and keep up the conversation.

"*Mur-patay*, man killed six Moslems," the old man explained. "*Pot-mur-patay*, ten Moslems killed. *Kaca-mur-patay* . . ."

"Thank you," McAusland said, "I . . . believe I have the general idea." The Thum of Hunza was a Moslem and he attempted to force his belief on the people in his territory, but it had long been suspected that the villagers in the high mountains were still openly pagan. However, this particular detail of their paganism had not been reported by the few ethnographers and explorers who'd previously had contact with the remoter tribes. Sickened, but curious in spite of himself, he glanced idly round the assemblage in search of a man with a gold headband. There seemed to be only one, a lean fellow with an evil expression. Besides the headband and the peacock feather, he was festooned with a clanking assortment of silver and gilt jewelry; as he turned towards them, McAusland saw two or three silver Koran cases—doubtless looted from the killed Moslems—and a strange circular ornament that seemed to have a glass face.

A glass face.

He felt oddly detached from his own limbs, his own movements. From some place removed from the dancing platform he watched, a passive observer, as his body rose and strode jerkily across the platform, pushing aside Kanjutis until he stood before the *kaca-mur-patay*. Yes, it was what he had thought it must be. One hand reached out and detached Gordon Westbrook's compass from the cord that suspended it about the Kanjuti's neck. He did not need to read the inscription to verify that it was the same instrument; it was the finest compass in Peshawar, of Swiss work, and McAusland had often regretted that such a good instrument should be wasted on an ethnologist with neither the interest nor the inclination to use it properly. Nevertheless he turned the compass over and studied, without really seeing, the words engraved on the back: *For Captain Westbrook, 7 December 1881. A gift from his wife on the occasion of our fifth wedding anniversary—L.W.*

The greasy Kanjuti before him snarled and reached for the compass. McAusland's fingers closed about it. "No. You can't have this." It was a damned ticklish moment, but he'd always been taught that it was fatal to back down before a native. They had to be brought to understand the natural moral superiority of the ruling race; all else followed from that. And the first rule was never to show doubt or fear.

He looked about the platform and spied Mohsun Khan, leaning back against one of the carved wooden pillars at the outer edge of the platform and laughing with his head thrown back and eyes closed to gleaming slits. Behind the pillar, there was nothing but empty space; the platform jutted out over the edge of the flat rock on which the whole village perched, and it was a long way down to the river.

"Mohsun Khan!" he called. "Please explain to this man that this is not an ornament or a toy. It was the private property of a British officer, and I must return it to his widow."

For a moment he feared that Mohsun Khan would refuse to translate for him. "I will, of course, reimburse him for the value of the trinket," McAusland added.

That concept, seemingly, needed little translation. Within minutes McAusland was surrounded by gesticulating, shouting Kanjutis, waving fingers and yelling numbers into his face. At least, he assumed they were numbers. He was all but deafened by the enthusiastic babel before Mohsun Khan roused himself and came striding to the center of the crowd, calling in authoritative tones for silence. The Kanjutis abruptly abandoned their bargaining session and clustered around Mohsun Khan, talking in lowered tones and glancing occasionally at McAusland in a way that made him feel increasingly nervous. The few words he caught did little to reassure him: "kill" and "the other Angrez" and "*rifle*," this last in heavily accented English.

When the Kanjutis began sidling round him again, McAusland decided he had pushed the natural superiority of a British officer far enough. Moral superiority hadn't saved Westbrook, had it? He was surrounded on three sides, but at least his line of retreat was clear. McAusland took three long strides back to the edge of the dancing platform, jumped to the roof of his temporary residence, went through the smokehole and picked up his rifle before anyone thought to bar his way.

The sound of gunfire echoed up the steep walls of the canyon above Kamdesh, sharp clapping noises that bounced and ricocheted from one side of the canyon to the other like bullets, until the echoes died away into a faint rattle high on the mountainside. There the last pattering echo of the shots alerted two travellers who inched along the stone face of the highest cliff, arms outspread to the wall, feeling with their toes for the narrow path of rocks crammed into crevices and cedar beams jutting out into emptiness.

At the first noise, Paluk froze where he stood, one hand outstretched towards Tamai. His cautious, shuffling progress had disturbed nothing, but when he stopped so suddenly a pebble broke free under his right foot and dropped into the abyss beneath them. The small sounds of its fall, bouncing off bare rock faces until it spun into the river so far below, were magnified in the stillness; then a second burst of gunfire echoed up the canyon and covered the noise of the pebble.

Ever since they began this perilous crossing Paluk had been cursing the KamKhels, their casual attitude towards roads, and the gods of these mountains in a steady undertone. Now he added a few remarks on Kanjutis and their tendency to engage in tribal wars just when any intelligent village would be celebrating the harvest and preparing for winter.

"No hope of slipping by unobserved now," he finished gloomily. "We'll have to go around, north again and to the east—there's another pass that way. A bad one."

"How much will that add to the journey?"

"A week. Maybe two. It's a long way to the next pass."

"And what villages are in our way?"

"More KamKhels. Some Yasinis—they're Moslems, not devil-worshipers like the KamKhel Kanjutis, but their habits are just as nasty. And a Kirghiz camp. Go on, will you? I don't want to be standing on this ledge until they wander up this way and notice us. They're not friendly to strangers even when they're nominally at peace," Paluk complained.

"Yes," Tamai said, almost under her breath. "I know."

Paluk swallowed the next few words of his complaint unspoken.

"You might as well go on," she said after a moment. "We can't take the northern pass, Paluk; if the Kirghiz were there last year, the northmen may be there this year. We'll just have to go through Kamdesh."

"Yes, but—" Again Paluk stopped himself. They had been too long on this exposed ledge; his back felt more naked and vulnerable with every slow minute that crawled by. Even if they had to shuffle all the way back around the cliff, after dark, he would prefer to finish this argument with Tamai on solid ground and with some cover between them and the Kanjuti village.

The argument finished, as he might have known, just as it had begun; they were going to do it Tamai's way. She didn't even seem to know there had been an argument.

"You can't shoot your way through a whole village of Kanjutis, you know, even with your *Martini-Henry* jezail," Paluk said at one point.

"*Rifle*," Tamai corrected him. "The tribe who make these jezails call them *rifles*. We must learn the correct words so that we can bargain with them when the time comes. And I don't mean to shoot anybody if I can avoid it."

"If you think we can slip past the village unobserved, when they're trying to kill the next village over and both sides have sentries out—"

"I don't. Paluk, stop worrying and help me! I have an idea."

Paluk shut up then and did as he was told, but he also started worrying seriously. Tamai's last bright idea had been that they should go south to find the Angrez tribe and buy more jezails—*rifles*—from them, and look where that had gotten them: on the fringes of a Kanjuti war. No, that wasn't quite fair. His crazy cousin had been perfectly prepared to set forth alone, over mountains she'd never seen and through passes she'd never crossed, with no more knowledge of the world outside Gandhara than a child's memories of terror and the tales told by caravan leaders. He'd had to argue half through the night to convince her that she hadn't a hope of success without the company of somebody like him. He might not be a caravan leader, but he was a travelled man, having been as far as the Kirghiz camp to the north and all the way to Bashgul, on the border of Chitral, to the south. Of course, in all these extensive travels he'd never encountered the tribe called Angrez, but there was no hope of convincing Tamai that she'd been taken in by a trader's fantastic tales. The best he could do was to go along with her until she gave up the search.

And having argued himself into that position, he was not going to turn about and run for the shelter of Gandhara at the first setback. Even if he did know, from twenty-odd years of experience, that Tamai's bright ideas usually got both of them into more trouble than they were worth. Even if he didn't have the faintest idea why she was now insisting that they unpack both their packs to get at a black wool blanket and her best embroidered sash.

Eventually her reasoning became clear to him, and that nearly started another argument.

"You can't get away with it."

"Yes, I can. These people are ignorant."

"But you failed your test in the Disciplines!" Paluk yelped, too scared for tact.

"Paluk. I don't have to *be* a wisewoman to get us through the village; I just have to make these Kanjutis *think* I'm a wisewoman. The point is not how much I know, but how much they don't know. They've never understood how the Disciplines work. They wouldn't begin to know what's wrong with my magic. And they *do* know that it can be very, very dangerous to annoy a wisewoman. Now if you'll just act a little more confident, we can walk through the village *and* the war and both sides will leave us strictly alone." Tamai looked up at her cousin with a strained smile on her thin face. She seemed very pale, but that might have been an effect of the fading light. "A little more respect would be appropriate, too. If I were really a wisewoman you wouldn't dare argue with me like this. *Would you?*"

On the last words Tamai rose to her feet and let the black cloak about her shoulders fall slightly open, exposing a band of brilliant color on the inside. Even though he knew the cloak was only his old blanket and the colored band was only Tamai's best embroidered sash, Paluk automatically glanced away as if he were really in danger of staring at a wisewoman's secret badges of rank. And that involuntary gesture, more than anything that Tamai said, made him feel that this masquerade had some chance of succeeding. All the same, "some chance" wasn't exactly the odds he liked to wager on when the stakes were his life and Tamai's.

"It's getting dark," he pointed out as they negotiated the hairpin bends and curves of the path down the cliff.

"I've—noticed." Tamai's voice shook as though she'd stumbled over a rock in mid-sentence. Paluk hoped that was the reason.

"They won't be able to see your wisewoman's cloak."

"I don't want them to get a very close look at it,"

Tamai said abstractedly. "Watch out, there's a break in the path. Take my hand till we're on solid rock again."

Her fingers were cold.

They were too close to the village now for Paluk to risk any more argument. He followed Tamai, keeping a respectful distance once they were past the worst parts of the cliffside path, and watching through the gathering gloom for any sign of movement to right or left.

Just as the first cluster of flat-roofed huts came into view, clinging to the mountainside below their feet, there was a shriek like a kite ahead of them and Paluk heard the sound of bare feet pattering down the path. Tamai swore and flung her hand out, too late to stop the boy. Fire blazed briefly from her fingertips and showed the child's eyes gleaming as he turned for a moment; then the darkness enshrouded them and the boy was down among the rooftops of Kamdesh.

"I *wish* you wouldn't do that in the dry season," Paluk jested.

"I, too." Tamai sounded weary and tense, and Paluk wondered if she'd known the fire would come just then, or whether it had been an accident. "Oh, well. If they use children as sentinels, it must not be much of a war," Tamai said under her breath. They had heard no more gunfire since that first outbreak of shots. Paluk wondered if they had made a mistake in choosing to walk openly through the village instead of trying to skirt it as they had the earlier KamKhel settlements.

Torches flared among the rooftops, and Paluk caught a glimpse of deep brilliant colors set off by the sparkle of gold and silver: green and purple brocades of Chin, turbans surmounted by swaying clusters of feathers, belts heavy with shells and silver and raw gems. Three Kam-Khel men in festival garb came up the path to greet them, bearing pine knots that flickered and sputtered with a fitful golden light.

"Well met, wisewoman of Gandhara," said the oldest man, and Paluk let out a breath that he hadn't been aware of holding. "You are wanted in the village. How did you come so quickly to our need?"

Tamai spoke only a few words of the KamKhel dialect, and those only when she cried out in nightmare; she could not possibly understand the men. Paluk stepped in front of her. "My lady is not to be addressed by common folk," he said loftily, "nor is it your place to question a wisewoman. I will communicate your desires to her, should you be found worthy."

The spokesman for the tribe lifted a pouch at his waist so that Paluk could hear the jingle of coins, but he was not so crass as to spill them out for inspection. "I think we can make an arrangement for our mutual profit," he said.

After hearing the Kanjutis' story, Paluk sent the Kam-Khels back down the path with a lordly gesture and announced that his lady would give them her decision when she was ready.

"You were right, Tamai," he said as soon as the torches had bobbed out of sight. "I can't believe it. You were right about everything! That merchant was telling the truth! Who ever heard of a trader who spoke truth? There *is* a tribe called Angrez, there really is, and they do have *rifles*. The KamKhels have one of them now."

"One *rifle* won't do us much good," Tamai pointed out.

"No, I mean they have an Angrez."

"Prisoner?"

"Ah—not exactly." The way the KamKhel told it, the Angrez had come into the valley alone and had grossly insulted the most important man in the village for no reason whatsoever. When the headman of the village tried to reason with him and gently point out his error, the Angrez had barricaded himself in one of the village houses and had begun shooting innocent villagers through the windowslits.

"I think I understand," Tamai said when Paluk had told her this version of events. "I expect what really happened is that they tried to rob him, he defended himself better than they expected, and now they don't know how to get rid of him without risking his shooting a few of their own people."

Paluk nodded. "Something like that."

"Well, I expect they'll figure out what to do about it eventually," Tamai said. "They could drop fire through the smokehole and try to smoke him out, or they could wait until he starves."

"I think they're in a hurry. They seem to be assuming that you sensed their need and magically transported yourself to this valley just in time to solve the problem. The headman is willing to *pay* us to get rid of the Angrez, Tamai."

"It's a trap," Tamai said at once. "They don't need to do that. They don't need a wisewoman to help them kill; KamKhels do that perfectly well on their own. What do they really want?"

"What I told you," Paluk insisted. "It's a gift, Tamai. They were trying to shoot him, that's true, but now they can't wait and they don't dare attack. They need someone to bargain for them—and who better than a Gandharan wisewoman? Everybody trusts our healers."

"Why can't they wait him out?"

Ordinarily, Paluk knew, Tamai would have rushed to help as soon as she knew the full story. But when it came to the KamKhels, she was unpredictable at best. She might not care to save a KamKhel life, even a very small one. In the end he decided he could only tell her the truth and hope that she understood the need. "The Angrez is in the headman's house. And so is the headman's only son. The child must have wandered in there during the feast and fallen asleep where he was used to sleeping, and nobody missed him until after the shooting began. That's why we haven't heard any more shots. Just about the time we started down here, the boy's mother missed him—and then they heard him crying from inside the house."

CHAPTER FIVE

[Extracts from the Political and Secret Correspondence series of the India Office Records, L/P and S/3, 1884, p. 392 et seq.: McAusland, James R., "Confidential Report on a Mission to Chitral and Beyond."]

At this juncture I felt that my position vis-à-vis my hosts, the Kamdesh Kanjutis of the KamKhel tribe, was unlikely to be resolved in a manner totally satisfactory to all parties. Although I had held them off for some time by firing from the various window slits and cracks in the wall of the ill-constructed room in which I found myself, it was clear that either lack of ammunition or the advent of darkness would soon make this tactic difficult if not impossible to sustain. I accordingly took advantage of the remaining moments of daylight to seat myself on the rude plank which, as I have said, ran halfway round the room and was evidently intended to serve as both bed and chair. Here, having first commended my soul to my Maker, I jotted down on the flyleaf of my copy of Tacitus a brief account of the events related in the first section of my report, together with my reasons for supposing, first, that Captain Westbrook's death could now be considered a certainty, and second, that my opportunities for doing further surveying in this area would be severely limited in the near future. I concluded these notes by stating that I felt a strategic withdrawal would be both tactically and morally appropriate but that I doubted my ability to execute such a manuever, and expressing the hope that these notes might be found some day by another Englishman who would then be able to communicate the intelligence contained in them, together with the rough sketchmaps and data concealed in the binding, to some official of Her Majesty's Government in India.

The writing of this account, brief though it was, was interrupted several times by the necessity to move to one or another of the slits in the walls for a brief exchange of shots designed to persuade my hosts that an immediate advance on my position would be inadvisable. Upon returning to my seat after one such excursion, I made a discovery that was, temporarily at least, even more disconcerting than the extreme difficulties of my present position.

I was not alone in the room.

The other occupant of the room, a Kanjuti baby of some eighteen months, must have crawled or fallen into the room while I was occupied on the dancing platform. Thereafter it had evidently fallen asleep under the bench on which I sat, and when I returned to this room, in some haste and with numerous other worries, I had taken the dim form which I glimpsed there for a pile of rags. The child had slumbered peacefully through several exchanges of gunfire, probably being accustomed to the sounds of warfare from its cradle, but eventually my repeated movements awakened it. The baby announced its presence in a manner I could not but think of as typical of Kanjuti hospitality. It bit me on the ankle.

Since I was wearing boots, this unprovoked attack was startling but not immediately painful. However, the Kanjuti baby began to cry rather loudly, doubtless out of frustration at having failed to draw blood from an enemy—that is to say, a stranger. I understand that under such circumstances one is expected to dandle the baby on one's knee. I accordingly executed this maneuver, but without result (unless you count the soaking of my undress uniform as a result; the child was *wet* as well as angry).

I bounced it up and down a few times, trying whatever appropriate soothing phrases came to my mind, such as, "Hush, hush, little darling." The child's roaring continued unabated until, by twisting its head to the right, it managed to seize onto one of my fingers, which it bit hard enough to draw blood before I wrested my hand free.

Whether the satisfaction of biting me silenced it, or whether it was soothed by my involuntary exclamation of, "Cut it out, you little bugger," which probably corresponds to a Kaffir term of endearment, we shall never know. At the time I was only grateful for the following minor ameliorations of my lot: the child had ceased crying, I had retrieved most of my left index finger, and the Kanjutis outside had temporarily ceased firing at the windows of the room in which I had blockaded myself. Even as I sat bouncing the child on my knee, darkness had overtaken us, and neither the Kanjutis nor I could have seen well enough for a further exchange of shots in any case.

After a few moments of peace it occurred to me that the cessation of active hostilities probably portended some attempt to creep up to the very walls of my sanctuary. I peered through the window slits and was astonished to see a native woman in a black cloak crossing the dancing platform, in full view of my line of fire, and making no attempt at concealment; in fact, she carried a burning splinter of pinewood in one hand to light her way. I naturally assumed that she must be the child's mother, and that the strength of her maternal instincts had overpowered her sense of self-preservation. (By this time I was ready to grant that the Kanjuti women must be subject to the strongest and most irrational instincts of maternal care known to humanity; how else to explain the fact that the brat presently rendering my sanctuary malodorous had not been strangled in its cradle?)

My own instincts of self-preservation were somewhat

atrophied by the disgusting odor emanating from the child's lower regions, but I was not yet entirely suicidal. I unbolted the trapdoor over the smokehole and lifted the child through the aperture, following after it in such a way that any Kanjuti meaning to shoot me down would necessarily have to risk the life of the child as well. The woman had meanwhile stooped to set her torch in a crack of the dancing platform, but she did not retreat as would have been the case, I thought, had she come only to expose my position to the Kanjuti marksmen.

"For God's sake, woman, take your brat and get it out of here!" I exclaimed in Urdu, following with the Kanjuti words *"Kolleh. Hittoo. Itsooyess!"* meaning roughly, "Here. Child. To take away!" Under the stress of the moment, what I had learned of Kanjuti grammar had entirely escaped me, and I counted myself fortunate to have remembered this much of the relevant vocabulary.

(I learned later, on consulting Major Biddulph's word lists, that I had erred in using the vocabulary of the Burishki Kanjutis rather than the KamKhel Kanjutis. It seems I should have said, *"Ani. Shudar. Nikaloyki!"* I mention this only to illustrate the extreme difficulty of communicating with people who cannot even manage to keep a common language from one village to the next, and who in any case would prefer to shoot the stranger rather than to parley with him.)

Fortunately my grasp, or lack thereof, of the Kanjuti dialects was of no significance in this situation, as the woman replied to my plea in Urdu as halting and ungrammatical as my attempt at Kanjuti had been.

"Not my child," she replied, and a look of ineffable sadness crossed features which I was now able to recognize as somewhat finer and significantly cleaner than those of the average Kanjuti woman. "You give back the child, Kanjutis let you go free, good?"

It dawned upon me that my erstwhile hosts had actually feared for the well-being of this small hostage.

"Madam," I replied, "a British officer does not make war on women and children!"

She appeared somewhat disappointed at this statement. At the time I assumed that she thought the less of me for lacking the bloodthirsty attitude of her people (remember that I still believed this woman to be a Kanjuti, albeit an unusually clean one); only later did I understand that my use of the term "British" rather than "English" had confused her as to my national identity. But I anticipate.

It was a strange parley that we held, there upon the rooftops of Kamdesh, lighted half by the red-gold flames of the pine torch and half by the silver light of the rising moon. The woman gave me to understand that her name was Tamai, that she hailed from a tribe some short distance away and that the Kanjutis had employed her as a negotiator to secure the return of the infant.

"In return for my free departure from Kamdesh?" By this time, as I have said, I had no doubt as to poor Captain Westbrook's fate, nor could I feel that I would be able to carry out any other part of my mission through hostile Kanjuti territory. Retreat seemed both sensible and extremely desirable.

"That is my intention," the woman said, leaving me in some doubt as to the Kanjutis' intentions. She suggested that she, her companion Paluk and the Kanjuti baby should all travel with me as far as the swaying bridge of cables by which I had entered Kamdesh. At that point we would leave the baby, but the Kanjutis would have been warned not to attempt retrieving the child until our party had safely crossed the bridge. I felt that the woman might be trusting overmuch in the Kanjuti sense of honour, but being unable to propose a better plan, I accepted hers.

Bringing up my gear from the room below, I followed Tamai and her companion across the rooftops and down the sloping rock. At every moment the back of my neck twitched with apprehension of a sudden attack from one of the carved wooden verandahs overhanging the path, but it seemed the Kanjutis valued this child more highly than I had dared to hope. I learned later that the child was the only son of the headman, whose house I had occupied, and that he had threatened any of his people who risked the child's life with being made a sacrifice to Zhiwud. (Details of the manner in which the pagans of Hunza and Kanjut worship Zhiwud will be found in Dr. Leitner's report to the Royal Geographical Society, 1866, v. l, pp. 413–415. The exact manner of the sacrifice is described in Latin, being unfit for repetition in plain English.)

We were still some steps from the bridge when Tamai set the child down in a crevice between two rocks from which it peered up at us, evidently too frightened to move. Despite my previous feelings about Kanjuti babies, I now felt some concern about leaving a baby so close to the gorge. "What if it should crawl out of this crevice and throw itself over the side?" I asked Tamai.

"We set a guard," she told me. Before I could ask which of us was to stand guard over the child, she flung out her right arm—which I now observed to be covered with a half-sleeve of thick leather—and gave a shrill cry which was answered, moments later, by the screech of a bird of prey. It came plummeting down among us like a hawk stooping to the lure, but greater than any hawk I have ever seen the Indians to fly: a full-grown golden eagle, whose weight should have knocked the slender hillwoman down if the bird had not slowed at the last moment, beating its wings to stop the full force of its downward plunge.

Tamai stroked the bird's head and whispered to it while it fixed me with such a baleful stare that I could almost believe it possessed of a human intelligence: just so, bright-eyed and hostile and wary, do the Kanjutis look when one enters their territory. Then she stepped back and let the eagle perch on a rock over the child's head.

"Dushmuni will not let the child wander," she assured me, "and she will give warning should we be followed."

Rather a novel idea, using a bird of prey to act as nursemaid! But at this point I was in no case to argue with Tamai's certainty. She had extinguished her pine torch, and the bridge hung before us, a slender double thread over an abyss shrouded in night. Tamai crossed before me, moving so nonchalantly and gracefully along the double line of ropes that I could not for very shame hang back. Behind me came the man Paluk, gripping the lower rope with his toes and holding the upper one with one hand only, that he might keep a rifle pointed back at the KamKhel village at all times. Whatever one may think of the manners and morals of these savage hill tribes, I am forced to admire the feats of mountaineering which they undertake daily, crossing glaciers and ravines as casually as an Englishman might stroll to his club.

On the far side of the ravine, once we had all crossed safely, the woman Tamai stooped and withdrew a short knife from her boot. Two quick slashes cut through the lower of the two ropes constituting the bridge, and the freed cable swung back to dangle harmlessly down the cliff before the Kanjuti village. She passed the knife once or twice above the handrope, but without allowing the blade actually to touch the rope, and then returned her dagger to its place of concealment before I could get a good look at the weapon. (Later I was able to examine it in detail. The ornamented hilt and the curve of the blade suggested a direct relationship with the Tibetan ghost dagger; see my forthcoming paper in the Reports of the Royal Asiatic Society for a sketch of the weapon.)

The man Paluk now took the lead and hurried us along a trail barely made visible by the risen moon. Within moments I heard the swish of wings through the night sky, and I thought I could see the golden eagle circling high above us.

As we travelled, Tamai explained her reasoning in the matter of the bridge to me. To have broken both ropes of the bridge, she said, would have caused the KamKhel Kanjutis serious annoyance and might have resulted in a war with her tribe. With the handrope left, they could send a man by daylight to repair the footrope, but they would probably not risk making the crossing by night. Besides, they would fear that she had cut through part of the top rope also, so that it might break when it bore a man's weight and so dash one or more of their number into the abyss. Kanjutis, she said disdainfully, liked such treacherous methods of killing.

"And your tribe does not?" I enquired. This was my first hint that she was not of the same people as those who had attacked me.

"What is yours?" she returned without answering my question. "British? I do not know this name."

I took the opportunity to explain, as well as I could given these people's ignorance, something of the might and power of the British Empire and the extent of the dominions over which servants of our gracious Queen hold sway. The woman Tamai did not exactly call me a liar outright, but her guarded responses made me feel that she was not quite ready to accept my word without question. Fortunately, from my extensive work with the Pathan tribes, I am accustomed to this little difficulty. Most natives cannot understand the importance of the British Empire, or our destiny in world affairs, until a few of their leading men have been brought to Jacobabad or even to Peshawar to see the works of the Raj for themselves.

However, Tamai's first questions showed that she was not quite as ignorant as I had assumed; she was only suffering from a minor point of confusion, easily cleared up. After questioning me in some detail about the location of my fellows (to keep matters simple I mentioned only the Vale of Peshawar; I doubted that this poor hill-woman could have comprehended the concept of the entire Indian Raj, let alone the ocean which lies between us and Home) she said that I seemed to claim the same territory as another tribe of which she had heard, the Angrez.

"You mean English?" I exclaimed.

"Yes, yes, although you do not say it right," she corrected me impatiently. "An-grez!" speaking loudly and slowly, as though I were a child or an idiot. "They have taken the ancestral homeland of my people. And they made your rifle. Surely you know of the An-grez?"

I did not understand this pretense that her savage tribe had some claim to the Vale of Peshawar, but I did manage to convey to her that I did, in fact, come of those people called English by some, but more correctly British by the rest. (As a Scotsman, I must be forgiven for insisting on this point.) Tamai nodded thoughtfully. "Good," she announced. "We search for the Angrez, Paluk and I. We will guide you to your home, and you will repay by telling your people to make us many good rifles like yours."

The eternal native desire for arms! Naturally I had no intention of putting up with these hillmen on my homeward journey, nor was there any possibility that we would agree to sell their tribe the arms I had just refused to the Kanjutis. But in my present circumstances—recall that we were travelling by moonlight along a path I had found difficult enough by daylight, that behind us were the KamKhel Kanjutis who had killed poor Westbrook and would have meted out the same fate to me, and ahead were the Bashguli Kanjutis who also held no very friendly feelings to me—under the circumstances, I thought it best not to quarrel with the woman.

I was, I must admit, quite weary, and the moon was high overhead, when at last we reached the narrowest point of the gorge. We had just paused, looking for the hand- and footholds which would allow us to creep along the cliff without descending into the water, when Dushmuni swooped down with a screech of alarm. At the same moment rifle fire echoed across the canyon.

Somehow we all found the narrow footholds in the side of the cliff without further delay. I have no very clear memory of the crossing of the next few minutes. The eagle was all about us, Tamai was calling to it in the same shrill tone she had used earlier, and bullets were breaking the very rocks to which we clung into splinters. A moment later, we had put one wall of the twisting gorge between us and our assailants, and had found somewhat better cover behind an outcropping of naked rocks. The eagle had disappeared; I learned later that Tamai had commanded it to circle overhead, where it might be able to warn us of any sudden attack, but to keep out of range of the Kanjuti fire at all costs. It seemed the Kanjutis had indeed risked a hand-over-hand crossing of the one remaining strand of their bridge, by night, in order to follow us and exact their revenge!

When I said as much to Tamai, she indicated that I was a fool to think the Kanjutis cared for honour and revenge; it was my rifle they wanted, she said. It was a fine weapon and would give a serious advantage to any tribe that had the possession of it.

I had the distinct impression that she herself might well have murdered me for my rifle had she not set her sights on a higher, albeit impossible, goal of obtaining many more such weapons from my "tribe." This did not seem a propitious time to pursue such a question, as we were all crowded together in this small space and in imminent danger of death, but I did feel grateful that I had not troubled to refute her original idea that she could buy arms from the British Raj when she first stated this plan.

Paluk rose to his knees and aimed his own long jezail up the pass through which we had come, but Tamai slapped the weapon down. She said that he was a fool to think of firing; he could not possibly aim in this poor light, and his shots would serve only to give away our position to our attackers. Much to my surprise, Paluk accepted this criticism without striking the woman. These hillmen are not half the *men* my Pathans are; I cannot imagine a Yusufzai hearing such impertinence from his woman without giving her, at the least, a bloody nose and a split lip for speaking to him in such a manner. Even if she did happen to be right.

He merely replied that our position would be much the worse if we were pinned down here until daylight, and said that it was a pity we didn't have a wisewoman to "cast the veil" over our attackers. I did not understand this last allusion but supposed it to be some local idiom; however, it seemed to be quite meaningful to Tamai. Her lips thinned and she snapped at Paluk in their own tongue, then settled back in the shelter of the rock and drew her blanket over her head.

A moment later we had a most amazing stroke of luck. The KamKhels had continued firing intermittently, although from the circumstance that none of their shots came anywhere near us I concluded that they were in fact unsure of just where in the rocky gorge we might have taken cover. Now a far-ranging shot must have dislodged some key bit of rock near the top of the gorge, for I heard a series of sharp cracks, then a rumbling roar, and looked up just in time to see what appeared to be the edge of the mountain toppling down upon us. Immediate action was necessary if we were not to be buried under tons of rock. Momentarily heedless of the danger from the KamKhels, I sprang to my feet. Paluk did likewise, but instead of running he took Tamai's blanket-covered form by the shoulders and attempted to drag her bodily away from the danger. Her body was quite rigid, as though she were experiencing some form of epileptic fit. Seeing his desperation, I seized the woman's feet and together we ran with her away from the rock slide, down the valley of Bashgul. She was lighter than I had expected and we were able to get well away from the area of danger before the rumbling ceased. I looked back and saw the rocky, narrow ravine where we had sheltered a moment earlier quite buried under an avalanche of boulders. The pass between Kamdesh and Bashgul was completely filled, and an ominous silence reigned where, only moments before, the air had been filled with the echoes of Kanjuti gunfire.

CHAPTER SIX

[Continuation of Lieutenant McAusland's report]

The remainder of our journey back to British India was, thankfully, almost devoid of incident. We had, of course, some difficult terrain to cover, some of it inhabited by the most treacherous and violent tribes known to humanity; but not until we were almost home, crossing the Malakand Pass, did we encounter any serious danger.

It may seem strange that, having earlier decided to reject the escort of the two natives Tamai and Paluk, I should now speak of "our party" as though it were a settled thing that we should travel together. The events of the next day gave me reason to think that they should be brought back to British territory for interrogation; and being ill-equipped to make them my prisoners, I allowed them to continue thinking of themselves as my "guides" until we should reach the first station in British India.

After the accidental destruction of the pass between Bashguli and KamKhel territory, we travelled some miles on down the gradually widening ravine and up the cliffs on the south side, finding our way by the sharp but deceptive light of the moon. We were all too tired for further conversation, and when at length my self-appointed "guides" indicated that they felt it safe to stop,

I composed myself to sleep on the rocky ground with as much comfort as if I had been in a featherbed.

The next morning dawned clear and bright, with only a slight overhang of clouds visible on the furthest mountain ranges. A cursory examination of my surroundings showed that Tamai and Paluk had led me to a high point which offered much better opportunities for surveying than the low path through the ravine which I had traversed only the previous day with my Bashguli guides. Paluk informed me that we were travelling this far out of the usual way in order to avoid contact with the Bashguli Kanjutis, who might be annoyed when they discovered that the pass offering them communication with their KamKhel neighbors had been blocked by a rock slide.

"But surely they cannot blame you for that," I exclaimed in surprise.

"Why not?" Paluk enquired. He frowned at his woman. "Tamai, I *wish* you would be more careful what you do," he said, for all the world as though he blamed her for the accident that had saved all our lives!

Much to my surprise, Tamai flushed and apologized in a low voice. She seemed quite cast down, and when Paluk began to lecture her in his own tongue I was moved by misguided considerations of chivalry to intervene.

"Look here, you don't suppose this poor girl caused the rock slide, do you?" I demanded of Paluk.

Both faces turned towards me at once, and it was the woman who spoke first, assuring me apologetically that she had indeed caused it, but that she had not meant to do so; she had only hoped to "cast the veil" over our attackers.

"Good God," I exclaimed. "Do you think you have some sort of magical powers, woman?"

"Yes," said Paluk.

"No," Tamai said at the same time.

They looked at one another, manifestly confused, and I felt it was time to take charge.

"Look here, old fellow," I told Paluk. "You may find

it useful to persuade the Kanjutis that your woman is some kind of a witch, but you can't carry that tale off with a British officer. Let's have no more of such nonsense!"

"How did you know?" Tamai demanded.

I tried to explain the concept of scientific proof to her, but she seemed unable to understand. She did not speak Urdu very well and it was impossible to convey abstract concepts. All I was really able to communicate was that there were no witches in the British Empire, and that we knew well enough how to deal with people who oppressed their fellow natives by trading on rank superstition.

By this time the sun had risen high enough to burn off the last traces of morning mist. Paluk and Tamai were ready to move on, but when I explained to them that I had to take some observations of our position first, they decided to stay with me. (God knows what they made of my surveying procedure, or why they wished to watch it at all. I fear I had not succeeded as well as I wished in explaining the scientific method.)

Accordingly, we all three climbed to the top of the cliff, from which high point I was gratified to see that I could sight on no fewer than three major peaks which would serve to fix my position. Unfortunately my instruments were exposed to a high wind which altered the direction of the ruler on the plane table, making it extremely difficult to decide on consistent readings. To supplement this data I therefore made an estimate of the angles between the peaks and my position, using Captain Westbrook's compass, which, as you will recall, I had retrieved from the Kanjuti headman of Kamdesh.

The woman Tamai observed these proceedings with deep interest, while her companion retreated some feet away from us, explaining that he did not feel competent to deal with the demons I was bringing out, should he by ill fortune attract their interest! My task would have been easier had the woman shared his fears; instead she observed intently, as I have said, and asked several not unintelligent questions. She seemed particularly interested in my difficulties with the plane table, and appeared disappointed that the compass was not equally affected by the wind. She demanded to know if anything at all could confuse the "demon" dwelling within the compass. Not feeling equal to a complete discussion of magnetic theory, I simply told her that it was protected against wind.

"And it can see through fog," she said with a queer air of pride at her own knowledge. "For the other man used it when the wisewomen cast the veil."

"What other man?" I demanded. "Did you know the man who owned this compass?"

"I do not know if his demon was the same as yours," she answered. "One bearing such a demon used it and tried to come into our country, but he failed and the KamKhels killed him."

"What is the name of your country?"

"Gandhara," she replied, with an air of thinking that I should have known such a simple thing all along. "Where else would a wisewoman come from?"

In my surprise at the discovery of her origins, I failed to remind the woman that I had seen through her pretensions to magical powers and that she had already confessed her fraudulence to me.

It was after this that, as I have said, I decided to allow these two to travel with me to the territory of the Raj, where they might be interrogated at leisure. It seemed quite probable that this woman had been an eyewitness to the cowardly murder of Captain Westbrook by his Kanjuti hosts, and I felt that her testimony should be recorded in the event that we decided to send a punitive expedition. What an irony, if it should be true that poor Westbrook had been killed on the very bounds of the mystery-shrouded land he had sought for so long!

I had as well other practical considerations for thinking that these two Gandharans, if such indeed they were, should be encouraged to open relations with the Raj. If their land did indeed lie on the further side of that occupied by the KamKhel Kanjutis, it seemed not improbable that through it we might be able to make contact with the caravan routes of traders with Chin. Was it possible that Gandhara could be a key to our getting a share of this lucrative trade with the Hidden Empire? Establishment of a British outpost in a valley near to the Chin caravan routes could give us direct contact with the caravans; we need no longer be limited to the few bales of silks brought down through Chitral and Swat by Afghan traders. Roads could be improved, passes controlled by strategic gun emplacements. Almost I regretted my own decision to turn back towards India from Kamdesh. Had I but continued on, might not mine have been the first feet to tread the future highway of trade through Gandhara?

Then again, had I gone on, I might well have fallen to the treachery of the Kanjutis like Captain Westbrook. Instead, I was returning, if not triumphant, at least bringing with me two guides whose services would indeed be invaluable—not in aiding me to reach India, as they thought, but in bringing a column of British troops back to the passes of their country!

Again I anticipate my own narrative, for it must be confessed that these bright visions of direct trade with Chin did not all at once occur to me. Only during the subsequent days of our travel towards India, when both Tamai and Paluk disclosed with naive pride that the wealth of their land came from its position, uniquely placed to serve as a staging-place between the caravans from Chin and the Chitrali traders, did I begin to see the advantages to the Raj of extending our protection to Gandhara.

As we travelled through the Bashguli valley and into Chitral, I began to perceive some advantages in the apparent reputation of Gandharans for some kind of magical powers. Although the woman Tamai did not claim that she herself possessed such powers, she encouraged the natives we encountered to think her a "wise-woman," as she styled the witches of her native land. The presence of the golden eagle, so uncannily obedient to her will, did much to reinforce that impression.

(Through most of our time of travel the eagle soared high above us, evidently using the currents of air to support it on lengthy glides that carried it without effort above the rugged terrain that caused us so much difficulty. But whenever the woman flung up her gauntleted arm, the eagle swooped down from the sky with an alacrity that astonished me as much as it did the rude tribesmen observing us.)

Whether because of the eagle's example or because of the existing reputation of Gandharan witches, both pagan and Moslem tribes deferred to Tamai with the alacrity born of respectful fear. They allowed our party to pass unchallenged—better yet, they often volunteered to escort us to the next valley by way of secret routes and passes which had been unknown to me on my journey into the interior.

Each night, when we camped, I made what notes I could on these routes. Unfortunately I was not able to take many compass bearings or other observations while on the march, being only too sensible of the unwisdom of permitting the Mehtar of Chitral or some other native potentate to imagine that I had come into his country as a spy, rather than on a simple mission of mercy to settle the mind of Captain Westbrook's widow. My lack of data supporting the appended sketch maps may not, however, be such a loss as at first I thought, since few of the paths we traversed would be suitable for an army's progress. Indeed, the more I learned of this difficult territory, the less I believed that we had any reason to fear an invasion from the north. If the harsh plateaus of the Kirghiz Pamir do not form a natural barrier to the Tsar's ambitions, the steep defiles and glacier-blocked ravines of the Hindu Kush mountains must surely do so. But these matters of political strategy have been argued by abler heads than mine, and should properly form no part of my report.

The respectful attitude of the natives was enhanced by their belief in Tamai's powers as a healer-shaman. It is a sad commentary on the superstitions of these remote tribes that, meeting a party led by a British officer, they should choose to forgo the remedies of modern science in return for the laying-on of hands of a mountain shaman! I was, however, not entirely unhappy about this choice, since I am untrained in medical science and since my supplies of basilicum powder and opium tablets had been severely reduced by native demands for the care of the "Angrezi hakim" on my journey into the mountains. Nor, must it be said, was Tamai's medical care much inferior to that which I would have given the patients. She had a surprising grasp of the need for cleanliness and for fresh dressings on wounds, which alone is two-thirds of the battle in caring for native patients; for the rest, I considered it little short of amazing that the natives' faith in her methods produced an alleviation of symptoms every bit as gratifying as the best English doctor could have hoped for!

Tamai's own attitude towards her "healing" work was equivocal at best. It seemed to me that both she and Paluk believed implicity in some forms of magical healing and similar superstitions, but that they did not think Tamai personally had the ability to do much for the patients who consulted her. At the time I was inclined to consider this belief a convenient way of maintaining their faith in the superstitions in which they had been raised without putting it to a practical test. How convenient to say always, "There are those in my land who can work this magic, but I am not one of them," rather than admitting outright that their vaunted "magic" does not exist at all!

After some days of comparing Tamai's simple and commonsensical healing techniques with her claims of great magical powers for the people of her country, I asked her in a jocular manner whether she did not consider that her own limitations rather disproved those claims. She considered my remarks with some care and for a moment I believed that I had made some impression on the irrational beliefs of her pagan mind; to my disappointment, however, she changed the subject almost at once and began enquiring about the parts and workings

of my rifle with that childlike curiosity which is always
such a prominent part of the native mind. She seemed
to labour under the illusion that I had constructed the
rifle with my own hands, like some tribal blacksmith beating out the metal for the barrel of one of their long and
inaccurate jezails. I tried to explain about factories to
her, but I fear the achievements of our industrial system
will always remain a closed book to the native. "So you
tell me that there are those in your country who have
the ability to make these *Martini-Henry rifles*, but you
are not one of them?" she summarized my explanation.

"Exactly," I replied.

Both she and Paluk seemed to find this extremely
funny, though they were never quite able to explain the
cause of their merriment to me.

We were nearly back to India by now, having passed
through the domains of Chitral and Swat so quietly that
I doubt the native potentates ever knew we had been
there. There was, I had to admit, some benefit in travelling with a Gandharan wisewoman; she had only to
announce her desire to move inconspicuously through
the area, and the superstitious natives agreed. True, we
had experienced somewhat more difficulty in Swat than
further north; apparently, although the fame of Gandhara
had spread this far, the people had not actually seen one
of the witches and were inclined to be skeptical about
her powers. In one such village, where the headmen had
the audacity to demand payment from us for the right
to pass, Tamai increased their respect for Gandhara by
lighting a circle of fires about the village. The flames
crackled impressively in the dry brush, and as the land
was too barren and rocky for there to be much serious
danger of the fire getting out of control, I must confess
that I rather enjoyed the sight of the villagers' reactions.
Later I quizzed Tamai about how she had achieved this
effect, assuming that she had employed some sleight of
hand unknown to me, but she only hung her head and
apologised for the incident, saying she had not intended
it to happen that way at all.

We encountered no more overt opposition until we reached the Malakand Pass; however, the attitude of the natives had been causing me increasing concern. At that point it seemed wise to me that we should take the narrow path of the old Buddhist pilgrim road, rather than exposing ourselves on the long open space of the pass proper. This was an error.

Within minutes of entering the narrow defile through which the pilgrim path winds, we were attacked by Latif Khan, a filthy bandit whom British troops should have put out of commission long ago, had not some pusillanimous politicians insisted that to do so would be to violate the autonomy of the native state of Swat. The bandit chief split up his men into two groups and bottled us up in the pass, and for some bitter moments I believed that I was to die within an hour's ride of British cantonments, a sacrifice to the insane policy of "masterly inactivity" which has for so long restrained our best men from taking those steps which are both necessary and desirable for control of the border.

The jezails of the natives may be inaccurate and awkward to load, but let enough of them be firing at a man, from close enough positions, and the sheer weight of lead will bury him if he is not killed by a lucky shot. Besides, more than half of Latif Khan's men carried British-made rifles, doubtless stolen from our garrisons at Mardan or Nowshera. As soon as the bandits attacked, we took cover in a space between the rocks on one side of the path. From this position I endeavored to hold off the men advancing from the head of the pass while Paluk fired at those who had appeared behind us. The eagle made screaming passes through the sky, beating off one or another of our attackers with each flight. This bought us some time, but it was clear that Tamai's pet would soon fall to a bullet from one of the native jezails.

It seemed to me that this would be an excellent time for Tamai to let them see the black cloak which was apparently the sign of a Gandaran witch, but when I turned to suggest this to her I found that she had fallen into another fit. She was sitting crosslegged under the blanket that served her as a cloak, rigid as a carving, and when I touched her cheek it was so hot that I had the illusion of scorching my fingers. Had we not been facing imminent death from other causes I should have been seriously concerned about having a sick woman on my hands.

It was at just this time, when for the third time in as many weeks I was commending my soul to my Maker, that certain events transpired which shook the whole of my former understanding of the system and transformed my scoffing into belief. These things may be difficult for one who has not seen them to believe, but I affirm, on my honour as an officer and a gentleman, that all occurred exactly as I shall set forth; furthermore, the troops from Mardan who so gallantly came to our aid in the pass must have seen some, if not all, of the workings of what I can only call Gandharan magic.

First the air quivered above Tamai, like a wave of heat above the desert in midsummer; then that same heat appeared to move through and into the rocks of the Malakand Pass, melting them and sending down a flow of fiery, liquid rock at the very feet of Latif Khan's horses. (The men from Mardan must have heard the horses scream; let them be questioned, if it is felt necessary to verify my account.) Before Latif Khan could rally his men, a wall of flames shot up from the bare rock of the canyon walls. These flames were coloured with many shifting shades of light, like the Northern Lights that shine over the Russian snows. The air echoed with the screams of tortured souls, and the flames seemed to writhe with faces that dissolved and melted into blue fire even as I looked upon them.

"*Shaitan!* Ride, brothers!" cried the bandit chief, and his horse bolted under him and passed right through the wall of flames. The rest of the troop rode hell-for-leather after him, and had I been mounted I confess that I might have been tempted to do the same. The heat within the canyon was rapidly rising to a point where it seemed we must all be consumed in the flames and molten rock.

Even as the bandits fled, however, the rocks cooled and the flames vanished from sight. Moments later, a detachment of troops from Mardan arrived, having been alerted by the sounds of gunfire while patrolling the border of British territory. They brought us back to Mardan and arranged transport to Peshawar for me and the two Gandharans, who should be interrogated by Colonel Vaughan or some other high-ranking officer as soon as possible, both about the routes through their country and about the—I can only call them miracles—which I saw with my own eyes in the Malakand Pass.

These things were done by the hillwoman Tamai, unarmed save for a black cloak and her travelling costume of coarse wool and leather: a young woman, alone, uneducated, in a strange country, with no props or helpers and no warning that some such display would be required. Scoffers may speak—as I had done, up to that moment—of fraud and superstition and sleight of hand. I can only repeat what I saw. Stones burned with living fire; the rocks beneath our feet melted; and Latif Khan, of whom it is said that he would ride through Jehanum for gold or rifles, fled the wailing flames like one possessed by demons.

My belief in the possibilities of Gandhara as a staging-post for British trade remains unabated; but I would recommend our people to proceed with extreme caution in our first contacts with these people. Whatever their true powers may be, they are not to be taken lightly.

The text of of Lieutenant McAusland's report breaks off here. A note transcribed in a different hand says, "The opinion of Lieutenant McAusland's superior officer, Major Josiah Phelps, is that the lieutenant was suffering from delusions brought on from heatstroke and that his report of these hallucinations should be suppressed in order to spare the young man later embarrassment.

"The men leading the rescue party from Mardan have

been interviewed in this connection. They say that they did hear some screams from the pass and that this, together with the noise of gunfire, prompted them to intercede, believing that the known bandit Latif Khan might be interfering with some Indian traders who would, of course, be British subjects and entitled to their protection. They found Lieutenant McAusland with two natives, having apparently driven off Latif Khan's bandits single-handedly, armed with nothing more than a rifle and a revolver. The native woman had been wounded in the shoulder and was suffering some kind of fit; the man and Lieutenant McAusland were unharmed.

"Sir Henry Morton, the Civil Judge for Mardan District and an amateur geologist, accompanied an investigative party to the Malakand Pass on the day after Lieutenant McAusland's battle. He reports that he found traces of once-molten rock in the canyon, but there was nothing to suggest that the rock melted recently; most likely it was a remainder from a great age of geological activity in the distant past. None of the other things which Lieutenant McAusland reports can be factually verified."

CHAPTER SEVEN

Tamai could imagine how a true wisewoman of Gandhara would have travelled to the land of the Angrez: unseen, cloaked in illusion, passing as lightly over the land as a breath of wind in the trees. As a wisewoman, Tamai was a fraud and a failure. She had made the journey the hard way. She'd climbed cliffs, jumped from boulder to boulder across streams, and balanced over swaying rope bridges, earthbound as any man, with blisters on her feet and hard, aching knots of muscle in her legs to bear witness to the long hard road they'd travelled from Gandhara. And all the way she'd been carrying a double load—herself with all her limitations, which was bad enough, and the cloak of lies she'd assumed in a bad moment outside the Kanjuti village of Kamdesh.

The single lie had spread like a noxious weed, putting down roots and sending out long tendrils to strangle the simple truth of her mission. First Paluk had argued that since her masquerade as a wisewoman had served them so well among the KamKhels, she should maintain the pretense while they passed through the other Kanjuti villages. Then the word had begun to precede them: a Gandharan wisewoman was travelling south, to heal the sick and protect the crops wherever she passed. It would have been most unwise, Tamai conceded, to disappoint the expectant tribes they met on the way south after those rumors had begun.

And finally, her own acceptance of the lie had bound her to the pretense she hated. What was to have been a brief masquerade to pass them safely through one small tribal conflict became a way of life, heavier than the pack of silk and turquoise she carried on her back, more demanding than Dushmuni's talons gripping her shoulder. With every step of the way south, the black woolen blanket that did duty for a wisewoman's cloak seemed to weigh heavier and heavier on her shoulders. People came to her for magical healing, and she cleaned wounds and changed dirty bandages for clean and prayed that Nirmali the Maker would not punish the sick and wounded because their "healer" was a fraud. They came to her to drive away the birds that stole their crops, and she sent Dushmuni on a plunging raid through the sky that frightened the crows and scattered them for a day. They came to her for prophecies and promises of a better life, and she told pretty lies that tasted salt and bitter on her tongue.

Being a cheat and a liar was, she thought, the last and hardest part of the price she would have to pay for the rifles that would save Gandhara. Leaving Gandhara, which she'd thought the worst of the price, had been only the beginning. Now she was no longer afraid of the world outside the valley. The world within her frightened her more: the capricious power that moved a mountainside when she called for a veil of illusion, the weight on her heart of all the villagers she'd cheated and all the lies she'd told, the numbing certainty that she had rendered herself forever unworthy of Nirmali's grace and Dizane's favor.

And all that, too, seemed well worth it when the small black-haired Angrez told them that the pass before them was the last of the mountains. Once up that rocky slope between the mountains, and they would see the rich land of the Angrez before them.

"It was our land before it was yours, Angrez," Tamai

said coldly when McAusland would have boasted of the wealth of his empire. But within herself she was trembling with fear and excitement. No Gandharan in living memory had travelled so far south; the centuries-old tradition of isolation in the shelter of the mountains had been too hard to break. Once, when Tamai was still a child, a young man had been exiled for some crime that the adults would not discuss with her. Bilizhe had cursed them when he set off and had said that he would go south to see the world of the traders; but he never came back.

She, Tamai, would see all that Bilizhe had dreamed of and that McAusland had spoken of while they journeyed, the cities and the caravans and the iron horses that ran on tireless legs through the nights; and she would come back to tell her people of the world beyond the mountains.

She was straining forward for the first glimpse of the land beyond the pass when Dushmuni, who had been soaring lazily on an updraft of sun-warmed air, stooped into the canyon with a shrill yelp of alarm. Even as Tamai reached for her jezail, the bandits thundered screaming towards them on horseback, and when she swung to seek cover she saw the others waiting behind them, laughing from the narrow end of the pass. They were trapped between two fires, and she had lied and cheated and forfeited the grace of the gods for nothing, for she would never fight through these two lines of dark, laughing men to see the land beyond the mountains.

The power reached through her with the anger, rising like fire inside her, until she felt she would dissolve in a pillar of flame. The need to hold her soul within her drove her to her knees, then down farther, crouching under the blanket, compacted like the stones under the weight of the mountain. Now she knew what she had only mimicked before, the force of the power that could dissolve a wisewoman if she did not prepare her body to contain it. Now she understood why the wisewomen sat crosslegged to work their magic, covered with their black

cloaks, all sense, all thought, turned inward. Who could
control this rising fire and still see the physical world?

On that thought, as if she had given a command to
her own spirit, Tamai did see the world outside her shel-
tering blanket, wavering and unclear and overlaid with
other images, as if the mountains and the rocks were
bones and the shimmer of power in the air were the
flesh of the world. Small things raged and spat biting
projectiles at one another through the worldflesh. That had
to be stopped. Tamai abandoned her physical body under
the blanket and moved through the overworld. This was
and was not the place she had left. The pass called Malakand was "here," but so were many other times and
places, and she was "here" in all of them at once. She
was a cedar growing on a snow-covered mountain slope,
and "here" became all the centuries of the tree's slow
life. She was an arrow flying through cold air to strike
its quarry; she was the markhor feeling the shock of the
arrow and bleeding its life out, and she was the young
Tamai who ran forward to retrieve the arrow and cut up
her kill. She was a lake of fire underneath the earth. She
was a terrified child screaming in pain at the ring of dark,
laughing faces around her.

Tamai filled her hands with the fire and threw it outward, over the "here" that was the Malakand Pass and
bandits attacking some people whom she ought to know.
The molten rocks that flowed into the lake ran through
her fingers and puddled on the canyon floor, drawn a
million years out of their time. The lake of fire grew
walls of burning color, twisting and flickering with the
faces of all Tamai's "here," and she took the KamKhel
faces she remembered so well and threw their life-fires
around the bandit-demons and heard them screaming as
they fled.

The flames were too high now, an intolerable dance
of light and heat and shimmering, intangible nets of a
power she could not control. The fires ran in rainbow
streams through her fingertips, but she could not weave
them into the patterns of peace and control. If she let

the flames run free, they would devour everything within the gorge, and now it seemed to Tamai that there were some people here who were not demons and who had once been dear to her, in one of the many folds and facets of "here." A white-faced, black-haired man whose hands shook and who repeated a stream of words in a strange tongue; another man, of her own tribe, whose face was familiar and beloved even though she could no longer remember who she had been when she knew him; an eagle with hackles as gold as the flames, soaring high above the pass and preparing to dive suicidally into the heart of the fires that blazed around them.

Dushmuni.

The name came to her as a word in a forgotten language, and with it she sensed the eagle's determination and devotion. Dushmuni's wings folded and she came plummeting out of the sky, talons upraised to strike and kill those who attacked them, and Tamai could not call to stop her.

And so she folded her hands about the ribbons of flame and drew the fire back into herself, the burning and the molten rock and the souls of her tormentors. As the flames vanished within her, so did the dazzling multiple sight of the overworld. There was only one "here" now, a barren gorge between cliffs, where an eagle plummeted in the canyon, a fleeing rider raised rifle to shoulder to take one last shot at the devils that had frightened his men, and two men on either side of her caught Tamai's body as she fell forward, burning, to meet the rocks.

Darkness took her.

Tongues of flame danced at the edge of the darkness; fire burned in her face and a glowing ember exploded in her shoulder. Sometimes her body was being jolted, and she moaned through the depths that had claimed her; then there would be blessed peace and stillness again. Words that she did not hear consciously, would not have understood if she had heard them, settled in her resting mind to be remembered and understood when the time was right.

"The man is my guest. The woman needs a doctor."

The same voice, a little later: "Damn your eyes! If the regimental doctor thinks he's too good to tend a native, tell him Colonel Vaughan will have him cashiered! This woman is carrying valuable information. And she saved my life."

Sounds in a strange tongue, meaningless, but the voice was familiar. The part of Tamai's mind that had learned the seven thousand lines of the teaching riddles and songs stored the noises, effortlessly, without even disturbing Tamai's still slumber.

Another intrusion, this time in Urdu, understandable even if the words did not have the clear grace of her mother tongue:

"What's the matter with her, Paluk?"

"Her soul is wandering."

"That doesn't cause fever."

"She called fire that she could not master. We have songs of one who died so, when the White Huns were too many for her to defeat with sword and spear."

Suri Khazara. A half-remembered melody danced in the darkness of Tamai's mind, twining around words in a beloved voice.

"She never mastered the Disciplines! She should not have tried!" That voice trembled, and a sense of tears unshed came through Tamai's dreams.

"Is it safe to move her?"

"Nothing is safe. There is no cure."

"The hell there isn't! Look, Paluk. I'm taking her to Peshawar. Someone I know will look after her there. And the colonel will want to talk to you. Now will you tell that damned bird that I don't mean your woman any harm?"

"You can tell her as well as I."

"Goddamnit! I don't talk to birds! Phelps thinks I'm crazy *now*; if he—oh, all right, what have I got to lose?"

Too many sounds. With a small whimper of protest,

Tamai sank deeper into the darkness. From time to time there was pain lancing through her, dragging her reluctant senses back to the "here" where her own hands had turned men to burning torches. Her body was being jolted in a box, and there were streaks of fire coming from her shoulder, and something bound her arm to her chest. But Paluk was somewhere near, and the first questing tendrils of consciousness brought her a sense of Dushmuni soaring effortlessly through the hot, heavy air that lay on her like a stifling blanket.

She fell back into the darkness again, leaving her aching body to endure the journey while her soul floated through the overworld. Past and present and future overlapped her like images forming in the prophetic smoke of a cedar fire. Lacking the Disciplines that would have allowed her to walk the overworld and use the power there, lacking the bonds to earth that would have kept her close to her body, Tamai drifted and spun like a dry leaf in the wind. She understood now how the wisewomen of Gandhara cast the veil to confuse intruders; all they had to do was to draw a little of the intricate and impossible branchings of the overworld into "here" where their bodies waited. Distortions of time and space were the least part of this world's changes: this was a realm not meant to be inhabited by humans, a collection of places that could not be understood in human terms. In the land of the dead and the unborn Tamai tasted music as honey on the tongue, rode the arching winds of love and desire into an explosion of colors that showered her skin with sparks of ice, fell ten thousand miles through a narrowing tunnel that twisted back on itself and wept as it turned until she entered the very realm of the gods. She saw Nirmali the Maker riding through the heavens with the sun on one shoulder and the moon on the other, and her fingers plaited the rushing mountain streams that spilled from the breasts of Lunang of the Waters, and she lay upon plowed land and felt the fresh green shoots of Dizane's grace growing through her body until she became the earth of Gandhara and the grain that fed the city.

A cold wind blew through the overworld, and the clear pale light about Tamai became a murky gray. The stalks of ripe grain withered and turned black as ashes; Lunang's breasts dried up and the naked rocks at the bottom of the streambed laughed at Tamai; the sun and the moon winked out like blown-out candle flames and Nirmali's face vanished into blackness. A stench of rotten carrion filled the air, and something behind the rocks was laughing and coming from Tamai. She fled down the endless tunnel, twisting and turning and weeping with fear. A voice somewhere far away was urging her on, calling her towards the light. She followed that voice and the overworld fell away around her, music and colors and fields and streams crumbling into ashes, and only the thing that laughed remained to follow her down the tunnel. Heat and blinding light burst on her and she felt something pinning her down like heavy weights, chains that ached like living flesh.

It was the weight of her own body she felt, like a trap closing about her. The heavy air of the plains did not imprison her so much as the clumsiness of her own arms and legs. Instead of drifting free through the overworld, she was bound to her body again, hardly able to lift her head. Pain danced through her arm and shoulder when she tried to move. It seemed unfair that the pain should move so lightly and quickly when she was so slow in her prison of flesh.

The smell and the laughter that had followed her through the overworld were gone now. Tamai lay quite still, eyes closed, trying to sense with her weak mortal senses what had been so clear when she left the body. Not gone, she thought. Waiting. Like a hawk waiting for a rabbit to come out of the tunnel. It sensed me and it came for me, but I am safe as long as I stay in my body . . . I think. . . .

A whisper of uneasiness tainted the thought. The teaching songs told of demons that had walked the Earth in times past. Some made bodies for themselves out of dead things, and that was why a wisewoman who kept a hawk never allowed her bird to eat carrion. Others had bodies of wood and metal held together by seven screws, like the one Dzo Tsungpa of Bod had destroyed by removing the screws while he distracted the demon with fantastic stories.

"But this one is in the overworld; it has no place in the worldflesh," Tamai whispered to herself.

"That is not," said a familiar voice beside her, "a very dramatic way to announce your return to the world. I shall have to make up some better first words for you to speak when it comes time to make the song of Tamai Fireweaver."

"Paluk?"

Tamai opened her eyes slowly, almost blinded by the glare of noonday sunshine. Paluk was sitting beside her, and she thought there were tears in his eyes, but the room was too bright and she could not be sure of anything. And he was holding her hand.

"Say something else," he urged now. "Anything. Just so I am sure you've come back. Dizane bless! We thought you would not return."

"I almost didn't," Tamai whispered. Her throat was dry and sore. "You helped me find my way back."

Paluk picked up a cylinder of water and brought it to her mouth. The outer edge of the water was hard and cold and smooth; the inner part was still water, cool and wet against her dry lips.

Tamai fell asleep in contemplation of this wonder, and when she woke again Paluk was still sitting beside her.

"Dushmuni?" she whispered.

"The little Angrez man took her to his house. I sleep there, too. I will bring her to you soon," Paluk promised. "Hungry?"

Tamai nodded. "And thirsty."

The magic cylinder of water was in Paluk's hand again. This time she studied it as he brought it to her lips.

"How did you do that to the water?" She felt stronger

now, and as hungry for understanding as for food and drink. "Can the Angrez teach a man to be a wise-woman?" Truly this was a land of wonders, if her lazy cousin Paluk could learn the Disciplines here! A faint hope grew within Tamai.

"In the land of the Angrez," Paluk said, "there is no need for wisewomen. This is a *glass*. It looks like water, but it is not water; it is made by men. They have many dozens of them, and any child can use them. They have also many *machines*, like the one that makes this wind to cool the room."

Tamai had been vaguely aware of something flapping above her head, something that looked like a kite tethered so that it could not blow away. An ugly kite, plain white with no faces of birds or gods painted on it to help it catch the air. Now she realized that the white square thing was not blowing in the wind, as she'd first assumed without really thinking about it; it was making the wind. A rope attached to the kite passed through iron rings on the ceiling of the room and down again, through a hole in the wall.

"They call that a punkah," Paluk told her.

"To cool the air? But it does not seem to me that this place is very cool," she said.

Paluk smiled and shrugged. "True, but we must not insult our hosts. Living on the plains as they do, perhaps they do not know what real air is. Tamai, when you are stronger, you must come with me and see what else the Angrez have done! This is a great city, greater than Gandhara, and it is all full of wonders such as we have never dreamed of! The Angrez are so rich that they have no need to hunt or to dig in the fields. A man could spend his entire life lying at his ease, with slaves or *machines* to do all his bidding!"

"It does not sound so wonderful to me," Tamai said flatly. "If they do not hunt or have harvests, how do they know which gods to thank for their good fortune? And don't they get bored lying down all day?" Something about Paluk's manner disturbed her. His eyes were glittering and he seemed almost too excited to sit still. Whatever the marvels of the Angrez city, they should not have distracted him from the task that brought them there; he should have been finding out how to buy *rifles*, not playing with Angrez toys and dreaming about a life of ease.

"These *machines*," she said abruptly. "Are they demons?"

Paluk shook his head. "No. They have no soulstuff. The Angrez McAusland showed me—he took one apart for me and put it back together."

"Like Dzo Tsungpa? He killed the demon by taking it apart while he told it stories?"

"No." Paluk's laugh was shaky and high pitched. "You can't stop these *machines* with words; I told you, they have no soulstuff."

"No?" Tamai looked up at the kite that flapped back and forth above her head, pushing the hot air of the plains into a lazy imitation of a breeze. "You white kite-thing. Stop!" she called, and then, just in case a demon of the plains could not understand Gandharan, she repeated the command in the halting Urdu that she used to speak with traders. "No move! Stop wind!"

The white thing faltered in its rhythmic flight; the rope attached to it twitched once and they lay still. Tamai grinned at Paluk. "I think these demons hear us well enough."

"It's not the same thing," Paluk said. "That isn't really a *machine*—at least, it is, but there is a man who makes the *machine* work. He sits outside and pulls the rope, and he stopped working when you called out."

"Well," Tamai conceded, "if it *is* a demon, it's a very small one and probably not dangerous." It did not smell like the thing that had almost caught her in the overworld, and she did not have the same sense of a living and malevolent intelligence about it. Perhaps Paluk was right.

"You will see," Paluk said happily, "when you feel strong enough to come out with me. Tamai, there is so much to show you!"

"All I want to see," Tamai told him, "is a caravan of *Martini-Henry rifles* heading up to Gandhara before the snows come. Have the Angrez agreed to sell them to us?"

Paluk looked away. "Not exactly. I have been to their council house," he said proudly. "They are ruled by a council of men. I asked about their wisewomen, and they did not seem to understand me."

"Perhaps they do not speak of such matters to outsiders," Tamai suggested. She knew that the Kanjuti tribes around Gandhara were ruled by men, treating their women rather worse than their beasts of burden; but they were people without magic, and savages. Surely no civilized city would be so foolish as to waste the talents of half its people by excluding them from council matters. And if the Angrez possessed as many marvels as Paluk thought, they must have some very powerful wisewomen somewhere in the city.

"Perhaps," Paluk agreed. "That Angrez who came with us said, though, that the men I spoke with had authority to decide all such matters."

This, at least, was not as unbelievable as his first statement. If the wisewomen of the Angrez were occupied in working the wonders Paluk spoke of, they might well ask the men's council to deal with trade matters, just as the men of Gandhara were left to decide when the herds should be moved up to summer pastures and when it was time to harvest each crop in its turn.

"The council leader is called *Colonelvaughan*. He asked me many questions," Paluk told Tamai. "I am not sure what he wants. He showed me some lines drawn with an ink-stick, on very smooth parchment, and told me they were pictures of the mountains; but they were only black lines on white parchment."

"Maps," Tamai suggested. Paluk, like most boys, had not had the patience to sit through the hours of schooling required of girls who might grow up to be wisewomen. And although the Council refused teaching to none, no one ever pressured the boys of the tribe to spend years learning to read the old language and memorizing the old songs. What use would they make of such an education? So Paluk had left the teaching house for the more immediate delights of hunting and working the land and chasing the girls who had proved too dull or untalented for the study of the Disciplines, and he'd never seen the scrolls treasured in the Council house with their maps of long-dead kingdoms and god-realms of the overworld.

"You have seen these pictures before?" he asked now. "You know how to read them?"

"Yes, of course," Tamai said. "How did you think I hoped to find the land of the Angrez when I'd never left Gandhara? I studied the maps in the Council house before I spoke to the Dhi Lawan."

Paluk's face fell and Tamai felt guilty. "But I don't think I would have made it without your help," she added quickly, "for the maps do not tell one very much about the land, and nothing about the tribes outside our borders. I did not realize how much I would need the help of someone like you, who had actually travelled far."

Paluk brightened, and another thought struck Tamai.

"And—do not tell the Angrez that I understand maps, Paluk."

"Why not? It will make their headman very happy. He was angry with me because I did not understand his pictures."

"I'm not sure," Tamai said slowly. "But—we are here to trade. Think of the Angrez as caravan masters. When you buy bullets for your jezail, or a ribbon for one of your girls, from a caravan master, you do not begin by telling him exactly how much silver you have to spend. I think our knowledge may be silver, Paluk, and we should not give it away lightly. It may be better, for a time at least, if they think I am as—" She bit her lip. *As stupid as you*, she'd been about to say, and that was not fair. Paluk was ignorant, not stupid—and she too was ignorant, as helpless as a little child, in this strange world. "If they think that I do not understand what they are asking," she said finally.

Paluk shrugged. "I don't see why we should not be
friendly. These Angrez are so rich, they will probably just
give us the *rifles*—and if they don't, we still have the
turquoise and silk in your pack to show them what riches
Gandhara can offer in return. But if you say so, Tamai,
I will not tell them anything more." He smiled and his
long face lit up. "I would rather go out and see the city,
anyway! Three days we have been here now, and I have
seen nothing except the Council house and this room."

Tamai felt like a selfish idiot. Paluk had been sitting
in one room of an Angrez house, holding her hand and
trying to call her spirit back, and when she did return,
did she thank him for saving her life? No, she started
right off demanding to know what he had found out and
why he hadn't done more.

"It's all right," Paluk said, and Tamai felt her face
grow hot. "I know what you're thinking, cousin. You're
wondering how you can ever thank me for my devoted
care over the last few days, and then you're wondering
how you can tactfully persuade me to go away and let
you alone so that you can think up some clever plan to
get the Angrez to give us all the *rifles* in their city. And
you don't want me to talk to the Angrez headman again,
because you're afraid I will say something that you don't
want them to know."

Tamai laughed. The effort made her shoulder ache
again, but it was worth it to know that she and Paluk
were still friends. "You are right about everything but
the clever plan."

Paluk stood up and brushed one finger along her
cheek. "That will come in time. As for me, don't worry.
These Angrez are very friendly. One of them has invited
me to come with him and see the city, but I was not
willing to leave you until now. But if you promise not to
go throwing your soul into the overworld again—"

"Don't fear," Tamai said. She remembered the smell
of rotting meat, and a laugh like bare stones clashing
together. No. She had no more taste for experimentation.

There was a sound of small winds whispering together

outside the room, and then a horribly pale woman appeared in the doorway. She had no braids, no jewels, no sash with jeweled and embroidered ends; Tamai could only tell that she was a woman because her strange costume was molded indecently tight to her torso, outlining the shape of her breasts. Below the waist the costume flared out into a bell-shaped skirt that made the woman look deformed, as if she had no legs at all.

Paluk looked uncomfortable and unhappy. "Tamai, this is the woman of this house. She has been helping me to care for you. She speaks our language, a little. She asked me . . . you know, about the other one with yellow hair, the foreigner with the demon. . . ."

"My husband," the Angrez woman said. She came across the floor with a smooth, gliding motion, as if she really had no legs. The full skirt of her costume whispered like small breezes playing through the leaves. Tamai repressed an instinctive shiver of distaste at the sight of this pallid, deformed-looking creature. She hoped the woman would not touch her.

"You see him. My husband," the Angrez woman repeated. She spoke Gandharan very badly, leaving off most of the word endings and mispronouncing the long glides of the vowels, but Tamai could just manage to make out her meaning. "Tell me what you see."

Tamai glanced at Paluk for guidance, but he had slipped away. What had he already told this woman? If the other foreigner had been her man, she would hate the Gandharans for having caused his death. This woman was old enough to have borne many children. She might be a very powerful wisewoman, strong enough to block the men's council of the Angrez from selling Tamai the *rifles*. It would have been better not to tell her anything at all.

"I know little of foreigners, O excellent and wise," Tamai finally said. She used the most formal mode of Gandharan, as if she were speaking to the Dhi Lawan herself. "I have come to trade with the men of your nation. It would not be fitting for a noble one such as yourself to be concerned with such small matters, nor would I dare to tell you what you can doubtless scry for yourself from any distance."

"You tell," the woman with the white face of a demon insisted. "Angrez not speak Gandhara talk. Only me. I speak for you to men—or no trade. This my house. No trade. No man." She pointed at the door through which Paluk had vanished. "No bird. No one help you here, hillwoman. Only me. Now you talk!"

CHAPTER EIGHT

[Excerpts from the journal of Louisa Westbrook]

1 October 1884:

I find it very hard to look at her.

It has been just two days since Lieutenant McAusland brought her to my house, although it seems much longer. At first he said only that this hillwoman had helped him in his journey, and that she was wounded, and that he did not think it was right for her to lie in the regimental hospital among the men.

Naturally I could not in charity turn away the wounded stranger from my gate; but seeing that the woman was in need of medical attention, I did wonder why Lieutenant McAusland thought my house more suitable than that of Mrs. Dr. Scully. After directing the *khansamah* and my ayah to see to the woman, I asked Lieutenant McAusland why he had brought her to me. I hardly dared ask if he had any news of Gordon. My husband was not with him, and I had a presentiment of the information Lieutenant McAusland would have to give me soon enough.

He told me then that she claimed to come from Gandhara, and that he thought it would be good if she awoke among those who spoke some words of her language.

"Gandhara!" I exclaimed. "Has she seen Captain Westbrook?"

Lieutenant McAusland shook his head. "I fear so," he said.

It was then that he gave me Gordon's compass, the Swiss-made one which I presented to him on the anniversary of our marriage. I began then, I think, to believe that Gordon truly would not return; but as Lieutenant McAusland thought this native woman might have actually seen him, I resolved to wait until I could question her before quite making up my mind.

She has been unconscious since she was brought in, suffering from a fever which Dr. Scully assures me is only a natural consequence of the gunshot wound in her shoulder. He showed me how to dress the wound, and I have bathed the woman and changed the dressing daily. Indeed, I have had to perform most services for her with my own hands, for shortly after she was installed in this house the most ridiculous rumours began to circulate in the bazaar. My servants claimed that this poor savage hillwoman was a witch possessed of great powers and that they dared not enter her room. They showed no such fear of the man who accompanied her, probably because he is staying in Lieutenant McAusland's quarters and they don't fear having to take on extra work on his behalf—so transparent are their little ruses! But they are so stubborn, and so prone to believe the wild tales they invent to terrify themselves, that I have found it easier to care for her myself rather than try to break down their superstitious fears.

Besides, I did not wish to miss any chance of interrogating her, should she recover consciousness. And so I keep vigil by her bed as much as I can, withdrawing only when her man Paluk comes to sit by her side—for it is really too much to share a room with two hill savages at once! The woman alone is quite fierce enough, on the evidence, to make any civilised person wary. We found two daggers concealed about her person when we cut her clothes off her, and she had been carrying a stolen rifle of English manufacture. What is more, she was accompanied by a monstrously large and fierce bird which Lieutenant McAusland claims is her pet and hunting companion. If a woman of Gandhara is such a warlike savage, what must the man be! I prefer not to further my acquaintance with the fellow.

He is with her now, and I have taken the opportunity to withdraw and jot down a few rambling notes in my journal and to read over the treasure which I received in the morning's mail—the first brief letter from my children.

Just touching this little sheet of paper makes me feel closer to my darlings. I can almost see Harry as he must have knelt at the table, tongue sticking out as he laboured to print his name in these big, staggering letters after the short lines which Alice penned for both of them.

The letter itself is very short and prim, quite unlike my darling romp of a girl. She says that they arrived safely and that Mrs. Thompson, who is to care for them, has a good Christian home and keeps everything very clean. I fear the words may have been dictated by this Mrs. Thompson, who enclosed Alice's brief note in a covering letter of her own. She tells me much about the state of the children's hair (tangled), clothes (too light for the English climate) and behaviour (too noisy for her taste), but nothing about whether they are happy, whether they miss their Mama, whether she cuddles Harry when he wakes at night with his bad dreams.

I will not weep over the letter. I am happy to know that they are safe in England; I must trust the good Christian woman whom my husband chose to care for them at Home.

2 October 1884:

This afternoon, while the man was sitting with her, she recovered consciousness. One of the servants told me that "the northern witch" was awake, and I proceeded immediately to the bedroom where the two of them sat deep in conversation. Their speech was so rapid that I could catch only a few words, and I was forced to reflect upon the irony which brought these two speakers of the Gandharan tongue to my door only after Gordon had lost his life in search of them. For indeed he is dead; I cannot but accept that, having heard the woman's story.

The man, seeming as ill at ease in my presence as I was in his, took his leave almost immediately, and I was left alone with the woman whose inscrutable native countenance might hold the secret of my husband's disappearance. I felt a momentary reluctance to question her, now that I had the chance. I remembered the warlike panoply of weapons we had taken from her unconscious body. Lieutenant McAusland had hinted that she might know something of Gordon's fate, but he had also made it clear that he believed Gordon dead. What had he been trying to say? Had I been nursing my husband's murderer? An unthinking revulsion constricted my throat and for a moment I wished that the woman had died rather than recovering to tell me a story I should not wish to hear.

In the end, I believe that I was able to conceal my distaste for the woman and to behave toward her as Our Lord commanded us to treat the least of His creatures. I questioned her gently but firmly, and made her understand that Lieutenant McAusland had good reason to believe she knew more than she had told him about the fate of my husband. She attempted to evade my questioning for some little while, but the effort tired her and she gave in when I told her that she should see neither her fellow tribesman nor the monstrous pet bird she had brought down from the hills until she confessed the truth to me.

I was gratified to find that my grasp of the Gandharan language was equal to the task of forcing the truth from this savage woman. Alas, my composure was not so great; I mean that I was not equal to hearing the story she had to tell in a manner befitting an Englishwoman. I was forced to leave the room somewhat unceremoniously in order to conceal my tears from her, and I fear that the servants are not unaware of my moment of weakness, for later I heard my bearer discussing the trouble that the "witch-woman" had brought on our house.

In fact, although this woman apparently believes that her people share some part of the blame for Gordon's death, I know that I ought to absolve her. In our enlightened age we know better, I hope, than to accept the native superstitions of witchcraft! I do not for one minute believe that her tribe actually cast a spell upon Gordon to make him lose his way in the mountains; accordingly I ought not to blame this woman for being the involuntary witness of his death.

But I do blame her.

3 October 1884:

I wish I had never heard this woman Tamai's story. It will haunt me till I die.

Over and over, in my dreams last night, I reenacted the dreadful scene as it was recounted to me by the hillwoman Tamai: Gordon crossing the river, losing his balance in the strong current and accidentally staggering back towards the shore where the Kanjuti tribesmen waited; then the fateful fall, the stealthy advance of the murdering savages, the knives raised and the blood of my husband mingling with the clear water of the river! I saw it all in my dreams, not once but a dozen times, and each time I dreamed that it was I who stood with the women of Gandhara on the cliff above the farther shore of the river; that it was by my will that Gordon fell to the Kanjutis; that it was I, and not Tamai, who watched and did not lift a hand or call out a word of warning to save him.

May our Lord forgive me! This morning I have been sitting in my room and writing this account because I can hardly bear to look at the woman, much less have her in the house. I have given orders to the servants that the hillman Paluk is to be admitted whenever he calls, with or without that great bird. More I cannot do; not today. When she is stronger I suppose I shall have to keep my promise to Lieutenant McAusland, and act as interpreter when the colonel questions her, but fortunately that cannot be for some time yet, as she will surely be some weeks recovering from her wound and the subsequent fever. Now that she is conscious again, Paluk may nurse her; I feel that I can hardly be asked to do more for the creature.

4 October 1884:

These natives do have amazing powers of recovery, doubtless on account of their coarser constitutions and the fact that civilisation has not distanced them from their animal nature. Just after dawn this morning I was awakened from dreams of my little ones by a thump and a crash as of something breaking in Alice's bedroom. Still only half-awake, I flew to her room with some dream-fuddled expectation of finding my darling there again. Instead, I saw the dark countenance of the hillwoman glaring at me from the floor where she had fallen, knocking over and breaking the porcelain washbasin in so doing.

Since the servants still pretended to a fear of entering the room, I cleaned up the debris myself. I would first have helped the woman back into bed, but she refused my aid. As she clambered to her feet, I began to understand some part of her problem. The dirty, bloodstained clothes in which she arrived had been cut away from her body by Dr. Scully and I had directed the sweeper to burn the rags. While she lay in bed I had seen to it that she was decently covered in one of my own nightgowns. Now that she tried to walk, the long skirt of the gown caused her no little difficulty. I suppose she had never worn skirts before; she moved like Major Phelps when he took the part of Mrs. Malaprop in our amateur theatricals, first striding out and then discovering her limbs inextricably entangled in the billowing muslin skirt.

"Look," I told her, "you must hold it like this," and I demonstrated the way of lifting the hem of the skirt a scant inch above the floor, "and walk with smaller steps, like this."

When she attempted to follow my instructions, her whole body shook, and I remembered that she must still be weak from the fever. I managed so far to conquer my natural repugnance as to offer her my arm for support back to the bed. Why this small contact should have troubled me so much, when for three days I had performed every intimate service for the woman, I do not know. But *then*, she had been unconscious, a suffering body in need of charity; *now*, she was looking at me with the bright eyes that had witnessed my husband's violent death, and I could not offer to touch her without feeling myself inextricably linked with Gordon's murderers.

In the event, my qualms went for nothing, for she refused support, and refused, also, to return to her bed. "I must talk to the *colonelvaughan*," she said, pronouncing the name all in a rush as if it were a single word.

"And so you shall," I said, "when you are stronger. Today, and for many days to come, you must rest."

"*Today* I must talk to him," she contradicted me. "The snows will come soon. And I am strong enough now."

As if to prove this statement, she continued to hobble up and down the room, leaning occasionally on the bed, and growing visibly paler with every step that she took. I left her engaged in the task, expecting only that she would soon collapse and have to be helped back into bed.

All this day she has continued with her self-imposed program, walking as much as possible and resting only when collapse was imminent. She has eaten the meals brought to her without appetite, but determinedly chewing and swallowing each bite as if it were medicine that she must force down her throat. And after eating, again the endless pacing, until I think I shall go mad from listening to her dragging steps as she forced herself up and down the length of the bedroom. I cannot but respect the determination which she brings to this task, although I do think it missapplied; if Colonel Vaughan had felt it urgent to talk to this woman, he would surely have informed us of the fact.

5 October 1884:

This morning she rose and dressed herself without assistance. I had meant to set the *durzee* to sewing a dress for her—some loose-fitting calico garment with long sleeves, such as the orphan girls at the mission wear, would have been quite suitable—but there was not time, and in any case I think she would have refused to wear "Angrezi" clothes after her difficulties with the nightgown. Instead she donned a festival costume from her pack. The costume consisted only of tunic and trousers, cut like the ones she had worn when she was brought in, but these garments were woven entirely of silk from Chin, with something that shimmered like moonlight brocaded into the fabric. The floating stuff of the tunic was girdled in with a wide belt of brocade, so closely ornamented with beads of silver and turquoise that the fabric was hardly visible, and around her neck she wore a king's ransom in precious stones set together with lumps of turquoise and carved bone, as if she esteemed the diamonds and sapphires no more than pretty sparkling beads to set off the bits of bone.

I must admit that the overall effect, though regrettably gaudy, was quite impressive. I was surprised to see her spoiling the look of the costume by strapping an armlet of heavy leather about her right wrist and a shoulderguard of the same stuff on her right shoulder, but I understood the reason when her cousin arrived.

On his shoulder, perching on a blanket secured there with straps, was the wild bird that had come down from the hills with them. (Dr. Scully tells me it is a golden eagle, and that these birds are not uncommonly used for hawking by the Kirghiz of the northern steppes.) I was rather surprised to see that the bird was neither secured by jesses nor pacified with a hood over its eyes, the more so as the man Paluk appeared quite nervous of his burden. As soon as the bird saw Tamai, it sprang from

Paluk's shoulder and glided to perch on Tamai's leather-covered wrist. (The wings were only half outspread for this glide, and so it knocked over only a few small ornaments, easily replaced. However, I resolved that in future the animal should not be allowed within doors.)

"I am ready now," Tamai told me, rather in the arrogant manner of a Maharaja issuing commands to his servants. "You may conduct me to the *colonelvaughan*."

"Colonel Vaughan will send for you when he wishes to see you," I told the impertinent woman, "and you will certainly not take your hawk into his presence."

"Where I go, Dushmuni goes," the woman said. "And we will go now to speak with the *colonelvaughan*. Where is he?"

I was still trying to explain to the woman that she could not simply command the time of the colonel of the regiment in this high-handed manner, when a bearer arrived with a note from Colonel Vaughan. He had been informed by Lieutenant McAusland, who had spoken that morning with Paluk, that the Gandharan woman was well enough to be interviewed, and he would be much obliged to me if I would put aside my plans for the day and come with her to his office.

When I translated this information for Tamai, she did not even have the good manners to be thankful for the colonel's prompt consideration; she merely smirked as if she had won an argument and waited for me to lead the way to the colonel's office.

I was fully sensible to the impropriety of my attending on Colonel Vaughan in his office, a lone female among men doing men's work (for I could hardly count my savage companion *en chaperone*). The colonel was most gracious in his assurances that no blame could attach to me, for far from thrusting myself forward into the affairs of the Raj, I had only come with the greatest reluctance and upon his express desire. All the same it seemed wrong to me. Gordon has always said that females have no business with affairs of state, and besides that, how furious he would be to find me usurping his place as the expert in Gandharan languages and customs!

I find it difficult to remember that there is now no possibility of his returning to be angry with me for this or any other cause.

We arrived at the colonel's office to find several members of his staff gathered there already: Lieutenant McAusland, Major Phelps, and several others. There was also a civilian gentleman, a Mr. Haverford, who was introduced to me as the private secretary of His Excellency the Viceroy. It had not heretofore occurred to me that so minor a matter as the interviewing of a hillwoman from an obscure tribe could engage viceregal attention, and I regretted more than ever that the responsibility for interpreting the woman's words should rest on my inadequate shoulders. But there was no help for it. Colonel Vaughan clearly had no intention of making himself foolish by translating English diplomatic language into the rough Urdu we all use for communicating with the natives; he preferred that I should be the one to suffer, trying to say these complicated things in my inadequate Gandharan.

When the talks began, fortunately, I was too much occupied with understanding the strange turns of the woman's speech, and with translating them into terms acceptable for the gentlemen gathered there, to remain in the least self-conscious.

After the introductions were over (and I fear I made a poor hand of translating military and civil titles into Gandharan terms), Colonel Vaughan began by unrolling a map of the Hindu Kush mountains and asking Tamai to point out the location of her home on the map. When I translated this request, she stared blankly at the paper and then, laughing, asked if the men thought a whole mountain could be rolled up in paper and carried from room to room.

This, at least, needed no translation.

"It is as I feared," said Colonel Vaughan. "The woman

is as ignorant as her companion. We will have to let her guide us to the valley."

When I transmitted the colonel's decision to Tamai, she did not even have the courtesy to reply directly; instead she began talking about her people's need for weapons. She had come to trade, she said, not to play games with pieces of paper. Her city was rich beyond the imaginings of these Angrez who could not even spare a little silver to brighten the ceremonial costumes of their councillors. For the right arms—she mentioned Martini-Henry rifles several times—she might be persuaded to share a little of the wealth of Gandhara with the Angrez. Until that was settled, she said, there was no point in discussing anything else.

Naturally I could not translate such a rude farrago of lies and demands. "She wants rifles," I told Colonel Vaughan.

The men laughed. Even I know that every hill tribe and savage state begins by trying to extort a gift of weapons from the Raj.

"Make her understand that it's impossible—" Colonel Vaughan began, but Mr. Haverford interrupted him quite rudely.

"Not so fast, Vaughan," he drawled.

Colonel Vaughan stared at him. "Good God! You can't seriously be suggesting that we arm the tribes?"

Mr. Haverford shrugged his elegant shoulders. In that company of military men, he seemed so slender and dandified as hardly to be worth any attention; but there was a suggestion of menace about him that compelled respect.

"Oh, it shouldn't be necessary to go that far," he murmured. "The poor woman has no transport, after all— and she hasn't mentioned cartridges. If she thinks she can load a Martini-Henry with lumps of lead, like an Afghan jezail, she'll be in for a sad shock."

"I wouldn't count on that," Lieutenant McAusland said drily. "She possesses one of our rifles herself—and she's a damned good shot. I'll wager that if you begin discussing how many rifles and where to deliver them, you'll find that an adequate supply of cartridges is also part of the deal."

"Well, well, no need to be so *specific*," said Mr. Haverford, but he seemed rather annoyed at this intervention. "I'm merely suggesting that we don't wish to cut off negotiations with a potential ally at this stage. If we have to promise her arms in order to get the concessions we want, that's not the same thing as actually delivering them. Later on the Gandharans will be happy to settle for a cash subsidy, like the Chitralis."

"Er—what concessions exactly did you have in mind, Haverford?" the colonel enquired.

The Viceroy's secretary responded with a list that had clearly been thought out beforehand, doubtless with the concurrence of his master. "Gandhara to be placed under British protection through our vassal, the Maharajah of Kashmir, who can also be responsible for delivering the subsidy in return for a yearly tribute to be decided later. Establishment of a British Residency in Gandhara. Accommodation for a picked troop of the Punjab Frontier Force to be barracked in Gandhara, the men stationed there to be changed on a regular basis, hardship pay and extensive leave—well, all that is our concern, not the Gandharan's. The main point is that we will protect the Gandharan state from now on."

"I don't recall their asking for protection," the colonel said, "and what makes you think this woman is empowered to make such grants?"

"If we consider her an envoy, and accept her invitation to extend British protection to the state of Gandhara," Haverford replied, "no blame can extend to us. Diplomatically speaking, that is. Any little misunderstandings can be straightened out later—*after* our men are installed."

Colonel Vaughan exploded at this. "Before you put a troop of *my* best men out in an isolated frontier outpost, too far away for decent lines of supply and communication, where they'll be a natural target for any native ris-

ing, you'll have to come up with something more than a
diplomatic line of reasoning, Haverford!"

"Oh, we have our reasons," Haverford said cheerfully.
"Didn't you read young McAusland's report? *I* did—and
it has been carefully studied in the Viceroy's office. He
is absolutely right about the usefulness of a British trade
depot in the mountains. Have you no vision, Colonel?
There's an empire to our east—an empire no British
agent has ever been able to penetrate. A world of wealth
unimaginable, of silk and pearls and tea. A world
bounded on the north by ice, on the east by oceans so
tempest-tossed that no ship of ours has ever reached the
Chin coast in one piece, on the south by the Great
Desert. A world whose only contact with the outside has
been by caravans threading their way through the mountains to Samarkand, where the Russians meet and control
the wealth that trickles from Chin."

"I am tolerably well aware of the situation of the Chin
Empire," Colonel Vaughan growled. I could not blame
him for sounding irritated. In his youth the colonel had
been a member of the Taklamakan Field Force that
attempted to force the Chin Empire to open its doors to
British trade. Most of the men of that ill-fated force
perished in the desert of Taklamakan, and the few survi-
vors—of which Colonel Vaughan, then a mere subaltern,
was one—came back with strange tales of dust clouds
that seemed possessed of demonic intelligence, of sands
that sang and lured their men into the desert, and other
ramblings that made even less sense. No, if anybody
needed to be told of the isolation of the Chin Empire,
and of our own country's desire to control some of the
lucrative trade which now passed almost exclusively to
Russia, it was not Colonel Vaughan; nor could he enjoy
being reminded of that harrowing experience in the
Taklamakan. Had it been proper for me to speak, I might
have warned Haverford that he was taking the wrong
tack entirely if he wanted to get the colonel on his side.

"If the Viceroy wants to risk men's necks to open up
a trade route," Vaughan went on, "let him send box-

wallahs. Commercials. The men who'll benefit. I am here, and my men are here, to protect the British Empire—not to pave the road for merchants. And I've yet to hear one good military reason for establishing a British outpost too far beyond our lines to be defended in case of attack."

"The Pamirs and the Hindu Kush are all that stand between us and Russia," Haverford replied at once. "Will you see a Russian army of invasion swoop down over India while you and your men lounge in cantonments in Peshawar, Colonel?"

"Lieutenant McAusland assures me that there is no road fit for an invading army through those mountains."

"Major John Biddulph, who explored the region some years ago, is of the opposite opinion. His report, also, has been studied in the Viceroy's office."

"Then let this Major Biddulph lead an army over the passes he claims to've found, and if he gets them through to Russian Turkestan, I'll believe his report."

"Colonel." Mr. Haverford's voice was silky, patient, indefinably menacing. "You know well enough that the Russians do not suffer from the same difficulties we encounter in the mountains. Their bases in Russian Turkestan supply the armies, and in any case their Cossacks can virtually live off the land. They have already conquered Turkestan. Now they are turning their attention to the Pamirs and the Hindu Kush. Do you really think that General Skobelev's appetite for conquest has been assuaged by gobbling up the cities of the plains? When his army is at the Malakand Pass it will be too late to argue."

"Nonsense! There's no reason to assume that the Russians have any intention of attacking the mountain tribes. The Pamirs and the Hindu Kush form a natural boundary for them, as they do for us."

"*Do they??*" Haverford had not raised his voice, but something in his quiet assurance captured everyone's attention. He turned to me with a courtly bow. "Mrs. Westbrook, might I trouble you to put some questions to—ah—to Miss Tamai, here, and to translate her answers?"

"I shall do my best, Mr. Haverford," I replied.

"Good. Ask her, if you will, just why her people so urgently need arms at this time."

"Have they decided what price they want to set for their *rifles*?" Tamai demanded as soon as I translated Mr. Haverford's question.

"Not yet."

"Then what have they been talking about all this time?"

I did not think the colonel had asked me here so that I could expose all the plans of the British Raj to this hillwoman. Although I was somewhat troubled by the ruthless tone of this man Haverford, I could not reconcile it with my conscience to tell Tamai exactly what was being planned for her people. Besides, it would be for their own good if they were brought under British protection. Like all natives, the Gandharans are doubtless incapable of ruling themselves and in desperate need of our civilising influence.

"The colonel has many matters to discuss which do not concern you," I said at last. "Answer the question, please."

Tamai sighed and launched into a story of the sort all too familiar to those of us who have lived on the frontier and who know the inhumanity of the tribes towards one another—a tale of crops and houses burned, women and children murdered, and a people facing famine in the winter snows. But there was indeed something different and troubling about Tamai's story, and when I had heard enough I raised my hand to stop her and turned back to the gentlemen, who had been waiting with commendable patience.

"I am afraid Mr. Haverford is right," I told him.

"Louisa—Mrs. Westbrook. I mean—I asked you here as an interpreter, not as an adviser!" Colonel Vaughan snapped.

Strangely, his disapproval did not put me out of countenance as it might once have done. Now, as I look back, I fear that even this brief contact with the world of affairs has made me somewhat unwomanly. At the time, however, I was only concerned with transmitting Tamai's story to those who could best judge the proper course of action for us to take.

"Tamai says that in the last two seasons her people have become aware of a new tribe from the north. Last season the new tribe conquered the Kirghiz of the steppes, and now they are attacking Gandhara. They have made no declaration of war, nor have they sent to ask for tribute; their only aim seems to be to control the valley of Gandhara itself. Tamai says that her valley lies directly athwart the caravan route to the Taklamakan, and that she supposes these new invaders want to control the trade which has made Gandhara wealthy."

Lieutenant McAusland sucked in his breath. "I told you so! Control Gandhara, and we'll bring the Chin trade south to India!" he interrupted me, most impolitely—but then he is a very impolite young man, self-centered and always in a hurry. I suppose being so short, and a Scotsman to boot, he feels that he will be slighted by his English fellow officers if he does not make himself noticed at every opportunity.

(Gordon would be most annoyed at my disgressing like this; but then, Gordon is hardly likely to read my journal now.)

"Tamai also says," I went on after silencing the lieutenant with a freezing stare, "that the men of this new tribe are tall and yellow-haired, that they ride horses and are mounted with modern rifles that can shoot much farther and faster than the tribal jezails. Unless our own armies have been attacking this mountain fastness, gentlemen, I can only suppose—"

"Skobelev and his Cossacks!" This time it was Colonel Vaughan who interrupted, but since I had concluded what I felt necessary to translate of Tamai's story, I did not raise my eyebrows at him as I had done to young Lieutenant McAusland. Besides, I doubt that he would have noticed. "By God, Haverford, you were right! The damned Russians are trying to sneak into India by the back door! This calls for strong measures!"

"Indeed," Haverford replied, and I felt certain from his smile of satisfaction that he had known exactly what Tamai had been going to tell us. I surmised at the time that he had been questioning Paluk, and he later confirmed this theory. He said that Paluk's Urdu was barely sufficient to get more than the basic components of the story across, but the fact of a strange tribe moving inexorably south, bent on conquest and armed with modern equipment, had suggested strongly that the Russians were expanding their territory again. He'd gambled on Tamai's backing up this story with more details, and his gamble had paid off richly. Once presented with a clear military objective, Colonel Vaughan completely reversed his previous attitude. Indeed, he professed himself ready to support the immediate dispatch of troops to Gandhara. I fear that as a professional soldier, he saw more honour in the prospect of a war than in the chance of opening up a peaceful trade route.

"I don't see why we need to make any bargain with the woman," he said now. "Open aggression from the Russians is all the excuse we need to march on Gandhara—the Hindu Kush are agreed to be within our sphere of influence, dammit!"

"Indeed," Haverford agreed. "There is just one small problem, don't you see, Colonel? Nobody can find Gandhara."

"Then what the devil do we pay the Survey Office for?" the colonel demanded. "Pundits, trigonometrical surveys, maps, sightings, native informants—by God, can't those blokes on the scientific side find one native state when we ask them for it?"

Here Lieutenant McAusland leapt into the fray again, bent on demonstrating his classical education and his reading in Arabic and Turki literature. He seemed to have spent the days since his return to Peshawar investigating all the classical references to Gandhara.

"Herodotus tells us that the Gandharans fought in Xerxes' army," he informed us, "and Gandhara was known to the Macedonians of Alexander's time under the name of Gandaritis. The Greek kings who succeeded Alexander in Asia established a kingdom in Gandhara, and at the peak of their power the Gandharans controlled all the mountains down to and including the Vale of Peshawar. This very cantonment may be built, for all we know, on the remnants of the civilisation created by Tamai's ancestors! But in the fifth century the White Huns devastated this area. The Chinese pilgrim Hsuan Tsang, who travelled through here in the seventh century, reports a tale that the remnants of the Gandharan empire had survived somewhere in the Hindu Kush mountains, but he himself did not visit their kingdom. The Barbur-Nama reports that Babur subjugated the mountains as far east as Chitral, and took tribute from the Kanjutis of the hills; but on the one occasion when he and his men tried to find Gandhara for purposes of exacting tribute, a snowstorm blinded them and sent them around in circles until they were glad to escape with their lives. Earlier in this century, Vigne and Masson both tried to find "the fabled kingdom of Gandhara" but Vigne became ill with some kind of falling sickness that caused him to lose his sense of balance, and Masson suffered hallucinations which he does not describe with any precision in his book of travel writings. The evidence strongly suggests, sir, that the Gandharans do indeed possess some mysterious power of confusing and disorienting those who attempt to discover their last remaining valley."

"Poppycock! Skobelev's Cossacks found it well enough, didn't they?" Colonel Vaughan snapped. "Don't tell me any more about 'mysterious powers,' McAusland." He turned back to Mr. Haverford. "All this tells me is that there've been a number of incompetents fumbling their way through the mountains in the last six hundred years. You've yet to show me one good reason why a modern scientific observer—like young McAusland

here, before he got water on the brain—couldn't locate
Gandhara by one of these processes of triangulation you
scientific chaps are always going on about. Or do you
think these tribal tricksters are going to cast a spell on
your plane tables and compasses?"

"Without arguing the merits of Lieutenant McAusland's beliefs, sir," Haverford replied, "may I point out
that the process of extending our known maps by trigonometric survey is a long and laborious one? Doubtless, in
time, we will have precisely located enough peaks
between here and Chitral to enable us to make fixes on
the remaining mountains of the Hindu Kush; and doubtless a process of elimination would then allow us to pick
out the exact mountains surrounding Gandhara. But this
will be the work of years, sir—and Skobelev is already
at the door! If you wish to thwart his plans of conquest,
we must move quickly—and we have, at present, just
two people in Peshawar who can guide us to Gandhara.
The man we have no hold over, for he wants nothing of
us. And you know what *she* wants." He pointed to Tamai.
"Sir, we—need—that—woman. And if I have to promise
her a caravan load of Martini-Henry rifles to get her
services as a guide, I'll promise them."

"We don't arm the tribes," Colonel Vaughan protested.
"That's basic to all frontier policy."

"I said I'd *promise* her the rifles," Haverford rejoined.
"Delivery is another matter."

"You'd better be damned sure they're not delivered,
then, or I'll ask the Viceroy to assign you picket duty on
the first convoy through the hills. Louisa—Mrs. Westbrook—tell the woman whatever will make her agree."

My conscience troubled me somewhat. It appeared to
me that Colonel Vaughan wished me to lie to the woman.
Fortunately I was able to choose words which should
have satisfied the colonel without actually lying to Tamai.

"The men of the council are discussing your request," I
told her. "Some do not wish to give your tribe the rifles.
It would help if you would agree to guide a few of our
people to Gandhara. They could help you transport the

rifles," I added, and I thought this suggestion no less than a stroke of genius on my part, for how else did she propose to get a load of rifles and ammunition through the mountains? She could hardly carry it on her back!

Unfortunately, it appeared that Tamai already thought this through. "There will be no need for help," she told me. "The Powindah traders will lead a caravan for me." These Afghan nomads customarily travelled into the hills in spring and back down in autumn, but I did not doubt Tamai's ability to persuade them to reverse their direction.

"Will they take the rifles all the way to Gandhara?" If our men could accompany the caravan, perhaps that would be enough to satisfy the colonel.

Tamai shook her head and tried to explain to me where the caravan's journey would terminate, but either her explanation was not clear or my grasp of Gandharan was not as good as I had hoped, for I was unable to make any sense out of her statements. I explained my difficulty to the gentlemen, and Lieutenant McAusland, for once, made a very helpful suggestion.

"I think she is talking about the Silent Trade," he said. "It is mentioned in the Tarikh-i-Rashid and in several other medieval documents. There are certain places, well outside the boundaries of Gandhara, where traders from India bring their goods. The Gandharans wait there with bales of silk from Chin and the traders lay out the goods they offer in return. When the Gandharans think the price is high enough, they put down the silk and take the grade goods. It is called the Silent Trade because nobody has to learn Gandharan to deal with the people, and apparently very few traders wish to learn such a difficult and complicated language."

He made this last statement with a little bow in my direction, and I was absurdly pleased by the implied compliment.

"Tell her that's not good enough," Mr. Haverford instructed me. "She must guide us to Gandhara—or there will be no rifles for her people."

"There'll be none in any case," Colonel Vaughan said.

Mr. Haverford contrived to have the last word. "There's no need to translate Colonel Vaughan's statement. If she chooses to understand my ultimatum as a promise of arms—well, it will be an unfortunate misunderstanding that can be cleared up later."

I felt somewhat troubled in mind as I translated Mr. Haverford's words, for I have always instructed Alice and Harry that to tell a lie by implication or acts is as much a sin as to lie in words. If Tamai believed Mr. Haverford, I should be a party to the deceit.

I need not have worried. Tamai responded to his demand with an ultimatum of her own. Before I could translate her most impolite and vigorous refusal, she had risen to her feet and left the room, the great eagle riding on her shoulder. Mr. Haverford put out his hand as if to stop her, but she had already passed; he was left with his mouth open, momentarily frozen in a somewhat ludicrous position. Colonel Vaughan, who had been sitting with his chair legs tilted back and his feet propped on the lower drawer of his desk, let his chair come down with a crash. For a moment I had the strange feeling that this ignorant hillwoman in her gaudy tribal rags had displayed more decorum and dignity than these gentlemen.

"She says," I translated, unnecessarily I fear, "that foreigners are not permitted to enter Gandhara."

"Damned cheek!" Major Phelps exploded. It was his first comment since the meeting started. I rather thought that all the political discussion had gone over his head; Major Phelps's political views begin and end with his oft-repeated statement that "the niggers have to be taught their place." Now he amplified on this basic philosophy. "Throw the native woman in the punishment cells for a week, Colonel. She'll be singing a different tune after you've taught her some respect."

The colonel's face froze over at this suggestion, and I realized that he felt no more fondness for Major Phelps than I did. "I hardly think that would be a suitable way to deal with a potential ally, Major Phelps. And need I remind you that there is a lady present?"

"No need to remind me," said Major Phelps with a bow towards me. "I'm always aware of the lovely Mrs. Westbrook. That dress is mightily becoming to you, ma'am. The black crepe sets off your fair English complexion."

Since I put on black for the first time only this morning, in sorrowful acknowledgment of Gordon's death, I found this remark in even worse taste than most of Major Phelps's comments.

A dry cough from the Viceroy's secretary recalled us to the topic of discussion and saved me from the necessity of finding some polite response to Major Phelps. "She'll be back," Mr. Haverford said. "She wants those rifles—not that they'd do her much good against the Russian Empire! But she'll have to deal with us for any help. Give the woman a day or two to realize that."

Lieutenant McAusland laughed quietly. "I wouldn't be too sure of that," he said, almost to himself. "She's very resourceful, Tamai is—and you chaps haven't seen the full range of her resources yet."

By common consent, we all ignored this veiled reference to the magical powers in which Lieutenant McAusland seemed to believe. It was embarrassing to see a British officer falling prey to some native superstition. But then, Lieutenant McAusland is Scots, and one understands that the Celtic races have always been rather queer and overexcitable.

CHAPTER NINE

The British cantonments, lying to the west of the old city of Peshawar, were arranged exactly like every other British station in India: barracks here, commissariat stores there, racecourse occupying one large level swath of ground and cricketground another. Radiating out from this central area were the officers' bungalows, laid out along tree-lined main roads and surrounded by little patches of gardens in which English daffodils languished and died (Mrs. Colonel Vaughan), or native cassia and jasmine flourished in a cheerful jungle (Mrs. Dr. Scully, who was born in India) or nothing very much grew at all (Mrs. Captain Westbrook, whose *mali* gave notice when he discovered that the memsahib had installed a Gandharan witch in the house and a savage eagle in the garden).

Less than two miles to the east, all this trim British tidiness and efficiency disappeared into the crowded, odorous, noisy streets of the native town. As usual in the early autumn, the Kabul Gate was jammed with the long lines of Afghan caravans coming down from the mountains. A long-haired, two-humped Bactrian camel, all but buried under its bales of carpets, gurgled and snorted and turned itself sidewise in the gate, thereby incurring the curses of the farmer behind it who was trying to goad his buffalo loaded with sugarcane through the narrow

way. "*Batchka! Batchka, O Apridiah!*" cried a horseman
whose path was temporarily blocked by the loads before
him. His horse swerved around the buffalo with an inch
to spare and he came trotting up through the dust, very
elegant in embroidered yellow Chin silk and silver-
trimmed boots. "Watch out, O Afridi! Thy camel's
mother—"

The suggestions he made about the camel's female
ancestors and their disreputable habits convulsed the
spectators and did not quite invite the Afridi camel-
master to begin a blood feud. Eventually the stubborn
animal consented to be led into the caravanserai, where
it kicked in a mud wall and tried to kill a few small boys
before responding to the Afridi's commands to kneel. But
by that time, the horseman had long since passed through
the gate and had vanished among the crowded, flat-
roofed houses of the native town.

Two hours, a bath, and several pegs of whisky later,
Vladimir Zernov lounged on satin cushions and regaled
his servant with the tales of his adventures as Mubarak
Khan, the foul-mouthed Afghan wanderer.

"You ask for trouble when you call attention to yourself
so, Vlad' Dmitrievich," his servant grumbled with the
confident familiarity of an old retainer. "Your father
always said that discretion was a spy's best tool."

"My father and his *discretion* are in St. Petersburg,
where they belong. He is a man of no imagination. Those
peasants were amused." Vladimir Zernov gestured
grandly with his whisky and splashed one of the satin
cushions with the drink. The cheap red dye that colored
the satin ran and puddled in the alcohol, leaving a cloud-
shaped white stain in the center of the embroidered
design.

"And is that why we swelter in Peshawar? For you to
amuse the peasants?"

"Stop grumbling, old man, and fill my glass. The British Political Agent for the Yusufzai has been on leave for
over a month, and Mubarak Khan has been making
friends among the Yusufzai while the Englishman plays in

the hills—shooting large animals, I suppose, or small birds. Some day I will show this Englishman how to hunt. Yes! His friends the Yusufzai and I will teach him something about the hunting of large animals. But I think he will not like the lesson."

Vladimir Zernov giggled. He had been hot and tired and dirty, and because he had been pretending to be a good Moslem, he had not had a drink for a month. Now he was clean and rested and there was whisky in his glass and later, if he wished it, there would be a girl. Perhaps two girls.

"He wasn't on leave." Josip blotted up the spilt whisky and refilled his master's glass.

"What do you know about it, old fool?"

"If you'd stayed in Peshawar you would know, too," said Josip with sour satisfaction. "The English boy came back with some very useful friends for the Raj: Gandharans."

"Gandharans! Here? I thought we took care of that man. What was his name? Bilizhe?"

"We did," Josip nodded, "and nobody suspected that he had any help in finding Paradise. These are new—don't you listen, Vlad' Dmitrievich? A man and a woman. The man is already an opium dreamer like Bilizhe, but the woman is treating with the English. If she leads them to Gandhara while you are playing at being a Pathan, your father will have something to say about discretion, Vlad' Dmitrievich."

"Your mother and her mother before her . . ." Vladimir Zernov cursed mechanically. Josip waited, impassive, until he had finished.

"So you were just saying about the Afridi's camel, Vlad' Dmitrievich. You're beginning to repeat yourself. And cursing me won't do anything about these Gandharans, will it?"

"If they lead the British there, before Skobelev has the valley, I may as well have spent the summer in St. Petersburg." Vladimir Zernov clenched his fist around the whisky glass. "Why haven't you taken care of them? Do I have to oversee every little thing myself?"

"Perhaps killing them is not such a little thing," said Josip. "I tried when they first came. The woman was unconscious then, and the man would not leave her side. They should have been easy."

"But?"

He shrugged. "They were inside the British lines, you understand? And the guards have been doubled; too many raids from your Afghan friends lately, too many rifles being stolen and copied. The first man I sent was caught by the sentries. He was trying to pick up a few rifles from the barracks before he did the work he was sent for. Fortunately, their first shots killed him, so they never guessed he was more than a thief. The second one got into the garden of the house where the woman sleeps, but her eagle took out his eye and he ran. He wanted to be paid for his injuries. Unfortunately," Josip said, "he died of them." A slow smile spread over his face. "Sad how a little wound will carry a man off in this climate . . ."

"Stop babbling, you old fool. What eagle?"

"The woman goes hawking with an eagle, or says she did, in the hills. It rides on her shoulder everywhere. And she is a fighter—quick, suspicious. She may be . . . difficult."

"But what about the man? An opium dreamer, you said?"

Josip nodded.

"He will be easy enough to deal with, then. A little something extra in his pipe, or some trouble in the bazaar. Let that wait until you have killed the woman. We do not want the two of them to die at the same time; even these thick-headed English might become suspicious, and the woman is the greater danger."

"Don't you listen, Vlad' Dmitrievich? I'm telling you, it will not be so easy to reach the woman. Two men have tried and failed already."

"The third man will not fail," Vladimir Zernov said.

He drained his glass, set it down on the thick, soft carpet, and leaned forward to grasp his servant Josip by the shoulder. His thin hand dug into Josip's flesh like the talons of an eagle paralyzing its prey. "Because the third man, Josip, is going to be you. And you are going to think of a very, very clever way to get to the right house in cantonments without arousing anybody's suspicions. Aren't you?"

Life in the British cantonments went on its usual slow way while those who had stayed in Peshawar through the hot weather waited for the cool winds of autumn. Everyone was tired and short-tempered from the prolonged hot season. Mrs. Colonel Vaughan dismissed her *mali* for letting the daffodils die, and Mrs. Captain Westbrook's *khansamah* Ali Melekh disappeared without giving notice. Fortunately, the very next day a man appeared with a chit attesting that the bearer was clean, sober, reliable, and the cousin of Ali Melekh who had been seized with the desire to make pilgrimage to Mecca. Louisa Westbrook hired the man on the spot, rejoicing, and Mrs. Colonel Vaughan hinted darkly about forged chits and the danger that they would all be murdered in their beds.

"The man is a positive jewel," Louisa told Mrs. Dr. Scully. "I'm sure Ali Melekh never kept the servants up to their mark the way this *khansamah* does; and the best of it is, he's not afraid of the Gandharan woman. He actually volunteered to clean her room himself, since the bearers are all too superstitious to go in there."

"Amazing!" Mrs. Dr. Scully fanned herself and glanced enviously at the slippered *khansamah* who glided noiselessly in and out of the room where the ladies were sitting, bringing tea and cakes and clearing away the dirty plates. "I don't know how you manage it, Louisa. I can never get one servant to do a task that they think is the province of another. It's a positive tyranny."

Louisa Westbrook smiled and accepted the implied compliment. She had not the faintest idea how she had "managed it" either, but she did know that such a prize servant was not to be passed by just because of Mrs. Colonel Vaughan's vague suspicions.

While the English ladies chatted on the verandah, Tamai sat cross-legged on the floor of her room and stared at the small wriggling black snakes that were the letters of English words. English books were ugly, so square and plain, and there was no natural relationship between the shapes of the letters and their sounds. But she had to learn this language somehow, and there was no one here whom she trusted to teach it to her.

In a week of meetings with Colonel Vaughan and his advisers Tamai had not advanced beyond her starting point. While Paluk explored the delights of the city, she went each day to the colonel's office, resolved that *this* day at last she would force an answer from the man. Always the slender man in the gray suit was there in the background, and when she looked at him she sensed danger.

And each day their different languages were like a wall between her and her intention. The Urdu words and phrases that Tamai had picked up from traders were adequate for bargaining over a string of beads or buying a loaf of bread, but she could not begin to explain Gandhara's needs with her limited Urdu vocabulary; she could only speak, as she thought, in Gandharan. As for the Angrezi *colonel* and the others, she suspected they suffered from the same limitation, for they insisted on using their own language to discuss the trade she wanted—if indeed that was what they were talking about. She couldn't even be sure of that. The Angrezi men spoke many words, but the woman in black who owned this house translated only a few grudging sentences for Tamai. And never did she mention any discussion of a price for the rifles.

She dared not remain dependent on this woman's translations. This Mrs. Westbrook hated the very sight of her, and Tamai could not blame her. The woman's feelings were so strong that in her presence, Tamai could sense nothing else but the Angrezi woman's hatred, thick and throbbing like an infected wound: *You saw my husband die. You could have saved him.* It was never explained to her in so many words, but somehow Tamai understood that the Angrezi woman had dyed her clothes black in mourning for her husband, the tall golden-haired foreigner who had gone down under the KamKhel knives; and every black ruffle on the woman's preposterous costume whispered reproaches at her.

There was a rustling sound, the faintest breath of moving air. Tamai jerked her head up and touched the top of her boot with one hand, then smiled and shook her head. She was too nervous these days, living in this strange place where she understood so little of what was going on around her. It was only the new *khansamah*, who moved so quietly with his soft slippers on the straw matting. There was no reason for the image in her mind, the thought of a snake slithering past obstructions until it could see its way clear to strike.

"Missy wish *chai*?" the man lisped.

Tamai shook her head. It was not his fault, she supposed, that she disliked the man so much. She was not used to being waited on; she hated the open spaces and flimsy screens of this English house, the sense that every move she made could be observed by the eyes of some servant she had never even met.

"Missy works too hard." The *khansamah* stepped into the room. Tamai felt crowded, even though he was nowhere near her. "Should rest, drink *chai*."

"T'ank you," Tamai said awkwardly. It would be easier to use her trade Urdu than to try speaking English, but she had to practice these strange English sounds if she was ever to use the language. "Maybe later."

The *khansamah* bowed and came closer, bending over her as if to put the cup on the low table where Tamai's book rested.

"Tamai? Tamai!"

Louisa Westbrook's high, clear voice cut through the

heavy air of the plains, and a moment later Tamai heard the rustle of her full black skirts.

"Come out for a moment, if you please. Mrs. Scully wishes to meet you."

The *khansamah* backed away rapidly. He was out the door and down the long hall before Mrs. Westbrook reached the room. Tamai drew a long shaky breath and stood up to *shake hands* with Mrs. Scully. This English way of greeting was reasonable, since it allowed both parties to be sure the other did not hold a knife in the right hand; but Tamai failed to see the point in practicing it with women as soft as those in a Moslem khan's harem, women who would have no idea what to do with a weapon if they held one.

After Mrs. Scully left, it was time for the daily visit to Colonel Vaughan's office. Once again the Angrez chattered among themselves while Tamai squatted on the floor, trying to make what she could of faces and tones of voice and the few grudging words that Mrs. Westbrook translated for her. It was impossible. She had been here for more than a week, and she was beginning to think that these people would *never* sell her the rifles Gandhara needed. Was this refusal to mention any price or terms some subtle form of Angrez haggling? Was she omitting some custom that should have been known to her—some sacrifice to the gods of this place?

If so, the Angrezi woman would never tell her.

Tamai closed her eyes and reached towards the spirits of the arguing men. Perhaps from the overworld she would be able to sense their intentions. It had been more than a week since that dream of being pursued had frightened her out of the overworld; she'd been wounded, too, and feverish; perhaps it *had* been only a dream. . . .

She'd been unconsciously braced against Mrs. Westbrook's hatred. There it was, a black, pulsating pool that tried to draw her down into its depths. There was something strange about the feeling there. There was anger burning in the black fires of the whirlpool, but it did not seem to be directed at Tamai. And she sensed guilt and shame as well.

And none of it, Tamai reminded herself, had anything to do with her. She moved through and past the black current, reaching for the thoughts of the men of the Angrezi council. Their soul-flames were puny beside the strength of Louisa Westbrook's misery. She could barely feel their presence. She reached out with all her powers of concentration, open to the slightest quiver of rational thought and will—

Something about as rational as an earthquake slammed into her. Tamai felt her physical body falling sideways, striking the leg of a wooden chair with a thump that made her sick, while a force infinitely stronger than Louisa Westbrook's soul-current seized and shook her. A sickly sweet stench of something long dead filled her lungs, and rocks clashed together and made words that she could almost understand.

I have you now.

"No!"

Tamai's physical body flung out its arms, awkwardly, spasmodically, and blue fire lanced from her fingertips. In the overworld the fire was a thousand times stronger. It met the rotten soulstuff of the demon and blazed up, blue and angry and evil. The demon had become the fire, instead of being consumed by it. Tamai reached down into the molten core of the worldflesh and drew good clean red fire through her fingers, cast it out like a net over the blue flames and drew them all together in one binding. Red over blue, blue over red, the flames swayed and twisted until, with a keening screech, the blue flames shriveled away from the cleansing fire. The flame that was Tamai glowed pure red, then gold, then white-hot. She screamed with the pain of the fire attacking her own physical body and fled the overworld.

"Tamai? Tamai!"

Hands gripped her shoulders, shaking her. Tamai opened her mouth, trying to tell the black-clad demon to stop torturing her, but only a dry croak came out of her parched throat.

"Are you ill?" It was McAusland, the little black-haired man, squatting beside her and speaking in his atrocious flat-voweled Urdu.

"There was an earthquake," he told her now. "Mrs. Westbrook has gone back to her bungalow to see to her servants. You fell and hit your head on a chair and you were unconscious for a short time. Can you understand me?"

Tamai nodded, glad that no more was required of her.

The man in gray said something in Angrezi, and the Colonel turned on him, saying something angry in reply.

"Colonel Vaughan says that you should rest now," McAusland translated. "We will talk more tomorrow."

He helped her up. Tamai was relieved to find that she could stand, though she was glad of McAusland's hand under her elbow. "I will take you to my bungalow to rest," McAusland told her. "It's closer. You can go back to Mrs. Westbrook's later."

The effort of walking was good; it anchored her in this world. Tamai felt almost herself again by the time they had crossed the wide, sunny road that separated the staff offices from McAusland's bungalow. She hoped Paluk would be there. He would help her to dress the blisters that throbbed along her arm and side, and would not ask too many questions; though he might be angry with her when he saw this sign that she'd ventured into the over-world again without any proper controls to protect herself from burning.

But Paluk was ill. He lay sprawled out on a cot at one side of McAusland's verandah, head thrown back, one arm trailing off at an angle that must have been uncomfortable if not painful; his eyes though open, were glazed over and he stared at Tamai without really seeing her.

McAusland swore softly at the sight.

"Is it the fever?" Tamai asked.

"No—it's—he should have more sense than to come back here in this condition!" McAusland swore again, under his breath, and his obvious irritation reassured Tamai. One was not angry with a dying man.

"Then . . . what is it?"

"Get him to tell you. When he wakes up." McAusland's black brows were drawn together, but Tamai sensed that his anger was still directed at Paluk, not at her. "It's about time it came out, anyway," he murmured. "One doesn't—I couldn't run to you with tales of his doings in the native town, could I? As if you were his nursemaid? Men don't treat one another that way."

"Evidently not," Tamai agreed, without really understanding what McAusland meant.

"Look. I've got to get back to the colonel—and, ah, other things. I'll tell the punkah-wallah to keep at it, keep the place comfortable—leave you two alone—you'll rest for a while—have a good talk with the boy—explain to him this sort of thing just won't do, right, Tamai? In the long run. Death in the long run. Your people seem especially susceptible to it. Look at Bilizhe." And McAusland was gone before Tamai could ask him anything more.

Her dizziness was gone now. She squatted on her heels beside Paluk's cot and waited. His eyes were closed now, and he seemed to be sleeping more naturally. She could wait. He had spent three days holding her hand, trying to call her spirit back from the overworld. She could wait as long as necessary for his spirit to return.

But when, scarcely an hour later, Paluk's eyelids flickered open again and he groaned and held his aching head and begged for water, she found all her patience hissing away like water poured on the stones of a hearth.

"*Ghangaz?*" she repeated when he explained what had made him so drowsy.

"The Angrez call it opium. It is a wonderful thing. It sends visions. I always wanted to know what it was like for the wisewomen. I have flown, Tamai. I have been in the overworld—with such lovely girls, and sweet music, and a garden. . . ." Paluk's head flopped back limply; he winced with pain at the movement, but his sweet, vague smile never faded.

"I have heard of this opium," Tamai said. "It is poison, Paluk. It makes fools out of grown men, and in the end it kills them." Had Bilizhe died of this drug? McAusland's words seemed to imply as much. "It is making a fool out of you now, Paluk, before it kills you. And you are growing soft and *fat*." She punctuated her words with hard, unforgiving pokes at his ribs.

"You don't understand," Paluk muttered sullenly.

"No? But I understand this much, my foolish cousin. To be a wisewoman is more than flying through the clouds and dreaming of pretty, peaceful gardens—it's power, and that power is not given to any bazaar-loafer with a few rupees to pay for a magic pipe, but to those who work, and use the Disciplines and—"

"And what," Paluk asked, "do *you* know of the Disciplines, Tamai? Or have I missed something in my opium dreams? Has your black blanket turned into a real wisewoman's cloak? Have you flown back to Gandhara to save our people overnight? We are both hopeless dreamers, Tamai. The difference is that I know it."

Tamai sucked in her breath and stood up. This drug was poison indeed, and not only to those who used it. It had taken away her gentle, lazy, laughing cousin, replacing him with a man who could cut at Tamai with a few perfectly chosen vicious words. She felt the poison in his words like a snake curling through her own body. It wasn't only the truth that hurt so much, the reminder that she was not and never would be a wisewoman. It was that Paluk, of all men, should choose to hurt her with this particular truth.

She turned away without a word and left the shady verandah for the wide, dusty street. The noon sun blinded her; starbursts of fire exploded in her head, and the street quivered beneath her feet.

"I have to get away from here," she whispered to herself. "*We* have to get away."

Shame and pain blinded her as much as the noonday

sun. Without quite knowing what she did, Tamai reached out for the world in which she belonged. The cool pine-shaded slopes of the mountains rose before her, and she slipped half in and half out of the overworld. Her body stumbled mechanically along the flat cantonment street that led to Mrs. Westbrook's bungalow, but her spirit flickered in and out of a place and time when she had been simply Tamai, a girl of the Gandharans, ranging the safe mountains within the boundaries of the veil, learning the spirit and the name of every boulder and spring and ancient tree.

She could not stay in that "here." Other times, other places swirled about her in the overworld. She was a frightened child being hurt by strangers; she was Tamai of a moment ago, tearing at Paluk with words as Dush-muni tore apart prey with her beak; she was the torch of flame that had been Suri Kazara when she called the fires of the overworld to fight the White Huns, and the fires consumed her.

And in every "here," she felt something pursuing her, something that smelt of carrion under the sun and that laughed as it came closer.

Before her, the white dusty street shivered like a wall of snow in the instant before an avalanche buries the traveller; behind her, there were cries of surprise, and the clashing of falling rocks. The earth shifted under Tamai's feet and the walls before her shook.

She knew these walls; behind them there was a neglected garden, an empty house, shade, sanctuary. Tamai watched her feet moving up the path and into the house, and as she concentrated on the simple task of putting one foot in front of the other, the shifting images of the overworld vanished. As she came into the house she heard the servants wailing and Mrs. Westbrook's sharp voice reprimanding them, but she was too exhausted to care what the trouble might have been. She stumbled into the room where she had lived and slept since she was brought to Peshawar. The bed was too high and too far away; she sank to her knees on the coconut matting that covered the floor. There seemed to be something queer about the angle of the punkah above her head, and the floor seemed to be tilted towards one corner; the overworld must still be distorting her senses.

Tamai brought the full force of her will to bear on staying in this world around her, where a slanting streak of sunlight lit up dust motes in the air, where the woven matting followed a regular pattern of diagonal lines, where a tiny painted image had rolled out from under a bureau and lay like an abandoned doll at the edge of the matting. She had no sense, now, of other times and places, of being a child or a goddess or a dying heroine. She was just Tamai, a barren woman in a strange country, who had quarreled with her dearest friend.

The house seemed very still and empty. McAusland had said something earlier about an earthquake. Perhaps that was what had happened again, just now. The servants must have panicked and run away; there were no bare feet padding through the house, no whispers beyond the flimsy partitions. Even the punkah hung limp and motionless above her head.

And the floor was still tilted at a subtly wrong angle. That was real, then. And it explained why the little image had rolled out of the corner under the bureau where it had lain unseen all this time. Tamai picked it up and studied it carefully. She felt shaky and dull from all that had gone on that morning, the voices of the Angrez weaving incomprehensible patterns inside her head, the quarrel with Paluk, the seductive pull of the overworld with its promise of beauty and its visions of nightmare. Soon she would have to get on her feet again and do—something—she was not sure what—but for now, she had barely enough energy to turn the little image over and over in her hand.

It was a figure of a man, about three inches high, dressed in a red coat and blue trousers and holding a sharp stick in his hand. Tamai looked more closely. The sharp stick was the tiny image of a rifle, with something shaped like the blade of a dagger projecting out beyond the end of the barrel.

A rifle. Sent by the gods? What chance had brought this image into her hand? Perhaps it was a sign from Dizane that she was about to succeed. Tamai blinked and stared at the little figure in her hand, waiting for some clearer understanding of the goddess's will.

"What are you doing with that? How dare you! Give it to me!"

A black-covered whirlwind swept into the room and snatched the figure from Tamai's open hand. With her pale face distorted by anger, her yellow hair disordered like snakes about her head, Mrs. Westbrook seemed to Tamai like the incarnation of an angry goddess whose image had just been insulted.

"I found it lying on the floor," Tamai said quietly. She was still drained from the quarrel with Paluk; she did not have the energy for another scene. Mrs. Westbrook had always hated her, and she could not blame the woman, and it was too late to try to change that; but she would not flinch from this anger or apologize for a harm she had not done. Still, it was only right to respect the beliefs of other tribes. She would have to try to make amends for any unintentional sacrilege.

"I think it must have been under this bureau. I had no intention of keeping your idol; it is of no value to me. I worship Dizane of the Grain," she said, speaking slowly and carefully to make sure the Angrezi woman, with her limited command of Gandharan, understood that no insult had been intended. "And after Dizane, my goddesses are Nirmali the Maker, Kshumai of the Herds and Lunang of the Waters. If my touch has defiled your idol, I will make what sacrifices are necessary to purify it." She did hope that Mrs. Westbrook would not ask for too much recompense; the Angrez would certainly want some payment in advance for the rifles she was about to buy, and she did not know how much the silk and turquoise she had brought from Gandhara would be worth in their bazaar. It was, she thought hopefully, a very small idol; surely one small goat, or maybe a chicken, would be enough to purify it?"

"Idol. Sacrifices." Mrs. Westbrook repeated in Gandharan, and then she said something in her own language. *"Heathen nonsense!"* Tears sparkled in her pale eyes and she bent her head over the little image. "You should go," she said without looking at Tamai. "Go back to your home. It is too much! The servants run away, and the Colonel tells me to lie to you, and every time I see you I remember how Gordon died—and now you take my Harry's toy for a *heathen* idol. Go! Just go away!"

Tamai thought dully that Mrs. Westbrook's Gandharan had improved greatly in the week of practice. Talent for languages was one of the first requisites for a future wisewoman, a sign of the verbal memory and linguistic agility required to master the pattern matrices of the teaching songs and the Disciplines. *If she were a girl in Gandhara I would recommend her to the Dhi Lawan for advanced study.*

A useless, pointless, ridiculous thought, like everything else Tamai had said and done since she came south to the land of the Angrez. What did it matter if this pale foreign woman had talent enough to learn the Disciplines? She was not Gandharan or Chin—she had no magic, she belonged in a world that knew no magic, and she hated all Gandharans for her husband's death. She would fear the mountains as much as Tamai hated this hot, still, dull world of the plains. There was no possible point of contact between them.

Tamai rose and bowed to the strange woman who had cared for her, nursed her, interpreted for her and hated her through these weary, frustrating days. Mrs. Westbrook would not look at her; her head was still bent over the little image of the red-coated soldier.

Running steps sounded in the hall, and the new *khansamah* appeared in the doorway. Something flashed in his hand; he raised the knife and brought it down in a deadly arc aimed at Tamai's head. Tamai cried a word of warning and threw herself to one side, and the long, heavy knife came down harmlessly on the matting. The bright arc of its passage sheared away a fold of Mrs. West-brook's black skirt. Tamai shoved the foreign woman down and behind her with one thrust of her hand. The desperate move sent her to one knee, barely able to twist and avoid the next blow of the *khansamah's* knife. A burning pain grazed down her upraised arm, scoring the blisters that the overworld had left on her flesh. She twisted and came up with her own sharp little boot-dagger in her right hand, pointing upward, and the force of the *khansamah's* clumsy rush carried him onto the small bright blade. The weight of his body thudded against the hilt and Tamai absorbed the shock in her crossed wrists and aching arms.

Slowly, very carefully, she lowered her arms before her. The man's body slid off the point of her dagger and tumbled to the floor like a sack of grain. Tamai wiped the dagger on the man's robe and returned it to her boot.

Behind her, she could hear the foreign woman breathing in short hard gasps. Tamai turned and completed the formal bow she had begun only seconds earlier. "You did not scream," she said. "This is good." She had thought that Angrezi women were all soft and silly like the sheltered harem girls in rich Moslem houses. Mrs. Westbrook had surprised her.

"I am not—brave." The woman's face was whiter than ever, and she spoke with an effort, but she had not forgotten her Gandharan words. "I would have screamed if I had had time. *You* were brave."

Tamai shrugged. "My people learn to fight. Yours do not." It seemed a small difference beside all else that separated them. "Shall I go now, or do you wish me to help dispose of this?" She stirred the dead man with the toe of her soft boot. "I think the servants have all run away. You may wish help before I leave your house."

"I—they will come back," Mrs. Westbrook said. She breathed more deeply now, and some color had come back into her face; but she avoided looking down at what was left of her new *khansamah.* "You saved my life!"

"He meant to kill both of us, I think," Tamai said drily, "and I was principally concerned with saving my own life."

"Which explains why you threw yourself in front of me?" Mrs. Westbrook extended one white, soft hand to touch Tamai's sleeve. "I was wrong to be angry with you. It—is not your fault that Gordon died. And you did not know what this little toy meant to me." She opened her other hand. The palm was marked with creases where she had clenched her hand around the little idol. She looked at it and spoke as if to herself, but still fumbling for the right words in Gandharan. "It was Harry's favorite soldier, you see. He cried when he left for Home because we could not find it. And I have been as foolish as Harry, crying over a thing that cannot be helped. I have been weeping because I could not see my children every day. But for you, I might never have seen them again. I owe you a debt I cannot repay—I cannot save your life, but perhaps I can help you with the colonel. I wish you would stay."

After a moment's hesitation, Tamai held out her own hand to the Angrezi woman. At the touching of fingers, she felt a strange shock, something like the sense of Dushmuni's feathered head resting against her own and transmitting an eagle's vision of a bright, clear world. Only now, it was Mrs. Westbrook's world she sensed. All the anger and guilt and shame she'd felt before were still there, but in this new moment of openness Tamai could feel what lay beneath that black current: strength of soul and quickness of wit, and a deep abiding love for two small bright sparks of life that seemed to be at once very far away and somehow deep inside the Angrezi woman herself.

This is what it is to have children and love them. Tamai had shared-sense with Sunik in Gandhara, but she had never known this; perhaps Sunik had kept this part of herself apart from Tamai, fearing to hurt her with the knowledge of what could never be. And even that sense-sharing had not touched her as deeply as this unexpected, unwished contact with the foreign woman.

"I did not know," she said aloud. "I did not guess." This new grief went deeper than the bitterness Tamai had felt all her adult life. Always before she had longed for children to help carry her wisewoman's power, so that she could be what she was born to be. This time she was only thinking that it must be good to love another being as wholly and uncomplicatedly as Mrs. Westbrook loved these two small ones. The pain of what she had lost without ever knowing it went through Tamai, worse than any physical hurt, but she was reluctant to break the contact with Louisa Westbrook. "Nirmali has blessed you," Tamai said at last. "I . . . I will never have children."

"I know," Louisa Westbrook said softly. The foreign woman moved closer, until their hands touched from fingertips to palm. When Tamai looked in the woman's strange light eyes, she saw mirrored there the knowledge of her own bitterness, the slow painful acceptance that the KamKhel rape had marred her for life. She should have felt angry at being stripped of her defenses like this, but there was something soothing in the silent communion.

If I could speak thus, soul to soul, with the Angrezi colonel, perhaps he would sell me the rifles.

But the chance of that was so small as to be laughable. This Angrezi woman was unusual. No wonder she had felt so bruised by Louisa Westbrook's mourning! The woman's spirit was very strong, and she sent it out all around her without even knowing what she did. Tamai had felt no such strength in the Angrezi men.

No, it was too much to hope that she could share-sense with the colonel. But she had to find some way to convince him of her cause—and she could not do that through an interpreter, even if Louisa Westbrook had ceased to hate her. There were too many tangled layers of guilt and concealment in the Angrezi woman's soul;

Tamai could feel the confusion, even though she could not tell exactly what it was about.

She would have to create her own solution. Had she really been thinking of running away? Tamai felt new strength coming into her—coming from this white-faced foreign woman whom she had despised for her soft hands and easy tears. "You can help me," she said. "Without lying, and without disobeying this Colonel Vaughan." She felt doubt and pleasure coming from Louisa Westbrook.

"I have been trying to learn from books, but that takes too long, and it is not the way of my people. Will you teach me? Teach me the Angrezi speech, so that I may know for myself what they say, and may plead my own cause in council."

"Oh, yes—yes, I can do that. But will it not take too long?"

"I think we can spare another week," Tamai said. Louisa Westbrook seemed to feel confused and doubtful again at this statement, so Tamai pulled her hand back and broke the contact. There would be time enough to show the Angrezi woman how one used the Disciplines to master new patterns. For now, there was the body of the *khansamah* to dispose of, and—now that she had broken free of Louisa's mind—Tamai could sense Dushmuni, agitated and confused in the garden, demanding to be reassured that her mistress was unharmed.

Tamai left Louisa Westbrook to deal with the returning servants and the dead body on the floor. Dushmuni was more important to her than a man who was already dead.

CHAPTER TEN

While his servant was away Mubarak Ali Khan had to go to the bazaar daily to buy his own food. On the fifth day there were tales in the bazaar which troubled Mubarak Khan greatly, though on the face of it a small disturbance in British cantonments should be of little interest to an Afghan trader. Indeed, Mubarak Khan received without much excitement the news that a servant of the British had run mad, attacking a widowed Englishwoman and her houseguest. When the seller of spices added that the Englishwoman's houseguest had killed the madman before he could do any harm, doubtless by the use of such *jadoo* as was known only to the northern witches, Mubarak Khan's hand trembled and he spilled the banana-leaf full of turmeric that he had just bought all over his embroidered shoes with the pointed toes. And when Amira, the widow who kept the vegetable stall, added that the colonel's wife seemed inexplicably pleased by these events and had laughed about it to the cake-seller, Mubarak Khan fell silent and left the bazaar without buying his onions and lentils.

In the privacy of his house, Vladimir Dmitrievich Zernov unwound his silk turban, swore, smoked from the Indian bubble-pipe which he was beginning to prefer to Russian cigarettes, and drank things forbidden to a True

149

Believer. That Josip should have failed in his mission was not the surprise it might have been, given the amazing luck that had already favored the Gandharan witch; that he should have bungled so badly as to get himself killed was also not entirely surprising, for he might well have preferred death at the hands of the Gandharan to reporting his failure to Vladimir Zernov. But the news that the English colonel was rejoicing, so openly that his wife spoke of it to the servants, could mean only one thing. Josip had been identified as a Russian agent, and the English were laughing at having killed one of their enemies.

And why was the English colonel allowing this news to spread to the bazaar, instead of keeping it all secret until he caught the man who had sent Josip? The answer to that was clear enough. If the colonel knew who had backed Josip and where to find him, Zernov would have been a dead man by now. No, Josip must have died without betraying him, and the colonel was spreading rumors in the hope that any remaining Russian agent would give himself away by trying to flee the city before he was arrested.

Wherefore, to flee the city would be most unwise; besides, he had no more wish to confess his failure in Russia than Josip would have felt to confess to him. But help was most definitely needed. These British might not believe in Gandharan witchcraft, but Vladimir Dmitrievich Zernov had heard tales of the strange forces encountered by Skobelev's men once they entered the mountains of the Hindu Kush. And what but magic could have enabled a native woman to kill an old Cossack soldier like Josip?

After some hours of deep thought, aided by the remaining whisky, Mubarak Ali Khan emerged from the house once again and made his way to the telegraph office. There he sent a telegram to a man in Cairo concerning some horses from the mountains which might, if captured and sold in the right quarters, be worth a great profit to the traders concerned. This message, reworded along the way, went from Cairo to Paris as a discussion of certain rare jewels; and from Paris to Moscow, apparently as a debate over the new fashions being unveiled in the salon of Worth; and there it was interpreted for the last time and sent to General Skobelev in plain Russian.

As a young girl, studying the Disciplines, Tamai had learned seven thousand verses in three languages from hearing her teachers recite them. Even the least talented girl was expected to remember a set of verses after three recitations. Tamai learned hers in one. From childhood she had had an instinctive understanding of how words could be used to shape the air to one's will. The Old Language, modern Gandharan, and the speech of Bod were three different sets of shapes and patterns. The Old Language was for lightweavers, the new speech for veils and illusions, and the language of Bod for controlling demons. Each had its particular set of characteristic shapes and patterns, and once the patterns were known, the words of the teaching verses slipped into place as perfectly as an eagle's glide cut through the air.

Listening and remembering the words that Mrs. Westbrook taught her was the easy part of the task she had set herself. The hard part was forming, in her own mind, the matrix of new patterns for the Angrezi speech. For days Tamai listened intently, not just automatically storing syllables as she had done before, but taking in every sentence she heard and fitting it against the matrices in her head. She sat like stone through the meetings with the *Colonel Vaughan* and his councillors, content now to let them talk at length while her mind captured the strings of sounds, raced through probable patterns and known words, fitted the known patterns into place and ruthlessly shifted the matrix to accept new understandings. The effort left her white and shaking by nightfall of each long day, with a headache that made bright spirals of light behind her eyes.

During those days of intense concentration, Tamai's

only respite from heat and sound and light came with the fall of darkness. Each night she slipped out to the garden, where Dushmuni quietly polished her beak on Tamai's sleeve and ruffled her feathers in contentment. Tamai would lean her aching head against the eagle's golden hackles and fill her mind with the memory of a soaring glide through the pure cold air of the hills, with the ice-blue of a glacier beneath and the ice-blue of the winter sky above.

One morning Tamai woke and found that the headache had left her, and that the world looked different. She was seeing with a double vision, but it no longer made her head hurt; she could call up either vision at will. When she thought in Gandharan, she saw a world of spirits and gods and demons, a world in which each object knew itself and could be called to its proper shape by the right words, a world hovering on the edge of the overworld where all things shifted like molten rock. When she held the empty matrices of the Angrezi speech patterns in her mind, the world became flat and dull and predictable, but with a marvelous underlying complexity of rules and gears and whirring *machines*.

While Peshawar sweltered under the autumn sun, the winds from the far north swept across the Kirghiz steppes and whistled through the narrow gorges of the Hindu Kush mountains. The first onslaught of bitter cold and snow caught a shepherd of the KamKhel Kanjutis by surprise, far from shelter with a flock that should have been brought down from the high grazing lands some days earlier. He cursed the slave whose slowness had delayed them.

"Clumsy plainsman, worthless large fool, canst thou not even follow a broad path down a little hill without thy mother's hand to guide thee?" The shepherd balanced expertly round a jutting rock that all but blocked the nine-inch-wide ledge on which he walked, reached back with one hand to guide a goat around the rock and added a few new and inventive curses. "Since thou must needs creep on hands and knees like a babe, then on thy head be it if the least of these my little goats is lost to the snow!"

The foreign slave made no reply; he had learned by now that defiance brought only the whip across shoulders or face. There was some excuse for his clumsiness in the mountains, for not only was he a plainsman, but his ankles were linked together by a securely knotted thong of raw leather that allowed him to take only short steps. The headman of the KamKhels had great hopes of selling this slave to his enemies, the northern tribe called Rus, for many rifles. The Rus had offered to pay well for information of Angrez travellers coming towards Gandhara; an actual Angrezi should be worth even more.

Still farther north, the cold wind that came across the Kirghiz steppes tossed away the tents of the Russian army and tumbled them in the air like giant kites. Officers and men huddled together round their fires, wrapped in filthy sheepskin coats that harbored, by General Skobelev's conservative estimate, more fleas in each sheepskin than an entire family of serfs would have supported at home. Skobelev himself did not object to a few fleas in moderation, nor did he feel that a little thing like having one's tent replaced by a snowdrift should cause a soldier with conquest before him to lose heart; but he could tell that his men no longer shared his certainty. He made a speech on the second day of the blizzard, painting bright pictures of Gandhara's wealth, guarded only by a few walls and some old women, waiting for the Cossack orgy of looting and massacre that was meted out to those who resisted conquest. The Russian soldiers grunted, picked fleas out of their own and their comrades' hides, and asked if there was any firewood that hadn't been soaked by the storm.

Skobelev had the loudest grumbler stripped and flayed with the knout. The sight cheered up his Cossacks somewhat, but the Russians only became more depressed. Rumors began to circulate through the camp. The Gandharans should have been starving by now; instead of being cheered by this thought, the soldiers whispered that Gandharan witches could live on air and sunlight. The snows that chilled the camp should have kept the Gandharan defenders inside their city, unable to send out witches who would disrupt the soldiers' aim with distorted visions; when Skobelev pointed this out, his own aide-de-camp said that the men thought the Gandharan witches had sent the snow, and it stood to reason that a witch wouldn't be kept indoors by a storm of her own sending, didn't it now, General?

One could not very well order the knout for a young officer whose illustrious St. Petersburg family had connections by marriage with the Tsar himself. Skobelev relieved his feelings by taking the sheaf of telegrams and dispatches that had just been delivered to the camp and retiring within his own tent to read them in privacy, while his aide-de-camp stood guard personally in the biting wind and wondered what news the general had received.

There was scant comfort in the messages. The Tsar could not understand why it was taking his best general so long to subdue this small savage city-state. The Tsar's advisers thought it a waste of time to keep so much of the army camped on the Pamirs through the winter. And the English in Peshawar had another Gandharan, one who wanted to buy rifles and who might be able to stay away from opium long enough to guide an English army through the Hindu Kush. A woman. A Gandharan witch, and apparently too strong in her magic for that drunken fool Zernov to control her. Oh, yes. The last dispatch from St. Petersburg said that the Tsar wanted to know why Skobelev had allowed a Gandharan to slip through his lines to make contact with the enemy. Was he besieging this city or wasn't he?

Skobelev twisted the dispatches into tortured shreds of paper. Hopeless—it was all hopeless. The Tsar and his advisers looked out on the flat, featureless plain of Russia, and drew neat pictures of besieged cities surrounded by trenches and breastworks and artillery. He would never be able to explain to them what it was like to make war in these mountains, where there was no track suitable to drag up even the smallest of his guns, where surrounding a city was physically impossible, where women in black cloaks appeared in the trees like birds of ill-omen and sent his men mad with their witches' spells, where any outpost or picket might be found in the morning with half the men's throats cut and the other half staring blind and mad at the sun.

He would probably never have the chance to explain. Skobelev read his own recall between the lines of the brusque, impatient dispatches. The Tsar was growing bored with this months-long war of attrition on a small and unimportant state; his advisers would argue that Russia already controlled the lucrative trade with Chin and would always do so, that Skobelev's desire for new conquests was causing him to exaggerate the strategic importance of this small mountain city, that they could always move south to take over the Hindu Kush and find a gateway to India some other year, some other time. The next message from St. Petersburg would command Skobelev to hand over his soldiers to some other general. He would die in disgrace, exiled to some remote corner of the empire. The string of victories he had given the Tsar, the cities and khanates of Central Asia that had bowed to Russia, the massacres of Geok Tepe and Khiva would all be forgotten; he would be remembered only as the man who had failed, in the end, to conquer some remote hill tribe.

He, the master strategist, the greatest general of all the Russias, had been left with only one strategy. He had to have a victory final enough to satisfy the Tsar, sudden enough to forestall the British. There was one way to accomplish that, and until this hour it had been unthinkable. Now Skobelev stared at the wall of his tent and saw with the clear vision of a doomed man that to a soldier, in the end, only one thing is unthinkable: defeat.

"Send for Li Kuang-hou," he commanded the young aide-de-camp.

He felt a small, sadistic pleasure in thwarting the boy's curiosity by saying nothing about the contents of the dispatches. But it was not entirely sadism. Soon the entire army would be speculating on why General Skobelev had finally chosen to accept the aid of his half-Khitai guide, the renegade from the Chin Empire who had all along been hinting that there were better tools than bullets when one fought witches. If he told his officers about the day's messages, they would understand why the mounting pressures from St. Petersburg and India had all but forced him to take this step. Therefore he could say nothing, for an explanation was halfway to an excuse, and to make excuses would be an admission of weakness.

When the Khitai guide was shown into the tent, Skobelev waited, hands folded, until the officer who brought him had withdrawn.

"So, Li Kuang-hou," he said, "I have decided to avail myself of the services you offer. Can you raise a demon for us tonight?"

The process outlined by Li Kuang-hou would take three days, and Skobelev did not blanch at the details; but he had to remind himself several times that he had killed men in war, had sacked cities and left women and children to starve or freeze. One more death should be a small thing to a soldier.

"Of course," the Khitai finished, "we could call a far stronger demon if you could get me a Gandharan baby instead of a Kirghiz one."

"Li Kuang-hou, if I could get into Gandhara, we would not be having this discussion!" Skobelev snapped. He tried to conceal his distaste for the man. "One thing more. Can you send instructions to someone else so that he can raise a demon for himself?"

Li Kuang-hou demurred. The process was dangerous even to an expert like himself. For an uninitiated one, who did not speak the language of Bod, the danger was far greater; one misstep and he would find himself controlled by the demon, not controlling it. What was the problem? Ah—a Gandharan witch to be killed? Alone, far from her people? Li Kuang-hou smiled and stroked his long beard. Even a very small demon, if brought to this plane, should be able to kill a single witch. It would suffice if the man in Peshawar sacrificed a goat instead of a child; and then there would be less risk of his raising something too strong for him to handle.

Tamai sat through this meeting with the Angrezi councillors as she had sat through all the others, quiet, squatting on the floor, speaking only to Louisa Westbrook and only in Gandharan. But this one meeting required discipline and self-mastery far beyond the effort of simply learning the language. She had to remain silent, apparently unmoved, while the Angrezi men spoke quite shamelessly about their plans to deceive her and take Gandhara for their own. Not Angrez, Tamai corrected herself silently. English. The man called McAusland had been right about that. She looked on him favorably. He at least had spoken truth to her; of course they had been speaking in Urdu, which perhaps was not so well adapted for lying as was this English tongue.

McAusland might be trusted; and Louisa Westbrook at least did not wish to lie to her, but Louisa had the strange habit of obeying men and could not be entirely trusted. As for the rest—pah! Tamai restrained herself from making a face. *They are as bad as those northerners, the ones they call Rus.* No. That was not quite true. The Rus had simply attacked Gandhara without warning. The Angrez wanted to wrap everything up in words. They wanted her to invite them to Gandhara, then they would twist her invitation to mean that Gandhara was "under British protection," which seemed to be a polite term for conquest. They meant to promise her the rifles she wanted, but to play games with the words of the promise so they could refuse to deliver the rifles and yet pretend that they had not lied.

And they wanted Louisa Westbrook to cooperate in all their shaded lies and half-truths, by telling Tamai just what little they wished her to know of their discussions.

On the whole, Tamai thought she had done somebody an injustice. These English were not just as bad as the Rus; they were far worse. No wonder they had no magic! People who used words as a tool to twist their meanings and conceal their deceits could not possibly understand how the right words, properly used, could take the shape of the worldflesh and change that shape in the air.

Now that she could understand both the English deliberations and Louisa's translations, she saw why the Englishwoman had found this translating such an onerous task. Colonel Vaughan and this Mr. Haverford proposed outright lies, demanded that Louisa tell Tamai things they had just agreed were untrue. Louisa changed their words and managed to speak truth to Tamai—just barely—the only lies were in the things she omitted. She would say that Colonel Vaughan was very eager to see Gandhara, and would not mention that the colonel wanted to visit it at the head of two regiments of English infantry. She would explain that the rifles Tamai wanted to buy usually fetched an extremely high price across the border, and would not explain that the reason was an absolute prohibition against selling modern rifles to tribes outside British India—a prohibition that the colonel and his advisers had absolutely no intention of contravening.

At the same time, Tamai noted with appreciation and deepening respect, Louisa was equally discreet about what she told the English. She had not, for instance, told them that Tamai no longer needed an interpreter. She had not exactly lied; she had just accompanied Tamai as usual and continued to translate to her as usual.

At least this Englishwoman with the strong spirit did not use words to lie. She used silences. And she did it very well. She had a difficult course to pursue, finding a middle ground between her duty to her tribe and the requirements of honor to a guest in her house, and Tamai respected the way she had chosen to manage the matter.

She was also very grateful. Because talking directly to Colonel Vaughan might prove useful in the end, but today Tamai was getting far more benefit from hearing the long unguarded discussions among the councillors, the words that were not meant to be transmitted to her at all. Take this matter of the price of rifles, for instance. If, as Colonel Vaughan kept insisting, they were not to be sold across the border for any reason, then how could these people in the same breath quote the current prices for rifles in the hills of Afghanistan?

She dared not ask directly, because she wasn't supposed to know about the laws forbidding the English to sell their rifles abroad; Louisa had never translated those statements. But this Mr. Haverford, the man from the other council, also did not seem very knowledgeable about the arms trade across the border. Colonel Vaughan took it upon himself to educate him, and Tamai watched and listened and stored away every word in her memory.

"Oh, it's not the thieves that are the worst problem," Colonel Vaughan declared. "Though God knows, they're wily bastards! Used to lose a sentry every fortnight or so. But we've pretty well put a stop to that. Here in Peshawar we issue old muskets to the night sentries. A native won't risk getting a load of shot in his face just to steal an outdated muzzle-loader like the one his grandfather already has. And out in the border forts, where our men need the long-range rifles, we chain the sentry to his rifle. That way, even if an Afghan thief does manage to sneak up quietly enough to kill the sentry, he's still got to drag the dead body away with him if he wants the rifle. Or cut it up on the spot—they've tried that occasionally."

Mr. Haverford looked rather green around the edges after this blunt exposition of the problem.

"Then, if the tribes can't get many rifles by stealing them, what is the problem?"

"Factories," Colonel Vaughan said. "Every six months we get word of a new one starting, usually just across the border where we're not supposed to go. Native-made arms never used to be worth much, but they're clever little fellows, and they stole too many of our rifles before we put in the new security measures. Some of these Afghan gunsmiths can turn out a rifle that's nearly as good as the old Enfields. I managed to burn one such factory on a reprisal raid last year, but there's a new one now and I haven't found out where it's set up."

"Then how do you know it exists?"

"Ghilzais—the Afghan nomads who lead the caravans into the hills. They always have the latest and best arms they can get. Need 'em, too. Old Yusuf Sabazai, the Ghilzai leader who camped here last month, had all his men armed with good new rifles—and *not* of our making. Told me a string of lies about where they came from, but *I* know there's bound to be a new factory somewhere back across the border." The colonel chewed his mustache and brooded on the injustice of the system that prevented a man from mounting raids across the border to put down troublemakers, and Tamai sat back on her heels and enjoyed her own meditations on the subject of contraband rifles.

By the time Skobelev's instructions reached Peshawar, the cold wind out of the north had already broken the spell of the long, hot season. The sky was gray and there was a promise of rain in the dampness of the air. The English community came back to life and began making noises about theatricals and picnics and gymkhanas and all the other amusements for which no one had any energy during the hot weather. The English ladies who had gone to the hills for the hot season returned, vowing that one could smell snow in the air of Simla.

Tamai, too, could smell the snow coming, and she worried that the passes would be blocked before she could make her arrangements and start north again. "If I should become ill," she said to Louisa Westbrook, "would you convey my apologies to Colonel Vaughan, and tell him that I hope to resume our meetings as soon as possible?"

Louisa agreed, and Tamai mentioned casually that Gandharans really liked to be left alone when they were ill, and perhaps if she did not appear at breakfast the next morning it would be better if no one disturbed her.

"My dear," Louisa said impulsively, "shouldn't you take Paluk with you? It might be dangerous."

Tamai looked her straight in the eye and said that she had never heard of anyone running into deadly danger from spending a few days in the seclusion of their own bedroom.

"No," Louisa agreed. "But I wish you would reconsider. British protection would be best for your people. You cannot fight the Russians with a caravan-load of stolen rifles!"

"I have no intention of stealing my rifles," said Tamai, with perfect truth.

Privately, Tamai thought that she had learned a great deal from Louisa Westbrook about the uses of silence in establishing a really good lie. This interchange had been rather too blunt by the refined standards of English liars, but then, Tamai didn't have their lifetime of practice, and she was in a hurry. The snows were coming in the north.

Vladimir Dmitrievich Zernov did not worry about the snow; there were other things on his mind. Despite the cool weather, he sweated profusely in the low-ceilinged room at the bottom of his house. This had probably been intended for a storage room; the floor was of hard-packed dirt, unadorned by carpets or floorboards. He had hoped that it would soak up the blood, but the dirt was packed down so firmly that the blood puddled and ran in little rivulets all over the uneven surface.

The dying goat, incongruously bedizened in a wealth of cheap tinsel and trinkets from the bazaar, lifted its head in one last spasm and gave Vladimir Zernov a reproachful look. For some reason, probably because of the little pointed beard and the tufts of white hair around its horns, the beast reminded him of Josip.

A funnel of darkness gathered in one corner of the room. Vladimir Zernov dropped his knife and backed away. The room stank of hot, fresh blood, but now there was something worse in the air—the smell of something cold and very long dead.

Thank you for giving me a body.

The goat's severed limbs and head quivered and turned into an impossible boneless mass, then were sucked into the dark tunnel.

It is not enough.

Lips trembling, Zernov stammered out the words he had been instructed to use, the ritual phrases of Bod which should have made the demon his servant.

A grinding sound of rocks being splintered against one another filled the room. *Little flesh-thing, that ritual is for one far weaker than I am. You thought to call a little imp? But I have been waiting for a body. There is one nearby who is danger to my kind, and I cannot defeat her in . . .*

The unspoken images matched no words in Zernov's vocabulary, but he caught a confused sense of shifting flames, forces beyond his imagination battling in a world where nothing had its own proper shape.

It had to be the Gandharan witch that had drawn this demon to answer his ritual. "I can show you the witch," he promised. "Bring her to me, and I will feed you whatever you desire."

The goat's head nodded above a whirling darkness of sparks and shreds of flesh and hair and bone. *Good. You will be a good servant. Lead me to the witch.*

CHAPTER ELEVEN

The caravan of Ghilzai traders led by Yusuf Sabazai was encamped south of the Suliman Khel pass. A troop of the Punjab Frontier Force, commanded by a lonely and bored young subaltern, overlooked the doings of the caravan from a mud-walled frontier fort. The annual migration of these nomads was one of the high spots of a routine based on cavalry drill, dust storms, rifle practice, and more dust storms. For some weeks in spring, and again in fall, the barren plain with its bleak mud-walled Wazir villages was transformed into a small, turbulent city. By night, the plain was bejeweled with hundreds of small fires; by day, the subaltern could watch the bold, handsome women of the Ghilzais strolling amid their black goat-hair tents. They went unveiled, with silver and coral braided into their long black hair, and they walked with a long stride that made their full, red-bordered skirts swing out like ringing bells.

Between the black tents, bearded men in long coats waved their hands and chaffered over Turcoman rugs, baskets of dried apricots, Chin silks and British printed cottons. The tiny mirrors embroidered on their sleeves danced and winked in the sun like a host of miniature semaphores, spelling out messages in an unknown tongue. The subaltern watched those flashing mirrors and wished that he dared go down among the nomads as Lieutenant McAusland would have done. He wanted to be like McAusland some day: to joke with the men in their long coats, flirt with the bold black-haired women, sip scalding black coffee flavored with spices and dip a hand into a mound of greasy lamb pilaf on a silver tray.

The subaltern had graduated from Sandhurst, the officers' training school in England, just six months before he was stationed in this mud-walled frontier fort and told how lucky he was to oversee a troop of native cavalry with no one to support or advise him. He had a rash of prickly heat all over the tender parts of his body where the tight new uniform chafed him; he had discovered in his first week at the fort that the Urdu picked up from grammar books in England bore little relation to the quick-flowing, allusive, often obscene patter of his native soldiers; and he was beginning to suspect that Sandhurst might not have taught him absolutely all he needed to know about commanding men in a hot foreign land.

He did not actually think that the long-haired mastiffs used to herd the Ghilzai sheep and goats would tear him to pieces if he went down among the black tents; but the traders might laugh at him—they would certainly laugh at his accent—and he would hold himself stiffly and feel foolish and the prestige of the British Raj would suffer on account of his desire to mix in with people whom he could not force to respect him and his uniform.

So he leaned on the parapet and wished he were like Lieutenant McAusland, who knew everything about the tribes and who was popularly believed to have command over several minor devils. And while he daydreamed, he completely failed to notice that a woman who was clearly not of the Ghilzai had ridden into the camp. This woman was dressed in silk tunic and trousers instead of the Ghilzai full skirts. She wore her hair in one long braid rather than down her back in silver-decorated streamers. And when she dismounted—rather stiffly—and threw the reins of her horse to a boy outside one of the black tents, it could be seen that the steed had an English saddle.

Now, a stranger entering a Ghilzai camp unchallenged is an unusual thing, and a native woman other than a Ghilzai who travels alone and unveiled through the land of the Wazirs is unheard of, and Lieutenant McAusland would certainly have noticed this double anomaly instead of leaning on the wall of the fort and dreaming.

Yusuf Sabazai greeted Tamai with the courtesy men extend to someone who may just possibly be able to destroy them by speaking certain words and shaping the air in certain ways. Which is to say, he was not delighted to have a Gandharan witch in his tent; but he feigned delight, and offered coffee and a dish of honey-dipped walnuts, and managed to repress somewhat his curiosity as to what a wisewoman of the Gandharans was doing so far from home. Then he recognized that this particular wisewoman was only Tamai, the barren one who had never passed the Disciplines, and he relaxed somewhat—enough to laugh without feigning when Tamai explained her desire to buy Enfield rifles from the men who made them for the Ghilzais.

"You told me that you came here from Peshawar," Yusuf Sabazai laughed. "There are the men who make our rifles for us. Is it not kind of the Angrez to equip us so well?"

"Colonel Vaughan spoke of arms factories in these hills."

Yusuf Sabazi's face was grave. "Yes. The Afridis of the Zargun Khel have their *karkhanas*. But I would not send a friend to buy from them. They do crude work without honor."

"Honor is found at the end of the barrel, and not in the silver mounting," Tamai quoted a proverb of the Ghilzai, and Yusuf Sabazai rolled about on his cushions and shook with, perhaps, a little more laughter than the quotation merited.

"Truly, the women of Gandhara are wise beyond the mortal lot," he said, watching Tamai narrowly out of the corner of his eye. It was *said* that this woman had no magic, but another proverb of the Ghilzai said that only a fool trusted an unbroken horse, an unmarried maid, or any woman of Gandhara. Tamai had changed since the days when she came to see his caravan at the boundaries of Gandhara, a thin girl hungry for knowledge of the outside world. There was a shimmer of power troubling the air around her now; Yusuf Sabazai had a sense of unseen presences whispering about them, and when he looked at her he could almost see the glimmer of unearthly fires. Who knew what she might do if he irritated her—for instance, by refusing to sell her some of his own rifles, which he needed for the defense of the caravan? Perhaps it would be best to let her buy from the Zarghun Khel after all.

"Is it permitted to inquire why the wisewoman desires to purchase rifles?"

"Yusuf Sabazai, you know I have no magic and should not be called a wisewoman," Tamai said wearily.

"I did not mean to offend!" If the woman wished to pretend that she was not attended by sprites and encircled with fire, far be it from Yusuf Sabazai to call her a liar. One did not survive some thirty seasons of trading up and down the passes of the Afghan hills and the Chitral mountains without learning a certain amount of tact.

"And you know, also, that my country is attacked by the Rus," Tamai went on. "That is why your caravan did not come to us at the end of the flood time—because you knew we had received no goods from Chin this season."

"I had heard certain rumors to that effect," Yusuf Sabazai admitted. A frown creased his forehead between the brows. So Tamai wanted to take the rifles to Gandhara, for her people to use in battle against the Rus! He would *definitely* not allow her to buy the trash made in the Zarghun Khel *karkhanas*; if he did, he would eventually have several hundred Gandharan wisewomen calling a blood-feud on him, instead of one woman angry with him now.

"Come," he said, rising abruptly. "I will take you to

one of these *karkhanas*, and then you will understand that their rifles will not serve your purpose."

It was only a short way from the nomad camp to the village of the Zarghun Khel where the rifles were being made, but a man like Yusuf Sabazai would not have considered walking. Tamai gritted her teeth and tried to ignore the complaints of her own aching muscles. Louisa Westbrook had very tactfully pointed out the mildest horse in her stables—without, of course, saying outright that Tamai might wish to borrow a mount—but no horse could be gentle-gaited enough to make riding a pleasure for a woman of the mountains, used to walking and climbing on her own two legs rather than splitting herself astride a large stupid animal.

She tried to think less about the trembling of her tired knees and more about what Yusuf Sabazai was saying. They were riding at a leisurely pace and he was engaged in equally leisurely conversation. But everything he said had a point, and the drift of all his polite smalltalk, Tamai realized, was that he was going to be little or no help to her in the search for rifles. The Ghilzai rifles had been acquired, by devious means which it was best not to go into, from various British military posts. He made it clear that he had absolutely none to spare—certainly not enough to serve Tamai's need.

When she accepted this statement without arguing, Yusuf Sabazai stopped sweating and began to think that perhaps his instincts had failed him. Perhaps it was true that she had no magic. Tamai seemed too *reasonable* to be a true wisewoman.

Within the baked brown walls of the village of Shalozan, Yusuf Sabazai spoke certain words in a voice too low for Tamai to overhear. A boy darted between two houses, a shrill voice was heard behind a window grille, and moments later a door swung open for them.

They passed through a house where the eyes of veiled women watched them from behind a carved screen, went down a winding narrow lane between crooked houses set very close together, turned several corners where they had to pass peepholes set into high walls of mud bricks. The skin on the back of Tamai's neck prickled, and she wished that she had brought Dushmuni, who could soar overhead and warn her if there were men with weapons behind those staring blind walls.

The rifle makers squatted in a flat open square surrounded by walled houses, working under the shade of an awning. At first sight of their finished products Tamai's eyes opened wide; the men appeared to be surrounded by racks of fine Enfield rifles, perhaps not the equivalent of her Martini-Henry, but far better arms than most of the people of Gandhara possessed.

"Trash," said Yusuf Sabazai, and taking up one of the rifles, he showed Tamai what he meant. The barrel which seemed so smooth from a distance was actually made of short iron tubes, each about a foot long. These tubes were roughly welded together and the joins polished to deceive the casual eye.

"And there is no rifling on the inside of the barrel," he pointed out. "See how they try to smooth it?"

Grinning, one of the workmen showed Tamai how he thrust a square bar inside the long welded barrel and turned it round and round to scrape off the larger lumps left by the welding process.

"Only five rupees Kabuli!" the master of the rifle shop said.

"Three," Tamai replied automatically.

"*None*," said Yusuf Sabazai. "This lady wants real rifles, O cheat of beggars and despoiler of thieves! Bring thy true Angrezi arms to show her, not these worthless imitations. Who supplies her tribe will become as rich as a Kalif."

The master of the shop smiled and spread his hands. "Who has true Angrezi rifles in these sad days? Thou knowest, O great Khan, that those dogs of unbelievers have resorted to unworthy tricks, such as chaining the sentries' rifles to their bodies or arming them with ancient muskets. It was always difficult to acquire good arms, but now it is ten times impossible! And this is a very good rifle that the lady is holding, this one which was made by my own son. It has already killed three men."

The Ghilzai trader snorted. "Without doubt, each of those three men was attempting to fire this misbegotten imitation of a weapon. I doubt very seriously that it has ever dealt death from the barrel. Show us a real rifle, shame of thy tribe!"

Not all Yusuf Sabazai's insults and bribes could shake the man's insistence that he had no Angrezi arms for sale—only these crude products of his workshop.

"Take care," Yusuf Sabazai warned at last, "that you do not offend a wisewoman of Gandhara, lest a *shaitan* come to despoil you of those rifles which you pretend you have not."

The man paled at the mention of Gandhara, but did not change his story. "If a *shaitan* could find Angrezi rifles in my humble abode, he would be wiser than I, who see none there!"

Tamai was thoughtful on the ride back to the Ghilzai camp. It was growing late, and she gladly accepted Yusuf Sabazai's invitation to stay with the nomads that night. Perhaps by morning she would have thought of some other way to get rifles without giving in to the treacherous plans of the English. Perhaps it would be best, after all, to buy a great many of the crude imitations made by the Afridis of the Zarghun Khel. True, some of her people might die when those ill-made barrels exploded; but they would all die anyway if she did not act soon.

The sepoy on night duty at the end of the cavalry lines was nervous. There was nothing before or behind him to account for this fit of nerves: no intruders slipped among the tethered horses behind him; before him, the Bara Road stretched out blank and empty, for all he could tell, all the way to Fort Bara. *Ghazis*, the religious maniacs who occasionally attacked British stations without regard for their own lives, usually came from the direction of the Khyber Hills; thieves tried to slip up to the cantonments through the Saddar Bazaar to the south. There was no reason to fear an attack of any sort on this peaceful road, with the cavalry lines to the left and a few officers' bungalows to the right. All the same, the horses stirred and whinnied uneasily in the still night, and their restlessness infected the sentry. He crouched, whirled, aimed his musket at a shaking in the darkness and then lowered it with an uneasy laugh. It was only the wind in the leaves of a large mango tree. The *rissaldar-major* would have something to say to him in the morning if he wasted ammunition and woke the barracks for such a target as that!

He relaxed and turned to pace the regulation steps back to the other end of his assigned territory, and there was something blocking his way: a whirling darkness sparked with fire and stinking of rotting meat, with a goat's head bobbing incongruously above the dark column.

His musket was sucked out of his hands into the spiraling darkness. Fire struck it; for an instant the shape was outlined in ghostly blue flames, then it had become a glowing molten mass somewhere within the demon. The sentry screamed; his voice, too, was drawn into the mass of carrion and trash held together by elemental forces of air and fire. His soul followed it; then his intestines wound through his mouth. Leisurely, as one savoring a fine meal after a long fasting, the demon raised by Vladimir Dmitrievich Zernov consumed the sepoy from the inside out, until nothing remained but a crumpled husk of skin and cloths. These were added at last to the whirlwind, incorporated into the demon's structure to give shape and coherence to some parts of its inchoate being. Now, as well as a head with rotting eyes, it possessed bonelessly limber hands and arms—four of them; it had no use for legs as such.

In the house with the barren garden, Louisa Westbrook slept alone. She had sent all her servants away for a day and a night, that they might not gossip about the fact that her Gandharan guest had mysteriously disappeared; for the fiction about Tamai's keeping to her room might deceive a colonel, but never a *khitmutgar* or an ayah. She slept blithely innocent of the fact that now her servants had two, not one, interesting items of gossip to retail: the Gandharan witch had left, and the memsahib had gone mad and had given them all an unearned holiday! But she did not sleep well, for Gordon Westbrook came to her in her dreams, with blood clotting in his beautiful yellow hair and a world of reproach in his sightless blue eyes. *Why did you not save me?* he demanded, and in the logic of the dream Louisa knew herself guilty of his death and had no answer. *Come to me now, my bride.* He opened his arms. His body was marked with many wounds, and the smell of death filled the air. Louisa screamed, but she could not wake; her open eyes saw sparks of fire dancing under a monster's head, and she still smelled the putrescent flesh that came closer to embrace her.

Dushmuni had been sleeping on her perch in the garden. She stirred and ruffled her feathers unhappily as the demon drew near. A sense of wrongness pervaded the night, and a smell of long-dead things offended her nostrils. Like the horses, she would have fled if she could. But the horses were locked within their stalls, and Dushmuni, though free to fly, was imprisoned by darkness. Eagles have essentially no night vision, and without Tamai's sight to guide her, Dushmuni was all but blind. She smelled the carrion and heard certain sounds: the breaking of an ornament in Louisa Westbrook's bedroom, the bubbling scream of a woman roused from nightmare into nightmare, the crash of splintering wood. She huddled on her perch, chilled by the knowledge of an enemy who could not be driven off by beak and claws, waiting for the dawn.

That same night, in Gandhara, the early snows came down in thick, wet flakes that turned the darkness into a whirling blindness of soft white patterns. Mirjan, patrolling the northern walls of the shrunken city, stared into the dizzying circles of snowflakes tossed by the winter wind until he could almost feel his soulstuff being sucked out into the black cold of the mountains. Was this how it was for the wisewomen, when they sent their spirits into the overworld?

Surely not. That must be something great and wonderful, not this cold, cramped boredom. He couldn't believe that the wisewomen in their two-sided cloaks suffered like ordinary people from damp seeping into felt-lined boots, and toes so cold that he was glad of an ache to prove they were still there, and limbs cramped and frozen from standing so still beside the icy stone of the northwest tower on the outermost wall. Mirjan beat his hands together on his chest to warm them, and blew on his frozen fingers, and reflected wryly that he had not really anticipated the ramifications of his new, honorable position. When the Dhi Lawan announced that the wisewomen remaining were too few to guard the city, he'd been one of the first men who volunteered to take a spell on the walls. He'd thought then of honor, and glory, and the ancient songs of heroes like Suri Khazara who'd died defending Gandhara from the White Huns.

Now, after a cold month of standing guard when he might have been at home warming his fingers on the growing swell of Chakani's belly, he tended to remember that Suri Khazara—may her name be honored—had, after all, died in that last battle. And the White Huns had destroyed Gandhara-of-the-plains anyway. And all deaths, glorious or not, were probably equally cold and lonely at the end—and—

"*Lunang keep us!*"

Mirjan shrank back against the cold blue tiles of the tower and shaded his eyes with one hand, a ridiculous gesture, as though peering through this snowblind night were like squinting into the sun. But he had to do *something* to pretend to himself that he could see more clearly—could make out the vast tumbled shapes of emptiness that were replacing the snow—

His right hand automatically grasped the copper chain about his neck, feeling for the little jade image of Lunang of the waters. The shapes were closer now: cylinders and funnels of darkness, with lumps like goats' heads turning blindly from side to side as if to smell out their prey. And now, almost too late, Mirjan called warning and beat frantically with both hands on the great warning-drum of brass and hide that hung from the tower wall.

"Demons! *Yush!* Wisewomen, to the north—to the northwest wall—"

"*Ma Mihter yoh nisai; pinjareshoh mus nisai,*" said a calm voice to Mirjan's right. The black-cloaked figure stepped forward, one hand upraised, and the cold white light of a wisewoman's working illumed the north wall. The light absorbed the glitter of melting snow on the walls, dulled the sheen of tiles fired in Nirmali's flames by long-forgotten arts, soaked up the points of brightness in the patterned brass of the drum. There were no reflections from witchlight. But it did show the moving shadows along the base of the wall and the dripping shapes that formed and re-formed as they blundered along their first real obstacle. The *yush* were oozing right along the wall now, scrabbling for purchase on the smooth stones, too stupid to retract the dead limbs on which they had stumbled across the snow.

Even as he watched, paralyzed with a fear that dried his mouth and turned his cold limbs to melted snow, Mirjan saw one of them blunder into the wall with the soft black stuff of its body. Too stupid in its fleshly form to make a plan, it was still able to take advantage of the accident. It sucked itself onto the tiles and began moving upward like a giant black leech adorned with bits of carrion. It snuffled quietly as it moved, and the patterns of moving sparks within it were exposed as its dead arms and legs were shoved aside to give more body-surface against the wall.

"*Um yette bes dusubah? Ja munna etaba!*" the wise-

woman beside him called out in a quavering voice. Mirjan could not see her face under the muffling folds of
the black cloak, but her voice was young and frightened,
and the smooth young hand she held out in the path of
the *yush* trembled.

He did not think less of her for that. He himself had
been in such a panic that he had forgotten to let go of
Lunang's image when he beat his fists on the warning
drum. The thin copper chain round his neck had snapped
and now dangled from his closed hand, as useless as the
little jade image he held.

Now, seeing before him a death worse than any he
could have imagined, Mirjan found his fright overlaid by
a strange calm. Fear was for those who had a chance to
live.

"Deshkulti, it will do no good to command the *yush*
in the Old Speech," called a thin, calm voice from the
next tower over. Mirjan raised his eyes and saw Kazhirbri
standing with her black cloak flung back, both thin old
arms upraised while she traced lines of fire against the
whirling snowflakes. The back-turned edges of her cloak
showed a rippling waterfall of color and pattern, all the
broad bands of embroidery she had earned in a lifetime
as a wisewoman of Gandhara.

Once he would have averted his eyes lest the sight of
those forbidden patterns bring him ill luck. Now it didn't
seem to matter. Mirjan laughed grimly. He sensed Deshkulti, beside him, turning in surprise. It didn't seem
worthwhile to explain the poor jest that had come to
him—that there was no need, now, to worry about
tomorrow's bad luck.

Instead he watched quietly, as Kazhirbri began a chant
in the language of Bod. The foreign words rang like
gongs in the night and the patterns of fire she traced
spread out like a shell from her outspread fingertips.
Mirjan could see that the *yush* turned aside from that
shell of light. But there was no one else to take up her
chant, and the pattern grew too slowly to cover the wall;
it was only sending the *yush* to the left, to his tower.

When he glanced down, the base of the wall just under the north tower was covered by a heap of writhing dark shapes, and three of them now had learned how to make their slow progress up the wall.

"They will be here before she finishes," said Deshkulti in despair. She leaned forward, gathering witchlight in her two hands, and hurled the dull white radiance down on the shapes of the *yush*. The topmost *yush* turned to watch the falling globe of light, and in turning, seemed to forget its direction; it began sliding sidewise across the tiled wall to follow the witchlight.

"Do that again," Mirjan said.

Deshkulti's hood had fallen back. She turned her head and looked at him for a moment; a pretty girl, somewhat too thin and tired, as were all the wisewomen, but with a fall of glossy black hair that would have shone like black silk in any natural light. Chakani's hair was like that, silk and Chin ink.

Chakani. Not yet a wisewoman. He breathed a prayer of thanks that she was home, safe with their baby inside her, not facing the *yush* on this dark night.

But no one would be safe if the *yush* crossed the wall, to feed at will on all the souls crowded into the diminished boundaries of Gandhara.

"It's not enough," Deshkulti said in the flat tones of despair. "Nothing we can do is enough."

All the same, she returned to the task, calling sphere after sphere of cold white radiance into being between her stretched fingertips and throwing them down among the seething mass of *yush*. The climbing demons slowed, turning their borrowed heads this way and that, and the shell of light around Kazhirbri's tower spread out and downward until nearly all the *yush* were beyond the barrier.

Mirjan began to breathe again, and to be conscious of just how frightened he had been underneath that protective calmness. "I damn near fouled myself there," he said, laughing shakily and wondering why his voice was so much higher than normal. "Kazhirbri is—Kazhirbri—"

Up to now he'd thought her a mean old woman, even if she was a senior of the Council. The narrow-minded, selfish old woman who'd played on poor Tamai's bitterness and sense of inferiority until she tricked Tamai into exiling herself on a hopeless errand. But tonight, Kazhirbri was a heroine, and her years of studying the arts of Bod had been justified all at once.

Mirjan was still trying to find words to praise Kazhirbri when Deshkulti swung round and made a gurgling noise that was choked off in the middle.

The far side of the north tower was still beyond Kazhirbri's shell of light; and over the wall on that side came a column of oozing darkness, spiked with horns and hide of dead animals and crowned with the wailing head of a human child. Between one breath and the next that darkness flowed round Deshkulti, ending her bubbling cry of horror and extinguishing the witchlight she had called out of the overworld. Mirjan could just make out its shapeless flow coming towards him, a shadow against the dim reflected light of Kazhirbri's magic. He flung up his closed fist before his face in an involuntary gesture of defense—foolish and hopeless—the jade statue of Lunang still clenched within his hand—

And a shower of bright sparks crackled around his hand and down the length of the demon.

The force of the blow, landing in nothing, sent Mirjan reeling forward. He tripped over Deshkulti's black cloak and fell onto something soft. Not a *yush.* He recognized that slowly, mainly because he was still alive and not a part of the *yush.* The *yush* that took Deshkulti had dissolved into a pile of carrion, and the others had retreated. Far behind him, from the next tower, he heard Kazhirbri's voice raised in a cry of triumph.

The *yush* had been destroyed in sparks of light when Mirjan swung his fist at it.

The hand that had been holding Lunang's image.

"Lunang saved me," he said aloud in a voice that creaked like an old man's, and then, "Lunang saved me, but not Deshkulti. Why?"

He still had no answer to his question when Kazhirbri's witchlight illumined the tower and he saw what he had been lying on; the smooth black coils of Deshkulti's hair, wrapped around the throat of the human child whose sacrificed body had been the core of the destroyed *yush*.

With the coming of morning Tamai was no closer to a decision. She had slept badly; in her dreams the stars in the night sky became whirling points of fire in a funnel of smoke, and the fire and smoke together laughed in a voice of doom and bent to Earth to entrap her. Dawn was a relief. She squatted by the first fire and drank hot, unsweetened coffee with Yusuf Sabazai and they spoke of unimportant things, the price of horses in Peshawar and the chance of snow in the passes to the north.

They were still watching the embers of the fire when a black speck appeared in the sky above the Ghilzai camp. Tamai looked up, then jumped to her feet. "Give me a saddle blanket! Or—no, that's too big—anything heavy that I can wind round my arm."

"Why?" Without waiting for an answer, Yusuf Sabazai stretched leisurely and called an order to one of the children hovering around the fire. The boy grinned and dived under a wagon, returning with a brilliantly embroidered strip of heavy cloth.

"That's too beautiful!" Tamai protested, but there was no time to seek out another arm guard. She wound the strip about her hand and forearm and raised her closed fist to the rising sun. Red silk flowers and shisha mirrors caught and sent back the morning light, and for a moment Tamai's upraised arm was outlined in fire; then a shadow covered the mirrors and the roar of a great bird's wings ripped the air apart. Dushmuni had stooped from her soaring height above the plain, plummeting like a bullet with wings folded until the last minute; then she spread her seven-foot wings like a sable cloak, fanned out the gold-tipped flight feathers at the ends and all but stopped her fall in midair. Even so, the force of her arrival was enough to have knocked Tamai off her feet if she had not been braced to take the eagle's fourteen-pound weight on her guarded arm. Three-inch yellow talons curved into the embroidered cloth and ripped slits between the sisha mirrors.

Yusuf Sabazai winced at the sight, not so much for the ruined cloth as for the thought of what it must feel like to have those talons clamped on one's arm. If Tamai had not found something to protect herself, Dushmuni would have ripped her arm to shreds without even trying, just from the sheer force of landing. Even now, Tamai must be bleeding from deep scratches where the eagle's talons had punctured the cloth; but she paid no attention. She stroked Dushmuni's golden hackles with one finger and murmured soothing words until the eagle was calmed; then she laid her head against the bird's. The woman's face should have looked soft beside the eagle's fierce jutting brows and wickedly sharp beak; but Yusuf Sabazai had the uncomfortable feeling that he saw, not a woman beside a bird of prey, but some not-quite-human creature leaning its own head against a magical mirror and seeing its inner nature reflected back.

Even as he watched, Tamai's face paled and her features looked indefinably harder, bringing her that much closer to an appearance of kinship with the eagle.

"Yusuf Sabazai, I must go now," she said when at last she raised her head. "Dushmuni brings word of grave trouble in Peshawar. The woman who gave me guest-right has been attacked, and by my enemies; they came under cover of darkness, so Dushmuni could do nothing to help her."

"She is dead? You make a blood-feud? One rifle, at least, I can lend you, and my sons to ride with you as far as Peshawar that you may not be attacked on the road—" Yusuf Sabazai began, but Tamai shook her head.

"No. Not dead. At least—" Her face seemed almost gray. "I think not. Dushmuni believes she was taken from the house; she does not know why, and she could not follow in the darkness to see where she was taken. And the enemy that attacked her cannot be fought with rifles, Yusuf Sabazai."

The Ghilzai caravan leader felt his own face growing still and gray, mirroring Tamai's. *"Yush?"* He used the word common to all the hill languages, the word that had come with the thing it described from the land of Bod.

"I fear so. It is a matter for a wisewoman, you see; and I must go alone."

"But—you said you had no magic!"

"That does make it more difficult," Tamai acknowledged with a flashing smile. Yusuf Sabazai felt a chill that had nothing to do with the winds from the north. He had seen this smile before, on the face of a man setting out to die in a battle against impossible odds.

"And if you don't know where this woman has been taken . . ." he began a last feeble protest.

"I will find her." Tamai raised her fist and the eagle scrambled up her forearm until it was sitting at the highest point. "Dushmuni and I will find her." She threw her arm up and the eagle took off with an ungainly sprawl of wings: a bird designed to soar from the mountains, clumsy and out of place here on the plains. Tamai, too, was out of place here, but there was nothing clumsy about her slender figure. Yusuf Sabazai watched with regret as she rode away, following the path the eagle had taken. He had always had a certain liking for this quiet, dark woman, and he was sad to see her going to her death. It was really a pity that she had no magic.

CHAPTER TWELVE

The narrow room had only one window, high up, with bars across the slit of an opening. There were empty shelves along one wall, and the tattered remains of a sack lay on the floor under the bottom shelf. The floor was hard-packed earth, stained dark brown in places. The room smelled of old blood and fresh green mould, with a hint of slimy secrets in the damp corners where insects scuttled.

Louisa Westbrook gave a little moan and shut her eyes. This was not real. It could not be real. The nightmares were getting worse; even, as now, when she knew she was dreaming, she could not wake from them. She had tried to wake herself up once, and all that happened was that Gordon had transformed into a rotting tower of darkness that laid flaccid hands upon her and laughed when she struggled. That part of the dream had been in her own pretty pink and white bedroom; she had smashed a vase on the monster's goatish head before the stench and the nauseating touch of those soft bulging hands overpowered her.

A door creaked on its hinges and Louisa discovered that she could move after all, even if only to cower a little farther back in the dark corner where she lay— where she dreamed that she lay.

The cold, damp wall felt very real. And there was nothing dreamlike in the face of the man who entered: a young man, with skin and hair dark as a native's, but wearing a loose white shirt and tight trousers like a European. Louisa pushed herself up to a sitting position against the wall and then, feeling as sore and tired as if she actually had been abducted and left on a damp floor for hours, she managed to stand. Even in a nightmare, she would not lounge on the floor with her skirts disheveled.

"Fool!"

"I *beg* your pardon?" Louisa said. Her voice quavered more than she wished.

"Oh, not you. Wait. Fool!" the young man cursed a companion somewhere behind him. "This is not the right one. I thought you knew her!"

The voice that answered came through Louisa's head without sound, without words. It was pure meaning, and it carried with it the feeling of rocks being crumbled to powder and screaming as they were destroyed, and it came out of the deep nightmares from which she had been trying to awaken. And hearing that voice through the vibrating bones in her head was what finally convinced her that this was no dream. *I know her in the overworld. How shall I know what shape she takes here? This was the only woman in the house you showed me. Perhaps you sent me to the wrong house.*

"Well, it's not her. Idiot! Son of a syphilitic she-camel!"

This is manifestly impossible. Demons do not consort with camels. The voice of horror was bored, perhaps sullen.

Louisa felt a quavering of faint, unworthy hope within her. She was not the one they wanted. Perhaps they would set her free. They would take someone else—anyone—she didn't care—only if she did not have to *see*, with her waking eyes, the thing that made that voice inside her head.

If you do not want this one, I will have her now, the voice proposed lazily.

"You may as well. I don't dare send her back—"

Louisa's knees gave way and she slid down the wall. She would have begged for her life if her tongue would only have obeyed her commands; but her mouth had turned to dry cotton.

"No. Wait. Let me see." The young man came down the short flight of steps leading into the room and gripped Louisa by the arm. "Stand up. Let me see you in the light." With his free hand he took her chin and turned her face toward the window. She let him move her, passive as a doll. If she did exactly what he demanded, if she did not anger him, would he spare her from the *thing* that waited outside that door?

"What is your name?"

She had to try three times before she could get her dry mouth to function. "L-Louisa Westbrook."

"Ha! I thought so." The young man sounded pleased. He, too, was standing in the light from the window, and Louisa studied his face anxiously for some hint of what he meant to do with her. He looked cruel, and the flesh around his mouth was pouchy, with little petulant lines that detracted from the handsome bone structure. Major Phelps had something of the same expression; and it was whispered that Major Phelps consorted with the native girls. From somewhere in her limited experience and copious reading the word "voluptuary" came to Louisa. Was *that* why he was studying her face so intently? Surely not. She was not the sort of woman one kidnapped for such a reason; why, Gordon was always telling her—*had* always told her, Louisa corrected her stray thought—that she was too thin and too plainly dressed and too careless of her hair.

But then, this man hadn't meant to abduct her; he had been looking for another woman.

"The Gandharan witch stays in your house, doesn't she?" the young man snapped.

Tamai? Louisa's incredulity spilled over into hysterical laughter. Dear God, she might be a thin little frump of a thing as Gordon was always saying, but what kind of voluptuary would want to kidnap *Tamai*, that taut bow-string of a woman in her sexless trousers, with a knife in her boots and a hunting eagle on her wrist?

A blow rang in her ears and rocked her head back painfully on her neck. Louisa tried to put one hand to her stinging cheek, but the young man held both her hands fast now. "Answer me!"

"Y-yes, she is my guest," she stammered, "but . . ."

"Very well." The young man nodded in satisfaction. "You have not done so badly after all," he observed over his shoulder. "These primitive people have some sense of honor between guest and host, and the bazaar loafers say that this woman has made a friend of the Gandharan witch. We will hold her here until the witch comes to get her back. I think we will put her on the rooftop; the witch's eagle will spy her well enough from there."

A darkness filled with sparks of light poured down the steps into the narrow room. The darkness filled her view and Louisa felt herself falling into it.

Sunlight beat on her closed eyes. Slowly, reluctantly, Louisa knew herself conscious again. She opened her eyes just a slit—she could bear no more. The blinding whiteness of a rooftop in the sun assaulted her senses: heat and light and something else hurt her. Pain in her wrists. While she was unconscious, someone—or *something*—had jerked her arms behind her and tied them together with a rough rope.

Was the man still here, watching her? It would be better to pretend she was still unconscious. But the sun was a torment beating on her unshaded head, and it would get much worse soon. She tried to roll into the shadow of the parapet. The rope around her wrists snapped taut, holding her where she was.

Something chuckled. Louisa wanted to faint again, but unconsciousness would not come. She heard steps crossing the roof. A pair of polished boots came into view beside her. It was the man, then, not—not that other thing.

"Awake? Too bad," he said, with what sounded like real sympathy in his voice.

"If you leave me in the sun," Louisa said, "I will die." She would not beg; it would be useless anyway. But she could say that much.

"You Englishwomen think any little discomfort will kill you," the man observed. "Your race is weak. Still, I do want you to last until the witch comes; she might not think it worth her while to retrieve your corpse."

He went behind her and did something to the rope, then pushed her into the shade and retied her bonds.

A grinding voice sounded inside Louisa's head, and she felt cold and nauseated in the Peshawar heat. *What if the Angrez come first?*

The young man chuckled. "I never knew demons were so slow," he remarked. "Almost as dull as the English. They do not *believe* in your sort, my stupid friend. And I left a torn Yusufzai turban, and a broken dagger, outside the sentry's post on the Bara Road. The English colonel will think this was a raid of the Ghazis, those fanatics who love nothing better than to kill Englishmen. He will go wild at the thought of a white woman held prisoner by natives. His men will be far too busy among the tribes, trying to get this woman back from those who do not have her, to pay any attention to a house in the Afridi quarter of Peshawar."

The flicker of hope in Louisa's heart died. This man was right. No one would think to search Peshawar for her; they would be looking for fanatics from the other side of the border, searching tribal lands and invading Yusufzai villages.

And she knew something else, too. The man who had taken her enjoyed destroying her hope. Enjoyed hurting her. Why else would he have spoken aloud, and in English? She could tell from the faint accent that it was not his native language. He was watching her face as he spoke, taking pleasure in her despair.

You think of many things, droned the worldless voice inside her head. *But you have made one mistake.*

The man looked over his shoulder. "And what may that be?"

I am not your friend.

The demon-darkness flowed forward until Louisa could see it. There was something vaguely menacing in the formless mass of shadows and carrion. *I hunger. You paid me only with a goat.* It is not enough.

"You had the sentry, too," observed the man.

It is not enough.

"Well? What do you propose? My servant is dead—and you can't take the woman; we need her to bring the witch."

I do not mean to take the woman. She is still of some use to me. You, on the other hand—

Louisa shut her eyes and put her hands over her ears, but not soon enough; not before she had seen the beginnings of the demon's feast. Her throat ached from hysterical screaming, but the rooftop was silent around her. The demon absorbed her screams and her fear like a tasty relish to the physical body of the man who had held her prisoner.

She never did learn his name; and so no one ever knew what had become of Vladimir Dmitrievich Zernov.

Tamai paid a boy in the bazaar to take her horse back to the British cantonments. There was no use in going there herself, she thought. These English did not believe in demons, and they would certainly not believe Tamai if she tried to tell them that her eagle knew what had happened in the house of Captain Westbrook. Besides, what help would they be? A demon made its body of things that were already dead or that had never lived; it could not be killed with rifles. Only a wisewoman of Gandhara could have helped her, and Gandhara was far beyond the snow-topped mountains to the north. In this, Tamai was alone.

Perhaps, she thought, not quite alone. She threw an anna at another boy and asked directions of him; for the price of a leaf-cone full of coconut sweets he served as her guide to the Ghangaza Khana, in the maze of narrow streets behind the Saddar Bazaar.

The dimly lit rooms of the Ghangaza Khana were filled with recumbent figures. Tamai stepped over and around dreaming smokers, repressing her disgust at the filthy mats on which they lay. Here and there a lamp burned, where a fresh pipe of opium was being prepared. The small flames flickering in the smoky, windowless rooms lit up the faces of the smokers in fits and starts, like masks appearing through the incense smoke of a devil dance in Bod.

She found Paluk tending one of these lamps in the innermost room. He lay at his ease on one side, intent on the bubbling pill of opium which he held above the flame on a steel needle. The mass of opium changed colors from black to golden brown as he revolved it on the needle.

When he looked up to see Tamai standing over him, he gasped and his hand jerked. The needle, with the bubbling pill of opium still on its tip, fell into the straw. Tamai's booted foot came down on it before Paluk could retrieve his drug. She ground her heel back and forth, crushing opium and straw and dirt together into an unpalatable mess.

"That cost me good rupees, that you have ruined," Paluk said sullenly. His speech was slurred, and Tamai thought this would not have been his first pipe of the day. "Did you come here to complain at me again?"

"No," Tamai said, "I came for help—but you must be awake to help me, not dreaming of the overworld."

She explained her needs as quickly as she could and was relieved that Paluk did not interrupt or ask needless questions. "Yes," he said when he had finished, "the owner of this house can find a private room for you. But it will cost many rupees—enough for a month of smokes in the common room." He looked wistful.

"And you will guard me?"

"Yes. I will not smoke again until you return from

the overworld," Paluk promised, "no matter how long it takes!"

"It had best not be long," Tamai said soberly. "I do not know how much time we have. And I do not mean to go into the overworld. That is too dangerous. But I have to follow Dushmuni's search, and I must be alone and undisturbed to do that."

Dushmuni glided and banked lazily on a current of warm air several hundred feet above the city, waiting where *otherself* had sent her. To her eyes, the city of Peshawar was a complex assemblage of tiny shapes displayed in perfect detail. From her soaring height above the city she could follow the movements of a caged songbird on a windowsill. Regretfully she catalogued the bird as *not-prey* and went on to examine every other detail in the street she was observing with equal bright-eyed interest. The pattern of colors in an embroidered scarf caught her eye for a moment, mimicking as it did the subtle change of color and texture in the plumage of a mountain partridge; but the thing did not move. *Not-even-food*, she thought, and as such, of even less interest than the bird in the cage.

Suddenly her senses were blurred over by the vision of a dimly lit room in which *otherself* sat immobile. Dushmuni sent questioning and fear outwards and was reassured by soothing feelings coupled with commands.

Look at the city, commanded *otherself*. *See for me. Find the demon.*

Dushmuni sent back a catalogue of complaints. What, she demanded, was there to see here? Nothing but useless trash: *not-food, not-prey*. She hated this place called a city. And she did not want to find the demon. An eagle preyed on other things, but to a *yush* she herself was prey. Why could they not go back out into the hills, where she could gain the height to soar from peak to peak, where she could dive and catch food in her talons instead of waiting for *otherself* to bring her dead rabbits and chickens from a butcher's shop?

Find the demon and find Louisa, insisted *otherself.*
*Look for clues. What is different? What is out of place
in the city?*

Gradually Tamai's intelligence overcame Dushmuni's
instincts, and they merged as one being, the woman's
sharp wits carried aloft on the bird's wings and seeing
with the eagle's crystalline clarity of vision. House by
house, street by street, Tamai sent Dushmuni in ever-
widening arcs south from the edge of the British cantonments across the jumbled bazaars and houses and tem-
ples and *serais* of the native town.

It was very hard to complete the arcs. Something
seemed to be pushing at her, shoving her away from
one particular quarter of the town. Tamai pushed back—
Dushmuni soared over houses she had been avoiding—
there was a brief vision of a woman in a black skirt, lying
curiously immobile on a white rooftop—Tamai felt the
thin fabric of "here" tearing against her push and her
spirit fell into the grayness of the overworld and Dushmuni's clear sight was lost to her. Instead she was all but
deafened by the cries of Louisa's strong but undisciplined
spirit.

*Go away. Go away. Tamai, where are you? Oh, dear,
I am so frightened. Go away. Don't come to me. Oh,
please, somebody come. No, don't come . . ."*

Louisa was terrified, babbling, possibly driven mad by
the sight of the *yush.* Tamai sent soothing thoughts to
her and the contradictory babble slowed, calmed, became
one desperate message of warning. *Don't come. I am the
bait to catch you.* Behind the fear was an image of the
yush, wearing a physical body composed of the shreds of
its victims and sacrifices, waiting to strangle Tamai with
four arms formed from a sepoy's limbs and four sets of
claws built of a Russian spy's arms and legs.

Instinctively, blindly, Tami fled that image and the
overworld and tumbled back into her own body. A corner
of the matting was in flames. She beat at it with the
torn saddle cloth she had been using as a gauntlet for
Dushmuni. It was only a small fire, nothing compared to

the disasters that struck around her when she tried to use her power in the overworld. But where was Paluk? And Dushmuni?

A questing tendril of consciousness reassured her that Dushmuni was still soaring over the city, banking and turning and playing in the updrafts, and that the eagle could locate the house where Louisa was kept at any time.

Tamai drew back into herself, shaken and frightened, and went to look for Paluk.

He was asleep in an outer room, a discarded pipe of opium by his side, hands flung out in drowsy abandonment.

There could be no help from that quarter, then. She would not be able to wake him in time—and even if she could, would she trust him at her back while she fought a demon in the overworld? A man who could not even keep watch over her body for an hour while she searched through Dushmuni's eyes? Tamai did not even bother to leave a message with the keeper of the Ghangaza Khana.

To follow Dushmuni's guidance through the city streets required some concentration, but nothing like the degree of rapport they had achieved while Tamai sat in the Ghangaz Khana. Instead of following a regular, boring, geometrical search pattern with no joyous kill at the end, now Dushmuni had only to guide Tamai towards their prey—a task she'd done often enough in the mountains. No strength of will was required to force the eagle to this hunt, only the fine-spun thread of concentration that let Tamai follow her through the streets of Peshawar.

As she walked, Tamai thought about what she had learned. She also tried to convince herself that she was not desperately frightened.

The demon wanted to bring her physical body to meet its own; that was the purpose behind kidnapping Louisa. That implied that it was afraid to meet Tamai in the overworld. She was afraid of that level, too; but last time, her fires had overpowered the demon's. Perhaps, even though she was not a wisewoman, the latent power within her was enough to conquer this *yush*.

But if she tried now to meet it in the overworld, it would threaten Louisa. So she had to get into the house somehow, free Louisa, cast herself into trance and draw the demon's soulstuff after her into the overworld, all before it could suck the life from her or Louisa in this world.

"Difficult," Tamai said aloud. "Definitely difficult. But not impossible." All the teaching songs and stories laid stress on the extreme stupidity of demons in this world; when they put on their bodies of decaying flesh, it seemed as if their minds began to rot and die also. They could be fooled, sometimes, by childishly simple tricks. Tamai recalled a few of those tricks from the teaching songs, and thought that one of them might work—especially as she was not alone. She had Dushmuni to help her.

A somewhat more difficult problem was the matter of controlling her time in the overworld. Strange things had happened, both to Tamai's physical body and to her surroundings, whenever she sent her spirit out. Fires started. Rocks fell. She burned from the inside. She lost her way and forgot to come back.

And all that was when she had someone by her who understood about the overworld and could call her back. Without Paluk, what were her chances of returning from this battle? Perhaps slightly worse than she had estimated when she set off from the Ghilzai camp this morning. Well, even then she had not expected to survive the encounter, so what difference did it make? No matter how bad the odds were, she could not die more than once in this battle. And if she died now, fighting a *yush* to rescue her friend, she would have earned Dizane's favor and Nirmali's grace, and perhaps she would be reborn into a body that could hold the power she found so troublesome and transmit it to children of that body.

                    *   *   *

The glass windows on the east side of Vladimir Zernov's house exploded inward with a crash. The demon lurched towards the broken window, four hands and four sets of claws outstretched to grasp its foe. Shards of glass lacerated dead skin; claws of bone and hair closed on empty air. Something screeched defiance outside, and a black foot with three long yellow talons smashed in the windows on the opposite side of the house. The demon lumbered this way and that, slow and clumsy and hungry, but unable to touch the enemy that taunted it with speed and sound and defiance.

Dushmuni caught an updraft and rose to a hundred feet above the house. Again she plunged downward with both sets of talons extended to attack another vulnerable point. Louisa woke from her trance of thirst and heat and fear and knew a moment's incredulous joy at the sight of Tamai's eagle streaking past the roof. The demon yowled in frustration and stumbled clumsily from room to room within the house, trying to grasp a foe that did what no human could do.

And Tamai slipped in through broken glass on the east side while the demon was busy on the west, ran light-footed up the stairs to the roof while the demon howled its anger at an attack from the north, cut Louisa's bonds while Dushmuni kept the demon circling the house.

There was no time to talk, no time to let Louisa voice the warnings she had been crying with her spirit.

"Hush," Tamai said quickly. "I know. You tried to warn me. I think you can get away now, while Dushmuni keeps the demon busy."

Louisa grabbed hold of Tamai's tunic with both hands, like a child who would not be taken from its mother. "I can't. I can't go down into the house. Not while that—that *thing* is there. I can't!" she repeated on an indrawn sob. "You don't know—you can't imagine—"

"Oh, yes," Tamai said. "I do know." Her own fear was screaming inside her head, telling her to leave this foolish Angrezi woman and get out while she could. She tried to unclasp Louisa's white fingers from her tunic, but hysteria gave Louisa greater strength than Tamai could master just then, with her own hands sweaty and shaking.

"If I ask Dushmuni to draw the demon up to the roof," she said slowly, "do you think you could run down the stairs and get away, very quickly?" She had to set her will to form each individual word. It seemed to take forever to get the sentences out. There was a clatter of glass below them. How much longer could Dushmuni keep circling and distracting the *yush*? Eagles were made for soaring and gliding long miles on the winds, not for continual short, daring flights and pounces and escapes.

"With you?" Louisa demanded.

Dushmuni alone could not keep the demon distracted for long. And what would they do when Dushmuni tired? What would this whole city of Peshawar do? Tamai imagined the Angrezi priest with his black coat and white neck-piece, the Angrezi soldiers with their *rifles,* trying to destroy this thing that came out of a world they did not even believe in. She laughed, and the high cracking sound of her own voice startled her. She was nearer the edge than she had thought.

But there was no one else to face the demon.

"No," Tamai said at last. "No, I—I have something to do here."

"I'm afraid to go alone!" Louisa wailed. "And . . . and what will happen to you?"

What, indeed? She could not hope to defeat the demon in this world; as soon as it saw her she would be sucked up like a tasty morsel. "I will have to fight it in the overworld," Tamai said slowly. "You had better go away before that begins. You—might be hurt."

"But what will happen to *you*?" Louisa insisted. "Won't you be hurt?"

"It doesn't matter," Tamai said. She felt angry at Louisa for making her spell it all out again. Once she'd made her decision, it would have been so much easier to go through with it without thinking. "Don't you understand, you foolish Angrez, it *does not matter* what happens to my body in this world! Here I am, not even a wisewoman, I don't know how to control the Disciplines, but I'm all this city has got so I'm going to go into the overworld, and I don't know how to find my way back and I have no one of my own here to help me come back. Why should I worry about this barren body? I won't be *using* it any more."

"But you do," Louisa said. She had let go of Tamai's tunic at some time, and her hands were clasped before her, white as her face, shaking a little. But her voice was perfectly calm. "You do have someone of your own here," she clarified. "Me. Show me how to help you."

Was it possible? Tamai remembered the communion she'd felt with Louisa, the touching of souls that had endured even when their bodies were apart. Through Louisa's soul she had even learned what it was to love children of one's body, the children she would never bear.

It could work.

"I shouldn't let you," Tamai said. "I came here to save you. If you stay with me we may both die, Louisa, do you understand that?"

Louisa said nothing, just looked at Tamai steadily and without blinking. And Tamai could not find within herself the strength to send her away.

She looked ruefully around the flat roof. Higher by a story than any other house in the street, it was not an ideal place in which to suffer even a small earthquake. But at least there was very little here that could be set on fire, and the low parapet might keep them from being shaken off the edge of the roof. "Some things that happen may seem rather strange to you," she said carefully. Really, she was lucky that this Englishwoman had kept her sanity; it was asking too much to show her anything more today! But what choice did they have? "You have read Lieutenant McAusland's report; well then, you know what to expect," she said. "Put out fires if they start. Try not to be thrown off the roof if it shakes. And keep hold of my hand, that I may find my way back to this world through you."

There was no time for more; the demon's angry voice was vibration that shivered through her skull and made the bones of her spine weep for pain. And it was coming closer. Tamai knelt and braced herself against the parapet, holding out one hand to Louisa even as she sent her spirit out to draw the demon.

The grasp of the Englishwoman's fingers was warm and strong. Tamai knew an instant's shock at the power of the link between them. The feelings that had come to her dimly, like sunshine through mist, now blazed strong as the noonday sun. It was like the link with Dushmuni; only now, instead of knowing the joy of soaring with the wind or the blood-hunger for prey, Tamai felt Louisa's self enter her: the terror of the last hours, the fierce desire to protect her friend, grief for the children she thought never to see again.

The outlines of the roof shivered and half dissolved around her. The *yush* was halfway out onto the roof now. Tamai could feel Louisa shrinking from its physical semblance of rotten meat and unspeakable darkness, but she herself could see through that body into the net of dancing sparks that was the demon's true self. It was beautiful in its own way: so many lights spiraling inward, beckoning her own soulfire to join in the dance, to be absorbed in the greater being of the *yush*, to go down into the perfect heart—

But there was nothing there. The lights were extinguished as they spiraled inward to the dead center. The *yush* was nothing but the soulfires of its victims, knew nothing but that blind desire to consume all around it. The dead emptiness at the heart of the dance made the whole pattern ugly to Tamai; and yet its pull was still strong, so strong, her own soulfire flickered towards it and she heard the demon laughing.

Somewhere outside and beyond all this, a screeching horror with outstretched talons shot past the thing on the roof, snatching bits and pieces of the clutching arms and claws as it went. Something that had been a man's arm, now a boneless bag of decomposing fluids, went free over the parapet. The demon threw up a tower of its dark soulstuff and brushed the eagle's wingtip, and two flight feathers were sucked into the tower. Tamai sensed the battle on the rooftop but could not follow it; she had her own battle to fight with the soulnet of the demon, and she was losing.

Dizane, Lunang, Kshumai, Nirmali, help me!

Four pillars of fire sprung up around Tamai and the demon. Each was composed of a net of dancing flames, like the demon's soulstuff; but these flames danced around and about and over and under the central pillars, drawing substance from the center and returning it in a joyous and endless cycle, instead of being sucked inwards to black nothingness. Each fire-pillar shimmered between shapes, showing sometimes a young woman, sometimes an old woman, sometimes a bending stalk of grain or an endless waterfall. One was a flame of gold that sometimes seemed to be a woman and sometimes was a sheaf of grain, and that was Dizane of the fields. One was a cool blue flame that rippled like water and showed the face of a laughing girl, and that was Lunang of the waters. One pillar burned red like blood and showed an old woman with a knife in her hand, and that was Kshumai of the herds, who also rules death and war. And the fourth pillar was the silver of the moon, and it had three faces at once, young and mature and old, and the sun and the moon danced in its soulnet, and that was Nirmali the Maker of All Things.

Tamai raised her hands and the four colored flames leapt up high and fierce and flowed together between her outspread fingers, braiding into a many-colored rope. The soulflames of the *yush* yearned towards that braid of fire, and Tamai could feel its empty need trying to suck them back into its own meaningless dance.

Somewhere far below this dance of the souls, a collection of rotting flesh and bones stripped bare collapsed into a puddle of corruption on a rooftop in Peshawar. The *yush* had thrown all its soulstuff into the overworld to fight Tamai as she held the flames of the Four Goddesses, and there was nothing left to hold its physical body together. Dushmuni alighted on the parapet and spread out her wings to their full seven-foot span in a slow triumphal unfurling. And Louisa clasped her hands together and looked upon her friend, who had jerked out of their handclasp and now knelt quite rigid beside the parapet.

"What should I do now?" she asked the eagle. "Oh, yes—yes. I remember. I must hold her hand." She reached to touch Tamai and snatched her hand back with a gasp of pain and surprise: Tamai's skin was hot to the touch. Very hot. Even as Louisa watched, blisters rose on Tamai's long slender fingers. Her body twitched and moaned, and a section of the parapet wall beside her cracked, leaned out over the side of the house, and very slowly came loose. Louisa heard it crash in the street below them. Another section of the wall began to give way; the whole house shook and the roof tilted down towards the broken place. Tamai's unconscious body began to slide towards the edge.

The rope of fire between Tamai's hands stretched, widened, became a curtain of woven soulflame. She cast it towards the demon's net of sparks, but it was too small; she could not cover the demon without letting the soulflame out of her own hands. Words from the teaching songs came unbidden to her lips, the refrain of the verses about Dzo Tsungpa Demonslayer. The language of Bod made shapes of fire about her, a burning wall of protection from the demon. Tamai drew the fire from the wall and wove it into her curtain of soulflame, but still it was not enough.

"*Nirmali, Mother of All, help me!*"

The silver pillar that was Nirmali the Maker shot up into the sky, through all the worlds at once. Through the transparent, shifting stuff of the overworld Tamai could see Louisa Westbrook kneeling upon a trembling rooftop, looking at a silver fountain that overarched the sky. Nirmali's pillar encompassed earth and sky, sun and moon and stars, and Tamai reached through the silver fire and caught strands from the sun and moon to weave into her net. Again she cast it towards the demon, and this time it covered the whirling tunnel of sparks and the tiny soulflames went free, singing with joy, into the greater light of Tamai's net and thence into the infinite silver stream that was Nirmali the Maker.

The worldflesh trembled and the sun was momentarily darker; then the streaming fires returned upward to their source, the light of the worldflesh was restored, and Tamai felt herself drawn agonizingly between two realms. Her physical body was burning and dying, but that was a faint distant pain. Much stronger was the call of the overworld, where she moved through all created places at once and was all her past and present selves. She swam upwards through air in the silver stream of Nirmali's consciousness and beheld all the worlds in their glory, like soulflames dancing eternally in the blackness of space. But one world of all was most dear to her, and as she looked it seemed to grow larger and larger, rushing upon her vision like Dushmuni stooping from the sky: first a blue and green globe, then a jagged height of snow-covered mountains, and finally a string of secret valleys in the heart of the mountains where a city of stone and blue-tiled roofs glimmered with welcome.

Not yet.

The voice was within her and without her and all through her being, a cool, emotionless command that Tamai could not defy.

It is not your time to go home, the silver voice sang. *Look at the worldflesh and see it as it is.*

Now Tamai's vision expanded past the boundaries of Gandhara. To the south she saw mountains and valleys filled with savage tribes and petty Moslem states, then the plain about Peshawar and the lines of the British cantonments.

Look farther.

South and east and west of Peshawar were other cities,

some linked together by iron tracks on which hundreds of people could fly from place to place. She saw armies marching and drilling, and she flew over green lakes bigger than the world and saw that the soldiers and the iron roads and the cities were repeated in countries unknown to the wisest of the Gandharan women. She recoiled from that power and fled to the north again, searching for her quiet, peaceful valleys.

There was no refuge to the north: where the Kirghiz had roamed their steppes and the descendants of the Osmanlis ruled their walled cities, another great power had moved inexorably southwards until its soldiers and its roads of iron reached right to the edge of the mountains. The White Huns had passed over Gandhara and Hund like a plague of locusts, devasting all in their path and driving the remnants of Gandhara into the mountain fastnesses to form a new city. But these armies did not pass. They remained, and where they stayed and built there was something worse than devastation—a flat new world without meaning or spirit, a complexity of wheels and *machines* as empty in its way as the demon's net of soulsparks had been.

These armies and others like them encompassed the world about Gandhara on three sides: north, west and south; and to the east there was only the clouded darkness of the Chin Empire, impenetrable even to the sight of the overworld: a place where the air bubbled with demons and dragons, where snows and sandstorms and tempests guarded the borders and blocked Tamai's vision.

From this height she could see no help for her people, no reason to return to the pain and frustration of her body in the worldflesh.

Let me stay with you, she begged Nirmali; but the goddess of the sun and moon spoke no more to her. In the place of the silver singing voice Tamai felt other calls, full of love and anguish, and something tugging at her through the worldflesh.

o   o   o

Louisa grasped Tamai's tunic as her body slid towards
the edge of the roof. The fabric parted under her hands
and crumbled like fine ashes. She threw herself forward
and locked her arms around Tamai's waist. The heat of
Tamai's body burned her skin, but she would not let go
until she had pulled her friend away from that dangerous
open space. And while she held her, she could feel
Tamai's heart beating, feel the pull of visions beyond her
imagining. Tamai was soaring like Dushmuni in skies that
were not of this world, and Louisa ached to follow her;
but she was not free to go.

Alice. Harry. Their laughing little faces rose before
her, as clear as if she were standing in an English garden
where they played. Alice threw a ball and Harry ran after
it on chubby little legs, tumbling into a bush and laughing
as he scrambled to his feet.

She longed to know the skies where Tamai flew; but
her children were in this world, and the place Tamai had
fled to was much farther away from England than any
part of India could be. Louisa felt the bonds that held
her to them as a physical force, sweet and strong as a
baby's greedy mouth fastening on her breast. She held
to Tamai while the house rocked and shivered and small
fires came out of nowhere, and prayed that she would
see her children again, and prayed that Tamai would
come back.

Something held Tamai to the worldflesh when she
would have soared free. She tugged irritably at the bonds,
but there was no escaping them. Louisa Westbrook was
mastering her, as she in her turn had mastered Dushmuni, and her desire to fly free was being subsumed in
this pale foreign woman's idiot devotion to her children.
Tamai felt that love and fought against it and felt the
silver current of Nirmali's consciousness flowing away
from her as she slipped slowly, reluctantly, back into the
worldflesh and the blistered, barren body of Tamai the
Gandharan.

And after all, when she opened her eyes upon the

physical world again, it was very sweet. The rooftop was cracked and the parapet was gone, and her hands hurt as though she had been holding them over an open flame, and there was a puddle of rotting flesh and stinking fluids where the *yush* had been; but the sky was very blue and the sun was warm and Louisa, her face covered with dust and streaked with tears, was beautiful in Tamai's sight.

CHAPTER THIRTEEN

[Excerpts from the journal of Louisa Westbrook]

10 October 1884:

Tamai has recovered from our unpleasant experience in the native town with a rapidity that would have astonished me, had I not had previous experience of her resilience and determination. She returned to consciousness and even spoke to me immediately after the demon's collapse, but shortly thereafter she lapsed into a deep sleep. Even as she slept I could see the blisters that had appeared on her face and hands beginning to fade away as if by magic—well, I suppose it *was* by magic, but I am not accustomed to thinking in those terms! I had no idea what to do; fortunately Lieutenant McAusland found us very soon thereafter.

He wanted to know how we had come to be there. I could explain very little of what had transpired, and of that little, I was not sure how much I wished to say. Given Lieutenant McAusland's credulity on the subject of the Gandharans, I hardly feared that he would disbelieve me if I spoke of being abducted by a demon and of battles in an invisible world which I perceived only through Tamai's mind. My fear was rather that he *would* believe me, and would spread the tale about Peshawar, and that I should henceforth be considered as unbalanced as the lieutenant.

I took refuge in tears. Even the lieutenant could not be so unchivalrous as to press a weeping (and possibly hysterical) woman for details of her traumatic experience. (Had he proved so unkind, I had already resolved to faint, no matter what damage was done to my mourning dress by the puddles of filthy liquid on the floor; fortunately this last resort proved unnecessary.) He carried Tamai down to a waiting *tikka-gharri* and escorted us home without asking any further questions. On the way home I ventured to cease sobbing long enough to ask how he had found us. His ears turned red and he murmured something about Tamai's eagle. It seemed to me that he had no more wish to admit having accepted an eagle's guidance than I had to claim an experience with a demon. I therefore suggested that we might both of us find it profitable to say as little as possible about the episode.

He looked at me strangely. "I had thought you hysterical with the shock of your ordeal, ma'am."

"And so I shall be," said I, "if you ask me any more questions! Do you understand me? Neither of us has anything to gain by making public assertions which the world will assuredly not believe."

"I understand you perfectly, ma'am—my previous experience has taught me that much."

He went on, however, to mention some journalistic acquaintance of his who might take us seriously.

"I have no desire to see my life displayed for public gossip," I told him. "If you talk to this journalist, young man, you may do so alone, without dragging a lady's name into the matter."

Lieutenant McAusland's neck turned even redder than his ears. "Your name is safe with me, Mrs. Westbrook. And since you seem to have recovered so well from your vapors, may I point out that it is quite inappropriate for you to address me as *young man*? You forget that I am quite three years older than you. There is no point in putting on the airs of an old married lady in a station where everybody knows that you were a bride of seventeen just eight years ago."

Eight years! How much longer it seems! "There is no question of putting on airs, Lieutenant McAusland," I said, now quite sobered from my momentary bout of acting. "In truth, I feel that a lifetime of experience separates me from that foolish young bride."

He had nothing to say to this, and we completed the journey in silence, speaking only when he carried Tamai into my house and deposited her on the bed for me. I attempted to express my thanks for his timely appearance, but he made nothing of it, saying that as far as he could tell he had been too late to be of any real help.

I had feared being alone in the house, but even before Lieutenant McAusland took his leave my runaway servants began to return, in twos and threes, looking remarkably shamefaced—as indeed they ought! I gave them to understand that they should be very grateful that I allowed them to return to my service, and that they should not be paid for the time when they were absent. They accepted these strictures with appropriately contrite expressions; indeed, the *khitmutgar* and my avah all but groveled in expressing the depths of their desire to be accepted in my house again. While doing so, they let slip their real reason for coming back. The English community here may be ignorant of the true events surrounding my dreadful experience, but it seems that every loafer in the bazaar had already heard about the demon. Since I had returned unharmed, my servants correctly concluded that Tamai must have vanquished the demon and that the safest place in Peshawar was the house where she stayed. Hence their sudden renewal of devotion!

I did not quarrel with any of this; I was too deeply grateful for a turn of events which permitted me to bathe and rest instead of sitting up at Tamai's bedside. For now, rather than being afraid of "the Gandharan witch" or murmuring darkly about loss of caste, my servants are all but fighting one another for the privilege of waiting

on her. I have left my own *ayah* to watch over her while
I rest, giving her strict instructions to call me if there is
any change in Tamai's condition. I had intended to sleep
after my bath, but find that memories of the terrible
experience so recently past disturb me too much; I have
therefore beguiled the time in sitting up to write this
brief account of our return home. I ought to, I know,
also record what passed in that house in the native quarter; but I cannot bear to write that down. It would make
real what I am determined to remember only as a horrid
dream.

11 October 1884:

This morning I found Tamai awake, sitting up in bed,
and with only a few flushed splotches on her cheeks and
hands to mark where the worst of the burns had been!
She claimed to be quite recovered but said that she
needed to talk privately with me. I dismissed the avah
and the two bearers who had volunteered to help her,
in the hope (doubtless vain) of discouraging them from
eavesdropping on our conversation. One is never sure
just how much English these persons understand, so I
resolved to converse with Tamai in my halting
Gandharan.

"But you speak very well," Tamai assured me when I
acquainted her of this decision.

"You are kind," I said ruefully. "Indeed, at one time
I was rather vain of my ability to acquire languages. But
observing your learning of English has quite disabushed
me of that conceit." (I did not actually speak quite so
fluently as this; my Gandharan is not equal to the task.)

Tamai looked at me thoughtfully for some time before
replying. Her measuring look reminded me of the *durzee*
when he is trying to decide whether I have lost enough
weight for him to suggest taking in all of my gowns, or
whether it would be more tactful not to mention how
thin I have become. I felt decidedly uncomfortable by
the time she spoke again.

"I think that you could learn as I do," she said at last.

"It would be hard for you, not having been trained from your first years, but I think you could do it. You have great power, and your love for your children is strong."

"What has that to do with anything?" I exclaimed involuntarily, and then began to laugh. "Really, I have been having the strangest conversations recently. Lieutenant McAusland wishes me to understand that he is quite three years my senior, and you want to teach me Gandharan. Does nobody wish to discuss . . ." And here I fell silent, for the truth was that I, too, did not want to talk about what had happened in that house in the native quarter.

"It is not wise to speak of the *yush*," Tamai said. "And it is not just Gandharan I wish to teach you—first you must learn the Disciplines."

I sighed involuntarily. Gordon was always complaining that I lacked self-discipline; now Tamai, too, was going to improve my character. Goodness knows it could stand some improvement, but I had hoped for—I hardly knew what—something to do with the flight of souls I had shared on the rooftop, the shifting world that called to me like a voice from my dreams.

Tamai reached out and touched my hand, and my doubts vanished. The world where she had flown and fought and almost lost herself was still there, within her—within me, too! I *knew* this in a way which cannot be described in words; it is something like the experience of grace by which we know Our Lord. Oh, dear, I suppose that is blasphemous. But it is, truly, the only way I can find to describe the certainty I felt within me as soon as Tamai's fingers touched mine.

"It is all there for you," she said softly. "More than for me—I cannot master the Disciplines, but you can. Will you learn with me, Louisa?"

16 October 1884:

I know that I have been neglecting my journal, together with all the rest of my daily routine. The truth is that Tamai has hardly granted me a moment to think of anything else but the lessons she is so intent on imparting. I should hardly be free to write this now, were it not that today's experience left us both so overwrought that we agreed to suspend the lessons for this evening. Even now I can scarcely believe that I, plain Louisa Westbrook of Surrey, have been privileged to work wonders—

But I should tell it all as it came about.

Tamai and I have been taking all our meals in Gordon's study, which she selected as the ideal place in which to work, and I have scarcely left the room long enough to change my clothing and let the ayah brush my hair. All my faculties have been required to absorb the new knowledge which Tamai is pouring into me; indeed, I should never be able to contain it all, were it not that I can feel my mind expanding almost physically as new worlds, new ways of seeing, appear to me. She tells me, and I cannot but believe her, that what I have learned so far is but the smallest fraction of what is taught to Gandharan girls who are chosen for the study of the Disciplines; yet even that little has already changed me irrevocably.

Much of what we do would be dismissed by Colonel Vaughan or any other educated man as "native gibberish." For once I feel that my restricted life as a woman has equipped me better than the colonel or Lieutenant McAusland to tread those paths which Tamai traced out for me. They, like my husband, have been accustomed to examine everything according to the dictates of a rational mind and a classical education, and to cast out as unworthy their consideration anything which does not fit the notions in which they were brought up. I, like most women, have had to discipline myself to tasks which often seemed boring or pointless but which were set by superiors whom I dared not question. When I was six years old I worked my first sampler; when I was seventeen and newly married, I learned to read household accounts in Urdu and to see that the *dhobi* laundered Gordon's shirts in the style he liked. Compared to such chores as these, learning by heart the syllables of the teaching songs which Tamai chants to me is hardly tedious at all.

And unlike sewing samplers or overseeing the *dhobi*, learning the teaching songs brings its own reward. As Tamai hinted in the beginning, with each cycle of songs that I learn, my vision of the world changes and the next learning becomes easier. In a matter of days I have become all but fluent in Gandharan. Tamai shakes her head over the impossibility of teaching me the Old Tongue and the language of Bod as well as Gandharan, for without these, she says, I cannot hope to master any but the simplest of illusions. Some day, I suppose, I must embark on these additional studies. But for today, I am too happy and too excited by what I have already achieved to concern myself over the tasks lying ahead.

Today's session began, like most, with my repeating the lines of the teaching songs which Tamai had chanted to me on the previous day. Today, however, Tamai stopped me halfway through the verses.

"Do you understand what you are saying?" she questioned me.

"Of course I do," I told her with some pride. When we began this course of study there were many words and turns of Gandharan speech which were unfamiliar to me, but by now I could follow all but the most complex sentences. "It is the song of how Nirmali the Maker shaped the world."

"It is, and it is not," said Tamai. "Listen to yourself."

Obediently I set forth again to chant the words I had learned by heart, reflecting as I did so that no rational man of my acquaintance would put up for a minute with Tamai's self-contradictory and oracular pronouncements.

"What did you hear this time?"

In truth I had been automatically reciting the verses without paying much attention to their meaning; I had been too busy congratulating myself on the patience with which I endured Tamai's meaningless commands.

"Much the same thing, I suppose," I answered, somewhat sharply. "They are the same words that I sang before."

Tamai sighed and looked up at the punkah. "In Angrezi—*English*," she corrected herself, "everything is always the same. The punkah is always a piece of white canvas, and never a cloud or a spirit. That is why you cannot shape the world in English." She pointed at the toy soldier which had occasioned our first open quarrel and the first stumbling beginnings of our friendship. One of the servants had set the little man on Gordon's desk, where with his musket on his shoulder and his painted eyes staring straight ahead he guarded my dead husband's papers very bravely.

"What do you see when you look there?"

"Harry's toy soldier, what else?"

"Can you see a real soldier, standing guard, breathing, ready to speak or to march away? Can you show me that man?"

"Of course not! I see what is *there*."

Tamai sighed. "A wisewoman of Gandhara, knowing the song of Nirmali's First Making, could raise a growing walnut tree from the empty shell and make you want to eat the nuts on that tree. But you, Englishwoman—you are so sure that you know what the world is, you can't even imagine a different shape, much less make it become real for a moment."

"There is something to be said for a predictable world," I observed. "We English do well enough in our way." The sense of mystery and magic which I had felt immediately after our battle with the demon had quite dissipated by this time, and I lacked faith that my stumbling through the teaching verses would ever grant me entry into the world that Tamai knew. I was beginning to long for the comforts of ordinary civilisation which I had ignored over the past few days—a cup of tea, a visit to the silk merchants in the bazaar to select fabric for a new dress, a pleasant conversation about fashions with Mrs. Dr. Scully and Barbara.

"I know that," Tamai agreed with me. "Lieutenant

McAusland tried to explain to me once, about the *scientific method*." She spoke these words in English, there being no equivalent for them in Gandharan. "Your people and the Rus have grown mighty in a flat world without shapers or changers. Gandhara will be crushed like wheat between the two millstones of your empires."

"Then you no longer plan to defend your country with rifles?" I enquired.

"No. Nirmali showed me that my plan was hopeless. I must find something else." She studied her hands for a few minutes while I sat silent, feeling for her dilemma but not knowing what to say. "I have no choice, have I?" she said at last with a crooked smile. "We cannot defend ourselves from the Rus. And you British cannot help us against the Rus unless I show them the way to Gandhara. I am only afraid that the price of your help will be the same as the price of defeat by the Rus. What difference does it make which empire rules us?"

"A great deal," I said hotly. "*We* do not seek to enslave or massacre your people. We want only a peaceful trade agreement between our countries."

"And British soldiers to live in our country, to enforce the terms of the agreement, and a British Resident to give orders to our Council," Tamai murmured. "Oh, yes," she said when I started at this blunt statement of Haverford's intentions. "I have been listening to the colonel and his advisers. Was that not what you intended, when you taught me English?"

"I suppose it was," I admitted reluctantly, "but now I feel that I have betrayed my own people."

"I think they will survive the betrayal in better case than mine will."

"If you are concerned about our plans," I told Tamai, "then you should make a treaty with Colonel Vaughan, establishing the limits of British power which Gandhara will accept, before you agree to guide him to your country."

"And will he keep such a treaty?" Tamai asked. Her voice was smooth as cream, reminding me eerily of Haverford, and she gazed across the room. "I have been listening to Lieutenant McAusland as well. I have heard of Native States that thought they were independent, of rajahs who invited the British to help them stay upon their thrones and found that they had lost throne and all . . ."

"Treaties are broken sometimes," I admitted reluctantly, "on both sides." Then I thought of something which ought to have occurred to me earlier. "Tamai, our people do not all speak with a single voice. You have heard Colonel Vaughan and Mr. Haverford and Major Phelps arguing, each with his views of what is best to be done. Promises made in secret are easy to break, but if all the people in the British Raj knew the terms of your treaty, then if it were broken there would be a great outcry and those who broke it would be forced to withdraw for the sake of our honour."

"But how is this possible?" Tamai frowned and tugged at the end of her long braid. "Nirmali has shown me how many are your people. I cannot go about the streets and speak to each one personally, as I might do about an issue before the Council in Gandhara."

"Tamai, my dear," I said, "you learn very quickly and your visions have shown you much truth, but there are still some things you do not understand about our empire. Let me tell you about *newspapers*."

This thought did not, I must admit, come entirely independently to my mind. When Lieutenant McAusland and I were agreeing upon the unwisdom of discussing our experiences with the public, he had mentioned that he knew of at least one man who might be inclined to give us a sympathetic hearing.

"A boy, really," he apologised. "No more than nineteen or twenty, but a very talented young man. Born in this country—his father's a museum curator in Lahore, and the boy came back to work for the *Civil and Military Gazette*. He spends nights prowling the native town in search of things to write up for the paper, and he's fol-

lowed more than one story to Peshawar—that's how I
first came to know him. He's told me of some deuced
queer things he's seen in the native quarter, things he
wouldn't dare put in an English paper. In fact, I've
already written to him about what happened in the Malakand," the lieutenant confessed. "Wanted to tell somebody who wouldn't immediately assume I had 'water on
the brain.'"

That phrase of the colonel's must have stung him. I
felt some sympathy for the lieutenant, but at the time
I could not see what relevance his friend's newspaper
experience had for me, so the subject dropped there.
Now, however, I wondered if this young journalist might
not be just the person to hear Tamai's story—*all* her
story.

I was not sure, however, whether Lieutenant McAusland's friend would be free to come to Peshawar on such
an errand, and so I made Tamai no promises; I simply
told her that if she *did* choose to make a treaty with our
people, it might be possible to find a journalist who
would publish the text of the treaty in his newspaper and
that this would make it very embarrassing for the British
government subsequently to break the treaty without
provocation.

"I do not know how much your government minds
being embarrassed," Tamai said glumly, "and I have no
treaty to offer, for the Council will never agree to admit
a foreign man—and if your Resident does not sit upon
our Council, his voice will be nothing in Gandhara. Try
the teaching songs once again, Louisa—and this time
listen to what you are saying: listen to the *shapes* of the
words."

At least the interval of casual conversation had somewhat rested my throat muscles. I began the chant again,
and found that this time I was too weary to think of
anything but the necessity of getting each syllable in the
long exhausting string of verses exactly right, on the
proper note, with my mouth shaped just so to produce

the peculiar resonances of chanted Gandharan. So fierce was my concentration that I passed beyond weariness; when all my effort was caught up in making the verses, then they seemed to come effortlessly out of my mouth and I had the dizzying sense of being one with the chant, unable to make an error. I was both the singer and the song, both the words and the shapes. I was not singing *about* Nirmali; I *was* Nirmali, making heaven and earth to divide the overworld. And at the same time I was the overworld being shaped into the worldflesh, and I was all the spirits that came to inhabit the shaping, and I was still Louisa Westbrook singing about all these things.

The air seemed to quiver around me and I stopped with my mouth open, on a rising note that had nowhere to go. Tamai had always stopped me before I reached the end of this section, and she had never taught me the next verses. Now she prompted me, one word at a time, lips moving in unison with mine.

It was the chant Nirmali had used to shape the overworld, repeated and magnified in my voice and the myriad voices of the spirits she called, and as the words echoed around me the toy soldier on Gordon's desk seemed to quiver and break apart into many thousands of pieces. Each of those tiny red or blue painted pieces took into itself one singing voice and grew again to the size of the original toy, then taller, larger, until an army of six-foot soldiers in the red coats of the Royal Lancasters marched across Gordon's desk and vanished through the walls of his study.

I came, unprompted, to the last dying lines of the chant and let my voice fall to a whisper as the soldiers disappeared from view. Tamai had no need to tell me the words now; there was only one way for the song to end, unraveling the shapes of illusion that had been woven together in the opening lines.

Tamai's eyes shone with unshed tears, and I had no need to ask if she had shared my vision.

"You will be greater than I," she whispered. "You will

take my knowledge and weave your own vision of the world. I hope—oh, I hope I have done right!"

So do I. This new power, even if it is only the gift to raise illusions, confuses and frightens me.

Tomorrow I will try it again.

CHAPTER FOURTEEN

Sheets of crumpled paper littered the floor of Colonel Vaughan's office. Mixed in with notes on troop movements and requisitions for ammunition were various flimsy pages bearing telegraphic communications from the Viceroy of India, the Lieutenant-Governor of the Punjab, the Prime Minister of England, an M.P. from Sussex who had toured India for three weeks in '63 and wanted to share his understanding of the subcontinent, and three newspaper editors who wanted to know how the Punjab Frontier Force planned to defend the frontier against Skobelev's rumored advance. Colonel Vaughan was giving all this sage advice exactly the consideration it deserved; that is to say, he complained to the gentleman from the Viceroy's office, kicked the telegrams into the pile of scrap paper on the floor, and would have kicked the journalists downstairs if they had been physically present to receive such treatment.

"The P.M., God bless him, says in his first telegram that we must resist the Russian advance with all due force. In his second he insists that we are on no account to mobilize the army. And in his third message he tells me that the Czar's representatives in London assure him Russia has no designs on the Hindu Kush, so I'm not to worry."

"You know what the Russian promises are worth," Haverford warned him. "In February of 1873 they gave us their solemn assurance that they intended no further expansion in central Asia, and in June of that year they took Khiva. In 1874 they said that Khiva marked the limit of their territorial ambitions, and by 1876 Skobelev was governor of Khokand." Haverford gave an involuntary sigh. "Governor at twenty-two!"

"And a mass murderer at twenty-seven," Vaughan growled. "I read the reports of Geok Tepe. The population was slaughtered where they stood. That was three years ago. Now we've got another set of 'solemn assurances' that he's not going to do the same thing to Gandhara—and there isn't a damn thing I can do about it."

"We'd be in our rights to send a relief force to Gandhara."

Vaughan growled inarticulately and shook his head.

"Don't tell me you're afraid of the P.M.'s displeasure!"

"Not in this matter. It's for the Government of India to decide," Vaughan conceded.

"Then I can only suppose," Haverford said silkily, "that you military chaps are going to tell the Viceroy you can't mobilize in time to relieve the siege."

"Of course we can!" Vaughan exploded. "We've got a quarter of the whole Bengal Army right here in the Punjab—cavalry, Corps of Guides, artillery, even a regiment of Gurkhas. General Kinloch has drawn up plans against any invasion contingency—he can have five thousand men here within a week."

"*Here* in Peshawar is one thing," Haverford observed. "Ready to march into the mountains is another. I've read Captain Younghusband's reports on his travels. In those mountains you can't count on buying food for the men or even forage for the animals; everything will have to be brought up from the nearest railway station—which is *not*," he added grimly, as befitted a man who had been jolted by tonga from Lahore to direct this conference, "not even as close to the mountains as

Peshawar. You're not going to claim the transport and supply could be arranged quite so quickly?"

"If the Government would give us free rein to collect any mules we need for pack animals," Vaughan said, "and lay on civil engineers to construct railway sidings to Nowshera, I'd guarantee—in General Kinloch's name—to have men, transport animals, commissariat and telegraph departments at Nowshera and be ready to march within two weeks after we get the word to mobilize."

"And from Nowshera?"

"Our best estimates put the northern valleys of Chitral at something over two hundred miles from Peshawar. Three weeks for a flying column, travelling light—say six weeks for an army large enough to withstand any force Skobelev can put into the field." Vaughan paused. "There's just one problem."

Haverford sighed. "I know. One hesitates to mobilize an army of that size to advance into unknown territory. I don't for one minute believe young McAusland's superstitious babble about Gandhara's having some kind of magical protection for its frontiers. But I do understand that you'd like to have guides or a corrected map before setting out to relieve the siege. All the same, Colonel, our office may have to direct the army to go ahead—with or without the girl's cooperation. Surely it can't be that big a problem to find one mountain city-state? Can't your chaps deduce its probable location from what we do know of the area?"

"Be my guest." Vaughan picked up a rolled tube of paper and spread it out on top of his desk, weighting the corners with whatever came to hand: a brass ashtray, a small statue of Kali, and two odd volumes of the Army Regulations for 1875.

"This," he said grimly, "is the best map we have of the northern Hindu Kush. It's a compendium of the notes made by Biddulph in '75, A.K.'s observations in '80, and the Pundit's work for the Great Trigonometric Survey. I haven't had time to collate McAusland's notes, but they won't add much."

Haverford stared at the map in dismay. A jagged network of peaks and passes filled the bottom half of the map, each annotated in a neat hand with its reported height. Some of the passes had no measured height; others were estimated at anywhere between two thousand and twelve thousand feet, while a series of dots showed how their locations varied in different reports. The spaces between mountain ranges were lettered with the names of the petty kingdoms and tribal holdings known to exist: Swat, Dir, Chitral, Bajao, Thana and other names quite unfamiliar to him.

If this was bad, the top half of the map was even worse. It was almost completely blank. Two recorded peaks and one river were marked; the rest of the space was marked with such discouraging legends as "Unknown Territory," "Unexplored Regions" and "No Reports."

After staring for some time he discerned a few faint cross marks penciled in. "What are those?" he asked, pointing to one of the penciled crosses. "Points on a road north?"

"Places," Colonel Vaughan said with grim satisfaction, "where, as nearly as we can make out, our agents have disappeared. You've got your finger on Gordon Westbrook's grave."

Haverford removed his hand as quickly as if he had touched a hot stove.

"My best guess," Colonel Vaughan said, bending over the map, "based on what McAusland can add to these notes, is that there's a tributary to the Chitral River running north-south along here, a mountain range behind it and—I *hope*—a pass somewhere through *here*. I'll take a battalion through here and maybe, if God loves us, there won't be too many hostile tribes in our way. Of course, that's not counting the Gandharans as a hostile tribe. Lord knows what our reception will be there." As he spoke, he stabbed a blunt finger at the map, tracing the probable route that a field force would take in the search for Gandhara.

"You will have no reception at all there," said a low,

musical voice behind the two men, "for your maps are very badly drawn. There is only one pass through the Shandur, and that is defended by the Hunza raiders. You will have to go north along the Tears of Lunang—your people have no name for that river—and almost to the Little Pamir, before you find a way into my country."

"How the devil did you get in!" Colonel Vaughan glowered at Tamai. "I gave orders that no one was to interrupt us. And what the—what—" He sputtered to a halt, speechless at the sight of his native Gandharan informant dressed like an English lady in a tight black dress with a flowing, beribboned skirt.

"Colonel," Mr. Haverford interposed smoothly, "there will be time later to investigate any laxity among the sentries. At present, let us extend our warmest greetings to Miss Tamai, whose advice concerning these maps will be invaluable." He stepped on Colonel Vaughan's booted foot as the colonel opened his mouth again. "I'm most gratified that you have chosen to cooperate with us, ma'am," he went on before the colonel could say anything that might change Tamai's mind. "And may I say that is a very becoming dress you have on?"

"I suppose you may," Tamai answered, "but why? I thought you wanted to talk about your maps."

Louisa Westbrook, standing silently in the corner behind Tamai, rolled her eyes to the ceiling and suppressed a groan. She had invested several hours of that day persuading Tamai that Colonel Vaughan and Mr. Haverford would be more likely to negotiate seriously with her if she dressed in European clothes and spoke English and did everything possible to make them think of her as a civilized person from a country deserving respect. She had spent even more time explaining that Tamai could *not* achieve the desired effect by borrowing some of her deceased husband's shirts and trousers. As for the efforts required to get Tamai into petticoats and stays, bodice and skirt and bustle, she hoped never in her worst nightmares to relive such a morning. Tamai had laughed hysterically over the undergarments, had been amazed to discover that three petticoats and a camisole did not constitute clothing enough without the outer layer, and had categorically refused to be laced into Louisa's second-best set of stays with whalebone reinforcements.

But the strategy had worked. McAusland's friend, the young reporter from Lahore, had not only come to Peshawar to interview Tamai; he had listened with every appearance of respect to her story, had taken copious notes, and had been impressed beyond all measure by the brief demonstration of fire-raising and trembling stones which Tamai had reluctantly given him. In Louisa Westbrook's mourning dress, speaking fluent English with a slight trace of some unidentifiable accent, Tamai was not a native girl with a curious story and some sleight-of-hand tricks. She was a representative of a civilization considerably older than that of England, bearing ancient knowledge that compared favorably with the mechanical marvels of English steam engines and drill presses.

That first interview with the reporter had been a test; now Louisa thought that Tamai was ready to take on the colonel and his advisers. And once they had got past Haverford's automatic social niceties, she seemed to be doing quite well there. She leaned over the map table—Louisa groaned again as Tamai extended her arm and a seam gave way in the tight black sleeve of her dress—and traced the true course of the river known to her people as the Tears of Lunang.

"Two weeks ago you did not recognize a map," Vaughan growled suspiciously, "and now you instruct us?"

It was the opening Tamai had been waiting for.

"Two weeks ago I did not choose to give you gentlemen the route to Gandhara for nothing," she said in her precise, barely accented English, "nor do I choose to do so now. I can fill in the blank spaces on this map for

you, and I can guide your army past the barriers which
have kept all foreigners from Gandhara. But there will
be certain conditions."

Louisa found herself a chair and sat down during the
inevitable haggling that followed. The colonel most
strongly resisted Tamai's very first demand—that the
young newspaperman from Lahore who had interviewed
her that morning be present during the treaty negotiations and that he should be free to publish a full account
of the treaty in the *Gazette*. By the time Tamai had
convinced him that there could be no secret negotiations,
he was too worn down to protest much over the terms
of the treaty.

Louisa rather suspected that Tamai had planned it that
way. Whatever magic she had used to distract the sentry,
so that the two of them could enter unobserved and
unannounced, could just as well have been extended to
cover the reporter. But she wanted Colonel Vaughan to
agree to the man's presence, and she wanted him
exhausted from that argument—and within ten minutes,
she had exactly what she wanted. The boy from Lahore
entered between two sentries and took a chair beside
Louisa.

He was not very impressive, this young man on whom
they were resting their hopes. Short, dark, with a bristling
mustache and thick round glasses covering much of his
face, he had listened a great deal this morning and had
said little. Now he was listening again, nodding in comprehension as Tamai outlined each of her requests. Louisa hoped they had done right in trusting him. They did
not have a wide selection of journalists to choose from.
Fifty percent of the staff of the *Civil and Military
Gazette* was perched on a straight chair in Colonel
Vaughan's office. The other fifty percent, the editor-in-
chief, was busy doing both his job and his subordinate's
in Lahore while this energetic boy followed a story to
Peshawar. She only hoped he would be able to get the
story straight once he had it.

Civil and Military Gazette

Lahore, Wednesday, 19 October 1884

New Series: No. 2,523   Vol. X

THE TREATY WITH GANDHARA

From our own Correspondent

PESHAWAR 16 Oct.—Imprimis the setting: an office in the Staff Building of Peshawar Cantonments, a desk covered with vague and contradictory maps, a floor littered with equally vague and contradictory telegrams giving the opinions of the Great Ones of our world about the new Russian advance which is rumoured to have approached the mountain fastnesses of the Hindu Kush.

Now the participants. On one side, Colonel Vaughan of the 60th Rifles, his staff officers, and a very sleek, smooth-spoken gentleman from the Viceroy's office. On the other, a slender young native girl from those mountains where the Russian advance presses most fiercely, and—evidently attending her *en chaperone*—a young Englishwoman, recently and tragically widowed by the savage tribes north of Chitral.

The object of the meeting: to hammer out a treaty specifying the exact terms under which the British lion might be invited to aid Tamai's home country of Gandhara against the advance of the Russian bear.

On the face of it, a most unequal match. How could this young girl speak for her countrymen? Would not Colonel Vaughan overbear her most unmercifully, pressing terms most disadvantageous to the free citizens of Gandhara upon this innocent from the hills? And would not her countrymen, in any case, repudiate such a treaty as being made by one with no authority to speak for them?

Such accusations are commonly brought in the native papers concerning our gentle and honourable dealings with the native states, and no doubt in due time we shall see letters from gentlemen with names like Hon. Babu Chanderji, M.A. (failed), making the same protests about our handling of the Gandharan question. But in the view of this correspondent, no such double-dealing occurred here. Whatever may have been the *intention* of the good colonel, the end result of the treaty was that he and his men were (to use a military metaphor which seems only too appropriate in the context) "rolled up, horse, foot and drums!" Indeed, the outcome of this affair may well be that it is our Government which protests at having been forced to accept a mere colonel of infantry and a Viceroy's aide-de-camp as spokesmen for the Empire.

The exact terms of the treaty are published below, at the insistence of Tamai, the Gandharan representative; indeed, a general publication of the treaty was one of the conditions on which she insisted and with which this paper and our sister journal, the Allahabad *Pioneer,* are only too happy to comply. For those of our readers who may be disinclined to plod though the fine print and nice distinctions of official language, the following precis may suffice.

We are invited to send a force of not more than five thousand men to advise the Gandharan Council in repelling the Russian threat, and to give notice to the Great Bear that Gandhara is hitherto to be considered within our sphere of influence, and an attack on Gandhara or any of her citizens as an attack on us. In this much, our military gentlemen and the lady from Gandhara were in agreement; but their sentiments on the subsequent clauses of the treaty left much to be desired.

It is customary, when taking a native state under our protection, to leave that state with a garrison of British troops sufficient to ensure that such protection will continue—or, to put the matter somewhat more plainly, to ensure that neither the neighbouring states nor the gentlemen who previously ruled the occupied state shall entertain any unwise notions about acting contrary to British interests. Our Resident in Gilgit, to take a case in point, is supported by no less than two regiments of Kashmir Imperial Service Infantry, a battery of four guns, and two companies of Sappers and Miners; a respectable total of some twenty-five hundred soldiers for a state whose total population of fighting men has been estimated to number no more than five thousand!

Such a garrison was rejected by the Gandharan representative as utterly unacceptable to her people. Instead, the treaty specifies that not more than twenty of our soldiers shall remain in Gandhara after the withdrawal of the Russian forces, these twenty to constitute a guard of honor for the British Resident who is also to remain in Gandhara to safeguard the interests of British and Gandharan citizens. This Resident is to be appointed by the Government of India *subject to the approval of the Gandharan Council*—a most unusual provision, this, and one which virtually gives the Gandharan elders the right of choosing their own Resident! But considering the difficulties which have been encountered in recent years by the ill-advised appointment of Residents unsympathetic to the interests of the native states in which they found themselves, one can scarcely quarrel with so reasonable a request (although Colonel Vaughan did so, at great length; your correspondent spares you the details).

The signing of the treaty having been performed with all due pomp and ceremony, the masculine members of this group withdrew to baptize the agreement with whisky and soda in the regimental mess, while the ladies retired in good order to celebrate, one presumes, with tea and cakes. The troops to be sent on the Gandharan mission have already been selected by General Kinloch and preparations for their departure, superintended by Colonel Vaughan, are well in train; my next dispatches will describe the expedition's progress through the snow-bound mountains and hostile tribes of the Hindu Kush and, one hopes, their happy arrival in Gandhara.

—R.K.

FROM: STEPHEN WHEELER, EDITOR, LAHORE *GAZETTE*
TO: RUDYARD KIPLING, SUB-EDITOR

STOP THIS NONSENSE ABOUT LATER DISPATCHES. GAN-
DHARAN STUFF WAS INTERESTING BUT WE NEED YOU

BACK HERE TO COVER DOG RACES AND REGIMENTAL GYMKHANA.

FROM: RUDYARD KIPLING, SUB-EDITOR, LAHORE *GAZETTE*
TO: STEPHEN WHEELER, EDITOR

RESPECTFULLY SUBMIT NEED FOR SPECIAL CORRESPONDENT TO REPORT NEWS OF EXPEDITION TO GANDHARA AND TREATING WITH RUSSIANS. NEW COMPLICATIONS ARISE DAILY. MY SOURCES REPORT THE TWO GANDHARANS QUARRELED BITTERLY AFTER SIGNING OF THE TREATY AND THE MAN PALUK HAS DISAPPEARED. THE AYAH SAYS HE CALLED TAMAI A TRAITOR AND THE DURZEE SAYS HE IS AN OPIUM ADDICT BUT I HAVEN'T BEEN ABLE TO FIND HIM IN THE GANGHAZA KHANA TO GET HIS SIDE OF THE STORY. THIS IS THE STORY OF THE CENTURY AND WE CAN'T LET IT DROP NOW. AND WHY DID YOU CUT MY STUFF ON TAMAI'S FIRE-RAISING?

FROM: STEPHEN WHEELER, EDITOR, LAHORE *GAZETTE*
TO: RUDYARD KIPLING, SUB-EDITOR

CUT MATERIAL ON FIRE-RAISING BECAUSE I DIDN'T WANT YOUR PARENTS AND THE REST OF LAHORE TO KNOW YOU WERE SUFFERING FROM SUNSTROKE OR HAD FALLEN FOR THE TRICKS OF A NATIVE CHARLATAN. YOU HAD BETTER GET BACK HERE IN TIME TO COVER GOVERNMENT HOUSE BALL ON THE 29TH OR I'LL ASSIGN YOU TO COUNTING THE PERCENTAGE OF LEPERS AMONG LAHORE BUTCHERS.

FROM: RUDYARD KIPLING, SUB-EDITOR, LAHORE *GAZETTE*
TO: STEPHEN WHEELER, EDITOR

WHAT ABOUT SPECIAL CORRESPONDENT?

FROM: STEPHEN WHEELER, EDITOR, LAHORE *GAZETTE*
TO: RUDYARD KIPLING, SUB-EDITOR

ALREADY HAVE ONE—AND IT'S NOT YOU. REMEMBER TIME I HAD YOU INVESTIGATE SANITARY CONDITIONS IN SLUMS DURING CHOLERA OUTBREAK? LEPER ENQUIRY WILL BE WORSE.

FROM: RUDYARD KIPLING, SUB-EDITOR, LAHORE *GAZETTE*
TO: STEPHEN WHEELER, EDITOR

WHO?

FROM: STEPHEN WHEELER, EDITOR, LAHORE *GAZETTE*
TO: RUDYARD KIPLING, SUB-EDITOR

CORRESPONDENT PREFERS TO REMAIN ANONYMOUS. AND
YOU'LL WISH YOU WERE TOO IF YOU'RE NOT ON THE NEXT
TRAIN TO LAHORE. SOCIAL COLUMN HASN'T BEEN WRIT-
TEN UP FOR A WEEK AND MRS. HAUKSBEE WANTS TO
KNOW WHEN YOU'RE GOING TO DESCRIBE HER MASQUER-
ADE BALL.

While the British cantonments from Abbotabad to
Mardan were tumbling like ants in an overturned ant hill
to answer the call of war, the Russian general paid out
bribes to certain rulers of hill states who should have
known better than to listen to Skobelev's promises. The
Thum of Hunza took the Russian money and promised
to do his share of making trouble on the narrow paths
that crossed the mountains from south to north.

Some of the Thum's new wealth went to reinforce the
loyalty of his chiefs and headmen in outlying districts,
half-pagan mountaineers whose loyalty was first to their
local gods of wind and water, second to the Thum of
Hunza, and last—a long last—to Allah, whose worship
had reached the mountains a scant six hundred years
previously. Silver, weapons and the promise of war were
a heady intoxicant to the men of the hills. On the night
of the full moon there were feast-fires glowing across the
mountains, and the warriors of many a remote village
danced in anticipation of the glory and loot they would
win in the coming war.

In one such village, the messenger who brought the
Thum's silver stayed to collect a slave captured the previous summer and destined for the great Russian general
himself. Delivery of that captive would mean yet more
silver for the headman; in anticipatory celebration, he

brought out his own jars of snow-cooled new wine and killed a goat for the feast.

The thin, pure notes of a wooden flute carried far in the crisp night air, and the thump of the dancing warriors' feet beat out a rhythm that wakened the hillside with the promise of war and blood, honor and riches. The wine forbidden by Allah blended with the opium brought from the south, which Allah had not thought to forbid, and the warriors stamped and shuffled their way into a trance-like state in which the severed heads of their enemies seemed to dance about and bow to them.

On that night of all nights, a slave might escape. Desperation and luck were on his side. The bonds that had been fresh and strong in the summer had weakened like any other leather in the course of a hard autumn following the herds, and the man who had watched him so closely at first had grown careless with the months of waiting. All the warriors of the village were at the dancing, and why should he be denied his share of the wine and the music? He left the slave alone in the storeroom, and he forgot to bar the door.

The moon was high when the foreign slave got up courage enough to push open the storeroom door. He was as well prepared as he could be for this escape; the thick woolen blanket that had been his bed was wrapped around his shoulders, and he had torn up grain sacks for cloth to pad his sandals. His pockets were stuffed with dried fruit and nuts. There could be no going back now, not after the wreckage he'd left in the storeroom. But freedom dizzied him; he reeled on the threshold, momentarily afraid to go forward.

The mountains were cold, silent and implacable, and the stars wheeled around the slave's head and seemed to mock him when he looked to them for direction. He had been too long a slave; in the months of suffering he had forgotten who he was, had forgotten how to reason and deduce his position from the clues of sky and hillside. And his fine compass had long since been taken away from him. He stumbled uncaring away from the village until he found a rocky defile where he had never been before, in a part of the mountains that his master feared. The defile was blocked at the far end by what looked, in the moonlight, like a heap of broken rocks.

The fugitive clambered up the rocks, desperate to avoid pursuit, and his hands ached with cold until he cut them and the hot blood stung him. He fell asleep between one footstep and the next, leaning in between two rocks, and woke in the morning to find himself in a dark green cavern of ice. He had climbed up half the height of the *Yush-mountain,* the mountain of ice that his superstitious captors claimed to be the haunt of demons. He laughed sourly to himself. Well, at least now he had a choice. He could stay among the crevices of the glacier until he died of cold and exposure, or he could find his direction from the sun, make for the south, and be killed by the savages who had first captured him or by some other tribe.

CHAPTER FIFTEEN

Civil and Military Gazette

Lahore, Wednesday, 2 November 1884

New Series: No. 2,537   Vol. X

DEPARTURE OF THE GANDHARAN FIELD FORCE

From our own Correspondent

NOWSHERA, 1 Nov.—The Gandhara Relief Force marched this morning for the Malakand Pass. The force of some five thousand fighting men, commanded by Brigadier-General A.A. Kinloch, comprises native and British troops of the Bengal Army, supported by the Gwalior and Jeypore Transport Corps. In the leading position this morning was Colonel D.B. Vaughan's regiment, the 17th Infantry, followed by the 1st Battalion of the King's Royal Rifle Corps, the 15th Sikhs, and the 37th Dogras.

Colonel Vaughan had the kindness to communicate something of General Kinloch's plans to this correspondent. Gandhara is believed to be about two hundred and twenty miles from the base of operations at Nowshera, and it is hoped that the Relief Force will be able to reach the scene of the Russian siege in six weeks. However, the country which this army will have to traverse is practically unknown, and the information provided by the Gandharan Ambassadress suggests that some of the roads may not be suitable for army transport. Although it is impossible to foresee all the difficulties which may be encountered, Colonel Vaughan has made every effort to smooth the way for the Relief Force. A company of the Bengal Sappers and Miners is to accompany each regiment on the line of march, to assist in road and bridge building. Lieutenant J.R. McAusland of the 17th Infantry, who accompanies the Relief Force in the capacity of Political Officer, is also to act as Consulting Military Engineer for the expedition. In this capacity he is to accompany the advanced pickets sent out to protect the column before each day's march and to send back reports to the Relief Force on the nature of the terrain to be traversed and the points at which the Sappers and Miners could most usefully be employed. Finally, to ensure the column's safe passage through the tribal territories of Swat, Dir, and Chitral, Colonel Vaughan has caused the following proclamation (ably translated into the appropriate native tongues by Lieutenant McAusland) to be sent to all the tribes concerned:

To all the people of Swat, Bajaur and Dir:

Be it known to you, and any other persons concerned, that Russian armies have forcibly entered Gandhara, which is a protected state of the British Empire under the treaty of 16th October 1884. In order to honor our treaty obligations, the Government of India have arranged to assemble on the Peshawar border a force of sufficient strength to overcome the Russian attack. The Government of India have no intention of permanently occupying any territory through which the Russian misconduct may now force them to pass, or of interfering with the independence of the tribes; and they will scrupulously avoid any acts of hostility towards the tribesmen so long as they on their part refrain from attacking or impeding in any way the march of the troops. Supplies and transport will be paid for, and all persons are at liberty to pursue their ordinary avocations in perfect security.

The Sam Ranizai, the Khan Khel Baizai, and the Mian Guls have already consented to allow the Relief Force passage under the terms of the proclamation; we have yet to hear from the Khan of Nawagai and the Tarkanri tribes, who inhabit the Upper Swat valley.

—*Special Correspondent with the Gandhara Relief Force, 1 November leaving Nowshera*

       °   °   °

[Excerpt from the diary of Louisa Westbrook]

3 November 1884:

Oh, dear. Colonel Vaughan and Lieutenant McAusland are both out of reason annoyed with me about my first dispatch, which I thought I handled quite creditably for one entirely unaccustomed to the journalistic trade. Colonel Vaughan complained that I had made him, and not Brigadier-General Kinloch, appear to be the real leader of the expedition; to which I could only reply that everybody knew perfectly well he *was* the real leader and had virtually worn himself out with the thinking, planning and managing of the multitude of details which General Kinloch had delegated to his management. I considered it very tactful of me not to say in my dispatch that General Kinloch was a senile old man who was evidently still trying to fight the Crimean War and who would probably, if he did totter to the front long enough to give a command, throw our forces away on a disastrous charge like that of the Light Brigade long before we reached Gandhara.

"Louisa, you don't understand war," Colonel Vaughan told me. "This ain't a cavalry force, so how the devil could we emulate the Charge of the Light Brigade? Damme—excuse me, ma'am—I knew it was a mistake letting you talk me into this nonsensical notion. Females have no business on a campaign. Now you keep my name out of future dispatches, or I'll send you home to tend to your fancy-work!"

As for Lieutenant McAusland, he had the temerity to complain that I had made him appear like a humourless, ambitious intellectual with nothing better to do than to pass examinations in engineering and languages and with no object but to put his name forward in every capacity.

I refrained from the obvious rejoinder.

All the same, *I* think I shall be a very good Special Correspondent, and Mr. Stephen Wheeler, the editor of the *Civil and Military Gazette,* is of the same opinion, for today I received a congratulatory telegram and a request for further details. It is indeed wonderful to see how the young officers seconded to the Communications Troops have managed to bring up the telegraph directly following our line of advance, stringing new wires as they go, so that we shall never be more than a day's march away from direct communication with our advisers in India. I shall have to make some mention of this in my next dispatch.

When I commented on this fact to Colonel Vaughan, he snorted and said that too much advice had ruined many a good campaign and that in his opinion this field force could do with less advice, less transport and fewer blasted lady journalists. Since I am the only Special Correspondent travelling with the field force, this comment was not only pointed but extremely rude; I did not pay him the compliment of replying to it. I fear Colonel Vaughan is still slightly annoyed about my insistence on accompanying Tamai. Naturally I could not explain to him that I was unwilling to cut short my study of the Disciplines when I had only just begun; he doesn't believe such things exist. I had to invent some other excuse for my presence.

Initially I thought that I had arranged matters rather well, so that nobody would complain of my accompanying the force. First I telegraphed Mr. Wheeler, the editor of the *Gazette,* to inform him that I should be going to Gandhara with the Relief Force and would be happy to send his newspaper daily dispatches on the progress of the campaign. Mr. Wheeler's acceptance of this offer was not quite so polite as I should have liked. He wasted valuable telegraph space in explaining, quite gratuitously, that he would accept my services only because he needed to get "that blasted boy," Mr. Kipling, back to his post in Lahore. Still, he did agree to use my dispatches. Armed with this agreement, I visi: l Colonel Vaughan on the day after the signing of the treaty and informed him that as Special Correspondent to the *Civil and Military Gazette*, I should of course be expected to accompany the field force on the march to Gandhara.

Colonel Vaughan raised a great number of ridiculous objections to this plan. His principal concern appeared to be the unsuitability of exposing a lady to the dangers of a military campaign. Fortunately I had had the foresight to bring Tamai with me; she was quite distracted by some quarrel she had had with her cousin and paid little heed to my conversation with the colonel, but her presence was of the greatest help to me in achieving my ends. I had persuaded her to dress as an English lady once again. When the colonel began this line of argument, I pointed out to him that Tamai was not only going to go with the field force but was going to act as guide, presumably to be in the forefront of any actual fighting. He could scarcely, in Tamai's presence, deny that she was a lady! And looking at her in my second-best black mourning costume, head demurely bent under a bonnet of pleated Khitai silk, he could not but accept the force of my second argument—that it would be most improper to allow a young lady like Tamai to travel alone with an army. Was this showing the proper respect to our Gandharan Ambassadress? Where, pray, did he expect the poor innocent girl to sleep? Was she to lie alone in her tent, exposed to the lustful advances of the native soldiery? Or should she lose her reputation by sharing the officers' quarters?

Colonel Vaughan blushed beet-red, implored me to stop talking so indelicately, and finally accepted my view

of the matter—that it was absolutely necessary for Tamai
to be accompanied by a respectable married lady who
cold act as her chaperone, to assure the Gandharan
Council that she had been escorted to her home with all
the delicacy and propriety they could expect.

Once that small matter was settled I was quite fully
occupied for the next two weeks in arranging outfits and
supplies for the journey northward. What to wear for the
journey was, of course, a subject for the gravest consideration, and I have had the most extraordinary bits of
advice from various inhabitants of Cantonments. Mrs.
Beecham of the Ladies' Mission is insistent that I should
wear a mask at all times for fear that the sun and wind
will ruin my complexion for life; Mrs. Dr. Scully advises
that I should have my sleeves made so tight that no
insects will be able to get up them; and Mrs. Colonel
Vaughan began to suggest some extraordinary costume,
to be made something like a gown, blouse, and knicker-
bockers all in one, to be sure of protecting my modesty
in the event of my having to scramble over cliffs and
rocky paths. For a few moments she was actually
betrayed into something like enthusiasm for my venture;
then she recollected herself and said that, of course, *true
propriety* would dictate that I stay at home where I
belong! (She did not think much of my argument that
Tamai required a chaperone; in Mrs. Vaughan's view,
heathens have no virtue worth protecting.)

In the end I had to make up my own mind about my
clothes. I requested the *durzee* to make up several dark
blue cloth dresses, lined with flannel, with a tight jacket.
They are made just like riding-habits, except that the
skirts just clear the ground, and the sleeves are so painfully small, I shall have the greatest difficulty in getting
them on at all. I retain my respectability by taking an
old black crepe dress for wear in the evening.

As for Tamai, she was too distracted by Paluk's disap-
pearence to pay much attention to these important questions. As soon as Paluk heard about the terms Tamai had
made with the Government of India, he quarreled bit-

terly with her, calling her traitor and many other hard names. That very night he disappeared, doubtless to seek oblivion in the khans where opium is sold, like poor Bilizhe—the Gandharan men seem especially vulnerable to this drug. Tamai has spent hours of each day searching the bazaars and trying to find out any rumours about Paluk, for she was most reluctant to leave without him; however, since the Relief Force required her services as a guide to Gandhara, she had no choice in the end.

Civil and Miliary Gazette

Lahore, Wednesday, 9 November 1884

New Series: No. 2,544   Vol. X

FROM THE FORCES ENROUTE TO GANDHARA

From our own Correspondent

JANBATAI PASS, 8 Nov.—The mountain range which we have been ascending for the last two days offers a vista of surprising beauty. From our vantage point high above the valleys of Swat we can look down upon orchards and fields nestled among the barren, rocky slopes. Autumn has tinted the ubiquitous willow trees with a myraid of shades in gold and russet, while the fruit trees in the close-packed orchards blaze out in all the glory of their autumn foliage and the prevailing red tones of the plowed fields echo these autumnal hues.

So far we have seen little opposition from those tribes reputed to be hostile; the mountains themselves may well prove to be our sternest enemy. Nevertheless, General Kinloch has taken all precautions against attack. Each night before we make camp he sends out parties of piquets to hold any high points from which hostile marksmen might take aim at the camp, securing the ground all round our camp for a radius of two thousand yards. In addition, a defensive perimeter is thrown up, making use of such materials as the terrain affords, usually consisting of heaps of sharp stones interspersed with thorny bushes. This perimeter is guarded throughout the night and no movement outside the boundary is permitted.

We are thus quite as safe as any peaceful citizens in Peshawar of Lahore, free to enjoy the novelty and the poetry of our surroundings. As darkness falls, the stars shine brilliantly down on the camp out of the black sky; on the hills above, we see the fires of the piquets like a promise of protection through the night; and all around the mule lines at the lower part of the camp there twinkle the fires of the servants, mule-men, chaprassis, kalassis and saises. The homely sounds of the men cooking their chapattis of flour and water mingle with the music of the cavalry trumpets and the bagpipes of the 1st Punjab Infantry; while nearer by, the steady tramp of the sentries' feet along the thorn-hedge boundary of the camp reassures us.

Possibly when we reach Gandhara, there to confront the *Russian bear* Skobelev, your correspondent may have scenes of stirring action to report; at present I can only say that all is going as smoothly as one might anticipate from the superb planning and attention to detail which have attended General Kinloch's expedition from the outset.

> —*Special Correspondent with the Gandhara Relief*
> *Force, 8 November at camp on the Janbatai Pass*

*   *   *

[Excerpt from the diary of Louisa Westbrook]

8 November 1884:

And I hope *that* makes the good colonel happy! Since my first dispatch he has had the impertinence to demand the right of reviewing my daily reports before I send them on to Lahore. He seems to want two things above all: first, that no shadow of difficulty be so much as hinted at, and second, that his name shall nowhere appear as the one man responsible for most of the arrangments which protect the troops from hostile attacks. Therefore I have—gritting my teeth in a most unladylike manner—given General Kinloch credit for the orders to send out piquets and protect the camp boundaries; and I have said nothing about the mishap with the tents, which was entirely due to the general's idea that we could save time by sending the transport and supply corps by a separate road from that taken by the main column. Instead, the entire mule corps got lost for an unconscionable length of time; we are lucky they were not all slaughtered by Tarkanri tribesmen, and last night's "camp" presented a scene of cold desolation entirely unlike the pretty ladylike picture which I have painted for the benefit of the citizens at home.

We halted at sunset, at the top of the pass, a flat tableland offering virtually no shelter from the biting wind but having, to the military mind, the inestimable advantage that we could scarcely be surprised in such a locale. Until the camp perimeter was built Tamai and I walked briskly to keep ourselves warm, but once the boundaries had been defined for the night we could scarcely move for fear of tripping over guide ropes in the mule lines or stumbling across sepoys who had rolled up in their blankets on the cold ground. Tamai considered this an excellent opportunity for teaching me the Discipline of Inbreathing, called *tumo* in the language of Bod—the forbidden land known to us as Thibet— whence it was brought to Gandhara.

"Major Phelps says that the best way of keeping warm is to squat down against a bank, wrapped in your coat, and keep your head down to conserve heat."

"I will teach you a better way," Tamai told me.

We found a quiet corner just inside one angle of the brushwood perimeter and sat crosslegged on the ground, facing one another. "First concentrate, find the center of your being and breathe from there," Tamai said.

The center of my being? I focused my wayward thoughts somewhere around the region of my navel, but despite my best efforts, my breath still proceeded into and from my lungs. I tried to draw deep, infinitely slow breaths. I imagined the air passing through my limbs, down to my poor cold toes and back up again. I told myself that I was one with the great waves of the universe, the eternal rhythm of Creation; and I was halfway to believing it.

Then a cacophonous jangle of scratches, clangs and caterwaulings interrupted the rhythms of the universe, and an obstreperously Irish accent wailed something about the misdeeds of the British in outlawing poor Irish who only wanted to kill and slaughter without hindrance.

"How can anyone concentrate," I exclaimed in annoyance, "when Lieutenant O'Keefe persists in playing that bl—that *infernal* portable gramophone of his, night after night!"

Tamai laughed quietly to herself. "You must not allow yourself to be so easily distracted."

"Stay," I said, half-rising from my cramped position. "If the gramophone has arrived, so may have the rest of the baggage. Shall we not go and see if our tents are ready?"

"The true discipline," Tamai said, "does not turn aside from learning for comfort. Besides, even if the baggage has arrived, it will take them some time to set up the tents."

There was much wisdom in what she said. I settled myself on the ground again and tried not to hear the Irish lieutenant's gramophone wailing about the outlawed "wearing of the green."

"As you breathe out," Tamai instructed me, "expel all pride, anger, covetousness and sloth from your being."

"I had not fancied myself prone to any of those sins!" I said, rather sharply, and Tamai laughed at my irritable tone. After a moment I too had to smile. I stood fairly self-accused of anger, at least, and doubtless the other sins were also present in my soul.

"Am I allowed to breathe in?"

"Yes. Draw into yourself the fire of Nirmali with each breath, until you can feel the warmth at the pit of your stomach."

Two weeks previously I would have found it laughable

indeed to suggest that the frigid blasts of air surrounding us could be transformed into inner fire, but since then I have learned a little from Tamai. I sat quietly, following her instructions and trying not to shiver overmuch, while she recited some syllables in the Thibetan tongue. Not having studied this language, I should not have been able to understand her chant; nevertheless, as I practised my regular deep breaths of the icy air and concentrated on following her instructions, it seemed to me that her words called up certain images that assisted me in my task. A wall of gentle heat surrounded me, making the world outside quiver with the illusion. As the heat grew stronger, I felt an answering fire within me, and the wall took on a rosy colour. Soon I could not see Tamai, nor did I hear her voice, but the rhythm of the chant went on and it seemed to me that I could understand each word, laying its own commanding shape on the universe, with an understanding that could never be translated into plain English.

I was no longer shivering, and the air I breathed seemed as balmy as that in an English meadow on a June evening. _I do not need this wall,_ I thought, and with the thought it vanished as if it had never been. All around me were the stars, glittering like lanterns hung very low in the black emptiness of space. For a moment I floated in that space, alone and unafraid; then I was sitting on the rocky plain where our exercise had begun, and all around me were the small sounds and movements of the night camp, and the sky full of stars had receded until it hung above me where it belonged.

The tents had been set up while I was in my trance, and Tamai had disappeared, presumably to unpack our things and make ready for the night. I felt that I ought to go and help her, but was selfishly unwilling to break the peaceful calm induced by the breathing exercise. I still felt perfectly warm and comfortable and in no need of shelter. The sepoys' cooking fires glimmered in the center of the camp. I turned away from them and went in the opposite direction, towards the cold and stillness and dark at the outermost edges of the defensive wall. The sentries recognized me and nodded without speaking; I think they, too, must have felt the unearthly calm and beauty of the scene before us. The moon was rising behind the mountains to the east, like a cool silver dawn that illumined the valley below us almost as clearly as in full daylight. At this altitude the air was clear as crystal, and the snowy peaks of the mountains sparkled in the moon's white radiance. I felt that nothing could please me more than to spend eternity in this still perfection, surrounded by these ice-capped palaces of Nature glowing with their unearthly silver brilliance, untroubled by common daily cares.

Unfortunately the farthest and highest point of the camp perimeter was occupied by Lieutenant McAusland, who was very busy about some of his surveying observations, rattling equipment, cursing *sotto voce,* and scribbling down numbers by the light of a shielded lantern carried by a stoical sepoy.

"Mrs. Westbrook!" he exclaimed when he became aware of my approach. His raw Scots burr grated on my nerves, effectually shattering the peaceful trance which I had achieved through Tamai's Disciplines. "You should be under shelter, ma'am—you will catch cold, or at the very least this air will give you chilblains. Here, let me give you my coat."

"I assure you, Lieutenant McAusland, there is not the slightest need for such a sacrifice on your part," I said, trying to put aside the coat that he was attempting to wrap round my shoulders. "I do not feel the slightest chill, and—"

I broke off only because the young lieutenant, in his clumsy attempts to wrap me up, happened to touch my bare hand. I suppose he must have felt for himself the warmth which pervaded my body, for he withdrew his fingers with a muttered exclamation in some tongue unknown to me, and I thought I saw some wariness in his expression. He nodded to the sepoy who had attended his scientific labors and instructed the man to return to camp, taking the greatest care of his precious equipment. "I will escort Mrs. Westbrook to her tent," he said.

"Lieutenant McAusland, there is not the least necessity for you to go to such trouble," I said. "Pray remain and complete your observations."

He fell into step beside me as if he had not heard my request, pacing the boundary of the camp with two long, lazy steps to every three of mine. He appeared not to have noticed that the direction of our walk took us around the perimeter rather than back to the tents, and I felt no need to point this out, since I was still perfectly comfortable. "Thank you, Mrs. Westbrook, but I have had enough of freezing my fingers and chilling my toes in the name of science. In any case, this curst moon makes my work impossible, for in its brilliance I can barely make out the stars I had been using as fixed points."

"How like you," I exclaimed, momentarily diverted, "to see in the moon only an obstruction to your surveying, and in this scene of crystalline magic only the danger of chilblains! Have you no sense of beauty, Lieutenant?"

"Too much for my own good," he mumbled, and then, hastily, as if ashamed, "I beg your pardon, ma'am—I should not have said that. You must understand, Mrs. Westbrook, that a sense of beauty and an admiration of romantic scenery are sentiments altogether too high-flown for a mere lieutenant. A colonel may possibly indulge himself in a moment's appreciation of the passing scene, and I suppose a brigadier-general might go so far as to pen a sonnet expressing his pleasure in it, but a mere lieutenant had best confine himself to studying the *Manual of Field Tactics.*"

I had not previously suspected Lieutenant McAusland of possessing this vein of dour humour, and—perhaps perversely—I sought to provoke him further. "Certainly no one can accuse *you* of being remiss in your studies, Lieutenant," I told him. "Indeed, you scarcely seem to have time for anything else. Do you not think that a little more time spent with your brother officers, sharing their pleasures and pursuits, would do as much to forward your career as the mastery of yet another native language or the production of a beautifully detailed map of some obscure corner of this subcontinent?"

Lieutenant McAusland halted in his tracks, and for a moment I feared I had offended him with my mild teasing. "You think me a dull, ambitious dog, Mrs. Westbrook, with no thought but to further my career."

"Oh, no!" I began my apologies, but he was beyond listening.

"You and Captain Westbrook have never attempted to live on the captain's official pay."

This was true. The income from my small inheritance supported us both in comfort. But it was not a subject I liked to discuss.

"You have probably never troubled to examine the rates of pay in the Army Lists, have you?" Lieutenant McAusland went on. "Why should you? *I*, Mrs. Westbrook, do not enjoy an independent income. My father's resources were strained to provide me the schooling of a gentleman. He died the year after I entered the army, and since then I have supported myself and my mother and sister out of my pay. And the pay of a lieutenant in the Indian Army, Mrs. Westbrook, is two hundred and two rupees *per mensem*. His expected expenses—what with spare polo ponies, dogs for hunting, drinks in mess and all else—are estimated by the Army Office at three hundred twenty-five rupees monthly. So there, Mrs. Westbrook, you have the explanation of why I shun my fellow officers' amusements. Quite simply, I cannot afford them.

"As for my independent studies, there too I am driven by such crass pecuniary motives as you would find quite beneath your understanding. My surveying and mapping work may earn me the honour of a staff appointment, in which case my monthly pay would no longer be limited by the Army Lists. In the meantime, my facility with languages serves to procure my family at home some little comforts—for that, too, is measured in monetary terms—or did you not know that!" He flung the words at me like bullets from a rifle. "For passing the lower standard examination in any native tongue one is awarded five hundred rupees. For the higher standard, the award is two thousand rupees. I have won this award in Bengali, Punjabi, Sindhi, Gujerati, and Tamil. I have also passed the examinations for the degree of highest proficiency in Arabic and Sanskrit, for each of which I have been awarded a grant of *five thousand rupees*—two years' pay, Mrs. Westbrook! Would you care to know how many more languages I plan to learn while I wait for promotion, and just how I plan to eke out my pay with the prize money?"

"There is no need to tell me these things, Lieutenant McAusland," I said with quiet dignity. "I apologise if my thoughtless teasing offended you, and—"

"Never that!" he exclaimed with such warmth that I was momentarily startled. "I only wished you to understand—not to think me such a dull dog—to understand that I would most happily engage in the social life of the regiment, were it not that my circumstances forbid it. It will be many years before I can think of—in any case, it is much too soon and quite improper to suggest such a thing—the news of his death having been such a recent blow to you—"

I began to fear that Lieutenant McAusland was stumbling upon the brink of a proposal to me. Such a speech would, indeed, have been most improper to one so recently and tragically widowed, and if I had the least vestige of propriety I ought, as an experienced married woman, to have found some way of turning him aside before he said something for which we should both blush in the light of day. Dare I record that I did nothing of the sort? I simply listened passively as the lieutenant's words came tumbling out; and though I had quite lost the sense of calm detachment which the breathing trance had induced, I was as warm as ever—perhaps more so, for my fingers were positively tingling and my cheeks felt quite hot.

Fortunately for us both, Lieutenant McAusland halted himself before saying anything which I should have had to answer definitely. "It *is* too soon," he said with an air of finality, "and in any case, even if my circumstances did not forbid it, the colonel would probably do so. You know what they say: 'Colonels *must* marry, majors *should* marry, captains *may* marry, and lieutenants must not even *think* of marriage.'"

"True," I said, struggling to subdue my odd sense of anti-climax. "So they say, don't they?"

I was at a loss to understand my own confused feelings, for up until this evening I would have said that Lieutenant McAusland was the most self-centered, ambitious and difficult young man it had been my pleasure to meet in India, and one whose company I would be only too happy to avoid. I reflected that I should probably enjoy the same sentiments tomorrow; it must have been the lieutenant's moment of passionate outbreak, baring his straitened circumstances and his excessive Scots pride to me all at once, that made me imagine I could ever have felt anything else for him.

We paced on in silence until a sentry's challenge interrupted our walk.

"*Rukko! Kaun jata hai?* Halt! Who goes there?"

We had paced all the way around the boundary of the camp and were now approaching the more strongly guarded opening where the guns and supplies had recently been dragged through.

Lieutenant McAusland gave the password and we parted, I to my tent and Tamai's company, he no doubt to collate his latest observations by the light of a candle in the tent he shared with the other young officers.

After this disturbing conversation I was restless and unable to compose myself for sleep. I found Tamai in our tent, half buried in a nest of blankets, and watching my every movement with bright eyes that seemed to understand all too much.

"You don't use the Discipline of Inbreathing to keep you warm tonight?" I teased, partly to take her mind off my own all too obvious agitation.

"No," said Tamai flatly. "It doesn't work for me. You make yourself warm; I only start fires. Did I not tell you that you would be greater than I?"

While Tamai lay in her blankets and watched the candle flame flickering on the wall of the tent, I scribbled a few notes for tomorrow's newspaper dispatch, unpacked and rearranged my clothes, and finally sat playing with Harry's toy soldier. I had superstituously brought this little red-jacketed fellow with us, both as a memento of my children and as a symbol of my first success with the Disciplines of Gandhara. This night I was too overwrought to use him as a focus for imagery or any other Discipline; I marched him up and over my blankets, positioned him behind a ridge of folded blanket to fire on an advancing line of straw enemies, and sent him up to my pillow to do sentry duty, all the while remembering the happy days when Alice and Harry and I had played such games on the floor like three children together. Gordon played no part in those memories, for he had always been involved with his regimental duties or shut away in his study, but all the same it was Gordon whose face I saw when at last I composed myself for sleep and blew out the candle.

"You are restless," Tamai observed after she had waited patiently through my twitching and tossing and rearranging the blanket seven or eight times.

"Yes. I suppose so. I cannot sleep."

"Soon we will reach the river where your husband died. You are thinking of him?"

"Yes—but not of that, not tonight," I replied truthfully. "I was remembering the day when Gordon threw away Harry's toy soldiers—all but this one, which must have escaped his notice where it lay under the bureau. It was Harry's fourth birthday, and Gordon said it was time for his son to become a man and stop playing with little dolls. He had bought him a real little brass cannon, you see, only a toy, but it could be loaded with powder and fired off just like a real one. . . ."

Harry had been all agog to fire the cannon off, but when he heard the explosion it startled him and he began to cry. Gordon slapped him and declared that a son of his should never show the white feather. He ordered Harry to take the match and fire off the cannon himself, and when Harry cried and tried to hide in my lap, Gordon dragged him off me and whipped him soundly for his cowardice.

"How cruel!" Tamai exclaimed when I came to this point in my story. "And how foolish, to think that a child can be made brave by hurting him!"

"It is right that children should be punished for disobedience," I said, somewhat stiffly. "Everybody says so." But it had not been right, surely, for Gordon to lose his temper so thoroughly, and to shout at Harry as if he were drilling troops on the parade ground?

"And did your son fire off the cannon?" Tamai wanted to know.

"Not then," I admitted, and then, "No—he never did. Fortunately Gordon had to go on duty that afternoon. As Harry was still crying, he locked him in his room, and told him he should have no supper until he fired off the cannon by himself. By nightfall Harry had made himself sick with crying. I told Gordon he was in no condition to be tested anymore, but he said that I had infected the boy with my weak, womanish ways and that it was time for a man to take over his training. He was going to whip Harry again then, but . . ."

"What happened?" Tamai prompted me softly.

"Oh . . . he changed his mind." In the darkness, she could not see my fingers running over the rough joining of the bones in my upper arm, the break that Dr. Scully had said might never knit properly. "The cannon was gone, you see, so there was nothing to fight over. I had given it to a beggar outside the cantonment gate and told him to sell it in the Saddar Bazaar. And . . . the next month the children went to school in England." I was crying now, and although the darkness in the tent hid my tears, it could not conceal the sobs that caught in my throat. "I had to get them away from him, don't you see? Everybody sends their children away when they are of an age for school—no one thought it in the least strange—I said it was because I feared for their health in the heat, and because it was time for them to be with other English children. But it was really because Harry was growing up. Gordon never paid much attention to Alice, you see; she was only a girl, and I suppose he did not care how she turned out. But he wanted my little Harry to turn into a man just like himself, a loud confident soldier, and Harry could never have done it; he is a quiet child and rather shy. Once he started paying attention to his son, Gordon would have bullied and beaten Harry until he broke his spirit as he had already broken mine!"

There; it was out, what I had never admitted to another living soul. But there was more, and I felt the bitter rush to confession overmastering me, somewhat I suppose as Lieutenant McAusland had felt his compulsion to lay bare his poverty to me. "Everyone thinks I was such a devoted wife to Gordon," I said, "because I would not accept the presumption of his death, and because I dream about him still. But it's not true, and I am ashamed to let you think it. I hated him. And I am still afraid of him, and I was afraid to believe that he was dead without actually seeing his body. But since *you* have seen him dead—"

Tamai made an involuntary brief movement at that point, like someone startled by a sharp noise; but there had been no sound outside. I wondered if she were disgusted by my confession. "Now," I said, "now that I know he is dead, I can begin to find some peace. Yes, I still dream about him—I dream that he has come back to me—but I know these are only nightmares. I am free now. I can learn the Disciplines with you. I can go to Gandhara. I can find out who I am and what I am meant to be in this world; and when I have done that, I can go back to England and be with my children again.

"I am free now!" I repeated, luxuriating in the sound of the words. "And I have you to thank for it—no, I do not mean that I blame you for Gordon's death, Tamai; but you have shown me that I am worth something in myself. I had thought myself worthless, and my opinions of no account, because that was the way Gordon treated me, and I thought that he must know, being a man and having the experience of the world that I lacked. But now—now I can do things that none of the *men* of the regiment can do! You do not think less of yourself for being a woman, or submit your every thought to Paluk's judgement; why would I be less than you? I trust *myself* now," I told Tamai, "and so, thanks to you, I am truly free."

She made no reply to this long speech, and I was somewhat embarrassed to press for one. It occurred to me that she might have been hurt by my mention of her cousin, whose mysterious disappearance had never been resolved; or that she might, despite my disclaimers, think I held her at fault in some way for Gordon's death.

Then again, she might simply have gone to sleep. It was just possible that the rest of the world was not as fascinated as I by the discovery of my own soul.

On this slightly lowering thought, I composed myself to sleep.

Civil and Military Gazette

Lahore, Wednesday, 16 November 1884

New Series: No. 2,551   Vol. X

LAST DISPATCH FROM GANDHARA FIELD FORCE

From our own Correspondent

KANJUT RIVER, 15 Nov.—This will be the last dispatch which can be sent from the Gandhara Relief Force for some time. Despite the valiant efforts of Lieutenants Wetherby and Burrill, seconded to the task of communications, and the no less heroic achievements of the Transport Corps, the difficulties of the road into Hunza are such that the progress of the Relief Force has slowed to a trickle. Today it was decided that Colonel Vaughan should move on ahead of the main body of the army with a handful of men (about four hundred), lightly equipped. Their errand is to arrive in Gandhara as soon as possible, to ratify our treaty with the Gandharan Council, and by the moral effect of their arrival more than by actual force of arms, to prolong the siege sufficiently for the arrival of the main relief force. Your Correspondent is to accompany this flying column, well in advance of the telegraphic line which is being laid down as the army moves. As the portable heliograph which Colonel Vaughan takes with him is of necessity reserved for the most urgent military communications, no further newspaper dispatches will be sent until the communications officers with the main relief force have brought the telegraph line up as far as Gandhara, by which time it is hoped that your Correspondent will be able to give a full report of the happy conclusion to this campaign.

The reader in the flat plain of the Punjab may find it difficult to understand how our armies can be so severely delayed by the terrain. Let me describe the territory over which we have been advancing for the past several days. We are marching through the gorge formed by the Kanjut River, creating as we go a narrow road along the side of the canyon where only a footpath existed before. This footpath is interrupted at intervals by *paris*, projecting spurs of the mountains falling sheer into the river. At each *pari*, a perpendicular wall of hard rock, the Sappers and Miners must be brought up to spend a day of blasting and gallery work to make the roughest of mule tracks. The natives were used to avoid these *paris* by climbing high over the cliffs by steep scaffoldings, but these ladders have mostly been thrown down and destroyed in advance of our movements, and in any case they would be impasable for mules. The Kanjuti, or Hunza, tribesmen observe our road-building activities from distant heights, but so far they have refrained from rolling down stones or taking other steps in active opposition of our advance. However, progress has been so slow that Brigadier-General Kinloch fears the main relief force may not reach Gandhara before snow blocks the passes; hence the decision to send a flying column ahead under the command of the capable Colonel Vaughan.

—*Special Correspondent with the Gandhara Relief Force, 15 November, on the Kanjuti River Road*

[Excerpt from the diary of Louisa Westbrook]

17 November 1884:

That may very well be the last dispatch I send in any case. It seems a pity—but I must not write too much, now, of my feelings; it must suffice to put down just what has happened, as plainly as I may.

The first day's march of the flying column began ill, with a number of arguments about just what items of equipment were necessary to bring with us. Lieutenant McAusland wanted to bring our entire supply of telegraph wire so that we might remain in communication with the rear, Dr. Scully insisted on medical supplies, and each of the other officers had some particular requirement on which they were most insistent. Eventually Colonel Vaughan ended the discussion by allowing each officer one pack horse to carry his tent and personal belongings. Some, like Lieutenant McAusland, will have stinted their personal goods in order to carry badly needed medical and military supplies; others—but I had best not say too much about the young man whose pack horse is burdened with, of all things, his beloved portable gramophone! This morning that choice seemed the height of folly; now, if I could laugh at anything, I would at least smile at Lieutenant O'Keefe's idiosyncrasies.

Once we commenced moving, the real problems of the march up the Kanjuti River gorge overshadowed any trivial dissensions among our little group. The closer we approach Gandhara, the worse becomes the unseasonably bitter cold. (Tamai says this is the work of her people, that the ability to raise storms and blizzards is part of their defense against the siege. Naturally I have not ventured to communicate this explanation to Colonel Vaughan.) The lower reaches of the river, where we left the main force, were still free of ice, but in the upper valley we began to find ice crusting over the riverbanks more and more thickly. To save the time that road-building would have consumed, we avoided the *paris* by repeatedly fording the river on horseback. Yesterday we crossed the river at twelve different points. The torrent was frozen over for a short distance from each bank, and the ice would bear a horse's weight at one step and break away at the next. The water in the center of the river was so thick with mud that it was hardly possible to make out the bottom, and our poor horses had to flounder across as best they might, slipping and occasionally swimming for it.

By the end of the day the repeated river crossings had left the horses' coats covered with long icicles that clashed together at every movement. I attempted to practice the Discipline of Inbreathing from my saddle, and had such success that my lower extremities were quite comfortable beneath the ice-covered layers of my skirt; but my heart bled for the men who had to march through the icy river time after time, holding their rifles and packs above their heads, until they as well as our horses were draped in long icicles. At evening, when we halted, Colonel Vaughan's frozen breath hung in long clots of ice from his mustache.

Even the Discipline of Inbreathing could not protect me from the accumulated fatigue of the day, and I fell rather than lay down upon my blankets as soon as the tents were made ready. Tamai excused herself, as was her habit, to practice the meditations of her Disciplines. Tonight I was too tired to accompany her. Indeed, I was wondering if I had not overestimated my newfound strength when I insisted upon accompanying the flying column to Gandhara. The sad truth is that I was not so strong, nor so free, as I had jubilantly proclaimed myself to be; Tamai was my teacher and my guide, and I feared that, if separated from her, I might sink back into my bad old habits of excusing all manner of frailties in myself, of looking to the men around me for guidance instead of discovering the truth in my own heart.

I was still lying in the blankets, drowsing in a stupor of fatigue, when the sound of footsteps rustling outside the camp perimeter alerted the sentries. Shouts and a brief explosion of rifle fire followed, then—as I sat up, trying to struggle back into the clothes which I had shrugged off earlier—I heard a hoarse voice which seemed to be accosting the sentries in English!

For a moment I cowered in the tent, unwilling to face this new crisis. Old fears sprang up and half-choked, half-paralysed me. I felt myself indeed as weak and helpless as ever I had been before Tamai became my friend.

"I will *not* be defeated by fear," I told myself. "For shame!" And so, once dressed, I crawled out through the low flap that guarded the entrance to our little tent.

On the frozen ground before the tents I beheld a scene out of a nightmare, or from one of Dore's illustrations to the *Inferno*. In the glare of half a dozen hastily lighted torches stood a ragged, bearded creature, half-naked and most horribly scarred upon his back and sides. His emaciated ribs stood out like those of a famine victim; clotted blood was caked alongside his face, obscuring features on which a snarl of pain and despair seemed permanently fixed.

But where blood and dirt did not cover them, the beard and the long, tangled hair were yellow as the light of the torches; and the voice that issued from those thin, snarling lips was one which I had never thought to hear again in this world.

Half-fainting, I fell back against the guy-ropes of the tent. Gordon had not noticed my presence yet; all his

anger was directed at the soldiers who had impeded his
approach to the camp. But how long would that last? I
prayed for strength and guidance, but there was no
answer in the stony hills to which I lifted up mine eyes.
I heard nothing but my husband's ranting.

"By God, I'll have you cashiered!" he was threatening
the sentry who had evidently fired upon him. "To fire
upon a British officer—"

His voice echoed from the barren rocks around us
until he was interrupted by the colonel himself. Colonel
Vaughan's face showed the shock he must have felt, but
he put his hand on Gordon's shoulder as if he were
counseling any of his young officers. "Come, now, Westbrook," he chided gently. "You gave no password, and
the man could not know you in the dark. I hardly know
you myself, man!"

I could have told him that such a reasonable tone
would have no effect on Gordon in one of his rages. But
it was not my place to interfere between two officers of
the regiment, even if I could have summoned up the
courage to call attention to myself. I shrank back into
the shadows, trembling uncontrollably.

"Don't know me? Maybe you don't want to," sneered
the apparition. "For your information, Colonel, this is
what a British officer looks like when he's been enslaved
and tortured for months while you and your cronies were
carousing in cantonments. You took your time about
coming to look for me, didn't you? Maybe you didn't
want me found."

That roused a guilty echo in my own soul, for assuredly
I had not wished for his return. I had not even pursued
the search for him with what vigor I might; I had only
wanted to be satisfied that he was truly dead.

And now I was justly repaid for my hypocrisy. Gordon
back! It was my worst nightmare come to life; nay, *worse*
even than that. For the ragged, emaciated man standing
before the colonel both was, and was not, the husband
I had lived with and feared for so long. The man I knew

had always had enough sense, even in the worst of his rages, to protect himself against the repercussions of his own temper. He would never have raised his voice or his hand to a brother officer, any more than he would have risked beating me past the point where my injuries could be explained away as the result of some accident.

It was one of the things I hated in him.

But this man—he was beyond such vicious self-control; there seemed too little humanity in him for me to hate him. His glittering eyes appeared as those of one possessed by a devil. Had he been wholly consumed by his sufferings and his anger? Was there nothing left of the man I had married?

Fearful though I was, I felt that I *must* know what Gordon had become. I drew closer to the circle of torches, taking one unwilling step after another, and Gordon finally saw me. "Ah, my dear wife," he said. "What a surprise to see you here. You look well, Louisa. Not too pale with weeping for your departed husband, I see? Maybe you've found better sport in cantonments without me. The good colonel must be enamoured indeed, if he drags his light-o'-love on an expedition like this—"

"Captain Westbrook, you dishonour yourself and your wife by such insinuations!" Colonel Vaughan interrupted. He turned to the officers behind him. "The privations which Captain Westbrook has endured have momentarily disordered his senses," he told them. "None of you have heard anything he had to say."

There was a general murmur of agreement which my husband interrupted, shouting out in his cracked voice some suppositions to the effect that I had entertained the entire group of officers in ways I would not repeat, even in the privacy of this journal. Shame and fear together left me speechless before his vile assault, the blood rushing to my face as if to give some appearance of truth to his wild stories. Would he say that my blushes proclaimed my guilt? I was beyond caring; I longed to faint, to be removed from this scene, but escape was not to be so easy.

Gordon's filthy accusations were interrupted at last by Lieutenant McAusland, who struck him on the point of the jaw with his fist, so hard that my husband staggered and then fell unconscious.

"Unfortunate," said Lieutenant McAusland, blowing on his knuckles. "Man's delirious. Must have fainted with weakness."

"He must have," Colonel Vaughan agreed. "Dr. Scully, you'll see to him?"

None of the officers would look directly at me; they all seemed determined to pretend that I was not there, that Gordon had not made his horrible accusations, in short, that the entire scene had never happened.

I would have been only too happy to share in their pretense. Unfortunately, this morning's light revealed that it was all too true. I am indubitably here. And so is Gordon. He has calmed somewhat after a night's rest and some medical attention, and he no longer feels compelled to shout out his vile accusations of me to the world. But I had a private interview with him just now, in Colonel Vaughan's tent, and I find him unchanged in all important ways, unless it is that he is grown harsher and more unreasonably suspicious of me than ever—or is it that I am no longer so inclined to bow down under his jealous accusations? I remember, as if from another life, that once I thought it must be my fault when he flew into his rages, and that if only I could comport myself as a meek and dutiful wife and avoid angering him, our married life would be peaceful enough.

I suppose I began to see the unwisdom of this submissive course when he turned his anger on poor little Harry, who had done *nothing* to deserve his father's wrath. And the months away from Gordon, surrounded by people who do not seem to find my behaviour outrageous and who do seem to have some use for me, have made it very hard for me again to bow my head patiently under Gordon's baseless accusations.

All the same, it must be done. Gordon made that clear enough. My role with the Relief Force is over now, for he says that no wife of his shall lower herself to scribble for the newspapers, and that he is perfectly competent to act as translator when we meet the Gandharans. He is not, of course—I can now see how limited his command of the language is, and how many errors he makes—but after all, Tamai now knows English perfectly, and I shall have to trust that she will keep Gordon from making too many mistakes.

He desired me to move into his tent and to live as his wife again. Fortunately the exigencies of the march make that impossible, at least for now. Colonel Vaughan explained that we had only one large tent for the officers, and one small one for Tamai and me. He could not countenance turning the Gandharan Ambassadress out of her tent, nor could he consent that I should sleep away from Tamai, for my presence was required as a guarantee that she had been properly chaperoned in the midst of this army.

How glad I am, now, that I hit upon just those arguments as a way to reconcile Colonel Vaughan to my presence with the Relief Force!

It has been some relief to pour out my feelings in the privacy of this journal. But even that will end when we reach Gandhara, when I have no excuse to avoid sharing a dwelling with my husband. I do not think that Gordon would approve of my keeping a journal which he was not allowed to read, and I dare not allow him to see what I have set down in the months since his disappearance. As for all my fine words about my new strength and freedom—what do they avail me now? Gordon is alive. He is still my husband; he controls my little income and has the right to my body and my children. Alice and Harry are in England, being cared for by a family of his choosing. If I leave him, I will never be allowed to see my children again. If I defy him—but that does not bear thinking of. I must learn again to submit and obey and keep silence; and now I must hide this journal and go outside to face him, for it is time to strike the tents and proceed onward to Gandhara.

CHAPTER SIXTEEN

The child was wrapped in ceremonial scarves of Chin brocade and Bod embroidery, with strings of glass beads around its throat and wrists and ankles, paper flowers all around it, a crown of gild-embroidered satin on its flat Kirghiz head. Its eyes were dull, the pupils enlarged with the dose of opium that had made it calm enough for Li Kuang-hou's purposes. It lay like a gaudy doll on an altar carved out of snow, against a wall of ice.

The glacier stretched on up between two mountains until it met the northeast corner of the Gandhara city walls, two miles away. The ice-blue tiles of the city, molded of starlight and winter wind in the days when the White Huns ravaged the plains, glimmered in the white winter light, as smooth and perfect as if they had been set in place yesterday. From that corner, the glacier curved on down between the mountains, inching forward through the centuries, patterned with cracks that showed the cold green heart of the ice.

The Russian camp was a mile below the leading edge of the glacier. It had been there for three weeks, ever since the combined attack of Russian riflemen and Li Kuang-hou's demons had driven the Gandharans back from their pastures and orchards to crowd into the shelter of the ancient walls.

The final assault on the city should have been over in another week. Instead it had gone on for three weeks with no perceptible progress. General Skobelev knew that the Gandharans must be hungry behind their blue walls, that the incessant pounding of the shells his guns lobbed over the walls must be breaking their nerves. But to all outward appearances, the fortress-city of Gandhara stood as calm and untouched as it had been on the first day of the siege. Skobelev's guns made no impact on the charms that held the blue tiles together; his riflemen, who had been so successful at sniping in the broken ground of the high pastures, could find no cover within range of the city and no point from which they could see to fire down inside the walls. His men had been ordered on three desperate frontal attacks and had failed three times, falling on the ice-coated slopes, disoriented and maddened by the Gandharan magic that made them all feel as if the world were turning upside down to spill them off into space. All he had achieved by those rushes was to put his men within musket-shot of the walls, giving the men of Gandhara a chance to shoot back at their enemies. The first bullets fired from Gandhara had been solid lead; the ones dug out by the surgeon after the last attack had been made of garnets within a thin lead coating. The Gandharans were running short of ammunition.

This information did not cheer the men noticeably. The true Russians were sullen, on the verge of mutiny; the Cossacks, in a situation where they could not use their horses, were even more unhappy than the Russians.

As for Li Kuang-hou's demons, they had so far been worse than useless. The stupid, clumsy constructs of dead flesh and living lines of force might be some danger to a foe they could touch, but the Gandharans had been despicably inventive in finding ways to destroy them from behind the shelter of their magical walls. The demons had lumbered up the icy slope straight into trap after trap, until Skobelev had refused Li Kuang-hou any more victims for his sacrifices. Throwing demons at the wind only depressed his troops, and the number of sacrificial victims required depressed them still more; they worried that some day Li Kuang-hou might decide Russians were more effective sacrifice material than Kirghiz nomads.

Li Kuang-hou had procured this last child himself, buying the orphan from a Kirghiz group that wanted to move north without the encumbrance of a motherless toddler. The child's relatives had been happy enough to be assured that Li Kuang-hou would give it a good life. "I promised that it would be treated like the other Kirghiz hostages," the Khitai said in his lisping voice. "So you see, General, I did not even have to lie."

Skobelev stared down at the drugged child on the altar. Its ceremonial wrappings outshone his own spotless white uniform with its wealth of gold braid and sparkling buttons. He took pride in keeping himself immaculate, whatever the circumstances of the campaign; the men had a certain faith that "the White General" would bring them through battles unscathed and unmarred like his perfect uniform.

This irrational faith had survived the losses they suffered in the siege of Geok Tepe, had survived seeing Skobelev's previous white uniform splashed with the blood of the victims when the town was looted. But would it survive another fruitless month of besieging a witch-city protected by ramparts of ice? Skobelev was beginning to have doubts. And these doubts, together with the news that a small advance force of British soldiers was marching directly up the frozen river to Gandhara well ahead of the slow-moving main army, had inspired him to give Li Kuang-hou's magic one last try.

"I have discovered how to prevent the demons from taking on corporeal form," the Khitai told him. "This has been our mistake. By giving them bodies to use, I put them in my debt; but by going into those bodies, they became so stupid that the Gandharan witches were able to trick them. This time I shall protect the child's body." He poured a little blue powder into the palm of his left hand, closed his eyes and shouted a few words of the

Khitai tongue into the air. The powder began to smoulder and to give off a foul odor unlike anything Skobelev had ever smelled before. Li Kuang-hou drew certain, broken, jagged lines in a pattern radiating out from the altar of snow, chanted a few words over each line, and dropped a pinch of the burning incense at each of the four cardinal points. He finished rather quickly and wiped his palm in the snow.

"Now I shall call a spirit of fire," he said.

"And what good will that do?" Skobelev felt his usual deep distaste for the man's ceremonies, but he refused to show any emotion to an underling. His policy on Central Asia was well known and often quoted: "In Asia he is the master who seizes the people pitilessly by the throat." He could not now betray his own policy of crushing all resistance without mercy. The death of one Kirghiz hostage was a small thing. Besides, this time the child was "protected."

Li Kuang-hou smiled but did not answer Skobelev's question at once. He threw his head back and extended his palms to the sky and began a deep-voiced, throbbing chant that built up in spirals of repeated rhythms until the inside of the Russian general's head vibrated in time with the words of the chant. He felt some pressure building in the air around them, a troubling of the sky that might presage a storm—or something worse.

The trembling of the air drew together, invisible except as it distorted the scene behind it, into a man-sized funnel hovering directly over the altar. The child screamed as its body arched upwards. The funnel of air became almost visible, flickering with heat and a memory of color around the edges. The child arched farther and farther, until its head almost touched its heels, and its thin high screaming hurt Skobelev's ears worse than Li Kuang-hou's chanting had done. Suddenly there was a sharp crack. The child's body fell back, limp and lifeless, and the open eyes glazed over.

"I thought you said it would be protected!" Skobelev cried.

"General, General. What is one girl-child against the fate of your entire army? I have kept the demon from drawing the child's body into its own corporeal form; that is what matters. The child died because its spine broke while it was struggling. That has nothing to do with the demon." Li Kuang-hou spoke soothingly, his eyes never leaving the funnel of air, while his hands traced a shape exactly corresponding to the funnel. As his fingertips met at the bottom of the shape, a spark of fire leapt from finger to finger and he exhaled sharply.

"There. It is done. A spirit of fire, bound to our bidding by the sacrifice it accepted, but without taking corporeal form from the body of the sacrifice. So it will regain the intelligence of this shape, but will still serve our bidding."

"Can it *do* anything without a body?" Skobelev demanded.

"One thing only," Li Kuang-hou replied, "according to its nature. What is the nature of fire?"

He gestured, and the quivering shape of air moved back against the edge of the glacier. The green ice hissed and seemed to shrink back; a cloud of steam rose, and there was a funnel-shaped cave in the ice.

Skobelev stared, then slapped his knee and laughed. "Spirit of fire! Khitai, you shall sit at my right hand when I enter Gandhara! Can this demon melt the ramparts of ice?"

Li Kuang-hou bowed. "As the general sees. But for so much ice, many demons or many days will be required."

"Take all the Kirghiz brats you want," Skobelev directed. "I will put you in charge of a troop of Cossacks to hunt them down. By tomorrow I want enough demons in this form to melt a glacier."

And if even a part of this glacier, which covered the headwaters of the Tears of Lunang, could be melted in a day, two of his problems might be solved at once.

The Women's Council Hall in Gandhara was built around the roots and trunk of a cedar tree that had been growing there when the first Gandharans took shelter in this mountain valley from the scourge of the White Huns. Lightweavings and watersongs kept the tree green and strong through the centuries, its branches above the Hall roof dancing in perpetual sun, its roots fed by a spring that rose to bubble and laugh in the pool beside the ancient trunk. The lower branches of the tree were woven into the fabric of songspells that protected the roof of the Hall. Its roots were intertwined with the carpet of red ground and turquoise flowers where the wisewomen sat in their meetings. The Hall could not be moved, not would the Council meet elsewhere, even though the strange new weapons of the Rus sent death flying over the walls of Gandhara to strike at random in the open spaces of the public square and dancing platform.

The women and men of Gandhara made a point of going about their business almost as if the humming shells did not exist, though they developed various ways of travelling across the exposed spaces where shells most often struck. Some scurried across those dangerous corners with heads bent; others walked upright but quickly as if on some extremely urgent business.

The Dhi Lawan regretted the necessity of scurring through the streets of her own city like a rabbit flushed from the snare. Not only was this undignified, it was hard on an aging body that perpetually ached somewhere or other. However, having attained the long-coveted position as head of the women's council, she had no intention of losing her place to a Russian shell. Dignity, for the time being, could take second place to survival.

Those few Council members who could be spared for this meeting evidently agreed with her, for they entered the Hall in various stages of exhaustion and disarray. The Dhi Lawan had made sure to be first in the Hall, to give herself time to catch her breath after the undignified dash across the square; now she watched the old women scurrying inside, gasping for breath and clutching their bony chests, and let her own calm impress them with her moral superiority.

Only five old women in black cloaks came, rattling around in the great open chamber like ancient dried nut meats within a walnut shell. The previous Dhi Lawan had presided over Council meetings where every turquoise-colored flower in the red carpet was the seat of a cloaked wisewoman. Where were they now? While she waited politely for her sisters in Council to catch their breath, the Dhi Lawan ran over the Council roster in her mind, paying a moment's tribute to each absent wisewoman. Some had died of short rations and cold weather and the exhaustion of holding protective spells over the City for months on end. Some, like Shushibai, had died bravely, in the forefront of the defenders holding off the Rus attack, before the Council had decided to surrender all of Gandhara save what lay within the high walls of the City. Some had died stupidly, refusing to hurry across the open spaces of the square where the Rus shells spattered their bones and blood across the blue tiles. And, of course, most of those still alive were at the northern wall, renewing the bindings of wind and cold and illusion that kept the Rus still at a little distance from their final victory.

"My sisters, I wish you to hear a man's voice in Council," the Dhi Lawan announced when all were seated, "not to advise us, but to give us information which may bear on our future actions."

All five wisewomen had been aware of Paluk standing behind the Dhi Lawan, but they did not acknowledge his presence until the Dhi Lawan spoke. Now he moved forward and waited, head bent and hands crossed over his bosom, until they signaled that they were ready to hear him speak.

"Sisters, you have been betrayed by a sister," Paluk began formally. "The one who left to save Gandhara has been the one who chose to lose Gandhara, and the one who loved her must be the one to bring the tale of her treachery. . . ."

The wisewomen listened without moving while Paluk told his story. Before long he had forgotten the formal cadences of Council speech and was talking as he would to another man, passionately, eyes wet with tears, hands shaking as he poured out the tale of Tamai's treason—how she had left him alone in the foreign city and at the mercy of poisoners while she turned herself into an Angrez, learning their speech and donning their garments.

"It seems that the man Paluk took this 'poison' freely," observed one of the wisewomen to the air of the Hall.

"And to learn an enemy's speech may be no more than wisdom," said another.

"Tamai should not have attempted to use the Disciplines which she has not mastered!" the Dhi Lawan said.

"If she learned the Angrezi speech within six days," said the wisewoman who had spoken first, "and the City of Peshawar is not in flames, then perhaps she has learned more control than she had when she left here. And if she *did* set the City on fire or bring its walls down, well, they are only foreigners; what is it to us?"

"She did worse than that," Paluk said. "You have not heard all my tale."

And what he had to tell them then, of soldiers marching north and Tamai guiding them, seemed damning indeed. There was a long silence after he had finished.

"The man may go now," the Dhi Lawan said finally. "Let the discussions of the women be for the women, and let the discussions of the men be for the men. He has done well to bring this news to us, but the rest is for us to decide."

"*Is* there anything to decide?" one of the wisewomen demanded as soon as Paluk had left. "If she has betrayed us as he claims—"

"Tamai would never betray the City!" another interrupted her.

"What are you going to do about it?" a third challenged the Dhi Lawan.

She thought that they were like unruly schoolchildren, challenging authority, longing for some show of strength from their leader. Had she been so argumentative when she sat on a woven flower and the old Dhi Lawan put forward her plans for the City? She could not remember now. Those days seemed so long ago. At least, she thought with a gleam of bitter laughter, there were some advantages to having such a miserable shrunken husk of a Council. Two hundred wisewomen would have argued all day and all night about what she proposed to do with Tamai. These five could be stared down by the strength of her will, the strength that had made her Dhi Lawan in the end.

"If she comes with rifles, and with no foreigners," the Dhi Lawan said mildly, "then Paluk was mistaken or lying, and she has not betrayed us; she has only fulfilled the mission on which she was sent."

"Without Council approval!" flashed one of the wise-women. "I said all along it was a mistake."

"And if she comes with a foreign army," the Dhi Lawan went on as though there had been no interruption, "then are we agreed that Paluk's story must be taken as true? And that we must act before that army has a chance to breach the walls of Gandhara?"

There was a murmur of assent.

"What shall we do?" one of the wisewomen asked. "It has been so long since we had any lawbreakers in Gandhara—we can hardly fine her as though she had been filching walnuts before the harvest!"

"She shall not be a lawbreaker," the Dhi Lawan said. "We shall stop her before it comes to that. This is my plan."

For a miracle, the five contentious old women listened and found the plan good, or at least were too weary to argue about it. The Dhi Lawan stood, pushing herself up with her hands resting on the arms of her carved chair. The swift motion made her head swim. She might be the Dhi Lawan and the head of Council, but she was also a tired old woman who had trouble forcing herself to eat the coarse barley soup that was the common ration in Gandhara now. "Go, then, in the Light of Nirmali, and may the four pillars guard you!" she blessed her five senior councillors.

There was a brief flash and swirl of color as the last wisewoman of Gandhara stood, the bright inner linings of their cloaks showing glimpses of their rich histories; then the black cloaks were all folded close, and there was only a line of old women making their way out of a hall much too big for the six of them.

In borrowed clothing a size too small for him, riding a mule hastily liberated from the transport division, Captain Gordon Westbrook might have been a figure of fun. But there was nothing amusing about the sufferings he had undergone as a prisoner of the Kanjutis, nor about the change in personality he displayed now. He had always been a serious type, but quiet and polite enough in the officers' mess, whatever the rumors might have said about upheavals in his bungalow and servants beaten for too little cause. Now he seemed unable to repress his anger; it burst out of him at the slightest halt. And mostly—there being few servants with the expedition— his rages were directed either at the mule he rode or at his wife. He had lashed the mule up one steep mountain path until it halted on the brink of a gorge, legs splayed out and quivering with strain, ready to hurl itself off with its tormenter.

"Gently, man, gently!" Colonel Vaughan counseled when he came up behind Westbrook.

The captain stared at Vaughan, blinked and ran one hand over his head. A measure of sanity returned to his eyes. "Bad form. Sorry!" he apologized brusquely. His shoulders stiffened and his whole body took on the rigid military bearing that had always characterized him in Peshawar. He was once more, to all appearances, the pukka officer, the brilliant young Captain Westbrook who lived by the manly code of the army and knew no doubts.

Tamai had dismounted and sidled around to the front

of the path, where she stroked the mule's foam-flecked nose and talked to it in low, soothing tones until it consented to move forward an inch at a time. Westbrook ignored her intervention and rode on, nose in the air, as if nothing had happened.

Lieutenant McAusland watched the incident with a creeping unease that kept him from interfering. He did not believe that Westbrook was really mad. He had sense enough to stop abusing the mule when Colonel Vaughan intervened; when he realized he was being observed and criticized, he had pulled himself together until he had the outward semblance of the perfect soldier who had left Peshawar so many months ago.

But McAusland felt as if he were looking at a shell, dangerously thin, over something worse than madness— something that knew how to disguise itself at will. He had never cared for Westbrook, but the antipathy he felt towards the man now was something more than the natural tension between the professional soldier and the political officer who spent more than half his time living with the natives.

It was probably, he thought, no more than the natural antipathy of a man who wants something another man has—something precious that the possessor, not valuing it, is likely to destroy. Westbrook—or whatever had come out of the mountains wearing Westbrook's name and face—had sense enough not to strike his wife in public. But that was the limit of his control. He spoke to Louisa as McAusland would not have spoken to the least of his servants, and each day she seemed to shrink back into herself a little. On the march into the mountains McAusland had just had a glimpse of what Louisa could have been before marriage to Westbrook broke her spirit. Now the pretty, confident, slightly pushy young widow who had begun to charm him on the way north had disappeared, changing back into the pale, shy little wife who never had two words to say for herself.

Only now he knew why she was like that. It was the only way to survive living with Gordon Westbrook.

He was almost relieved when they reached the narrow ravine where Tamai's magic had blocked the path to Hunza warriors. Here they would have to leave the horses and mule, under the guard of a few soldiers who were to await the coming of the main force; the path ahead, Tamai said, was too difficult for the animals. Westbrook agreed with her, although he looked as if it hurt him to find sense in anything a woman said. McAusland reflected that at least now he would not have to watch Westbrook maltreating his mount. Then he wondered how the captain would treat Louisa, now that he could not take out his mad fits on an animal. And then the sepoys who had been detailed to move the stones announced that a way had been cleared, and they went on towards the Hunza village where McAusland had first seen Tamai.

The villagers offered no opposition to the army's passage. McAusland, going forward with the advanced patrol, found the same pattern repeated here as in all the other villages they had marched through: empty streets, houses vacated so abruptly that the ashes of the cooking fires were still warm, and an eerie sense of unseen eyes watching from the still heights of the cliffs.

"It doesn't make sense," he complained to Colonel Vaughan. "I can understand their hiding the women and children, for fear we might take them and sell them as slaves, but where are the men?"

"Nonsense! What would make them think we'd take slaves?"

"It's what they would do if they had the chance," McAusland pointed out. "That's one reason there aren't more caravans coming up from India. Too many of 'em disappear in this region."

The high cliffs on either side of the river gorge made him feel as if somebody were always looking over his shoulder. He shivered involuntarily and, just for a moment, missed the flat sunbaked plain around Peshawar with a passion that surprised him. His own casual statement about the dangers to the caravans echoed in his ears like an unintentional prophecy. It seemed all too possible that the mountains would open up and swallow this small force of a few hundred soldiers as if they had never been. They would hardly be the first to disappear in this rocky wilderness.

After that village, the only possible path led up and away from the river gorge, narrowing until it was little more than a goat-track, then only a narrow ledge high above the sparkling thread of the ice-rimed river. Tamai took the lead, insisting that there was no other way to her country. Captain Westbrook roused himself from his internal mutterings of anger and betrayal long enough to confirm her statement, or at least to say that he had found no better path.

"And that," said McAusland sourly, "is *another* reason why the trade with Gandhara is not great. Some of the Gilzai traders are relatively sane. Has it occurred to anybody that this is a marvelous place for an ambush?"

"Don't worry," Tamai said. "Even the goats can't get higher on this cliffside than we are. The ambush would have happened back where we left the village."

McAusland inched his way along behind Tamai and offered up a brief prayer for those who followed; then, thinking of the army so many miles behind them, he made an even more fervent prayer for the Sappers and Miners, who would be charged with the task of creating a road out of this unpromising rock.

All his misgivings vanished when he rounded the protruding corner of the cliff and caught his first glimpse of the vista on the far side. Here the ledge broadened and offered room for two or three to walk abreast. Before him stretched a chain of valleys linked by the glittering thread of an icy green river, walled by mountains that rose to snowy peaks, the whole vista rising imperceptibly into the mists at the horizon. Above those white mists, barely perceptible in the distance, he could just see flashes of blue fire where the sun glanced upon tall, conical, blue-tiled roofs and narrow towers.

It was a city out of fable, the sort of great discovery

that every explorer dreamed of making one day. The blue spires promised him the secrets and the wisdom and the magic of the centuries. The pilgrim Hsuan Tsang and the conqueror Babur, the explorers Vigne and Masson had all searched in vain for Gandhara. And where they failed, he who least deserved it had been granted success.

"If this is what Westbrook saw," he exclaimed, "I don't blame him for risking his life by trying to get there!"

"It is not," Tamai said flatly. She was frowning. "He saw nothing but clouds. *You* should see nothing else." She glared at him. "How can you penetrate the guards we set on our City?"

As more members of the party worked their way around the perilous corner, they too stopped, stared and exclaimed in surprise.

"It's not just me," McAusland pointed out. "We can all see it. . . . Are you saying we should not? How can you conceal a city of that size?"

"You have seen what I can do," Tamai reminded him. "And I am not even a wisewoman. We keep—kept—our City walled by air and illusions." She scowled at the line of glittering blue towers. "What *have* the Council been doing?"

McAusland had no answer to that question, and only one hypothesis, which he hesitated to voice. Could they have come too late? Could Skobelev have taken the City already, destroyed the wisewomen and their defenses together?

As they made their way down the mountain to the river called the Tears of Lunang, Gandhara's tributary to the Kanjut, the blue towers of the city seemed to vanish into the mist. It could, McAusland thought, have been the renewal of a spell that had only trembled for a moment under some attack. Or it could simply be that the clouds were thickening and another storm rising.

There was no snow that night, but the next day, as they approached the place where Gordon Westbrook had forded the Tears of Lunang, they seemed to be marching into winter. Where the Kanjut River had been half frozen over at the banks, the Tears of Lunang presented a solid icy surface beneath which nothing moved. That was as good as a road; they made better time than before. All the same, something about this early winter worried McAusland.

"It's not *natural*," he grumbled when, for the third time in as many hours, he had to correct the column's tendency to wander away from the riverbed. Nothing should have been simpler than to follow this narrow gorge to the source of the river. Yet the men at the rear kept straying, apparently unable to tell the main gorge from the little intersecting nullahs where mountain streams had trickled down to join the river. And when they were stopped, they claimed indignantly that they had only been following their comrades—who, meanwhile, were trudging up the riverbed without looking back. McAusland himself found it extremely difficult to follow the river. The whiteness that covered everything seemed to radiate light into his eyes, dazzling him and making him too dizzy to tell where he ought to go. Only constant reference to his compass, and an obstinate refusal to believe that the needle lied, enabled him to keep going north instead of turning aside into one of the tributary paths.

Tamai, by contrast, was happy and confident. "Of course it is not natural," she assured McAusland. "Did I not tell you that Gandhara is well defended?"

"I wish you'd tell them to call it off," McAusland muttered. "Don't they understand that we're *friends*? We're coming to save their city, not to besiege it!"

Tamai looked back along the long line of men struggling through the snow, each with a rifle and a pack. "My people may find the distinction a little difficult to understand," she said softly. "I hope I can explain it to them."

Colonel Vaughan had hoped to reach the City of Gandhara that day, but by the time they reached the frozen expanse where the river could be forded in summer, he had to give up that ambition. The men were barely able to stand; marching on was out of the question.

"Tamai, can't you do anything?" McAusland appealed when Colonel Vaughan announced that they would have to make camp where they were. "These are your people we're trying to save—if they slow us down, it will be at their own cost."

"I could go on into Gandhara," Tamai said. "The illusions do not affect me. Perhaps I can persuade them to admit your people."

"Can't you stop the . . . illusions?"

Tamai shook her head. "I might be able to shield a few of us, if Louisa will help me. But I cannot be sure of the consequences."

McAusland looked up at the mountains beyond the ford and thought about trembling rocks.

"Sir," he said urgently. "Colonel Vaughan! Sir! If you want to use Tamai, move the camp back. Up the slopes."

"Where?"

McAusland tried to point to a safe place. But his hand would not obey the command of his eyes, and the barren hill he would have chosen for a campsite shifted, wavered, and then slowly and majestically turned upside down. McAusland sat down abruptly in the snow. It felt good, the solid ground under the snow. He did not think it would throw him off . . . not just yet, anyway.

Tamai knelt beside him. "What is it?"

He could barely understand Tamai's question. "Avalanche," he said between bouts of strangling nausea. "If you . . . if the rocks shake . . ." Walls had come down in flat Peshawar. What might Tamai's magic do to the snow on the mountain peaks?

"Yes." While McAusland tried to regain his sense of direction, Tamai showed the men what she thought would be a safe place for the camp. McAusland followed her back to the spot she had selected, on a cliff high above the river, and found that he felt much better . . . as long as he was walking or climbing *away* from Gandhara. No wonder the City had gone so long undiscovered! He felt a grudging respect for Gordon Westbrook, who had fought the wisewomen's illusions alone, with no one to tell him what they meant, with nothing to guide him but the evidence of his compass and nothing to support him but his own stubborn will.

Then Westbrook announced that he did not see why he should let his wife go off with Tamai and the colonel, and that he had a good mind to forbid her doing any such thing. Colonel Vaughan talked about insubordination, Tamai tried to explain that she needed Louisa's help to work her countermagic, and Louisa went very white and quiet and said nothing at all. In the end Tamai reluctantly agreed to try to shield five people instead of three: Colonel Vaughan, Captain Westbrook, Lieutenant McAusland, Louisa and herself.

"I see why you had to let Westbrook go," McAusland murmured in the colonel's ear as they were preparing to set out, "but why me? Not that I'm objecting, mind you," he added hastily. "I'm most grateful for the opportunity, but if it makes things harder for Tamai—"

"I'm not adding you to the group for your benefit," Colonel Vaughan muttered back. "I'm bringing you along to keep me from killing Westbrook."

"Why would I want to do that?"

The colonel fixed him with a paralyzing glare. "Consider it a direct order. Oh, and you're not to kill him either. Consider that another direct order."

When he turned back to face Gandhara, within the protective shield of Tamai's magic, McAusland found that his vision had cleared and he could look at the river valley like any other place, analyzing its strong and weak points and mentally planning just how he would move forward against a hostile force. It would have been an extremely difficult position to take, and he began to understand why Tamai had initially bargained only for a caravan load of rifles and ammunition. If all the approaches to Gandhara were like this one, a handful of determined men with modern rifles should be able to hold off an enemy indefinitely.

They were standing on a frozen river, with precipices hundreds of feet in height rising from either bank, and only a narrow crack between the cliffs to indicate the path by which they had marched to the river. A zigzag path up the cliffs on the opposite side was the only approach to the City, and that path was overlooked by jutting precipices where a single rifleman could have picked off the advancing enemy at his leisure. He would not have cared to have the assignment of storming such a place; if the approaches to Gandhara from the north were equally difficult, McAusland wished Skobelev joy of his self-appointed task.

Louisa and Tamai walked across the frozen river a few steps ahead of the three men, holding hands and chanting in a low undertone that rose and fell like the moaning of the wind in the high passes. Once Louisa stumbled over some obstacle hidden under the snow, and her hand jerked out of Tamai's grasp. Tamai kept moving ahead as if nothing had happened, but her voice started to rise higher and higher, and in the corners of his vision McAusland sensed strange things happening in the valley. An ice-covered tree branch sticking out of the snow burst into flames; the hillside to the left of them quivered with power. He caught Louisa's hand and helped her catch up with Tamai.

Tamai's fingers were limp and passive and very hot. As soon as Louisa touched her wrist, though, her hand seemed to come to life, clasping Louisa's so tightly that the knuckles turned white. Louisa's face showed the pain she was feeling, but she entered the chant with a low, clear, pure voice that gave no hint of cold or fear or pain, and as her song wove into Tamai's the flickering flames disappeared and the hillside was quiescent. But McAusland could still sense something wrong around them—a troubling in the upper air, as if invisible forces battled there, buffeting them with rough gusts of warm air.

Hot air.

Very hot.

A British officer did not panic; but a British officer might usefully employ his mind in analyzing any change in a hostile environment. It seemed that Tamai's chant shielded only the minds of the little group, not their bodies, for McAusland could feel the gusts of heated air quite close to him. They were fortunate that the wise-women attacked only with magic; he wouldn't have wanted to feel bullets as close to him as these furnace-blasts of wind. They might not pose any direct danger, but he was beginning to feel uncomfortably warm. Sweat trickled down his neck and itched unbearably under his woolen collar, and his feet were slipping on the ice. . . .

When they set out, the ice had been quite hard. Now it was covered with a slick film of water, and McAusland heard cracking sounds beneath his feet. He sincerely hoped the ice would not break before they had crossed the river. It should not be dangerous at this time of year, the water would be shallow enough, but a wetting would be decidedly unpleasant, and there was something he was overlooking—something about the time of year. It was hard to concentrate. There was Tamai's chant, and Louisa's voice weaving in and over and under in a complicated harmony, and the discordant cries of—well, it was only the wind, he supposed. And that distant roaring sound, was that also the wind? Now what had he been thinking about? The time of year. Yes. Rivers flooded in the late spring and summer, when the snow melted. In the warm air. The warm air—

"Run!" McAusland shouted at the top of his voice. Skidding and slipping on the ice, he threw himself forward and caught Louisa Westbrook around the waist. The chant broke off abruptly, and the world tilted sideways, but he was moving too fast for thought or illusion to catch up with him. Louisa's slender body was a dead weight that pulled at his arm. He went down on one knee, pushing her ahead of him. Rough spots in the winter ice abraded his knee and the palm of his hand, but the ice ahead was melting even as they slid towards the shore. They came to a halt in an icy puddle over rocks, and McAusland got to his feet somehow, pulled Louisa up and ran for the bank. In a distant corner of his mind he was aware that his vertigo had vanished and that he could see the bank and the cliffside path ahead as clearly as ever. But he had no time, now, to analyze this fact. He was out of breath and there was a roaring in his ears and they had to get up—how high? When would it be safe to stop?

Two months ago he had travelled down the Kanjut River valley with Tamai and Paluk, making notes of everything he observed from the position of an unknown peak to the height of the flood debris left along the sides of the cliffs. Twenty feet. Were they that high yet? The path was murderous, nothing more than footholds going nearly vertically up the cliff, and Louisa was hampered by her skirts. McAusland stepped sideways to give her more space and his left foot slid into space and he went down on one knee. There was a scree of tiny pebbles here, dragging him down. Louisa looked back at him, saying something that he could not hear over the rushing of the waters. He looked up and saw Tamai's hard brown hand closing over Louisa's wrist, dragging her forcibly up to the next hairpin turn in the path. A puff of blue-tinted smoke swirled around their figures, momentarily veiling them from his sight. Cannon fire? He had heard no shots. And he was slipping down the steep slope. McAusland clawed the cliffside and gripped the rocks with his fingertips and found firm footing again. Westbrook and Vaughan were waiting for him. Fools. Chivalrous fools! Couldn't they guess what that rushing sound meant?

"Get on up the bloody path!" he yelled at them, furious that they should waste their lives being polite.

Westbrook planted both feet in the path, grasped McAusland's arm and hauled him back up to solid rock. Together they hurried up the path, closely followed by Colonel Vaughan. Behind them the roaring grew louder. McAusland looked over his shoulder and saw the ravine closing like a sliding box, a wall of rocks and logs and muddy water pushing forward into the ford. The water hit the far end of the ravine with a crash that threw boulders and whole trees back and forth, tossing crazily on the surface of the water not ten feet below his scuffed boots.

Colonel Vaughan squatted on the path and observed the flood with detached, scientific interest. "Impressive! Quite twenty feet above your estimate of the highest flood line, wouldn't you say, McAusland?"

"Oh, quite." Panic was a wonderful thing, and it was a damn good thing he'd been too frightened to stop at a logical point. The logical stopping-place was well under water.

"How do you suppose your friends *did* that? Must have been a damned lake somewhere upstream, what? But why wouldn't the lake have been frozen, too?"

"I . . . I really couldn't say, sir." McAusland passed the back of his hand over his forehead and leaned against the cliff, looking up at Louisa. Gordon Westbrook was holding her firmly by the arm. After that mad scramble for safety and a hairsbreadth escape from death, the man didn't appear shaken at all. And he had even taken time to haul McAusland out of his dangerous place. McAusland felt a grudging respect for the captain.

Louisa did not look quite so calm. She was white-faced and shaking and her pale blonde hair had come loose so that she was dribbling hairpins and strands of hair all over the front of her sensible blue travelling costume. And standing behind her, like a wall blocking the way to Gandhara, were three old women in long black cloaks— and nobody else. After a moment of slow, difficult thought, McAusland realized what was wrong with this picture.

"Where's Tamai?"

Louisa's eyes glinted with tears. "Oh, James, they took her away—the others did—and they say her fate is not our concern. I think I got that right. I'm almost sure I understood them. But it doesn't make any sense, does it?"

"They? The others?" McAusland felt as if his brain, as

well as the rest of him, was only moving at half speed. If that.

"There were two other women here. They told Tamai she had to go with them. Didn't you *see*?" Louisa demanded.

"I was otherwise occupied." McAusland steadied himself with one hand against the cliff face. He noticed without much concern that his palm left bloody streaks on the rock. "Trying to get away from the flood your friends caused. Want to ask them why they did that? All right, maybe they drown visitors as a hobby, but didn't they even consider the fact that they could have killed Tamai, too?"

In reply to this question all three of the old women spoke at once, as noisy as chattering magpies. McAusland was too tired to try and pick out the few words of Gandharan he might have recognized in that babble, but one word recurred so often and accompanied with such vigorous gestures that he had no doubt as to its meaning.

"*Yush*," the wisewomen kept saying. "*Yush*."

CHAPTER SEVENTEEN

When Tamai opened her eyes again, blue cedar smoke had come from nowhere, a mist between her and the Angrez, and a black-cloaked wisewoman stood on either side of her. Beyond the veil of blue smoke, Louisa was looking upwards, a puzzled frown on her face, as if she could not see Tamai at all.

"Let me go to her," Tamai said.

The older of the two wisewomen brushed silvery threads of hair back from her forehead, and Tamai recognized her. It was Sharo Daki, who had taught Tamai her first verses of the Teaching Songs. When Tamai left, a season ago, Sharo Daki had been a round-faced, happy grandmother with a young laughing face under her silver hair. Now she was bleached to bones and sun-dried skin and her eyes were too weary for laughter. "You are to come with us. The Dhi Lawan will speak with you."

"And with my companions?" But the smoke was thicker now, a blue wall between them. Even Dushmuni had disappeared; Tamai could not see the sky where the eagle soared. And she felt powerless to resist the compulsion of the wisewoman's dry fingers laid on her wrist.

"All has been arranged," Sharo Daki said. "My sisters will care for them. You are to come with us to the Earth Tower until the Council can hear you." She looked back, as though her eyes could penetrate the veil of smoke and wind to see the soldiers encamped across the river, on the high bluff above the floodwaters. "Oh, Tamai," she said sorrowfully, "how could you? *I* did not believe it—"

A warning hiss from the other wisewoman stopped her, and the three of them preceeded in silence into Gandhara. Tamai sensed the City walls and the dark arch of the opened passageway, but no details could pass through the veil of smoke that had been cast about the three of them. She strained her eyes vainly for one clear sight of the blue-tiled roofs and narrow stone streets that she had loved all her life.

It was absurd to feel so lost and lonely, simply because she had been separated from these Angrez whom she had known for so short a time. Her home was here; her friends were here; all she loved was within these blue walls. Tamai lifted her chin and set a pace that made her companions wheeze to keep a step ahead of her. She need not slink into Gandhara like a lawbreaker returning to judgement. Surely there would be time to explain, to make the Council understand her motives. The Dhi Lawan, who had sent her to find the Angrez, would not condemn her for having brought help in a different form from what had been expected.

Tamai clung to this thought until the wisewomen brought her to the door of the Earth Tower. The door swung open and she tasted the cold despairing scent of air kept too long between damp stone walls. "When am I to see the Dhi Lawan?" she demanded. "My news is urgent."

"It is not for you to ask, nor for us to answer," said the younger wisewoman. "There are many urgent matters demanding our attention." Tamai recognized her now; Mirujai, Kazhirbri's daughter, youngest of the High Council and one of those who had spoken against letting "the freak Tamai" be tested in the Disciplines.

That Mirujai should have been sent to meet her was a bad sign. That Sharo Daki did not overrule her was

worse. Tamai entered the Earth Tower without pro-
testing, though the ancient cold within made her shiver.
They barred the door afterwards, leaving her alone there.

Her prison was a single circular room, quite empty,
with smooth walls stretching up to broken places high
above her head. The Earth Tower was not really made
of clay bricks; centuries ago the hand-molded clay had
been replaced by timbers carved in the form of the
earthen bricks, and then the wood had been replaced by
stones carved to the same shapes. Long before Tamai
was born those stones had weathered on the outside to
smooth anonymous surfaces that bore no memory of the
Earth Tower's origins as the first stronghold built by Gandharans fleeing the White Huns.

From the outside the Earth Tower was not impressive:
an ancient stump of a keep in the oldest part of the
City. Gandhara-of-the-mountains had grown around the
fortress, first in earth and timbers, then in stones, and
last in blue tiles fired in Nirmali's own kiln of sun and
moonlight, and very few among the people of Gandhara
now paused to consider the history of the tower. Most
of them disliked the place, though they could not have
said why, and children in their play avoided the Earth
Tower without any command from their parents.

Tamai herself had never before been inside it. Now
she paced the circular room and traced the carved shapes
of stones imitating clay bricks, and watched the passage
of a ray of sunlight that sometimes fell through the open
spaces at the top of the tower. The recent history of
Gandhara was written in those jagged openings and in
the piles of rubble that littered the floor. The chance-
sent shells that the Rus occasionally lobbed over the City
walls could do no damage to sunforged tiles bound in
place by spells older than the first Dhi Lawan, but when
they hit common stone or wood they shattered rooftrees
and walls. One such shell had brought down a part of
the Earth Tower, leaving an irregular hole in the wall
high above Tamai's head. Dushmuni soared and stooped
through that hole and landed with a rush of wings on a

projecting ledge of stone. Tamai reached up with an unspoken cry of joy. Dushmuni had found her!

But in the same moment she recognized that her own chaotic feelings were upsetting the eagle. Dushmuni's crest feathers were raised and her eyes were bright and wild.

"I know, I know," Tamai murmured absently. She raised one arm and Dushmuni polished her beak against Tamai's sleeve for a moment before breaking off to hop along the stone ledge, uttering short choked-off screams that perfectly expressed the frustration Tamai felt. *Not-fly not-see not-move not-good!* Dushmuni screamed inside Tamai's head. *Why why why why* ...

"I suppose," Tamai said aloud, "the Council did not perfectly comprehend the difference between armed Angrezi friends and armed Rus enemies. Well, we were afraid that might happen, weren't we? But I had thought they might at least give me a chance to explain!" In her frustration she sent Dushmuni the image of the two black-cloaked wisewomen who had escorted her to this tower, cutting her off from her Angrezi companions, and the eagle screamed in rage and raised one taloned claw as if she thought she could pounce on the image like a rabbit.

"Softly, softly, my love!" Tamai tried to send calming thoughts and images, but it was difficult to overcome the turmoil of her own mind. The eagle continued to sidle up and down her stone perch, making quick darting movements with her beak, bating half off the perch and rustling her feathers and generally behaving like a bird about to go into screaming yarak—ready to hunt, needing to hunt the largest and most difficult prey she could find.

"*Dushmuni,*" Tamai said sharply as the eagle's blood-lust and the multifaced images of mountain prey coalesced into one deadly vision. "*No.* You will *not* hunt the Rus. There are too many of them, and they have jezails that can kill you where you soar in the sky!"

Dushmuni screeched once, nipped at Tamai's tunic and tore off a shred of dark brown woolen cloth. Tamai

stood perfectly still, eye to eye with the eagle, impressing
the force of her will on the hunting bird until Dushmuni
subsided into a sulky bundle of ruffled feathers. Then
Tamai withdrew into her own thoughts again. She
needed to speak with the Dhi Lawan. Why were they
keeping her waiting like this?

The rapid crackle of musket fire came to her ears,
muffled by distance and by walls of thick stone. So. The
Rus were very close, now—it sounded as if they were
actually attacking the City walls. There would indeed by
other matters demanding the Council's attention; she
could hardly expect a hearing while the wisewomen of
Gandhara were engaged in battle. If only she could *see*
what was happening! Should she send Dushmuni? No,
in her present mood the eagle would never be able to
restrain herself to the role of a mere observer.

If Louisa had been there, she might have risked going
into the overworld to learn what she could of the battle.
But alone—Tamai shook her head. She had infinitely
more power than when she had left Gandhara, but without Louisa to keep her linked to this world, she stood in
as much danger as ever of losing herself in the overworld.
Or of pulling the stones of the tower down upon her
own head—or shaking the walls of the City loose, she
thought, considering the wider field of danger. No, for
Gandhara's sake as well as her own, she dared not try to
use her power. Had the wisewomen trusted to that, when
they locked her in here? Or had it simply not occurred
to them that Tamai the freak, the barren, might be able
to call enough power to shake this tower and, for all she
knew, the foundations of Gandhara?

Unanswerable questions, and worse to think on than
what was going on outside. Tamai listened intently, trying
to follow the battle from the few muffled sounds she
heard. The shots stuttered out in brief rapid bursts, echoing off the stones of the City so that she could no longer
guess which side was which. Then there were shouts,
splintering wood, cries of dismay in the Rus tongue, a
ragged cheer in Gandharan—she pictured the scene to

herself and thought that a scaling ladder must have been thrown down just then. How had the Rus come so close as to attempt scaling the walls? *What* was the Council doing to let them so near? Fists clenched, Tamai alternately paced and squatted on the stone floor, waiting out an endless afternoon. She could have been at the walls, helping to defend the City; she could have been guiding four hundred British soldiers with rifles of their own; but no—the Council in their great wisdom and fear of outlanders had thrown her in here to wait their pleasure! She was being treated as a traitor, when all she had ever wanted was to be a tool in the defense of her City!

Tamai pounded one clenched fist against her knee, taut with frustration, until a brief, disorienting image from Dushmuni stopped her. She saw herself as she appeared to the eagle, black hair springing loose from her braid, thin shoulders tense, eyes bright and angry. Beside that picture Dushmuni sent a series of brief flashes of prey hiding or scurrying for cover—a rabbit diving down a hole, a deer running across open fields for the woods.

Tamai laughed unwillingly. "Yes. All *right*! You've made your point—I am in yarak, too. And they won't let me hunt! What shall we do, Dushmuni?"

The eagle cocked her head as if listening to something far away. Tamai listened, too. She heard no more gunfire. And the golden line of sunlight on the wall opposite the broken place had faded to a pale lavender light.

"Night," she murmured to Dushmuni. "The battle is over—and the Rus have not broken through, I think, or we would be hearing other sounds." There were footsteps in the street, men speaking in low weary tones, the moaning of a wounded man being carried to his home—now that she was listening again, Tamai could make out the heavy double steps of men keeping time as they carried a heavy burden down the steep street. Somewhere in the distance, a woman's voice rose in a keening chant for one of the day's dead. Closer by, the voices of young girls took up one of the Teaching Songs, weaving melody and harmony together in a braided strand of sound that lifted up the spirit of the City.

Tamai began to sing the second verse with them, but the muscles of her throat clenched and she could not get the words out. When she tried to force her voice out, a slashing pain doubled her up and she fell forward on hands and knees, retching on an empty stomach.

She could not sing the Teaching Songs. The cold of the earthen floor seeped up through her legs, chilling her body as she considered the implications. Some dark magic built into the shape of this tower kept her from using any power. She felt sure that an attempt at any of the chants of the Disciplines would bring on worse punishment than she had just experienced; even thinking about it made her feel nauseated. She could just barely keep the thought on the edge of her mind while she concentrated consciously on other things, the dimming light against the wall, the black sheen of Dushmuni's feathers, the thread of melody against melody outside . . . ah. She could not sing with them, but she could still listen, and the song of Star's Daughters was a healing one that lightened the heart. Tamai gave herself to the music and let it heal her as it would. She was still absorbed in the song, floating on the high counterpoint of Star's Seventh, when the door of the tower swung inward and a pine-knot torch blazed up with yellow light, casting long shadows on the stone walls. Behind the torch, Tamai glimpsed a thin, bruised face with a blood-clotted bandage over the forehead.

"Mirjan! How good to see you!" For a long betraying moment Tamai had not recognized him; now she was overly warm in her greetings for fear he would guess what had kept her silent. He looked worn and tired, like a man who had been sick a long time. Like Sharo Daki, he had aged years in the course of a single summer's war.

"They sent me to bring you to Council," he said heavily, as though he had not quite heard her.

"It's about time! No—" Tamai caught herself. "I am sorry. I did not mean to criticize the Council."

"They have had," Mirjan said, "a few other matters to concern themselves with today."

And I could have helped, if they had let me. But Tamai did not speak the thought aloud. It was not Mirjan's fault that the wisewomen of Council were overly suspicious of all foreigners, preferring isolation to the possibility of help that did not come from a Gandharan. Hadn't she felt that way once? Hadn't she thought herself very noble to leave Gandhara and go among outlanders? As if it were some great sacrifice she was making?

Mirjan glanced curiously at her as they stepped forth from the Earth Tower.

"You've changed," he said.

So have you. "How?"

"Quieter. I was expecting you to jump on me with some sarcastic comments about the idiocy of Council for not trusting you completely just because you bring another army to sit on our doorstep."

Mirjan's speech underscored how her action must seem to the Council. And they had not even heard about her treaty yet—or had they?

"Have they spoken to the Angrez *colonel*?"

He shook his head. "Who has time to speak with foreigners? We have enough trouble with this Rus tribe, without having the Angrez on our walls as well." He shook his head again. "How did they force you to bring them here, Tamai? Was it very bad?"

Tamai tried to swallow. Her throat seemed suddenly very dry. "It's not like that, Mirjan. They have come to help us against the Rus."

"Gandhara stands alone." Mirjan sounded as closed and sure of himself as she had felt, two seasons ago, before she knew what the Rus were—or the Angrez.

"I do not think that we can do so any longer," she said, "but I shall save my voice for speaking before the Council. Let us talk of other things. How has the autumn gone?"

It was a foolish question; she could read the answer in the empty streets, scarred from the random impact of shells, and the empty houses on either side. She could read it in the sight of the few children who scurried from alley to passageway to catch sight of her on her way to the Council Hall: children too pale and too thin, children who had been cooped up within walls with not quite enough to eat and with nowhere to run and play.

Mirjan raised the torch slightly and let her look around, then shrugged. "As you see. They keep us penned close, these Rus, and they have killed a few of us. But now that we are within the City walls, the wise-women bring down storms on them. Snow and ice will drive them home soon enough."

The air around them was warm as on any summer afternoon. Tamai looked at Mirjan, her eyebrows raised, and he shrugged again. "The Rus are using fire-demons," he said. "Today they changed the weather and flooded the valley. If they stay in demon-form, I suppose the Council will have to go into the overworld to fight them, but today we have been too busy with the Rus soldiers."

"You sound very confident," Tamai said. She did not want to frighten Mirjan; but she had met a demon in the overworld, and she did not feel as certain as he did that the wisewomen of Gandhara would be able to defeat them.

Mirjan gave her a tired smile. "You have not seen how well we've been doing. Plain Gandharan men and women have learned to fight the demons when they take on bodies in this world; I don't think our wisewomen will do less in the overworld."

Tamai shivered in the unseasonably warm air, remembering rotting flesh, soft boneless limbs and dead eyes that saw her all too clearly.

"How do you fight them in this world?"

"I was afraid at first," Mirjan confessed. "And they took some of us while we were trying different things. But Kazhirbri is a specialist in Bod magic, and she had some good ideas. The old stories guided us. The Teaching Songs are right—when they take on flesh, the demons are very stupid. Any bright bit of color or new song distracts them. Then, if you hit them with a stream of running water—though that's difficult to arrange—or if you can throw bands of *leluril* about them, they make a bright fountain of sparks, and—" Mirjan laughed. His laughter had a grating, awkward sound to it, as though he had almost forgotten how. "No more demon!"

For some reason, Mirjan's description of demon fighting reminded Tamai of her Angrez friends. The army that marched into the mountains carried rolls and rolls of *leluril* wire—they called it *copper*—and somehow they sent voices back to Peshawar along that wire. McAusland had tried to explain to her how all this was done, by some Angrez *machine* called *electricity*, but Tamai never could follow his explanations. But she remembered the bright shower of sparks he had made during one demonstration of this machine.

Tamai shook her head impatiently. Angrez *machines*, mountain demons, *leluril*, sparks—what difference did all this make, even if she could puzzle it out? And Mirjan was still talking, being very cheerful in that tired strained voice as he described the anger of the Rus general's Khitai adviser when he saw his demons discorporating into sparks.

He glanced sidewise at Tamai. "But I suppose this is nothing to you, who've seen all these fine things in the outlands. Your Angrez masters doubtless have many tools for fighting demons."

"They are—not—my masters," Tamai said between her teeth, "and I am impressed, Mirjan. I saw only one demon when I was in the outlands, and it terrified me. Although," she added, to be perfectly honest, "the Angrez do have many servants that *resemble* demons, until one learns better. They call them *machines*."

"Hmm. Well. I suppose different people have different names for demons," Mirjan said gravely.

"It's not—" Tamai began, and then stopped, frustrated. She had not realized until now how greatly her sojourn in the outlands had changed her. She could remember arguing just like this with Paluk, when she had the evidence of the Angrez *machines* before her. And now she was a prisoner before the Council, and Paluk—what had happened to Paluk, and how could they ever forgive her for leaving him in that foreign land? Silly, useless tears stung Tamai's eyes, and her vision blurred just as they arrived at the Council Hall. The pale shadowless light of magic lit the long Hall, and the red and turquoise carpet blurred through her tears into a field of flowers.

"Go on," Mirjan urged. "This is not a place for me. You will have to go in alone, Tamai, and it will—it may look better for you if you are not forced to enter."

CHAPTER EIGHTEEN

Once, Tamai would have marched into the Council Hall, fists clenched, to demand an accounting of the wisewomen for having locked her up just when they stood in most need of the help she brought. Now she entered with head bent, arms crossed over her breast, and sank to a kneeling position in the center of the flowered carpet. While she had thought herself to be teaching Louisa Westbrook the Disciplines, the Angrezi woman had been teaching Tamai something too—such as the value of appearing quiet and meek and biddable while you went about getting your own way. If such methods could persuade the men's Council of the Angrez to let Louisa accompany an army of men, perhaps they could also persuade the women's Council of Gandhara to let that army defend their walls.

At any rate, said the mocking ghost of her younger self, *it is worth a try*.

For a small eternity she heard nothing but the subdued rustle of the wisewomen's black cloaks and the crackle of flames. At last a familiar voice spoke. "Tamai, formerly of Gandhara, do you submit yourself to the Truthspeaker?"

Formerly of Gandhara! Tamai's head came up with a snap and she stared unbelieving at the woman who sat beneath the tree of Council. Between them a fire of cedar bark glowed in a bowl of polished *leluril*. The ruddy curve of the metal reflected and magnified the small dancing flames. A thin haze of blue smoke distorted the features of the woman who had taken the Dhi Lawan's seat, but Tamai saw her all too clearly through the smoke.

"What are you doing in that place, Kazhirbri?" she demanded. "Where is the Dhi Lawan?"

"Do you submit yourself to the Truthspeaker? You should consent, child," Kazhirbri advised her. "The spell of Truthspeaking is required in a case for the High Council, and I am told that it can be painful for those who do not submit to it willingly."

"The High Council," Tamai said slowly. That explained, perhaps, why the room felt so empty. Only half a dozen wisewomen sat around her. "Does that mean—are you ready to discuss my treaty with the Angrez?" But they had called her "formerly of Gandhara." That must have been a mistake. Perhaps they thought she had taken service with the Angrez.

"We are here," said Kazhirbri, "to let you speak for yourself before you are exiled."

"You cannot exile me!" Tamai leapt to her feet, fists clenched. "You have not the power! I demand to be heard before the Dhi Lawan! *She* sent me to the Angrez; let her hear me now!"

There was a disbelieving murmur from one of the cloaked wisewomen. "*Did* she?"

"It is possible," murmured another one. "Halvidai was always too interested in outland ways, if you ask me. Remember, when she was still quite junior in Council, she spoke against exiling Bilizhe?"

Tamai's heart felt cold within her. Halvidai had been the name-in-life of the Dhi Lawan, never to be used once she became Daughter of Light and head of the Council. And they spoke of her now in the past tense. She stared at Kazhirbri.

"She who was Dhi Lawan cannot speak for you now,"

Kazhirbri told Tamai. "She was shot by one of your outlanders—"

"By the *Angrez*?" This was a nightmare. Tamai could
not believe that McAusland or Colonel Vaughan would
have been mad enough to shoot at the people they had
come to save, no matter what had gone on at the boundaries. Gordon Westbrook, though—

"Angrez, Rus, what difference does it make?" Kazhirbri snapped. "I am now the Dhi Lawan."

*You, the Daughter of Light? You, who cannot even
lightweave?* Tamai did not speak her instinctive denial
aloud, and in her thoughts she blessed Louisa Westbrook
who had taught her the value of keeping silence. If the
Council had allowed someone as limited as Kazhirbri to
assume the cloak of the Dhi Lawan, then something had
gone badly wrong in Gandhara.

But at least it seemed that Kazhirbri had misled her;
it wasn't one of the Angrez who had killed the previous
Dhi Lawan. Tamai relaxed slightly. Perhaps it was not so
bad as she had thought for a moment. If the Angrez had
fired on Gandharans there would be no hope of a treaty.
But she still had to deal with this woman who had
usurped the Dhi Lawan's position, who had always hated
her, who considered all outlanders as a single enemy.

Maybe, she thought, it was *worse* than she had
thought. More complicated, anyway.

"I ask you now for the last time, Tamai, formerly of
Gandhara," Kazhirbri repeated slowly, "do you submit
yourself to the Discipline of Truthspeaking?"

Tamai sank slowly back to her knees, crossed her
hands over her breast and bowed her head in assent. At
least, if she spoke under the power of that Discipline,
the Council would have to believe her—and then, surely,
they would understand why she had acted as she did.

But understanding did not mean agreement. They
could still repudiate the treaty and exile her. And while
the voices of the wisewomen around her picked up the
clear notes of the Truthspeaking chant, holding each one
until it stretched out in a vibrating eternity of pure

sound, Tamai reflected that Louisa Westbrook's techniques of silence and agreement did not, after all, guarantee that the Angrez woman would always get her own way. Angrez law still made her the property of her husband.

And if Louisa could not break free from that law, then Gandharan law would probably exile Tamai, no matter how well she spoke or how many Council members she persuaded.

As the last low notes of the chant died away, Tamai lifted her head again. She could feel the room charged with the power of the Discipline; it was like living light in the walls and in the roof and in the growing tree in the center, like light in her throat and on her tongue. No word that was not true could be spoken in Council while the power of the chant lasted. She understood why Kazhirbri had counseled her to consent; the light that filled her would have felt like fire if she had fought against the strong flowing current of the Discipline.

She was ready to speak now, to explain why she had felt that only a treaty with the Angrez could save Gandhara, to explain how the terms of that treaty could be fulfilled without breaking with Gandharan tradition. But Kazhirbri forestalled her.

"You have been accused of treason against Gandhara."

"Who accuses me?" Tamai demanded.

Kazhirbri's eyes evaded hers. "Is it important? You are condemned by your own actions. But since you insist, you shall see the man."

She knew then what she had been trying not to know, ever since she was arrested on the cliff. They had been waiting for her; they had been warned that she was bringing soldiers, outlanders; they had already judged her a traitor. Tamai did not want to look as Paluk entered the Council Hall.

He stood straighter than he had in Peshawar, and the sleepy haze that had blurred his features was gone now, and he looked proud and desperately unhappy.

"You were more than a brother to me," she said qui-

etly. "Was this what it took to make you find your man-
hood, Paluk? You could not give up the drug when I
begged for your help, but you could give it up to betray
me?"

Paluk shook his head. There were tears in his eyes; he
let them fall unashamed. "In Peshawar," he said, "I forgot who I was for a time, but now I have remembered.
I have broken free of my *ganghaz* dreams, Tamai. You
are still dreaming, and you have done worse than I—you
have brought your poison back to Gandhara."

"I was sent to find help, and I have brought it." *And
what have you done for Gandhara, that you presume to
judge me?* The words were as loud in her head as if she
had spoken them aloud; and Paluk winced as though he
could hear her thought.

"You have brought armed men to conquer us—you
have guided them to our gates, you have thrown away
our greatest protection. If Gandhara falls to outlanders,
does it matter what color uniforms they wear?"

"The Rus found us without my help," Tamai pointed
out, "and so would the Angrez have done, sooner or
later. By guiding them now, I have bought their aid—
for they *have* come to help," Tamai insisted, "not to
conquer. We have a treaty—if the Council will recognize
it—" But the chance of that now seemed very slim.

"We went south for rifles, not for an army! You were
going to help the men of Gandhara defend our own City.
Are we slaves of the Kanjutis, to cower behind walls
while the other men fight to see who shall hold
Gandhara?"

Tamai began to understand. "Paluk," she said quietly,
"you wanted to do a great thing for Gandhara. So did I.
But this matter is too great to be ended by a few of us
sniping at the Rus with bought rifles. Don't you see that?
The best thing any of us can do for Gandhara, now, is
to find a way in which we can live at peace between
these two great empires—for we cannot live at war with
them, Paluk; I know that."

"You know nothing!" Paluk almost spat at her. "There

are worse drugs than *ganghaz* in Peshawar, and you have
taken them. You are drunk on the wealth and power of
the Angrez; they have bought you with their *machines*."
He reached out one hand to Tamai, across the expanse
of red and turquoise flowers that separated them, and
she could have wept at the look in his eyes. Not hatred.
That would have been easier to bear. He didn't hate her.
He thought she was a traitor to Gandhara, but he was
still her friend and her loving cousin. "Tamai," Paluk said
softly, "I know you hate me now because you are still
dreaming of the Angrez life, but when you wake up and
remember who you are you will be glad that I stopped
you. All I want is for you to come back to us, Tamai. I
want everything to be as it was."

He spoke truth, or what he believed to be truth; otherwise the Discipline would have closed his throat around
the words. And what he believed was damning to her.
Tamai's shoulders slumped and she stared at the pattern
in the carpet. She had lost Paluk. She was about to lose
Gandhara. What was there left to fight for?

"My nephew speaks truth," Kazhirbri announced. She
looked sorry for Tamai, but there was no mercy in her
words. "You left Gandhara secretly; you returned only to
lead foreign soldiers here. When your outlanders encountered the Veil, did you not know that the wisewomen of
Gandhara meant to keep them out?"

"I did," Tamai conceded. "But—"

"Did you not use your own power—such as it is—to
shield the outlander leaders from the Veil so that they
might cross over into Gandhara?"

Even now, Tamai thought, Kazhirbri could not refrain
from mocking her for her aberrant power, for the lack
of control that was her grief rather than her fault. She
felt heat building within her, even though she had said
nothing to violate the Discipline of Truthspeaking.
Hadn't Kazhirbri understood what she had tried to tell
Paluk—that guiding the Angrez to Gandhara was the
price of their help? "Yes, I did as you say, but only
because—"

"No more needs to be said." Kazhirbri sat back, veiled by the drifts of blue cedar smoke. "The Discipline of Truthspeaking rules within these walls. Paluk has spoken truth; you have spoken truth; by both voices you are condemned. I name you—"

"No!" Tamai cried. "You have heard your truth and Paluk's, but not mine. You must know what I intended."

"I think," Kazhirbri said, not unkindly, "we know enough, Tamai. Do not make this more painful than it must be."

There was a rustle of black robes around the Hall.

"Perhaps we should hear the child," one woman murmured.

"She has hardly spoken."

"What can she speak but Truth?"

Before Kazhirbri could interrupt again, Tamai began her story in a torrent of unplanned words, pouring out all she had learned or guessed since she met Lieutenant McAusland in a Hunza village. She reminded the wise-women of her Angrez *rifle*, with its fine workmanship and uncanny accuracy; and then she told·them that the Angrez had many more of these things than she could count, made for them in places called *factories*, and that they had as many red-coated soldiers as they had rifles—thousands and tens of thousands of men. She told them about Peshawar, a city of square white houses and red-walled forts and ancient mosques, and she explained that this one city contained more people than all the valleys of Hunza and Nagar and Chitral—and all these people under the rule of the Angrez—and then she told them what Lieutenant McAusland had told her, that Peshawar was but one city of many under the Angrez in India, and that India was but one country of many in the Angrez empire.

"Marvelous! And you have seen all these things with your own eyes, child?" Kazhirbri's dry, ironic voice took all the strength from Tamai's telling, made her into a child piling wonders upon exaggerated wonders to impress the grownups.

"Some things I have seen. Some I have been told."

"And, of course, these Angrez always speak truth—even without the Discipline to guard them!"

A subdued laugh echoed Kazhirbri's words. Tamai spoke without thinking. "And *all* of this have I seen in the overworld, where Nirmali showed me the power of the Angrez and Rus empires, that I might return to warn Gandhara!"

There was a silence more ominous than the previous laughter, broken finally by Kazhirbri's ironic voice.

"A-maz-ing," she drawled, and her lips twitched just slightly at the corners. "The girl who could not master the first and simplest of the Disciplines returns to Gandhara as the personal favorite of Nirmali the Maker, having seen empires holding tens of thousands of cities, and each city filled with wealth unimaginable. What a charming story!"

"It is true!" Tamai cried. "I speak under the Discipline; how can you accuse me of lying?"

"I am sure that by now you believe your own dreams," Kazhirbri said. "But it is time to awaken."

"Let me show you, then!" Tamai challenged. "Come into the overworld with me, if you dare, and see the worlds of the Angrez and the Rus for yourself!"

"Child, you betray your ignorance of the Disciplines. Even in the overworld one cannot wander more than a few leagues from the body."

"*I can,*" Tamai said, desperately, without hope of being believed.

"You can do nothing!" Kazhirbri snapped. "You failed the first test—you have never passed through Nirmali's waters—you are useless as a man, and like a man, you imagine fantastic deeds to make up for your helplessness."

"Oh, no," Tamai said. "I have not imagined *this.*" She stretched out her hands and did the only thing she could think of to compel belief. Fire sprang to each fingertip, blue and green and golden—

And the rooftree of the Council Hall shook, and the walls groaned as if they were about to fall. The flames sputtered to nothingness while a wave of nausea wrenched her stomach and the room seemed to spin around her. She fell to one side and heard Kazhirbri speaking words of power that formed an invisible wall about her in the air. When she could kneel upright again she understood Kazhirbri's commands.

"You will not attempt to use the Disciplines against us," Kazhirbri was saying, softly but with an undertone that shaped the words into lines of force binding her down. She glanced up at the assembled wisewomen. "Tamai's problem has not been solved; if anything, from what Paluk tells me, it has grown worse. When she attempts to use her power, she cannot control the results. We cannot risk fires in the city, still less the destruction of our walls from within."

There was a murmur of assent. The momentary trembling of the Council Hall had impressed them all with the need to control Tamai, who was no wisewoman and would never be one.

"I have made long study of the spells binding the walls of the Earth Tower," Kazhirbri informed Tamai. "It was raised by our founders as a place of refuge against the *yush* who infested the mountains when they came, and in the shaping of the tower they bound spells that prevent any power from being used. I can place those same restrictions on you here, as you have seen, or I can accept your word that you will not attempt again to use the power."

Tamai nodded. It was all she could do; the light that had filled her with the Discipline of Truthspeaking was now replaced by a sullen, leaden silence that pressed down upon her and choked her.

"Very well." Kazhirbri's wrinkled fingers traced brief patterns in the air, untying the bindings of the spell, and Tamai felt the muscles of her throat loosen. "On pain of immediate and perpetual exile, you are bound by your word not to use any power of the Disciplines."

"During this hearing," Tamai prompted, and Kazhirbri glared at her.

"Do not presume! The binding stands as I have spoken it."

Tamai nodded. What else could she do? But the choice was like a new weight upon her heart. Kazhirbri meant to persuade the Council that this ban should be absolute—not just for the hearing, but for all time. Tamai had been manipulated into that brief use of her own power just to give Kazhirbri that excuse. Now, unless the Council reversed the ban, Tamai would be forced to choose between her citizenship and the use of her power. Eventually, Tamai knew, she would choose exile, even if the Council did not impose it on her today.

But there was still a treaty to be fought for, even if Tamai would not stay in Gandhara to enjoy the results of that treaty. And she still had a chance to convince the Council of the importance of the treaty, even if she could not show them directly what she had seen in the overworld.

"Paluk?" Tamai turned to him. "Never mind what you think of *me*, Paluk. Tell the Council what you have seen of the Angrezi Empire."

"I saw one city," Paluk said cautiously. "The Angrez claimed that they had many such cities, but I do not know whether they spoke truth."

Kazhirbri nodded. "They are strong, no doubt. But they are not invincible."

"I never said they were." Tamai felt the weight of the Council's disbelief pressing her down into the soft rich pile of the flowered carpet. "But they are many times stronger than Gandhara, and so are these Rus. And both empires have *machines* with which they can find us despite the veil. I do not believe that Gandhara can stand alone against both powers. In return for a few concessions, the Angrez will be our friends—"

"A few concessions," Kazhirbri mocked. "Yes, Paluk has told us of these promises you made. We are to allow foreign soldiers within the City—"

"Only a few, to guard the *British Resident*," Tamai protested, and knew even as the words left her mouth that she had been manipulated again into saying what Kazhirbri wanted her to say.

"Ah, yes. This *British Resident* of whom you speak. Paluk has warned us of this. You wish an outlander to rule the City, to override the will of the Council and of the Dhi Lawan."

"No." Tamai glared at Paluk. "You have been wrongly informed. The Angrez wish only to have a voice in Council, not to rule us. And I do think," she said, knowing that this must anger the very people she wanted to convince, but not knowing how else to state her case, "I think that we need such an adviser, Dhi Lawan, for we have been hidden in the mountains too long, and we do not know enough of the world. If we had understood who and what the Rus were, for instance, when they first came upon us—if we had then had a treaty of help and friendship with the Angrez—how many of our people might have been saved!"

"You are not called here to attack the Council's management of the war," said Kazhirbri, "but to defend yourself from charges of treason—which you have not done. Rather you have confessed to everything of which you are accused—and more—you admit that you promised the Angrez what was not in your power to give, that one of them should join our Council!"

Tamai bowed her head. "I hoped that the Council would approve the suggestion. The treaty states that the *British Resident* shall be chosen by Gandhara, and not by the Angrez themselves; and there is one who might be acceptable—"

Kazhirbri snorted. "In a nation ruled by men, who could be acceptable to us? No *man* will ever join the Council of wisewomen!"

"No." Tamai felt the beginnings of hope leaping within her. For once she had played Kazhirbri's game better than the Dhi Lawan herself, manipulating the other woman into giving her the opening she wanted. "I would not propose a man for the position. There is a woman with the Angrez."

She heard the rustling of black cloaks behind her, but dared not turn to guess what effect her proposal was having.

"A woman trained in the Disciplines," she added, "as worthy as any Gandharan to join the Council of wise-women. Will you refuse such a one? She *is* a wisewoman; she will love and defend Gandhara as the home of her power. But she is also an Angrez, and she will advise us as we join the world outside the mountains." Now Tamai could bear it no longer, kneeling and speaking only to Kazhirbri, whose closed face reflected a mind locked against any ideas coming from such a source. She stood and turned to face the women of the High Council, and for a moment the brilliance of their inner cloaks struck her into awed silence. Here in Council the wisewomen sat with their cloaks folded back, openly displaying the wealth of embroidered and woven bands which were their history. Each cloak was all but solid with color: interlocked vines of green and blue for the Veil, streaks of deep pure red for Songspeakers, wreathing spirals of burnished *leluril* for demon binders, glimmering stars of moonlight for lightweavers. Individually worked images tumbled among the bands, commemorating episodes of great power in each wisewoman's life: Nirmali smiled from a cloak of stars, Dizane grew from a field of ripe grain, strands of water spun into thread made a waterfall for some victory over drought in years long past.

How dared she argue against these women, as far beyond her in the power as she was beyond an Angrez boy-child? But they *were* women, and above the glory of their opened cloaks Tamai saw faces she had known all her life, some of them belonging to women she had loved well. She named them over in her mind as she spoke: Mirujai daughter of Kazhirbri, blind Akhanai, Jakunei the mother of Sunik, Sharo Daki who had given Tamai her first Teaching Songs, and all the others who now sat in judgement upon her. "Listen to me, sisters; hear my words. There is a world beyond the mountains, and it is coming to us. The *guns* of the Rus are only the beginning. Too long we have been hidden away in these mountains, too long we have known only Gandhara. Will we hide like frightened children, will we sing songs to keep the sun from rising, or will we join our sisters beyond the mountains and greet the new world like brave women of Gandhara?"

"Silence! Respect the Council!" Kazhirbri commanded.

"No."

It was Jakunei who contradicted the Dhi Lawan. There were tears in her eyes. "My daughter Sunik was the first to die before the Rus. The children of my daughter cry in my house for their mother. You do not speak alone, Dhi Lawan; it is time for you to hear the will of your High Council. I say, I who have buried a daughter in this war, that we should call the Angrezi woman before us. If she can help us stop this war, I am not too proud to take her hand."

"An outlander woman." Kazhirbri's voice was thick with scorn. "Taught by Tamai, who could not herself master the Disciplines—what could *she* teach anyone?"

"Let us judge that for ourselves." Sharo Daki entered the debate. "Tamai may not have mastered her own power, but *I* gave her the words of the Teaching Songs, and if she knows them now as perfectly as she did in her girlhood, she may have taught this woman well enough."

"And if there are errors in her teaching, can we not correct them?" asked Akhanai, the oldest of all the High Council, who saw the world only through the power that brought vague senses through her milk-white blind eyes. "The issue is not whether Tamai has trained this woman perfectly in all the Disciplines, but whether she *can* be trained. Our law is that only those who can master the Disciplines may join the Council. I do not recall," she said with a sweet smile directed somewhere in Kazhirbri's direction, "that we have any law specifically prohibiting an outlander woman from joining us. In fact, the law does not rule out an outlander *man*, if he had the power. What will you do, Kazhirbri, if we find that the Angrezi have wisemen as well as wisewomen?"

"Ridiculous—" Kazhirbri began, but this time she was interrupted by the swinging of the brass-bound doors at the end of the hall. A young woman hurried into the Hall, her black cloak swinging open around her to reveal a novice's single thin band of turquoise embroidery. Behind her, the opened doors framed an arch of darkness set with stars.

"Forgive this interruption, gracious ones," she apologized as she knelt at the very edge of the thick carpet. "There is a message from the outlanders which must be answered tonight."

"Which outlanders? Rus or Angrez?" called Akhanai, turning her blind head towards the kneeling novice.

"Both. The Rus say that they used today's battle, while our wisewomen were busy defending the walls, to move their *guns* up to the edge of the glacier above the City. And the Angrez say that if we do not sign a treaty with them tonight, the Rus will destroy the City at first light."

The women of Council drew in their breath silently. "Nirmali aid us!" Jakunei whispered under her breath.

Kazhirbri's dark eyes flashed with malicious triumph. "So. It seems they work together now, Rus and Angrez. These are the people you wish us to take for friends, Tamai?"

"There is a mistake," Tamai said. She felt as blind as Akhanai, feeling her way through treacherous passages. "There must be a mistake. Who brought this message? Who translated it?"

Kazhirbri shook her head. "We do not have time to deal with you now, Tamai. We must spend this night finding a way to heal the evil you have brought into the City." She raised one hand and called out a sharp command that echoed through the Hall.

"At least let Louisa Westbrook come before you," Tamai begged as two young men came through the opened doors to escort her back to the Earth Tower. "Let her speak the Angrez message to Council in her own words." Surely Louisa would be able to correct whatever terrible mistake had been made. She could not believe the Angrez would ally with the Rus against her people.

The wisewomen who had spoken in Tamai's behalf were silent now, averting their faces as she was led past them. Only Sharo Daki put out her hand to delay Tamai for a moment. "Do not despair," she said. "The Council can do no more now. Tonight we will call Nirmali down to our aid."

"Not I," said Tamai. "I have been forbidden." She might as well be exiled already. Tonight the wisewomen would dance to Nirmali, and she would be locked in the Earth Tower, forbidden to join hands with them.

"Tonight you will not dance with us," Sharo Daki conceded. "But remember this: all who should call Nirmali will be with us, else we will fail."

Tamai wondered, as she was led under the star-lit sky back to her prison, which interpretation of Sharo Daki's statement was meant to comfort her: that she had no right to dance for Gandhara now, or that without her the sacred dance must fail.

CHAPTER NINETEEN

Ever since the departure of Colonel Vaughan's flying column, Brigadier-General Kinloch had been chafing at the slow pace of the main army. When he received a heliograph message announcing that the column was actually within view of Gandhara, his impatience overrode all constraints. He had never imagined that Vaughan would reach Gandhara while he and his men were still methodically building a road through the Kanjut River gorge. Letting the man get a day or two ahead of the main force was one thing, hardly more significant than sending out an advanced patrol to clear the way ahead of snipers; that was what Kinloch had envisioned when Vaughan talked him into this plan. Let the mad colonel and his suicidal men clear the way, then Kinloch would march in at the head of the relieving forces. He would still be the acknowledged leader of the expedition.

But at the present pace, based on the reports that had been sent back by heliograph, it would take the army *weeks* to reach Gandhara. When the story reached the Indian press, the damned journalists wouldn't be writing about Kinloch's relief of Gandhara; they'd be falling over one another to tell the story of Vaughan's lightning march and the weeks during which his gallant little force defended Gandhara against the Russian siege.

It was intolerable. "Transport! Supply! Sappers! Bridges!" Shouted out in Kinloch's hoarse Scottish brogue, the words sounded like curses—which, his aide-de-camp considered fatalistically, they might as well have been. Certainly the orders that followed were likely to be the death of them all.

"We've been mollycoddling this army, letting the men take their ease while the damned Sappers build a high road through the mountains for them. Who's in charge of this force—me or that damned Southron, Hammond?" The young officer who had replaced Lieutenant McAusland as head of the engineering corps had the misfortune to be English, which invalidated anything he had to say in Kinloch's opinion. "What are we, an army of invasion or a group of ladies on tour? We're here to invade the country—let's bloody well get on with it! No more road building. We'll take the paths the bloody natives use. If they can get their caravans through the mountains we can take our soldiers the same way," General Kinloch decreed, and neither Lieutenant Hammond nor anybody else attached to the Gandhara Relief Force had the strength of spine to argue with him.

"Och, well, he'll see the error of his ways soon enough," opined the general's aide-de-camp when an expostulating Lieutenant Hammond dragged him out to view the terrain immediately ahead. The valley at this point narrowed until the river was shut in between nearly perpendicular cliffs. A small group like Vaughan's could, Lieutenant Hammond supposed, have managed to work through the gorge by crossing and re-crossing the icy river to take advantage of the narrow banks that appeared first on one side and then on the other. For the army that followed, such a course was manifestly impossible; the banks were already broken down in several places where Vaughan's column had marched, and the first company to follow them would destroy what was left of the riverside path, leaving no footing at all for the men and animals that came after.

"What were you proposing to do at this point?" the general's aide-de-camp asked Hammond.

"The same as McAusland did at the last such gorge," the young Englishman told him. "Unload the mules, set the men to work making a road round the base of the cliff by throwing rocks into the river until we get to a decent broad stretch of path again. Carry the loads over that causeway, lead the mules, take the screw-guns apart and have a party of four carry each piece, then repack and camp on the far side of the gorge."

"Take days. The general'll never stand for it," the aide-de-camp said. "He thinks—"

"I know," Lieutenant Hammond interrupted. "He says we can take the path the natives use. Have a look."

He pointed upward. The aide-de-camp followed his gesture, blanched, and chewed his mustache. Halfway up the cliff, a narrow shelving ledge offered just enough room for a string of men in single file.

"We'll *never* get the Gatling gun across yon!" he burst out when he had recovered his breath.

"*I* know. Kinloch's mad," said Lieutenant Hammond. "Will you tell him, or shall I?"

"It ought," said the aide-de-camp, "it ought to be left to somebody more senior than us, old man. Nobody less than a colonel ought to be charged with telling a briga-dier-general he's off his nut."

But as the only colonel who had accompanied the relief force was at present many miles north of the army, about to descend into the valley of the Tears of Lunang, there was no one with the rank and force of character required to argue Kinloch out of his obsession.

By noon, about the time that Vaughan's flying column was stumbling blind and dizzy over the frozen river, the leading men of the Gandharan Relief Force were feeling equally dizzy at the top of the path pointed out by Lieu-tenant Hammond. One by one, feeling their way with outstretched hands, the soldiers inched along the side of the cliff and cursed or prayed according to their inclina-tions. The baggage and ammunition mules did not do so well. General Kinloch had refused to take the time to unload the mules and redistribute their loads among the men. Terrified, braying, unbalanced by their loads, the mules stuck out their legs stiffly at the worst possible moments, staled on the narrow path and delayed the passage of the rest of the army. With depressing regularity one of the animals would lose its footing and go screaming down the face of the precipice, clattering against the rocks and braying in terror until the fall brought a merciful end to its sufferings.

In mid-afternoon one wheel of the Gatling gun went over a crumbling bit of shale that gave beneath the weight of the heavy machinery. The gun fell into the gorge, dragging two mules and a man to their deaths with it, and General Kinloch at last gave up his obsessive drive to the front. If his screw-guns went the way of the Gatling, he would arrive at Gandhara with no artillery at all with which to confront the enemy. That could be even more embarrassing than waiting in the rear while Vaughan rescued the City. He gave the order to withdraw, issued a sharp reprimand to Lieutenant Hammond for the misjudgement which had led him to recommend the cliffside path, and complained bitterly about young officers who thought they could do anything and who had wasted half a day during which the engineering corps could have been building a road through the gorge.

The retreating army left a river gorge littered with dead mules and horses and spilled baggage, an attraction to the vultures and a depressing sight for the men who would now have to drag the corpses out of the way of the road they would start building in the morning. Apart from that, General Kinloch's little tantrum appeared to have accomplished nothing at all.

He might have been cheered by the news of the flood that had just swept through the Tears of Lunang valley, leaving Vaughan and a few others stranded on the Gandhara side of the river with the rest of the column encamped high on the opposite side; but since the mountain range that now lay between the forces cut off heliographic communications, the general did not even have the satisfaction of knowing that Vaughan's relief force had also failed to reach its goal.

The flooded waters of the Tears of Lunang raced on into the Kanjut River gorge and recoiled with a crash from the walls of rock. White foam spurted up from the churning surface of the water as it filled the gorge; boulders and uprooted trees ground against the rocky sides of the riverbed. The fire-demons that had followed the flood south, curious to see the destruction they had caused, now shot high in the air to avoid the splashing waters. Then, as the flood turned and the wall of muddy water and boulders moved down the course of the Kanjut, the demons floated after it in the hope of some new amusement. The memory of their debt to the Khitai master grew fainter with every mile, and they saw no harm in pursuing their pleasure until nightfall before they returned to his service.

A Hunza shepherd saw the troubling of the air above the river gorge and fell flat where he lay, praying that he might escape the notice of whatever *yush* were abroad. His luck held; at the moment the demons still remembered that they had been commanded not to take on corporeal form.

A little farther down the gorge they came to the rough, pebble-encrusted head of the glacier where Gordon Westbrook had spent a cold night after his escape from the Hunza village. The chilly air in the crevices of the glacier was alive with their kind, *yush* bound to the place by ancient magics. The fire-demons saluted their brothers but swept on in the path of the flood without pausing to interchange energies. Below the glacier, where the river ran between steep cliffs, the water was being driven into a deadly rushing torrent and there was promise of more amusement from the souls encamped on the far side of the gorge.

The rushing of the waters threw up the army's debris, dead mules and burst baggage sacks, to flounder among the rocks and tree limbs carried from the beginning of the flood. The baggage was of no interest to the fire demons, nor did they care about the broken Gatling gun that now lay under the waters, but the carrion corpses were an irresistible temptation. The master whose word had bound them was very far away; this flesh was close and undefended, and it had been too long since they had tasted the delights of the sensory world.

First one, then another, slipped down to the high ledges where the mules' bodies lay, dry enough now that the first rush of weather had passed. The gorge was still flooded, but the wildly splashing waters had calmed and the fire-demons could now reach the debris near the top of the cliff without exposing themselves to the running water.

While the men of Kinloch's army scrambled to escape the flood waters, things beyond imagining took shape in the shadowed river gorge. The fire demons constructed bodies for themselves out of the broken parts of the mules, looked upon the world through dead eyes, heard its sounds through long floppy ears that had been shredded by the pebbles in the flood. Lazy swirling lights in a smoky blackness inhabited the spaces between limbs and ears and eyes; unnecessary bits of the carrion, tails and intestines and hooves, floated in that darkness until the demons had transformed all the unneeded parts into pure energy.

Having taken on corporeal form, they were hungry for more bodies to incorporate; but in these slow clumsy shapes their intelligence was also slowed. They stumbled about the gorge for a while, torn between the sense of all the living bodies and souls in the nearby camp and the draw of their Khitai master's command to return. In their fire-form they had known defiance and flashing laughter and quick, wordless communication, and it had seemed a little thing to slip farther and farther away from the one who had provided their first sacrifices. Now a deep wordless call reminded them that they were not, after all, entirely free. They had taken the Khitai's sacrifices and used the souls of his captives to bind themselves, however loosely, to this world. Now they must obey his commands or give up that binding and return to the overworld, where there was not nearly so much rich food and amusement to be had.

Such a loss was too painful to risk. And besides, were there not more bodies in the upper reaches of the river? The red-coated ones camped above the Tears of Lunang; the black-cloaked ones within the walls of blue tiles. All these they could consume while on the way to their master.

Moving more slowly than in their forms of air and fire, but much more swiftly than men or mules, the fire-demons returned up the river valley.

CHAPTER TWENTY

[Excerpts from the diary of Louisa Westbrook]

26 November 1884:

This afternoon has seemed interminable: kept in this one house, not allowed to leave, with no one to tell us where Tamai has disappeared to. We could not even find out how the battle went. But evidently the Russians have not taken the City—not yet—for it is dark now, the sounds of battle are over, and we have been left undisturbed.

We have had our first visitor, a young woman in a wisewoman's black cloak. She lit the lamps for us—I could not quite see how she did it, but I do not think that she had fire at her finger's ends like Tamai. However, she said nothing of Tamai when I questioned her; she had come, she said, to ask us for a translation of a communique from the Russian general.

Skobelev's ultimatum was written in clear French, and I could easily have rendered it into Gandharan, but Gordon assumed that this was his prerogative. I peeked over his shoulder while he was writing and saw that he had made three or four minor errors of inflection, and some poor choices of words, in the first sentence of the translation; but when I attempted to point this out he ordered

me upstairs, saying that there was no need for me to
interfere in men's business. I had the impression that
neither Colonel Vaughan nor Lieutenant McAusland
would have supported him in this, but, of course, they
could not interfere in our private affairs—any more than
Gordon would have permitted me to "interfere" by cor-
recting the Gandharan!

So here I am, exiled to the upper room of the house,
with only an oil lamp and my journal to keep me company. The men have an easier time of it with this waiting.
While I can only worry and scribble, they are quite occupied with bickering—I mean, with planning their diplomatic strategy—and deciding who ought to remain
behind as British Resident.

We have been accommodated in one of those steep
narrow houses, one room built on top of another in
the slope of the hillside, such as Lieutenant McAusland described to me from his visits to the Hunza
villages. This house is shaped just like the Hunza
wooden huts but differs in a number of details, the
most significant of which, to me, is its state of immaculate cleanliness.

Instead of being made of wood and packed earth, like
the Hunza houses, this building is walled with stone, and
the walls are faced inside and out with small hexagonal
tiles of a brilliant blue color. The roof-tree is a beam of
mountain cedar, and most of the simple furnishings—
stools, low tables and bedsteads, a storage chest and a
few deep bowls—are carved of the same wood, polished
until its reddish hue gleams in the firelight, decorated
only by the twists and rings of the wood's natural grain.
The harsh simplicity of this stone and wood is softened
for the mountains' cold climate by a wealth of woven and
embroidered cloths whose deep hues and subtle patterns
seem to dance and glow in the flickering light of the fire.
The bedstead on which I sit as I write this is covered
with a deep, rich cloth in which strands of some light,
warm golden fiber intertwine with white wool. I cannot
tell exactly what the golden stuff is, for it eludes examina-

tion in a most vexing way—every time I try to separate
a strand, I find myself holding only plain white wool—
but it imparts a soft sheen and an inner warmth to the
whole coverlet that makes it pleasanter to the touch than
the finest Kashmir shawl. It seems almost a sacrilege to
put my shoes on such a thing; I have left my boots at
the door and am curled up on my feet, scribbling with
one hand while the other hand is ready to cover this
journal with a piece of embroidery, should Gordon suddenly desire to come and see how I am doing.

Not that I anticipate any such interruption from him,
for he is quite absorbed in affairs of state. I can hear the
gentlemen quite clearly through the ladder-hole which
connects their room with mine. Ever since they received
General Skobelev's ultimatum they have been going over
and over the same issues, with never a clue as to whether
our hosts mean to agree to the treaty signed in Peshawar
or to repudiate it—and us—in favor of the Russian
dominion.

"So this whole afternoon's assault was just a feint to
distract the Gandharans while he— Yes, of course,
madam, pray do come in, what can we do for you? Westbrook, what does she want?" I heard the scraping of
stools across the floor as the three gentlemen stood up.
I peeked through the ladder-hole and saw an old woman
in a black cloak wandering around the room as if she
had forgotten what she was looking for. Eventually she
picked up a distaff wound with some shimmering white
fleece, which I should dearly have liked to have examined
more closely, and took her departure. "A feint while he
moved his cannon into position," Colonel Vaughan finished his statement at last.

"So it seems," Lieutenant McAusland agreed.

"Damned uncanny, the way he was all set to take
advantage of that unseasonable hot spell— Yes, of course,
pray do come in, madam, we are but guests in your
house. Say something polite, Gordon!"

This woman looked over the room as thoroughly as
had the previous one and then asked something which I

could not quite make out from my listening post. "*Awa, awa*," Gordon said impatiently in his rough Gandharan. "Yes, we all here, nobody leave house, all Angrez here now!"

I suppose I must have sounded like that, or worse, when I first spoke to Tamai. It was very kind of her not to laugh at me.

I wish I could ask one of our visitors what has become of Tamai, but I fear to arouse Gordon's anger should I once again intrude on the gentlemen's discussion. Ever since his unfortunate escape—oh, dear, I mean his *fortunate* escape from his *unfortunate* captivity—his temper has been on a hair-trigger; but although he has spoken rather offensively to me from time to time, up to now he has not struck me before others, and I do not think I could bear the humiliation if he did so now.

"I wish to God the Council would finish their deliberations!" McAusland burst out. "Are you sure they understand the gravity of the situation, Westbrook? Did you tell them exactly what the Colonel recommended?"

"Of course I did! Do you think I can't translate a few simple sentences into Gandharan?"

My husband's voice rose in a way I remembered all too well. I crept off the bed and positioned myself at the very edge of the ladder-hole, thinking that if necessary, to create a diversion, I might pretend to fall through the opening. Fortunately my help was not required; the tension was interrupted by yet another visitor, this one a silver-haired *grande dame* who wore her black cloak like a queen's mantel. She did not trouble to hold her cloak together—I suppose it does not matter what foreign men may see of the wisewomen's code—and as it fell open I caught my breath in wonder at the brilliance of the embroidery which covered the inner layer. Bands of bluegreen silk alternated with spiraling figures that seemed to have been woven with copper thread, well-nigh filling the underside of the cloak. From what little Tamai had told me of the wisewomen's code, this woman must have been very high indeed in the Council.

"Deuced pretty embroidery that lady has on her cape," Colonel Vaughan commented. "Wonder why they don't wear it on the outside, where it would show. Curious ways natives have. I wouldn't mind sending something like that home to Adelaide—she could cut it up for a fire-screen or whatever. Westbrook, ask her how much she'd sell it for."

I really thought I should have to "fall" at this point to prevent Gordon from offering such an insult to a senior wisewoman of the Council. Fortunately, he had to consult his notes to find the right words, and while he was still looking over the vocabulary lists and mumbling to himself, the woman said something curtly and stalked out.

"What did she say?" the colonel asked.

"Sorry," Gordon excused himself, "I couldn't quite make it out. The old hag mumbles too badly."

In fact she had spoken clearly enough, but in the High Speech of Council, which Gordon could not have learned from his informant Bilizhe, and I suppose the unfamiliar inflections confused him. However, though I could translate the *words* well enough, the *sense* was another matter. She had only said, "I see no one here!"

I cannot suppose she meant it as an insult, but it would be hard to propose another interpretation. In any event it was not a comment requiring any reply on our part, and so I felt I could with a clear conscience leave the men to get on with their deliberations. The tense moment had passed, and I returned to my couch to continue this journal entry.

Lieutenant McAusland's innocent question has reawakened my own concerns about our communications with the Gandharan Council. I fear that Gordon may not have translated General Skobelev's communique and our recommendations accurately. I do not know this for a fact, for I was not allowed to see his translation, but I have the gravest suspicions—which, of course, I dare not voice. The Russian threat was simple enough, and I don't doubt that he did an adequate job with that; all General

Skobelev's elegant French boiled down to "Surrender by dawn or I'll destroy the City."

The general could not, of course, have expected anyone in Gandhara to be able to read and reply to a message in any European language. He must have sent the message only so that he could claim, later, after he had taken the City and massacred the inhabitants, that all the diplomatic forms had been satisfied. However, we have had two strokes of luck: first, that the Gandharan Council was willing to invite us to translate the message; second, Colonel Vaughan's recognition of this opportunity to make our own case. He requested Gordon not only to translate the Russian communique but to add, in writing, that he strongly recommended the Gandharans reply to Skobelev by announcing their treaty of mutual aid with the Government of India. Once Gandhara was known to have accepted British protection, the Russians would not dare attack the City for fear of provoking an international incident.

It is this part of the message which I fear Gordon may not have translated with perfect clarity, for his attempts to converse with Tamai on our journey hither have shown me that his mastery of Gandhran does not extend to the complex and subtle forms of polite intercourse among this most civilised people. He speaks Gandharan just as he does Urdu and Punjabi, knowing no mood but the *imperative*, no phrases but those suitable for addressing servants. I greatly fear that all Colonel Vaughan's diplomatic phraseology may have been translated as a blunt command to the Gandharans, something to the effect that they must submit themselves to us before the Russians conquer them. But what could I do? Gordon would have taken my interference in the matter as the gravest insult.

I can only hope my suspicions may be unfounded, that he may have translated Colonel Vaughan's recommendations appropriately, that the Council will see the sense in agreeing to this treaty and that their agreement will be enough to protect Gandhara.

And this last part is far from certain! Even should the Council agree to the treaty and name a British Resident this very night—will Skobelev honour such a treaty, if he guesses that the entire British presence in Gandhara consists of just three men (for I can hardly count myself as part of the diplomatic party)? Or may he not rather choose to attack at dawn, whatever the answer he receives, and trust in his artillery to force a breach through which he can conquer the City and massacre the inhabitants, effectually destroying any evidence of a treaty?

If this has occurred even to me, a weak female unversed in military affairs, how much more forcibly it must have struck the three gentlemen sitting in the room below! It can only be their tactful desire not to alarm me which keeps them from discussing the problem openly. Instead they are engaged in settling among themselves who shall remain in Gandhara as British Resident once our troops and the Russians have withdrawn. Even now, as I listen to them, the same arguments are advanced over and over again. Colonel Vaughan naturally assumes that he, as the senior officer present, would be the natural choice. Lieutenant McAusland protests that the colonel's seniority and military expertise render him overqualified for such a post, that he cannot be spared from the regiment in Peshawar, that a minor outpost like Gandhara ought rather to be left to some young officer who would hardly be missed at home. Gordon tends to agree with McAusland but with the proviso that the Resident, whoever he may be, ought to be fluent in the Gandharan tongue. A few minutes ago they came close to quarreling over the matter.

"One can always find an interpreter," Lieutenant McAusland said. "More important, to my mind, is that the Resident should be somebody with previous experience as a political officer. Now, my work with the Wazirs and Baluchis—"

"You can hardly compare presiding over a dusty tribal

jirga with managing the affairs of an entire independent state," Gordon interrupted.

"At least I've done *something* besides sit in my study and write a dictionary!"

"So have I!" Gordon's voice was rising again. "I have already spent some months in these mountains, McAusland, and without any honour guard of British soldiers to keep me safe. And I've seen some damned queer things ... damned strange.... Have you ever looked into the heart of a glacier? You'd think it would be all cold and black, but there are lights and living things in some of those crevasses. You should spend a night on the glacier, McAusland; then you'd know how Skobelev changed the weather ... dancing lights ... a terrible beauty ..."

He did not sound angry now, but I was chilled by the quiet emptiness of his voice, the hypnotic rising and falling rhythm of his words. I felt as though the man I had married—harsh, impatient, soldierly Gordon Westbrook—as if this man were sliding away quietly into some wintry fastness of his own thoughts, and as if the voice that now spoke belonged to someone I had never even met. At all costs, I felt, someone *must* interrupt that voice, before it said something none of us could bear to hear!

"Aren't you forgetting one thing, gentlemen?" I called through the ladder-hole. "The choice of the Resident is up to the Gandharan Council, not to us!"

"Dammit, Louisa, we know that's what the treaty says," Colonel Vaughan called back up, "but we've got to have a Resident in place by dawn, and nobody's so much as *seen* us yet, let alone talking and deciding who they'd rather have stay on!"

Strictly speaking, this statement of the colonel's is not quite true, as any number of Gandharans have seen us, beginning with the two women who escorted us to this house. Still, I understand his feeling. He has been waiting in hourly expectation of being called before a meeting of elders in some formal Council house. He has hardly noticed the repeated interruptions by visiting wisewomen, and I suppose it is not really important to explain to him that the insignia upon their cloaks mark them as among the leaders of the City.

But it has now been some time since our last visitor. I wonder whether we shall hear any more tonight? And if no agreement can be reached, what will the dawn bring? Oh, how I wish Tamai were here!

The moon is rising now; its white light spills through the narrow opening in the roof of this room and quarrels with the gold of the lamplit circle. Below me, the men are smoking and talking, evidently bent on staying awake until we hear some more word from the Gandharans. I suppose I ought to sleep, but the brilliancy of the moonlight and the rhythmic drumming that has begun somewhere in the City combine to keep me awake—more than that; I suffer from a strange feeling of nervous expectancy, a tension not unlike that one feels in the days of lowering clouds just before the monsoon breaks upon us. It is unfortunate that Dr. Scully is with the field force on the other side of the river; I'm sure he would give me some laudanum for this nervous condition.

The drumming is louder now. I cannot think how the men can ignore it; I feel as if my very bones were being changed by the subtle, insistent rhythms. Tamai has spoken to me of the Gandharan dances and their importance, but I never understood how compelling the call of this deep music could be. There is a flute playing now, a thin sweet melody that dances with the moonlight and calls down the stars, and I can smell the cedar smoke of the fires around the dancing square. Intolerable to be trapped within this small room, when the moon and the cedar fire and the flute are all calling to me!

Gordon has not looked in on me since he banished me to this room like a naughty child. Perhaps he would not notice if I went on up to the white rooftop for a few minutes to listen to the music.

I have just been up the ladder to the roof. The music is clear and very sweet. The houses here are crowded so close together, and the slope of the hill is so steep, that I could quite easily step from rooftop to rooftop until I came to the street leading to the dancing place. What am I thinking of? This is madness! Gordon would surely divorce me if he caught me creeping out of the house by night to dance with a group of natives.

Every song Tamai taught me is echoed in the double dancing drumbeat. Everything I ever wanted to know is hidden in the secret voice of the flute.

I cannot possibly go. They would not allow an Englishwoman to join their secret rituals anyway.

I cannot stay.

27 November 1884:
I left the men in the room below to their endless debates and climbed the ladder to the rooftop. Outside it was cold and bright; the unnatural heat brought by the passage of the fire-demons had passed away, leaving only the cold brilliance of a clear moonlit winter's night behind. Fortunately I had had the forethought to bring my old travelling cloak with me, the faded red one which the *durzee* had dyed black when I put on mourning for Gordon; after all these years in the heat of the Punjab it was very little worn and still quite serviceable for this journey into the unknown mountains of Gandhara.

When we were hurried through the City to our house, I thought it presented as sad an aspect as any place torn by the horrible weapons of modern war, with roofless houses standing empty around the devastation of the Russian shells, with an air of neglect and sorrow and poverty overlying everything. But the moonlight silvered over the scars of war and presented me with a scene of unreal beauty. The flat stone rooftops of the City were

all pearl and shadow under that pure light, and the conical blue-tiled tops of the towers shone with a moving,
ever-changing sheen that was almost, but not quite, filled
with colors.

Once I stood on the rooftop, the direction of the dancing place was clear. I felt like a ghost or a shadow as I
moved lightly over the roofs from house to house, drawn
irresistibly forward by the double beat of the drums. The
moonlight was quite sufficient to show me where broken
roofs or missing parapets might present some danger,
and I soon reached a point where the rising street was
only a few feet below the level of the roof on which I
stood. Still, the jump was greater than I would choose
to attempt, and for a moment I resisted the tingling call
of the music in my blood as I tried to gauge the exact
distance I would fall and to see whether there were any
steps or ledges that might aid me to reach the street (for
I did not quite wish to go through some stranger's ladder-
hole and pass uninvited through the smoky darkness of
their home).

My dilemma was solved by three young girls who were
hurrying along the narrow street, arms linked, singing
as they went. The song was something about the seven
daughters of a star, and the melody was one that lifted
my spirits so that I laughed aloud for the sheer joy of it.
To imagine me, plain little Louisa Westbrook, here at
the edge of the earth, learning magic and hearing the
songs of a secret city!

The girls must have heard my laughter, for one of
them looked up and raised her arms to me. "Come down
and dance with us!" she cried. Kneeling on the roof, I
rested my own hands on hers, then leapt lightly down to
the street. Her hands were hard with manual labor and
the strength in her young arms was more than enough
to help me alight; all the same, perhaps because I was
still possessed by the strange jubilation that the song had
induced in me, I felt almost as if I were floating rather
than falling.

The girl who had helped me down from the low rooftop took my arm, and now there were four of us together in the street, three singing the song of Star's Daughters and one with her throat aching for the pure joy of being there. My cloak floated out behind me, the beat of the drum grew louder and more insistent, the street widened, more women joined either end of our line, we moved sideways and forward and swayed to the music, a forest of carved pillars grew around me: I was on the dancing ground of Gandhara, in the circle with the women of Gandhara, dancing to honour the light of Nirmali that silvered all about us.

How long we danced there I cannot say. The circle of women widened, swayed inward, undulated serpent-like about the empty space in the center of the dancing ground. The tempo of the music changed with the songs, now quick and almost martial, now a smooth gliding fall with a queer little catch at the end of each measure. Some of the Teaching Songs were known to me from Tamai's tutoring, and I lifted up my voice with my sisters around me. Others, like the song of Star's Daughters, were new to me, and I hummed the melody in the back of my throat and followed the steps of the women on either side of me until I felt as if my feet were rising above the dancing ground.

Moonlight spilled like a rope of pearls across the uplifted faces of the dancers, and the warm gold of torches encircled us like a necklace of golden beads against the night. Nirmali's cloak of stars and darkness was spread across the sky, and we reached out our bare arms to call her down among us. No longer cold, I dropped my travelling cape and pushed up the sleeves of my dress so that I could join in the calling.

On a last crescendo of frenzied backbeats the drumming stopped abruptly and the torches around us were extinguished. The moonlight seemed infinitely brighter, the silvery rays became narrow shining ribbons of pearly light, almost palpable against the blackness of the night. Three old women moved into the center of the dancing circle and raised up their arms to the sky. The ribbons of light slipped through their fingers and spiraled into a single dancing plait that turned about an invisible axis, seeming to be a serpent, a woman, a growing tree, a rising and falling cascade of silver light.

For a moment I forgot entirely that I was a foreigner, that I had no business there and should remain in the background to avoid detection. Nothing seemed to matter but getting close to that living fountain of light. I moved forward like one in a trance, and the circles of women with their arms linked parted like waves to let me through.

I was almost there when I found my way barred by the silver-haired woman who had last inspected us. Her face was grim and forbidding; her open cloak glimmered with serpent-like tongues of copper.

"Why are you here?" she demanded.

My tongue would not move; my lips were frozen.

"Angrezi woman, why are you here?" she repeated, and still I could not answer.

Her third questioning was harshly triumphant. "Outlander, what place have you among us when we call Nirmali? Go where you belong!"

That name unlocked my tongue. "I have never had a place anywhere," I said, not knowing where the words came from, "unless it is here. I have never had a home, unless it is with Nirmali. I can call to none for aid, if I cannot call to Nirmali."

There was a whisper all around me that grew like the swell of an ocean wave. I had the feeling of having, all unknowing, passed some test.

The woman who stood before me seemed disappointed that I had answered correctly—if so I had done. But she stepped back, saying in grudging tones, "Then find Nirmali, foreign woman, if it is true that she calls to you as she does to us."

The three dancing women were gone, and so was the fountain of moonlight. In their place I beheld a narrow passage, stone stairs worn smooth with age leading down into darkness. Far, far below there was the glimmer of water, as of an underground pool that reflected the last faint rays of the moon. The air that emanated from the passage was not as cold as the fresh mountain air of the night aboveground, but something in it chilled me to the bone: I thought I could catch the scent of dank waters too long imprisoned, despair, old age, death, unimaginable centuries in darkness. I drew back involuntarily, and my interlocutor smiled. If I failed to enter the passage, would I fail a second test, and would that please her? And what then?

"I—I cannot see my way," I stammered in excuse.

"There will be light enough," said the old woman, "for what you have to do." She gestured upwards with one arm; I looked up and could not see the moon in the sky, or Nirmali's cloak of stars; only the blackness of stones overhead. To my left and right I felt the solid damp coolness of stone walls; beneath my foot, the smooth worn edge of a stone stair rolled off into nothingness. I had already entered the passage, even while I thought I was refusing to do so. And it was not quite dark; there were pierced copper bowls set in the wall to either side of me. Through the patterns of holes I could see the dull glow of dying embers, giving off just enough heat to waft their wisps of blue smoke upwards. The scent of burning cedar was strong around me, and what I had taken for the old woman's black cloak was only an eddy of smoke in the darkness of the passage. And I was very cold; my teeth chattered and I could feel all my limbs trembling with the cold. It was worse than the evening Tamai and I had spent on top of a snow-covered pass while we waited for the tents and the baggage to catch up with us.

Remembering her teaching of that evening, I drew in deep, slow, even breaths and tried to feel the warmth within me. What had she said? "Expel all pride, sloth, anger and covetousness as you breathe out."

"Go on, go on!" I jumped as the old woman chattered behind me. How had she come there? She prodded me with her bony fingers and I braced myself against the pressure.

"Let me *alone*," I snapped. "I can't concentrate!"

"Better to fail now than later," she told me. "Far, far better, Angrezi woman, to give up now. Do you want to go back to the light? You can only reach the true light by moving forward. What do you want? Where do you think you are going, Angrezi woman? What do you think you are doing here? Why have you . . ."

Her questions were unanswerable; I stopped trying to answer them. I took in a deep breath of the smoke-filled air and imagined the cedar tree that had grown to make the wood of that fire. As I pictured it in my mind, the nagging of the old woman grew faint and faraway, something that could not really stop or hurt me.

Life must be hard, even for a tree, in these high stony hills. The cedar would have dug its roots in between the stones, bent itself before the storm winds, endured through seasons of bitter cold. It would have been a twisted little tree, not tall and graceful and stately, but it would have survived in the place where it belonged.

I let my long-held breath sigh out of my body. The old woman's voice was now a dim echo far behind me. And before me, going down into the darkness, a long line of copper lamps filled with burning embers glowed to light my way; five, ten, twoscore, a hundred lamps glowed ahead of me. I put aside my certain knowledge that the passage could not be so long or so deep, and stepped down onto invisible stairs that led ever downwards.

Breathe in, hold the warmth, let it out. Breathe in, fan the flame, let it grow. Be the flame, grow in the flame, breathe the flame. The rhythm of the Discipline matched with my steps. The passage narrowed until my skirts caught on rough bits of stone projecting from the walls. I knew now that there was no way but forward. I tugged at my skirts and felt the good, sturdy wool pull free of whatever had caught it, but the way before me was even narrower. There were no lamps at this point; just the

stone closing in on me, pressing on my shoulders, and
the gleam of moonlight on water far below. I turned
sideways and wriggled through the narrowing spaces until
my dress caught and I could go no farther. I could hardly
breathe now; I lost the comforting rhythm of the Discipline and felt the chill weight of stone pressing on me.
There was no gleam of light behind me, where I should
have seen burning lamps and the moonlight shining in
at the opening of the stairs.

I edged back into the darkness of the open passage,
where at least I had room to move. I fear I was not
thinking very clearly at this point, for the sensible thing
would have been to go back; but all I could think of was
the clear pool of moonlit water. How thirsty I was! I felt
sure that one drink from that pool would quench my
thirst and soothe my dry throat. Nothing else seemed to
matter. Scruples of dress and propriety, so weighty in my
other life, here seemed quite foolish. With fingers already
stiff and clumsy from the cold, I stripped off the sturdy
blue wool walking costume which I had commissioned
so happily in Peshawar.

Light filtering through from the lamps on the far side
of the passage showed me my ridiculous self, thin, covered with goose bumps, exposed in my chemise and
white petticoats. For a moment I faltered, and painful
memories long buried caught me by surprise. I relived
every humliating and embarrassing moment in my past,
from school days to my wedding night. If anyone saw me
here, half-naked in the middle of some native ceremony,
it would be worse than anything I had ever experienced,
worse even than Gordon's look of disappointment when
he saw me for the first time in my fine lawn wedding
nightgown, worse than all his remarks in the ensuing
years about my unattractiveness and unwomanly nature.

And going back, giving up my chance to drink of that
living water, would be worse yet. Once firmly decided
on that, I was able to put the painful memories in their
place—not forgotten, but unimportant compared to what

lay before me. And I found, too, that without my bulky skirts I was able to squeeze through the passage without the least difficulty. On the other side I resumed the Discipline of Inbreathing and soon felt myself growing quite warm despite my half-clad condition.

Again the passageway narrowed, and this time I had to strip off every remaining stitch on my body. The rock was cold and rough against my bare skin, and even without my petticoats I felt that I could not force my way through. I leaned against the wall of the tunnel. The tears on my face were the only warm thing about me. This time my past memories did not hurt so much; what kept me from going forward was a crushing weight of despair, the certainty that nothing would be any better in the future. No matter what I did, I was doomed to tread the same weary circle, shrinking, placating, never quite good enough.

Pain and loneliness and rejection. Had my life really been so sad? I tried to remember happier moments— my wedding day itself, the Indian sunshine and the good wishes of Gordon's friends and my brief flowering of joy before the pain and uncertainty of the night. The birth of my darling babes, so pink and rosy and perfect when I held each one in my arms. The closeness I had felt with Tamai, our spirits twining about one another in the overworld.

All these things seemed only dreams now; reality was the knowledge of my own unworthiness and loneliness, as unyielding as the stone about me.

"No!" I said aloud. "It may be pointless and useless, but I *will not* be stopped now!" The harsh rocks scraped my skin, but I pushed my way through.

There were no more lamps on this side; there was no need of them. The roof of the tunnel was open to the sky. Above me was Nirmali's cloak of stars; before me, a half-circle of shallow steps descended into the still waters of a pool whose waters were alive with living silver, a pool of light. I walked down until I could kneel on the lowest step. I reached out cupped hands to take

up a mouthful of the water, but it ran through my fingers
like light, colder than ice, taking my breath away.

"There is no way to Nirmali but through Her grace,"
said a hateful voice behind me. The old woman was back.

"How can I drink of the water?" I demanded, almost
in tears. I had given up so much to come here, fought
through so much, was I now to be cheated?

"You cannot."

"But then—"

"You must become part of Nirmali's grace."

Shivering, I rose to my feet. I wanted to shout at the
old woman that she was a cheat, that I hated her and all
her tricks. But years of training kept me silent. When
had defiance ever availed me anything? Perhaps if I was
quiet and did not make her angry, she would stop tor-
menting me.

But when I turned to beg her for mercy, she was gone.
In her place stood my husband, not tired and travel-
stained as I had last seen him, but standing to attention
in the full glory of his regimental uniform.

"What a fool you are, Louisa," he said. "I suppose I
ought to be used to that by now, but I do wish you would
not make *me* look foolish, too. What will people say if
they hear you've drowned yourself in some pagan rite?
Come along, now. There is still time to hush this up."

His voice was so clear that I could almost believe he
was really present. If I had not known that he did not
have a full set of regimentals with him, I would have
been terrified into instant submission.

"Go away," I said. "You are a trick of my imagination.
You are not really here."

He smiled, most unpleasantly, and stepped forward
with one arm upraised. I could not help flinching. "Ah,
but I *am* here, Louisa, dear. Wherever you are, there
am I also."

"That is perilously close to blasphemy!"

"And what do you call what *you* are doing?" he
enquired. "Stark naked, bleeding and filthy, about to
immerse yourself in some pagan parody of baptism—

Louisa, I am warning you now, you had best give up all this folly at once."

It was exactly what he would have said if he had known where I was at that moment. And hearing his voice, even in imagination, awakened me to the dangers and folly of my position. Gordon would never forgive me this escapade.

"Come along, now." He reached forward as if to take hold of my arm. I did not quite feel his hand on me, but I did feel all the old pains flare up. My arm ached as if it had just now been broken, my forehead was hot and swollen from the infected wound I had after he threw the teacup at me, and all down my side the bruises where I had fallen down the stairs came to painful life. If I moved, would not everything hurt worse than ever before? Perhaps, if I held very still, he would not hurt me anymore. Perhaps some day I would learn how not to make him angry—if I kept quiet and did nothing foolish—perhaps he would look at me again with the loving smile he had shown me on our wedding day, and I would again feel real and desirable and worthy of love.

And I would never taste the water of Nirmali's pool.

"No," I said aloud. "No, I will not go back. You are not real. You are nothing but an illusion."

"So is this magical pool of yours," he replied.

I stepped back from him, right into the icy water, and his hand had no power to hold me. I still felt every separate ache and pain of our years together, except where the water numbed my feet, but I did not feel his hands upon me. He seemed to be shrinking as I watched.

"Nothing but an illusion," he taunted me, and his voice echoed like a tiny bell in a vast cavern. "Illusion—illusion—all is illusion."

With each word he shrank until I was looking down at an image of Harry's toy soldier. A wrinkled hand picked up the toy and set it on a ledge at eye level.

"Illusion," repeated the old woman who had been taunting and teasing me all the way.

Had it been she who spoke with Gordon's voice? Had she been trying to tell me something, a hidden message behind those angry words? He had threatened me with "drowning in some pagan rite."

"Then," I said, "I will choose which illusion I follow."

I stepped down into the pool and found that I had not, after all, reached the lowest step; the flight of semicircular steps continued down into the water. It rose about my thighs and a fit of violent shivering overtook me. The old woman laughed and puffs of smoke whirled about my head. Her laughter went on and on, changing from an old woman's harsh cackle to the innocent pealing laughter of children at play. The faces of Alice and little Harry arose before me and I felt again all the grief of my parting from them. How hard it had been to go through with that decision! Even on the day when their ship was to depart I had felt more than once that I *could not* go through with it. It was too hard. To send them away from me, perhaps forever, to be reared by strangers—how could I give them up, the one sweetness in my life, my innocent babies?

But they could not be left to Gordon's rearing. And so I did it. And so, even now, I stepped forward into the icy waters of the pool at the bottom of the world. I had torn my children from me for their own salvation. Nothing could be worse than that; certainly not a little cold water. Indeed, the touch of the water now seemed almost soothing. It rose as high as my heart, lapping about my body with a whisper of promise, and wherever it touched me I felt no more pain. "You have not lost them," the water whispered. "They are always a part of you. How else were you able to guide Tamai from the overworld? They are part of you, and you are a part of Me." A joyous sense of wholeness of all things swept over me, and I sank into the waters with no fear, even as they closed over my head.

I could feel nothing under my feet now, but I did not sink down into the water; something buoyed me up. And all was light before me. The water was one pool of glorious light, and ahead of me, as I mounted the steps on the other side, two brilliant lights together almost blinded me. I could just make out the figure of a woman with the sun on her right shoulder and the moon on her left, riding the sky and dropping her cloak of stars behind her; and then there was nothing but the gold of the rising sun, and the pale crescent of the moon in the western sky, and the faces of my sisters coming to embrace me.

I was fully dressed again, even to the cape which I had discarded so long ago. And when I looked behind me, pool and stairs and lamps had all disappeared. I might have thought the long night only a dream, but for two things.

The hem of my cloak, where it hung free and was not warmed like the other clothes by the heat of my body, was dripping a few drops of an icy blue water that shone like moonlight.

And right across the bottom edge of the cape, on the inner side, a zigzag line of embroidery shone with the colors of the rising sun.

The horrible old woman who had teased and provoked me into the passage now stood before me again, her face impassive, framed in the glory of her cloak of turquoise and copper bands. I knew her now, and I knew what her greeting was worth. On one side of her stood a woman with milky blind eyes, on the other, a withered grandmother whose hair was moonlight combed and piled high. Behind her, rank on rank of black-cloaked women awaited me. They looked down at the hem of my cape and their eyes were wide with wonder.

"Welcome to the Council of Gandhara, sister," said the Dhi Lawan.

I had seen Nirmali riding across the sky to bring the dawn, with the sun on her right shoulder and the moon on her left.

And that dawn would also bring the Russian army's attack on Gandhara, if we did not move to stop it now.

I knew now, by Nirmali's grace, what might serve to save the City.

"Sisters," I said, "the Council has a treaty to sign. And after that, we have another task—and all must be done before the sun has finished rising. Will you trust me?"

CHAPTER TWENTY-ONE

[Continuation of Louisa Westbrook's diary]

As I hurried back from the dancing place, followed by the Dhi Lawan and her two most senior Council members, the wisewomen who remained in the square began moving to a low humming chant that sounded the way rain clouds smell, all heavy and moist and threatening. The gold of dawn was blotted out by gathering clouds, and we passed through damp, gray streets where drops of chilly moisture gathered on the stones of the broken walls.

"How long can they hold back the dawn?" I asked the Dhi Lawan.

"Not long. We are not what we were."

I prayed it might be long enough. As we walked, I asked my companions about the wording of the treaty and found that my suspicions were correct: Gordon had changed recommendations into demands, warnings into threats. Had I not answered the call of Nirmali's Dance, this morning the Council would have expelled us from the City and fought the Russians alone.

Even now, despite my best efforts to explain the real meaning of the treaty and of our presence here, I felt a lingering distrust from the Dhi Lawan. One of the other wisewomen let slip that they had been about to expel us from the City the night before, but that Tamai's pleadings had convinced some among the Council to test me first. (I say "let slip" because the Dhi Lawan ordered her to keep silent just as I was about to ask what had become of Tamai and why she had not come back to us last night.)

As we drew farther from the dancing place and nearer to the house where my compatriots slept, I could feel my courage and the joy of Nirmali's grace leaking away from me. I was tired and cold and bedraggled and in no state to explain myself to my companions. I could only hope that I would be able to get out my story to Colonel Vaughan, and retrieve the thing I had come for, without too much unpleasantness or too many questions.

I was not to be so fortunate. Scarcely had we reached the lower doorway of the house when Gordon blocked the way. He was unshaven, tired, travel-stained—a far cry from the dapper officer in regimentals whose illusory image had confronted me at Nirmali's pool.

He was also very angry.

"What the devil do you think you've been playing at, Louisa?" he shouted before I had so much as reached the doorway. "Sneaking out behind my back again? You may have got away with it in Peshawar, my lady, but there are no lying servants to protect you here!"

Despite my best resolves, I flinched. My eyes half-closed in anticipation of a blow, my shoulders raised, I became again the pitiful white-faced cringing *thing* that Gordon's anger always made of me.

"Get inside you——!" he shouted, using a word with which I would not defile the pages of this journal, and to enforce his command he reached out with one hand to take me by the arm. His fingers closed on the site of the old break, where my bones had ached all summer, and I gasped in anticipation of the jagged pains which any blow or violence to that arm brought on.

But no pain came; none, that is, but that occasioned by his holding me too tightly now. The arm was whole again as if it had never been broken. I remembered those moments of healing in the pool.

Nirmali, why could you not heal my spirit as well as my body? I thought. Whole in body I might be, but I still lacked the courage to stand up to Gordon. I was still leaning away from him, resisting his attempts to draw me into the house, but I dared not prolong that resistance. In a moment he would strike me across the face; I could see his free hand rising now. I squeezed my eyes shut against the sight of the coming blow, and golden suns and moons danced across my closed lids.

Nirmali was everywhere; within me as well as in the sky or in her pool. And I betrayed her grace by cringing like this. As I thought more of how to serve Nirmali, and less of my foolish self, the strength I had prayed for was given to me.

"Let me pass, Gordon, or I shall have to hurt you," I said in a strange, cool voice that I scarcely recognized as my own. Time seemed to have slowed around us; Gordon and I were in a bubble where nothing moved, locked together by his anger and my fear. But within that bubble, I had all the time in the world to reach out for the exact words I needed from the Songs of Discipline. Between one breath and the next the lines of power traced themselves in my memory. I sang the first verse and behind me the three wisewomen joined the chorus. Gordon let go my arm and reeled backwards as if he had been struck himself, clutching at the wall of the house for balance.

With two more verses I could bring him to his knees, dizzy and retching and aware of nothing but the world swinging under and above him like a top spinning out of control. Why did I not go on? I could remember nights when I had lain awake, sick with pain and suppressing my sobs for fear of disturbing him; nights when I thought nothing could make me happier than to hurt him as he had hurt me.

Now I could not recapture that fierce desire. Gordon was a pale, trembling man in dirty clothes, and when he

looked up at me I saw fear in his eyes, and—and I could
not bear it. He was not made to be afraid of anything or
anyone; it was his courage I first admired in him, and
now I was destroying that, and what would be left when
I was through? No one should be able to do that to
someone else. What he had done to me did not make it
right for me to break him.

I moved my hand downwards in a sharp, cutting gesture and the wisewomen broke off their chant. "It is all
right," I told Gordon, though I knew nothing could ever
be right between us again. "If you do not strike me, I
shall not harm you."

"Fine words!" Gordon sneered, but his countenance
had not yet regained its normal high color. "Go inside,
my fine lady. I'll deal with you later."

As it happened that I needed to search through my
pack, I did go inside, but I had no sense of obedience
to his command.

I had to pass through the lower room, where Lieutenant McAusland and Colonel Vaughan were still asleep,
and climb the ladder into my room above. Fully sensible
of the impropriety of such a proceeding, I made as much
haste as I might, and was back down the ladder before
either of these gentlemen was fully awake. Gordon was
waiting for me at the foot of the ladder.

"I did not give you permission to come back," he said.
He did not try to strike me this time, but blocked my
way with his body so that I could not pass without some
violence. "Go back into your room and stay there!"

"Gordon, I *cannot*," I told him. "I must talk with Colonel Vaughan, and then I must return to the dancing
place. *Please*, Gordon, let us not quarrel now. There is
too much at stake!"

Lieutenant McAusland stirred and mumbled something in his sleep. Gordon glanced over his shoulder at
the disturbance and I tried to slip past him, but he
caught my wrist and twisted it downwards so sharply that
I could not repress a small cry of pain. Almost before
the sound had left my lips, Lieutenant McAusland was

out of his bed. What happened next was so quick and so confusing, I scarcely know how to recount it. Naturally I averted my eyes for fear of seeing the lieutenant *en deshabille*. He shouted something in Gaelic and I think he must have struck Gordon, for there was the sharp sound of a blow and then Gordon released my wrist.

"Gentlemen! Gentlemen!" Colonel Vaughan's voice cut through the angry sounds. "McAusland, make yourself decent. Westbrook, put your fists down. That's an order. Two orders. By God, you'll obey me *now* or I'll see you both cashiered on our return!"

When I dared to look up, Lieutenant McAusland was at least half decent, having pulled on his regimental trousers. Gordon stood in a threatening attitude between us, fists clenched, and there was a light in his eyes that terrified me; but before the colonel's steady gaze he slowly lowered his fists and his face took on the expression I once thought *firm*, but now would describe as *mulish*.

I was ready to sink from having been involved in such a scene, so improper in every way, but there was no time to allow personal considerations their way. Colonel Vaughan was sitting up, white hair rumpled from sleep, with a blanket of white and golden wool drawn over his shoulders. A lesser man might have appeared comic in such a situation. "You need to talk to me, Mrs. Westbrook?"

"It's about the treaty. The Council is ready to sign it," I told him. "The Dhi Lawan—that's the head of Council—is waiting outside with two others."

"They are, by God! And not before time." He glanced out the door. "What is it—just before dawn?"

"Just after. The day is cloudy." I saw no need to explain to him what had produced the low-lying clouds and fog that were our last defence.

"Then there's no time to waste. Go and talk to the—what did you say—Dilawan, there's a good girl, and tell him I'll be out as soon as I've made myself decent."

Gordon did not move from the foot of the ladder.

"Westbrook," the colonel said sharply, "pray allow your lady to pass! That's an order!"

Gordon moved back a step, shoulders set rigidly as if he were on the parade ground. His eyes blazed in a face still marked by unnatural pallor. "Go on, Louisa," he taunted me. "Disobey me if you will, meddle in men's affairs—you're no wife for me. Tonight's escapade is cause enough for me to divorce you. You'll be disgraced. A laughingstock. *And,*" he said in a voice so soft I could barely hear the words, "I'll take steps to see that my innocent children are protected from your influence."

I never doubted that he would do it. Colonel Vaughan's direct order, the Discipline of the Veil—these things might force him to give in now, but what would they avail me when we were back in a civilised land— meaning, I thought bitterly, a land where law was made by men, for men? To get Harry and Alice away from Gordon's rages I had consented to having them placed with a family chosen by him. It would be a very little matter for him to persuade this family and an English judge that I was an unfit mother who should not be permitted contact with the children.

I had known all this from the moment I first set foot on the roof. Harry and Alice were Gordon's last and greatest hold on me, greater even than my own fear. He would not lightly give up such a victim as I had been to him. I had thought to buy my children's safety by sending them away. And ever since he returned from the dead, I had thought to buy my right to the children with submission to his whims.

How could I have thought that I could do that and at the same time seek my true home with Nirmali?

How could I bargain for my rights to the children with the lives of all Gandhara?

"You—will do—what you must," I stammered finally. "And—so will I."

I was crying when I came out of the house. But I came out. And with me I carried what might be the salvation of Gandhara; for Gordon had been too angry to stop me from bringing away what I had come for.

A moment later Colonel Vaughan came outside, fully dressed in his uniform and as dapper as if he were about to visit the Viceroy. "Told *him* to stay in the house, out of our way," he said, jerking his head back towards the empty doorway. "Don't let his threats worry you—sort it all out when we get back to base—tempers frayed, eh? Tempest in a teapot." But his eyes were sad for me, belying the heartening effect he'd wished for his words. "Now, my dear, dry your eyes, and let's sort out this muddle—if we can—if we have time."

The clouds that had rolled in so thick and low at first were thinning now. "We don't," I said, more firmly than I had meant; the colonel looked startled. "If you want to save Gandhara, Colonel—please, this will sound very strange, but there just is not time to explain. You must go *now* to parley with General Skobelev. Tell him that the Gandharan Council have signed a treaty with you."

"But they haven't," Colonel Vaughan pointed out. "They haven't named a Resident, either—oh, well, I suppose that can be settled later . . ."

"They have agreed in principle to a treaty. And to the presence of a Resident." I looked at the waiting wise-women and repeated my statement in Gandharan. They nodded solemnly. "These ladies are members of the High Council," I explained. "You can tell General Skobelev of that agreement—and then, Colonel, tell him that during the night the Gandharan Relief Force arrived, bridged the river and invested the town. Tell him you can match his army with your own, and that if he thinks to take the town by force he's got a long and bloody war in front of him. Ask him if he thinks the Tsar wants to go to war with England over this one little country. Ask him—"

"All right. Yes. I see." Colonel Vaughan nodded and hummed to himself. "Tell the truth, Louisa, I was thinking rather along those lines myself. Worst that can happen is, he won't believe the bluff, and then we're no worse off—eh?"

"Colonel, I *promise* you he will believe your statement," I said. I was shaking all over and in no case to demonstrate how I meant to make the bluff work, but fortunately the colonel took my words only as the sort of encouragement a soldier's woman ought to give a man going on a hopeless mission.

"Damme, but I like your spirit, Louisa!" he exclaimed. "If we get out of this tight spot alive—by God, if I weren't a married man—damme, I'll find some way to see young Westbrook don't harass you in the courts, m'dear. *Whatever* you were doing last night." He paused, and a look of concern came over his manly features. "But, I say, Louisa. What if they ask me to pledge my honour as an officer and a gentleman that the army's really here?"

"You must do your best to ensure that such a request is not made, Colonel," I told him.

There was no time for a formal leave-taking. I watched the colonel stride away, soldierly and erect as ever, even though his only errand was to deceive the enemy with half-truths and whole lies.

The Dhi Lawan and I were back at the dancing place before Colonel Vaughan had passed the City walls. From this platform in the center of Gandhara, as the clouds lifted, I could see the mountain that guarded the northern walls of the City, and the cluster of men and tents marking the position of the Russian artillery partway up that mountain, on what had until yesterday been an impassable sheet of ice.

The Dhi Lawan took on herself the task of explaining to the assembled wisewomen what we were to do, leaving me free for a few minutes to watch the colonel's progress towards the enemy camp. As first one and then another wisewoman diverted her attention from maintaining the veil of clouds and mist about Gandhara, I could see more and more detail in the thin winter sunlight. There was the colonel's white head and the blaze of his dress uniform; and there, high above him, were the Russians with their guns trained on the City. The light sparked and glanced off bright bits of metal around the gunners' position; and in the center stood a broad-shouldered man in Skobelev's infamous white uniform. He was too far away for me to make out his features or any details of the uniform; presumably the reverse also would hold true, and I thanked God for that as our task began.

The song of Nirmali's Shaping began in my own throat, with four low strong notes that set the tone for what was to come. I could no longer watch the mountain for a sight of Colonel Vaughan; all my attention must be bent on the little figurine I had brought away from my pack. Harry's red-coated toy soldier had travelled many miles from his home. Now, set atop a post of the dancing platform for all the wisewomen to see him and take him as a model, he was to be set the hardest task ever asked of a single gallant little soldier: he was to be the sole defence of the City.

He grew now to man-height, staring stiffly ahead, surrounded by others whose faces and uniforms I could not make out. For a moment I thought of how pleased Harry would have been with this illusion, how he would have clapped his fat little hands and begged me to do it again. A lump rose in my throat; the song faltered and the images began to dissolve into shapeless columns of mist.

Nirmali had promised that the children were always a part of me, no matter how we might be separated in this world. I had to put my faith in that promise, now, to put aside my fear and grief, to think of nothing but the task at hand. I took up the song again, singing through an aching throat, and the effort of concentration helped somewhat. As my sisters joined in the Song of Shaping, those other images multiplied a hundredfold and details came out sharp and clear: pipe-clayed belts, polished buttons, shoulders set squarely at attention, gleam of bayonets on the ends of their rifles. Even to me, who had begun the illusion and who now stood in the center of it, it seemed that the central gathering place of Gandhara was full of British soldiers.

How long must we maintain the illusion? I prayed that

Colonel Vaughan would finish his negotiations quickly—and especially that he would remember to insist that General Skobelev abandon his position above Gandhara.

A bird soared high above us. I glanced up, hoping against hope for a sight of the black wings and golden hackles of Tamai's eagle; but it was too far away for me to make out any detail, and my moment's inattention cost us dear. When I looked down at the illusory soldiers again, the colours of their uniforms were running together and their heads were melting into featureless blobs, like wax dolls left in the sun. My sisters of Gandhara could copy whatever illusion I created, but only I could bring the necessary realistic detail to the images.

If I could put Alice and Harry from my mind, I could also put off my growing concern for Tamai. My sisters, so much wiser than I in the ways of the Disciplines, had already abandoned their bodies under their black cloaks, sending their spirits into the overworld where they could maintain the illusion without distraction from bodily aches and pains. I sank down under the tree at the center of the dancing space, drew my travelling cape over my head and joined them. I had not time to be afraid; their minds touched mine like hands drawing me into the dancing circle, and then I was free of the world, safe from interruption, with nothing before me but the single task of keeping the illusion of the soldiers spinning before Skobelev's eyes.

How long we remained in that dancing emptiness I could not tell. Now and again I remembered Alice and Harry, but the pain of knowing that I had lost them in this world was eased by my sense of the bond that joined their souls to mine. How could we be truly parted, when my love for them was what made my path back to the world strong and safe whenever I needed it?

Then a different kind of need blazed through the overworld, like a pillar of rolling fire. I felt Tamai's presence. For a moment I thought she had come to join us in the dance of illusion; then she was far away, too far for me to reach while my mind stayed locked with my sisters', falling into the infinite sky of the overworld and burning as she fell.

I could not know what had befallen her or where she was now. I could not go to her aid. All the strength of our joined minds was now bent to maintaining this single illusion; break one link in the circle, and all would collapse.

CHAPTER TWENTY-TWO

With the first half-light of dawn Tamai sent Dushmuni to spy out the land for her. The link between their minds broke when Dushmuni flew out through the broken top of the tower, as if the Earth Tower would not let Tamai exercise even so much of her power as was needed to keep her bond with an eagle soaring high over the City. Tamai lived Dushmuni's flight in her imagination: black wings outstretched to catch the currents of rising air, soaring in diminishing circles higher and higher, becoming one with the winds.

But imagination was not enough; she was bound to earth. Standing at the base of the stone wall, Tamai let her head sink until her forehead rested against the stones. Even the free flight of the mind was forbidden her now. The tower was dark and hopeless; the first light of the sun had been blotted out by clouds and mist and there was no way to mark the passage of time. She began to think the eagle had been gone far too long, long enough to survey Gandhara and half the world besides; then she reproved herself for doubt. But the question remained. Would Dushmuni return to this prison, having tasted the wind again?

I came back to you yesterday, when you were first prisoned here and I could not hear your mind. The thought was not quite in words; Tamai felt the reproof, saw an image of a mother eagle returning to a nest to feed her young. The opening high above her head was filled with black wings churning the air in a dramatic last-minute stop; then a twelve-pound mass of black and golden feathers, wings tucked tight, fell through the tower to land full force on Tamai's shoulder. The eagle's weight knocked her to one knee.

That hurt! She let Dushmuni feel the memory of her fall.

And you hurt me. Again Tamai sensed the image of the mother eagle returning to the nest, this time mingled with an aura of faint reproach.

"You're right," Tamai said aloud. "I should have trusted you. Sometimes, these last two days, I've felt as if the world were falling away under my feet. I don't know what I *can* trust in."

Dushmuni rubbed her beak up and down Tamai's sleeve, then leaned her head near to Tamai's and shared images of what she had seen outside. Tamai winced at the crystal-sharp view of Gandhara's scarred walls and broken roofs. But there was worse outside the walls: spoiled fields, half a mountainside stripped to bare stumps of trees where the Rus army had been cutting firewood, soldiers encamped in the near pastures, and everywhere the burnt remains of the isolated cabins where herdsmen and huntswomen had once lived, outside the walls of Ghandara but still citizens.

The field of view dipped and turned suddenly, leaving Tamai dizzy until she adjusted to Dushmuni's memory of a quick banking turn to carry her south on a warm updraft. There, encamped on the high bluff across the valley of the Tears of Lunang, were the redcoats of the Angrezi army. Dushmuni's curiosity had carried her on down the river valley, past that camp. What had she been looking for? The main army? There was no good way to ask, and Tamai hesitated to interrupt the flow of memories that was giving her at least some faint illusion of the freedom of the sky. She relaxed and let the stream of images flow by: cliffs, deep shadowed gorges, fortified villages, springs trickling down to join the river. And as she watched, something of Dushmuni's sensations during that long reconnaissance came to her: a deep unease, a certainty that something was not right in the south. Could it have been the signs of the flood that disturbed the eagle so? That wall of water from the half-melted glacier had crashed through the valleys to the south, breaking trees and carrying along a tide of mud and boulders with it, scarring the land where it passed.

Tamai stiffened at the sight of moving things coming up the valley, moving clumsily but much faster than any man. Most of them clung like flies to the side of a sheer cliff far above the remnants of the floodwaters. Tamai thought she saw mules' ears and hooves, and sparks of light, but the eagle's memories showed her no clear details. It seemed Dushmuni had been afraid even to look closely at the things on the cliff. But that distant glimpse was more than enough.

Abruptly the view spun away again and Tamai saw air, clouds, the glistening line of the river far below, the blue walls and broken roofs of Gandhara, a crowd of brightly dressed people in the open square around the dancing place, the higher buildings of the northeast quarter, the dark opening in the Earth Tower. A thrust of powerful talons pushed her against the wall as Dushmuni, her memories transferred, launched herself upwards to her favorite perch well above Tamai's head level. The eagle settled on the outthrust stone ledge and stared down at Tamai.

"Yush," Tamai said softly. "Yush in the valley. Many of them, and all in bodies. Well, we can take care of those, can't we? Mirjan was saying—"

Not if they weren't warned. The wisewomen would hardly be on guard against an attack from the south. If the yush came over the walls while everybody was repelling another of Skobelev's attacks—and before the demons even reached those walls, there were the Angrezi soldiers on the bluff, and the villages between here and

the place they had seen, and nothing to defend all those
people from the insensate hunger of the *yush*. They
would have to be warned; everybody would have to be
warned, somehow. And Dushmuni couldn't speak to anyone but Tamai, and the door was barred—

Tamai looked up at the gray light coming in at the top
of the tower. She began unwinding her embroidered
sash. It was the finest garment she possessed, woven on
Gandharan looms with a weft of Khitai silk for color and
a warp of north wind for strength. "Isn't it lucky," she
told Dushmuni, "that I decided to dress as well as I
could for my—triumphal—entry into Gandhara? Come
down for a moment. I need your help."

The first few people Tamai saw in the streets gave her
a vague glance, as if they almost recognized her but were
not quite sure it was her, and she blessed the bitterness
that had made her so reclusive during her last years in
Gandhara. *And,* she thought with grim amusement, she
might also thank Dizane for the speed and secrecy with
which the Council had arrested and tried her. Most people in Gandhara "knew" she had gone south, and therefore weren't expecting to see her hurrying through the
narrow tangle of streets between the north gate and the
dancing square. And hardly anybody knew that she had
been arrested by order of the Council. As long as she
didn't meet a wisewoman of the High Council before she
managed to get her warning across, she should be all
right.

Her luck ran out in the Street of the Oryx, only steps
from the square. There was a powerful hum of magic
called out and amplified all around those streets, the air
fairly crackled with it; Tamai's loose braid was turning
into a spitting mass of dry hair and she could feel the
fire trying to come through her. Half her wits were occupied with trying to damp down her involuntary response
to all the power in the square before somebody accused
her of defying the Council's ban, the rest of her mind
was trying to figure out what to say when she did reach

the wisewomen in the square, and she walked straight into one of the two men in Gandhara who knew exactly where she was supposed to be at this time.

"Tamai!" Mirjan's hands came down hard on her shoulders. His voice was low, almost a whisper. "What are you doing here? How did you get out? Look, I can't leave to take you back to the Earth Tower, not now, there's something very important going on in the square. You'd better slip back by yourself now and hope no one sees you— How did you get out, anyway? I thought the Earth Tower was spelled against your power."

In the midst of her worry Tamai found that she still could enjoy a moment of triumph. "It is spelled," she said. "The wisewomen of Council were so intent on keeping me from using my power, they forgot that anybody can climb. The top of the tower is all broken open from Russian shells, didn't any of you people notice?"

And that was enough on that subject, no need to mention her raw, scraped hands or the ache in her shoulders or the fact that her best sash of windstream and silk would never be the same again after an eagle's talons had gripped the fine soft stuff and dropped it over a projecting stub of masonry in the broken place. And certainly there was no need to discuss the three times the sash had slipped free from its precarious hold before Dushmuni managed to drop it where it could catch well, or how hard she'd fallen one of those times. Tamai pushed back the knowledge of bone-deep aches in knee and side and shoulder, the stinging of hands scraped raw against the rough raw edges of masonry, and gave Mirjan a battered but cocky grin.

He didn't seem to appreciate her accomplishment; he was worrying again about her chances of getting back in the same way she'd come out before anyone else discovered her escape.

"Mirjan," Tamai said patiently, "I can't go back. Not yet. Dushmuni has shown me something I have to warn the Council about, and I can't reach them from inside the Tower. And I can't call them from the overworld, because it'll be exile if I use the Disciplines." Not to mention that without Louisa to guide her back to this world, she would probably never find her way back to her body. "So—since every wisewoman in Gandhara seems to be standing in the dancing place this morning—I have to go there. Now will you let me pass, or do we have to fight? I don't know if I can still throw you or not, Mirjan, but I know I will if that's what I have to do to get past you."

Mirjan flushed darkly. "I don't know either. But *will* you slow down and listen for a bit? I thought you'd changed, but no, here you go again, stubborn as a three-year-old, so damn sure everybody's out to do you down and so damn ready to fight—look, Tamai, you interrupt the Council now and it's the end of Gandhara, understand? Didn't you wonder why they'd set guards round all the streets leading to the dancing ground?"

"It may also," Tamai said wearily, "be the end of Gandhara if I *don't* interrupt the Council. There's an army of *yush* in physical bodies coming from the south. They'll suck up the Hunza villages and the Angrezi soldiers and then they'll be over our walls. The Council has to call out everybody to guard the south valley. And no, I didn't realize the place was guarded all round—this was the first street I tried. Just my bad luck I had to run into you."

But she listened anyway while Mirjan told her what he knew of the morning's work: that the Angrezi Colonel Vaughan was even now negotiating with Skobelev, claiming that he had an army already in Gandhara, while the linked minds of Louisa Westbrook and all the living wisewomen of Gandhara created the illusion of that army around the reality of a single battered toy soldier.

Tamai sighed and shook her head when he'd finished. "You're right. We can't interrupt them."

"But," said Mirjan with a slight smile, "fortunately, we don't need the wisewomen to fight *yush*, not if they're in their bodies."

"That," Tamai told him, "is what I was counting on. So far I have not actually broken any Council laws."

"Breaking out of the Earth Tower?"

"They didn't *tell* me to stay in there," she pointed out. "They just assumed I would have to, since it was spelled against me. All that is forbidden to me is to use the Disciplines. If we fight the *yush* with songs and noises to distract them, water and *leluril* to break up the forces that hold their stolen bits of bodies together—in all that, I break no binding of the Council's. But I need the wise-women to call everyone together . . ." Or did she? Tamai began to smile. Perhaps she had been as foolish as the Council, thinking there were no powers but those the women of Gandhara called from the earth and the over-world. For fighting demons in this world, men would do as well as women; and she knew where there were men enough, if she could just persuade them to follow her.

"*Leluril*. Yes." Mirjan frowned. "Now that's a problem. We've already turned most of the bowls and trays in the city into ammunition."

As Mirjan fretted, Tamai felt light and new strength flowing through her. All their problems could be solved in the same place. "I know where we can get *leluril*," she told him. A memory tugged at her mind—Louisa angry, in a cold place, complaining that she could not concentrate. "And music, too—but we must hurry. Come with me."

"I have to stand guard on the square," Mirjan said automatically, and then, "Where?" Already he was scanning the streets for a kinsman to replace him.

"I go to the house of the Angrez first, then to the south gate," Tamai called over her shoulder. "Meet me there."

There was something wrong in the house where the Angrez had been quartered. A brooding silence hung over the bottom room; Lieutenant McAusland was study-ing an old map with great intensity; Captain Westbrook had a fresh bruise on his jaw. Tamai ignored the signs of strife. Quarrels between the Angrez were none of her business, not now. She explained to McAusland what she needed and was pleased to see his ready comprehension; after all, he had never seen the *yush* raised in Peshawar, only its stinking remains after Tamai drew its spirit into the overworld. But he had seen enough, one way or another, to believe what she told him now of the danger facing the army and the southern villages.

Captain Westbrook was another matter. Tamai would have been happy to leave him out of the planning. She could expect neither understanding nor belief from this hostile Angrez, and she did not have time to explain the world to him. Sullen, abstracted, he stared at the wall while she talked to McAusland and seemed likely to ignore the two of them. But at the last minute he heaved himself up and announced that he would accompany them.

"*Yush* are demons," he said flatly. "I've seen demons. In the glacier. No offense, McAusland, but you need somebody who can direct the field force. Tactical experience."

When they reached the south gate, Mirjan was there—but not alone; to Tamai's appalled sight, it looked at first as if all the young people of Gandhara were with him.

"Not all," Mirjan reassured her. "Just the wounded. The others will stay on guard around the square, in case Skobelev doesn't believe our illusion."

And indeed, nearly everyone there limped, or wore a tattered bandage, or swung along with a crutch and a stick to take the place of wounded or missing limbs. Tamai felt tears prickling her eyes at the sight. Mirjan's little sister was there, cheerful as always beneath a bandage that covered her right eye and half her cheek. Others there she recognized, one by one, and wished she hadn't: so much beauty, strength and grace marred forever! Did they hate her for having escaped the worst of the siege? Better not to ask that.

"Right," she said briskly. "Now, you are experts in fighting *yush*, not I, so as we go along to the Angrez camp you must instruct . . ." Her voice stopped in her throat. At the back of the bedraggled crew was one man who stood straight and looked at her from an unmarred face. She would have thought him unwounded, but for the dull emptiness in his eyes. She could not keep up her brisk confident talk with Paluk staring at her like that, with all that lay between them choking her.

Gordon Westbrook looked at Tamai with a question in his eyes. He was expecting her to go on. They all were. She shook her head and glanced at Mirjan. Couldn't he go on for her? It was his experience they needed now.

Westbrook drew in one long breath and straightened his shoulders and lifted his chin. From a brooding scarecrow of a man he managed to transform himself—almost—into the officer of the Raj who had fought and danced and drunk through twelve long years of regimental service in the Northwest Province.

"Right," he said. "You, and you—" He jerked his chin at Mirjan and Paluk. "Tell us what we need to know—as we go on—make plans, what?"

He spoke in short, jerky rushes, like a man still fighting his inner demons. But he seemed to be paying attention to what they had to say. And as the military aspects of the problem engaged his man, he became more and more the officer of the regiment, less the demon-haunted wreck who'd come out of the Kanjut hills. As they went down the precipitous slope to the river valley, he shouted out questions in his broken Gandharan.

"Routine," he said in an undertone to McAusland. "Hill fighting. Tactics. Saw something like this in the Black Hills of Waziristan, back in '79."

"What, *yush*?" McAusland exclaimed, startled.

"No. Same lie of the land, though. Coming up a nullah. Superior force. Anyway, rather fight your *yush*, whatever they are, than Waziris."

"By God, *I* wouldn't!"

Westbrook might be operating mostly on automatic recollection of past engagements, but even on that level he was more efficient than the Gandharans, who had no history at all of military organization—nothing but the old ballads of Suri Khazara and the White Huns. And whatever his private troubles, he was able to put them aside, at least for the moment, while he thought out the tactics required for the coming battle. By the time they reached the valley, he was able to give orders and make the beginnings of a plan. In passing out his commands he used a tone the Gandharans had never heard from a mere man—but he expected, and got, obedience. By the time they had forded the river and started up to the Angrezi camp, Westbrook had shaped the tattered crowd of irregular forces into something resembling a coherent troop; he had learned more than any of them singly knew about the technique of fighting _yush_; and he had made most of them laugh at least once and had given them all the feeling that victory awaited them.

"He is good at what he does," Tamai said wonderingly to McAusland.

"Yes. Damn shame he's such a bastard the rest of the time, isn't it?" McAusland's fist rotated slowly and Tamai noticed that the knuckles were scraped. "Of course," he said in an undertone, "he's good at _that_, too."

Gordon Westbrook continued to display his best side when they reached the Angrez camp. With a few words he had the sentry who challenged him and the subaltern who managed the camp under his spell, obeying his orders without question—and some of those orders must have seemed exceedingly strange to men who had never faced an enemy like the _yush_ coming up the valley. No muskets? No forming square? No chance to charge the foe?

"Think in terms of _guerilla_ warfare," Westbrook told Lieutenant O'Keefe. "Surely some of you studied the Spanish campaigns of the Peninsular War?"

"You're expecting us to take tactics from a war that's seventy years old?"

"The enemy we are facing," Westbrook told the young lieutenant, "is much, much older than that." For a moment his mask of control slipped and Tamai saw black, endless despair where his eyes should have been. Then he shook himself, like a man shaking off an attack from behind, and she thought that she must have been imagining things. "You've got the telegraph wire ready? Stripped the insulation off? Good. And the portable phonograph—it was clever of you to think of that, young lady," he told Tamai.

The faint patronizing tone of his words set her teeth on edge. So, too, did his insistence that they had no time to advance down the river valley to save the villages immediately downstream. But when she saw the depth and thoroughness of his preparations, she had to agree. The man might be a bastard, but he knew what he was doing. In this brief walk from Gandhara to the river camp he had not only mastered the principles of fighting *yush* in their bodies, he had also translated those principles to a form which four hundred sepoys and three officers could use. Within the hour he had men and equipment dispersed about the river valley where the ambush could do most good. If they had spent that time marching south, as Tamai first wanted to do, they might not even have reached the first village downstream; and they would have faced the *yush* as a vulnerable column of straggling troops, not as a deadly ambush.

The Gandharans were dispersed, one or two with each group of sepoys, so that in each group there would be somebody who had seen *yush* before and would not panic at the sight of the moving carrion. Farthest downstream, where they would be first to confront the *yush*, two small groups crouched behind rocks. Mirjan and Captain Westbrook commanded the sepoys on the left bank; Tamai and Lieutenant McAusland were sent with the group on the right bank. "That way," Westbrook said to her in his atrocious Gandharan. "Have one in each lead party who have see *yush* before, and one officer who command troops do right thing."

"Your reasoning is tolerably clear to me," Tamai said in English.

Once they were all in place, there was nothing to do

but wait. Tamai thought of it as a form of hunting. Sometimes you had a long and tiring stalk before there was any sign of your prey; sometimes you had to wait for long hours before the prey moved into range.

Dushmuni was not fond of this form of hunting, and indicated as much, emphatically, with bird language that even McAusland could follow—ruffled feathers, wings outstretched and folded again, great talons kneading a rock with force that would have paralyzed a man's shoulder. Finally, with some misgivings about letting the eagle fly free in her state of yarak, Tamai allowed Dushmuni to soar above the valley. The eagle quartered the hillside above the waiting troops methodically, flushing and devouring small game as if she had not eaten for weeks. After she had taken a brace of red-legged partridges she calmed down and rode the wind currents to a soaring position high above the watchers. Tamai followed her flight, exulting in the sensation of freedom, the warm air like a pillow supporting her, the colder down draft rushing through her extended pinions. The Tears of Lunang glittered like a braid of silver and moonlight between the rocky cliffs; the world from this height, filtered through an eagle's vision, was tiny and precise and very bright.

And marred, along the southern edge, with a foulness like oily smoke. Tamai shuddered with Dushmuni's abrupt plunge through the air, wings folded, falling like a rock until at the last moment the powerful wings beat the air and talons still red with the blood of the last partridge gripped Tamai's shoulder.

McAusland looked at Tamai's set face, nodded once, and waved his arm in a wide sweeping signal to the watchers across the valley. Ten men on either side of the river tightened their grip on the lines of wire that now strayed across the river bottom. Gordon Westbrook dashed from the cover of his rocks to the sandy spur where Lieutenant O'Keefe's portable phonograph sat cranked up and ready for action. He tripped the lever holding back the tone arm and made it back to shelter before the first grating sounds echoed across the valley.

A cracked voice, scratchy with sand and wind and the accumulated small mishaps of campaign, began a light baritone rendering of "The Last Rose of Summer."

And the *yush* came around the bend in the cliff, clinging to handholds in the sides with the feet of mules and the rotting fingers of dead men.

A low monotonous noise beside her disturbed Tamai's fierce concentration. McAusland was deathly pale beneath his tan; his blue-black hair was like ink above the sickly pallor, and his lips were moving in a continued low-voiced invocation of his gods.

The *yush* were close, now, passing right by their hiding place, intent on investigating the box that made sounds. The Angrezi baritone who had made the music, five years and several thousand miles away, sang on undisturbed as the carrion bodies gathered around the flaring horn of the gramophone.

"Our Father which art in heaven . . ." McAusland muttered under his breath.

"Lunang, forgive me that I have defiled Your waters with these things!" Tamai murmured.

The first song ended in a grating screech and the *yush* began to lose interest even before they had all come down from the cliff. A long tail of wire appeared, straining against the river's current, making an ominous black line behind the demons. Across the river, Gordon Westbrook cursed the sepoys who were about to panic and raise their wires before all the *yush* had drifted into the trap. He stood up and waved his arm, gesturing emphatically: down! not yet!

Some of the *yush* began to turn heads full of glassy dead eyes towards the place where Westbrook and Mirjan hid. The Irish baritone began a new song dripping with martial pride and sorrow for a lost race. *"The harp that once through Tara's halls the soul of music shed. . . ."* The demons turned back to poke at this fascinating new toy.

More *yush* appeared, and yet more, and then the cliffs were empty and the sands around the portable gramophone were black with them, like a swarm of flies gathered on a piece of meat in the sun. Gordon Westbrook stood again and raised his arm emphatically.

This time one of the *yush* on the edge of the crowd stared at Westbrook and began to move towards him.

"*Now hangs as mute on Tara's walls as if that soul were fled,*" sang the baritone.

"Down, man!" muttered McAusland. 'Why doesna' the fool get down where they'll not see him?"

The sepoys positioned on each side of the river hauled at their lines. Rows of copper wire, glistening with water, rose from the muddy current; looped themselves round improvised stick-pulleys, became a net that closed on the assembled *yush*. Sparks showered from the edges of the crowd of demon-bodies, and rotting bits of mules fell to the sand amid pools of dark stinking liquid. The *yush* in the center, closest to the gramophone, pushed and struggled to get out, and in so doing, pushed more of their fellows onto the nets of deadly *leluril*.

The tinny musical voice went on as if its audience were still entranced. "*So sleeps the pride of former days, now glory's thrill is o'er.*"

"As foolish as any human mob, aren't they?" said McAusland with satisfaction.

But one side of the net had not quite closed, and the *yush* that had been looking at Gordon Westbrook, together with a few that had been standing near it, oozed through the gap in the wires unharmed. McAusland jumped to his feet and yelled directions at the sepoys. The second and third sets of men in ambush swung into action, rising from the high slopes to cast nets of telegraph wire down directly on the free-moving *yush*.

The sands around the gramophone were now a mass of semi-liquid putrescence in which hoofs and ears and a few bones lay while the machine poured out its lament unheeding. "*And hearts that once beat high for praise, now feel that pulse no more.*" On the hillside across the river from McAusland and Tamai, the last *yush* were being netted, one by one, too stupid to see the menace in the lines of copper wire that dropped around them and dissipated their soulforces. Only one remained free of the net.

But that one had almost reached Gordon Westbrook.

"Why doesn't the man *do* something!" McAusland's nails were digging into Tamai's arm.

Tamai thought she knew. She could still remember the *yush* she battled in Peshawar. The pattern of lights in darkness that held the demon's soulstuff was like a net to draw the onlooker in. Gordon Westbrook would be staring at that whirling obscenity now, feeling its call as Tamai had felt it, fighting the desire to join the pattern with its promise of something beyond human imagining.

Only Nirmali's grace had saved her from that deadly embrace.

Gordon Westbrook did not know Nirmali. And if he was calling on his gods, Tamai could not hear him. But she could see his face clearly enough from where she and McAusland lay concealed. He was looking full at the *yush*, and he looked like a man welcoming a friend he had never hoped to see in this life.

Even as they watched, he took two steps forward, right into the darkness and corrupt ever-moving life that was the *yush*.

"Dear God!" McAusland breathed. "It's got him!"

Another syrupy verse poured out of the gramophone. *"No more to chiefs and ladies bright, the harp of Tara swells."*

The circle of copper wire that the sepoys cast down at the *yush* floated down onto emptiness. The demon moved aside at the last minute: then, with incredible speed and agility, it made straight up the cliffs towards the ledge where the sepoys were hiding. As it went its form seemed to lengthen in some places and shorten in others, until the fat cylinder of blackness with its stubby mule-limbs was transformed into a man-shaped cloud, hideous, rotting, and yet retaining something of the athletic grace that had characterized Gordon Westbrook's movements.

The head of the *yush* now had a definite shape, too; a scornful, long-nosed, Angrezi profile, with living eyes that blinked and scanned the cliff as intelligently as any hunting animal. And it seemed to know exactly where its prey was hidden, and exactly how to move to evade the last coils of telegraph wire and to block the path by which the sepoys might scramble to safety.

"The chord alone that breaks at night, its tale of ruin tells."

Just above the demon, a man in a red coat stood up, shouted something in Punjabi, and threw himself right over the ledge with a bayonet gripped in his right hand, stabbing forward into the demon's body. The *yush* moved swiftly to take the blow of the bayonet in an arm built of a dead mule's skin. The bayonet stabbed through the flaccid unresisting stuff and the sepoy fell on, into the heart of the churning blackness, and his cry was turned into a gurgling lament that seemed to echo on forever between the two walls of the gorge. Two other sepoys leapt from the far end of the ledge into the river. One fell between rocks, where the current rushed green and strong, and Tamai did not see what befell him after that. The other landed on a boulder at the water's edge, one leg twisted under him at an unnatural angle. The *yush* changed direction and began flowing down the side of the cliff. The sepoy saw it coming and his hands scrabbled frantically at the sides of the boulder as he tried to drag himself away from the demon. "That's Mirza Abdullah," McAusland groaned. "He saved my life in Baluchistan. I can't let him—"

He broke cover and ran forward, skipping and jumping over the rough ground, waving his hands and shouting at the top of his voice over the metallic song of the phonograph. "Will you come and fight, then, damn you!"

"McAusland." Tamai caught up with him at the water's edge. "It won't come. It knows that the running water will kill it, as surely as the *leluril*."

"I thought you said the curst things were stupid!"

"This one ... has drawn intelligence from somewhere." And Tamai thought she knew where. Gordon Westbrook hadn't been consumed like the other victims of the *yush*; he had walked forward, hands outstretched, accepting its unspoken offer of power and knowledge beyond the mortal lot. What they confronted now, across the river, was only half a demon. The other half consisted of Gordon Westbrook's keen military intelligence, now turned against his own kind in the service of the *yush*.

The *yush* ignored McAusland after its first skeptical glance towards him. It bent over the wounded sepoy; Tamai could see the life being sucked out of him. McAusland waded into the churning water, shouting like a madman. He would cross in a moment, and then the *yush* would take him, too.

"Come on, damn you!" he shouted back at Tamai. "We've got to take this thing now, before it gets any more of us!"

"Thus Freedom now so seldom wakes, the only cry she gives . . ."

Tamai sank to her knees at the side of the river. She had no black cloak to draw over her head, not even a sash to cover her eyes, and this time Louisa Westbrook was not there to bring her back. She cast one quick regretful glance at a world that suddenly seemed too bright and clear and perfect to leave. The wonder of the sky and the red rocks above her head, the crisp winter air and the icy shock of the river current joined in one moment of perfect beauty.

"Is when some heart indignant breaks, to show that she still lives."

If she looked any longer, the world would seduce her back into life, draw her in the way the demon's promise had caught Gordon Westbrook. Tamai laid her head on the smooth, sun-warmed surface of an ancient boulder, shut out the light with an arm crooked around her forehead, and went into the overworld. Her last coherent thought was that even if she had expected to survive this journey, she would come back to exile for breaking the

Council's binding; so it really did not matter that there was no one to draw her back.

The fabric of the world trembled and became transparent, a fine-stretched gauze on which tiny figures moved and spoke incomprehensible words. When Tamai moved, her hands shredded the gauze, and it burst into flames where she touched it. She stood very still, wondering what damage she had done already. Around there the overworld shifted and changed shape continually, a fluid melody of colors and tastes and fierce burning needs that sucked her towards them. She swayed towards that hunger and rocks tumbled somewhere far away; a demon laughed; and Gordon Westbrook's blue eyes looked at her from a cloud of smoke and fire.

Too late, little native girl, his mind mocked her. *I know all your tricks now, and much more. Nothing can stop us now.*

What do you want? she screamed at him. *Is this what you want—to be a* yush? *To feast on souls and carrion? To be called to the service of any Khitai or Bod master who spills enough blood in your name?*

That is what a demon is. His thoughts were calm, instructing her, but without passion behind them; as if it did not matter what she thought, who would so soon be crushed out of this world and the other one. *I am more than that. The demon has not consumed me. We have joined. You cannot imagine the power that lies before me now. Will you share it?*

Tamai shook her head, and water spilled through a new opening in a cliff somewhere on the painted gauze stuff of the other world.

You can have power far beyond those Disciplines of the Gandharan witches. In that world you are a barren freak, forbidden to use what little powers you have. Join with us and know the root of all things, the shapes of all words. Somehow the dancing lights within the cloud reflected the demon-Gordon's message, spiraling and splintering into patterns too dazzling and too complex for Tamai to grasp in the brief time before they changed again, promising all the secrets of life to the one who had time to know their structure. *You can be stronger than any of this precious Council*, Westbrook hummed at her—or was it the *yush* speaking? What did Westbrook know of the High Council? *You will be able to unravel the light that the Dhi Lawan weaves, unbraid the strands of Nirmali's hair and leave the world in darkness. They will be afraid of you, these people who rejected you and called you freak. They will worship you.*

For a moment all the demon's lights and shadows joined together in a picture of Gandhara reborn, a Gandhara where Kazhirbri wept and acknowledged that she had never been Lightweaver and should not have usurped the position of the Dhi Lawan; a Gandhara where all the wisewomen in Council knelt to a Tamai ten feet tall and made of shadow—a Daughter of Darkness to replace the Dhi Lawan, the Daughter of Light.

And in the eternal night beyond the walls of Gandhara, Nirmali wept that Her daughter had forgotten her, and the universe was unbound, light from darkness, water from land, until all was level nothingness under this monstrous Tamai-demon.

Tamai felt the heat of her stay in the overworld consuming her physical body. Even in this world, blisters were rising on her hands and face. So much fire within her, so much useless power—and the Council had forbidden her even to experiment with it, to discover what she might be able to do!

Come, the demon purred, and this time it was all *yush* and nothing at all of Captain Westbrook—nothing except the blue eyes and the intelligence. The soulstuff was all *yush. Come. Join us. If you do not, we will crush you utterly.*

But if it—they—could do that, why were they trying so hard to persuade her?

Perhaps there was still one last use for the fire within her. Tamai reached deep within, to the place where her childhood pain and terror burned hot, and drew fire out of her own soulstuff. The flames braided through her fingers and scorched her skin in both worlds, and the *yush* seemed to have moved back a little.

Foolish little girl! You will only burn your own people in the other world. Be careful what fires you start there.

The danger of fire, for once, seemed relatively slight. Fires on a barren cliff, where winter had killed what little vegetation might grow, where a melted glacier had flooded the whole valley only the day before?

"I think *not*," Tamai said in her own physical voice, between clenched teeth, and the bones of the riverbed stirred and wakened to her voice. *Nirmali, Dizane, Lunang, Kshumai, help me now!*

With each holy Name a pillar of living fire grew between this world and the underworld. Nirmali's was silver light, Dizane's was green and constantly growing with new leaves and buds, Lunang's was water colder than the glacier's ice, Kshumai's was red as blood. Tamai stood in the space within the four pillars and the *yush* with Gordon Westbrook's mind crouched outside and yammered words that she could no longer hear, and she braided the fire of her own soul into a net that spun out around her, around and over and through the four pillars. The braided strands of flame danced around the *yush* and its sparks whirled in counterpoint, too many and too fast for her to catch.

Even if you live, you will go to exile! What are these people, that you would throw yourself away for them?

"I," said Tamai, "will not be the first to taste exile." Her fingers wound through the net of fire; she reached into the four pillars of living soulflame, silver light that flared through the bones of her hands, green soulstuff that ran tendrils of growing vines under her skin, essence-of-water that chilled her blood to crystal, red blood of Kshumai that spilled like fountains from her own veins. Each touch was exquisitely painful, taking her apart piece by piece and remoulding her in the shapes of the four Goddesses at once. It was more knowledge than she could hold, closer to the Goddesses than she dared walk, and they would destroy her for daring to

weave with their lights; but the four strands held firm like
fine-spun thread, and between her fingers they became a
skein of multicolored fire that opened out as wide as the
night sky and then closed like a hand over the bright
sparks of the *yush*.

The last thing to disappear was one of Gordon Westbrook's blue eyes, looking reproachful.

There was no time to savor her victory. Her hands and
face were hot and cold at once, burning with light and
freezing with water, bleeding for Kshumai and being
healed by Dizane as the four Goddesses possessed her
together. There were fire-blisters all over her body, and
her braid smelled of singed hair, and she was falling—
falling away from the perfect space between the four
pillars, and weeping and fighting the hands on her body
that insisted on drawing her back to the world where all
her burns would hurt like any other fire.

CHAPTER TWENTY-THREE

Fire all around her, cracked lips, a throat raw from silent screams. Someone was holding her blistered hand so tightly that a throbbing agony rose through her arm. A strange land danced in her dreams: a cool green place inhabited by two laughing, white-faced children. She longed for the cool mists of that land, but the way to it was through the aching hold on her burnt hand. Through the world where dead *yush* and living Angrez soldiers and wisewomen of the High Council all would ask questions she could not answer.

"She's trying to say something."

The voice was urgent, well-loved, familiar. Tamai opened her eyes the barest slit and sun dazzled her.

"Try to drink this, Tamai. Jakunei says it is a healing potion."

Tepid, bitter water trickled between her lips. There was a sourness in it that stung her throat, but she was so thirsty that she swallowed anyway. She tried to ask for more, but she was so tired. Sleep took her, and before she could force her lips to shape the words she was drifting back into the shadowy space between the over-world and this world, between Nirmali's grace and a misty green land where foreign children played.

Movement, aching, new pains, and the world swaying

366

under her. Tamai looked out onto dusk and saw the side of the hill moving beneath her head, falling away into nothingness. She tried to cry out that they must not penetrate the wisewomen's veil, that she would not fight the decree of exile; but her throat was still too sore for speech.

All her senses were tangled together. She tasted sun and moonlight. There was a blanket under her right hand, rough wool; the coarse threads made a noise like a drum under her fingers. Whispering voices swayed like pillars of shadow around her.

"Look at her there, what she has done for us! How can you speak of sending her away?"

"She may die of it."

"If she dies then there is nothing to argue about." The third voice was a thin wire of *leluril*, harsh and resonant. She who had been Kazhirbri, who was now the Dhi Lawan. Through her deepest dreams Tamai knew that voice.

"And if she lives?" It was one of the whispers again, flimsy and insubstantial as smoke wreathing about her head.

"If she lives . . . the law is the law." The copper wire of Kazhirbri's voice wound about Tamai's spirit, bound her, left her suspended outside the gates of sense and time.

Outside Gandhara, forever.

Blue smoke and golden light in a bowl of polished *leluril*, the sides pierced in a pattern of diamonds. Cedar beams above her head; a sunwoven coverlet, light and warm and soft, over her body. The foreign woman still knelt beside her, holding Tamai's blistered fingers between her two white hands. Her face was tired and drawn, but now Tamai could remember her name.

"You look tired, Louisa," she whispered. "You should sleep."

The Angrezi woman burst into tears. Beside her, some-

one else was crying. Tamai tilted her head back a fraction
and saw Paluk and Mirjan.

Memory returned. Louisa was supposed to be guiding
the wisewomen of Gandhara in their greatest illusion.
What was she doing here?

"The Rus?"

"General Skobelev has retreated. He agreed to our
terms last week."

"Last week!"

"You have wandered long," Paluk said quietly. "The
Angrezi woman has been here with me all the time.
She—brought you back—when I could not." The words
seemed almost dragged out of him. Tamai lay quietly on
her couch of cedar boughs and considered Paluk's face.
He had aged, as they all had. In Paluk's case she did not
think this was entirely a bad thing; he would be slower
and steadier now, a man they could trust. But some part
of her mourned her gay, feckless cousin.

"Can you forgive me?"

"There is nothing to forgive," Tamai whispered. "You
did—what you thought best for Gandhara—I, too."

Louisa gave Tamai a watery smile through her tears.
"You don't know how wonderful it is to hear you speaking
to us again. When Lieutenant McAusland brought me to
you, all burned and broken—I came as soon as I could—
we all thought it was too late—Tamai, if you ever do that
again I will *kill* you!"

Tamai moved slightly under the sunweave, took the
pitcher by her bed and drank more of Jakunei's bitter
healing tea. The pain that lanced through her body at
each motion was almost welcome, a proof that she was
indeed alive and in her proper body again. The blisters
of the soulfire were healing already; tonight she felt no
worse than someone who had been caught in a fire, by
next week it would be little more than a bad sunburn.

But that was quite enough. And there were bone-deep
pains that spoke of things shifted in her body that would
never be quite the same again, and in the back of her

mind were memories that could not be shown to anybody else—not even Louisa—especially not Louisa.

"I don't think you will need to make good that threat," she said wryly. "A second time like this would probably kill me without your help."

She lay quietly, sipping the bitter tea when she could and letting strength come back into her body, while Louisa and Paluk and Mirjan vied to tell her what had happened in Gandhara while she was wandering in the overworld. Louisa was formally appointed British Resident now, and Colonel Vaughan had asked Lieutenant McAusland to stay on as her military attaché.

"Not quite the post I'd hoped for," the lieutenant confessed, "but . . . well, it's better than being sent back to Peshawar and away from all this. I want to learn more about Gandhara."

"The climate here is much cooler than in the plains." Tamai wondered briefly if Louisa had lost her mind, to make such an idiotically obvious comment; but her next sentence explained it. "Gandhara should be a good place to raise children—an excellent place for us all to live, don't you think?"

An excellent place to live. I never asked for any other. A pain that had nothing to do with the changes in her body stabbed once through Tamai. She lay very still and carefully did not think of the children she would never see in the streets of Gandhara, or of the fact that she herself would not be there to see Louisa's happiness when she brought her son and daughter home. Of course. Gandhara was far from the heat and sickness of the plains, and there was no more need to protect the children from Gordon Westbrook's uncertain temper; Louisa would have Alice and Harry with her soon, and she would be happy again.

It would be a shame to mar her happiness by asking questions, just now, about the inevitable exile that would follow Tamai's flagrant disobedience of the Council's ban.

Instead she asked how Colonel Vaughan had felt about using Gandharan magic. McAusland and Louisa smiled

at each other and told the story in alternativing sentences. The colonel had apparently managed to make use of
Louisa's illusory soldiers without ever quite admitting to
himself what was going on; by the time he returned from
the Russian camp, Louisa said with a bubble of laughter,
he was already discussing the curious effects of heat
waves and the mirages he had seen as a young man in
the Taklamakan Desert.

Gordon Westbrook was officially described as having
died a hero's death, throwing himself before the enemy
to save the Gandharan Mirjan from an attacker. Lieutenant McAusland had written an affecting account of the
occurrence; it was expected that Captain Westbrook
would be awarded a posthumous medal.

Tamai looked questioningly at Mirjan when she heard
this version of Westbrook's death. He looked back and
raised one eyebrow. "There may be some truth to the
story," he pointed out when Louisa was out of the room.
"I was nearest the *yush* after the Angrezi captain, and it
chose not to take me."

"Yes . . . " Had Westbrook retained something of his
humanity for the first seconds after he merged with the
yush? Enough to turn him aside from the first prey the
yush found? If so, Tamai thought, he must have spent
several long seconds being absorbed with the *yush*, for
the unholy pair of them had shown no such mercy to the
sepoys on the ledge above. She wondered just how long
those seconds had seemed, and shuddered, and tried to
forget the memory of blue eyes in a face composed of
carrion and moving lights. She would not begrudge Gordon Westbrook's shade a medal or any other honor that
might help him rest in peace now.

After the stories were all told she drifted back into
sleep—a natural, healing sleep this time, from which she
was awakened by the noise of people arguing in whispers.
Paluk was sitting on the floor beside her bed; Mirjan
stood beside him, facing Jakunei and blind Akhanai of
the High Council. Louisa was nowhere to be seen.

"We don't leave," Mirjan said, "until Tamai sends us away."

"This is not a matter for men!" hissed Akhanai. "Tamai has been summoned to the Council. The Dhi Lawan is waiting."

"If the Dhi Lawan wants to exile Tamai for breaking a Council ruling," Paluk said, "she'll have to exile me, too."

"And me," said Mirjan, "and my wife and our child-to-be."

Lieutenant McAusland came down from the upper room. "I think the new British Resident would also not be pleased with this action." McAusland's voice made a threat of the statement. "Is not she a member of the High Council by the treaty? And is not the High Council to vote on any case of exile? As her military attaché—"

"*Men.*" Jakunei made a disgusted sound deep in her throat. "Will you solve everything by making war? Your Resident has voted with us on this matter."

"Please." Tamai's voice was scratchy, but at least it obeyed her now. "Jakunei is right. I will abide by the decision of the Council. Will you help me to the Council Hall?" She would have liked to have walked on her own feet to receive the sentence of exile. She would have preferred to be able to walk proudly out of the City as soon as the inevitable words were pronounced. But if the Dhi Lawan was not disposed to allow her that much time to heal, Tamai would not humble herself by begging for it. Nor would she see Louisa's first days as British Resident, the treaty and the peace they had worked so hard to bring about, ruined by a quarrel over her fate. When she went into the overworld to fight the *yush* she had gone willingly enough, knowing the price might be death or exile. Having been spared death, she would not be so ungrateful to Nirmali and Dizane as to balk at paying the lesser price.

But it was very hard to know that Louisa, too, had voted against her. Even understanding that it was the only thing she could do—that Louisa could not possibly begin her tenure as Resident by quarreling with the Dhi Lawan—Tamai felt as if she had lost a friend.

Paluk and Mirjan carried her to the door of the Council hall, but they were not allowed to enter. Tamai managed to stand erect. Sweat sprung out on her forehead and a wave of dizziness swept over her. She would have fallen but for Lieutenant McAusland's supporting hand under her elbow.

"Thank you," Tamai said after a moment. "I can stand now—and—I must go in alone."

The dimness of the Hall was the shadowy darkness of a forest of cedars, tall and fragrant and reaching up to the sky. The trees moved as Tamai passed among them, shivered and became a forest of women in black cloaks, each wisewoman holding fresh branches of cedar in her hands, each one bowing her head and sinking to the red flowered carpet as Tamai passed.

The Dhi Lawan and her sisters of the High Council stood in a semicircle at the end of the path Tamai trod. At one end of the semicircle, in a humble place appropriate for the newest member of the High Council, stood Louisa, wearing a black cape over her full-skirted Angrezi dress. All the Council members wore their capes folded open, so that each woman was framed in her secret history: peacock blues and greens of Lunang's waters, copper spirals of demon-binding, pale moonspun threads of lightweaving dazzled Tamai's eyes. Louisa's cape was one of the plainest there, decorated only with two bands for her two children, the red thread of initiation, and a shimmery lightwoven image of a British soldier for yesterday's achievement.

Tamai wondered dully that they should show the secret glory of their cloaks to one facing exile, almost a foreigner already; but she was too sick and too desperately unhappy to care why the Council did what they did. And after the first glance, she could not bear to look at Louisa again; she kept her eyes on Kazhirbri in the center of the group.

Kazhirbri looked remarkably sour-faced for someone

who was about to enjoy her final victory. Was it that difficult for her even to look at a freak like Tamai, somebody whose aberrant powers called into question the whole system by which Gandharan magic balanced the forces of the overworld? Tamai felt an irreverent urge to tell Kazhirbri, "Cheer up, I won't be around that much longer."

Instead she bowed her head politely and waited for the Dhi Lawan to speak.

"The High Council of Gandhara has considered your case," Kazhirbri said, drawing out the words until Tamai wanted to shriek with impatience. "You have broken a solemn binding of the Council."

"I do not dispute it."

"Some of our wisewomen consider that there may have been cause."

"I do not dispute the Council's ruling." Did Kazhirbri think to provoke her into an argument she could only lose, an argument that would force Louisa to take sides against her or lose face with Council? Was that the point of this agonizingly slow proceeding?

"Apparently," Kazhirbri said, sounding as though each word cost her a tenstring of pure sky-blue turquoise, "apparently, while in violation of our binding, you demonstrated certain—unusual—powers which the Council feels should be recognized and studied more fully. In view of the fact that you used these powers in defense of Gandhara . . ."

The pause was long enough for Tamai to feel a cruel stab of hope. Could Kazhirbri mean that she was not to be exiled after all?

"And," Kazhirbri went on at last, "in view of the fact that none of the existing Disciplines provide for control of these particular powers . . ."

This time the pause was so long that Tamai had to look up. As she raised her head, the wisewomen of the High Council moved together, lifted up a ripple of black folds from the ground and opened a cloak whose inside was slashed by a single broad band of fire and light.

Flames stitched with sun and candlelight, couched down with threads of gold and *leluril*, seemed to leap from the lining of the cloak like living fire.

"Tamai Flameweaver," Kazhirbri said, sour as ever, "the High Council of Gandhara has voted—not unanimously, I assure you—to waive the formal tests which are usual at this time. You are to join your sisters in Council as a wisewoman of Gandhara."

BUILDING A NEW FANTASY TRADITION

The Unlikely Ones by Mary Brown
Anne McCaffrey raved over *The Unlikely Ones*: "What a splendid, unusual and intriguing fantasy quest! You've got a winner here...." Marion Zimmer Bradley called it "Really wonderful ... I shall read and re-read this one." A traditional quest fantasy with quite an unconventional twist, we think you'll like it just as much as Anne McCaffrey and Marion Zimmer Bradley did.

Knight of Ghosts and Shadows
by Mercedes Lackey & Ellen Guon
Elves in L.A.? It would explain a lot, wouldn't it? In fact, half a millennium ago, when the elves were driven from Europe they came to—where else? —Southern California. Happy at first, they fell on hard times after one of their number tried to force the rest to be his vassals. Now it's up to one poor human to save them if he can. A knight in shining armor he's not, but he's one hell of a bard!

The Interior Life by Katherine Blake
Sue had three kids, one husband, a lovely home and a boring life. Sometimes, she just wanted to escape, to get out of her mundane world and *live* a little. So she did. And discovered that an active fantasy life can be a very dangerous thing—and very real.... Poul Anderson thought *The Interior Life* was "a breath of fresh air, bearing originality, exciting narrative, vividly realized characters—everything we have been waiting for for too long."

The Shadow Gate by Margaret Ball
The only good elf is a dead elf—or so the militant order of Durandine monks thought. And they planned on making sure that all the elves in their world (where an elvish Eleanor of Aquitaine ruled in Southern France) were very, very good. The elves of Three Realms have one last spell to bring help ... and received it: in the form of the staff of the new Age Psychic Research Center of Austin, Texas....

Hawk's Flight by Carol Chase
Taverik, a young merchant, just wanted to be left
alone to make an honest living. Small chance of
that though: after their caravan is ambushed Taverik
discovers that his best friend Marko is the last
living descendant of the ancient Vos dynasty. The
man who murdered Marko's parents still wants to
wipe the slate clean—with Marko's blood. They try
running away, but Taverik and Marko realize that
there is a fate worse than death . . . That sooner or
later, you have to stand and fight.

A Bad Spell in Yurt by C. Dale Brittain
As a student in the wizards' college, young Daimbert
had shown a distinct flair for getting himself in
trouble. Now the newly appointed Royal Wizard to
the backwater Kingdom of Yurt learns that his
employer has been put under a fatal spell. Daimbert
begins to realize that finding out who is responsible
may require all the magic he'd never quite learned
properly in the first place—with the kingdom's
welfare and his life the price of failure. Good thing
Daimbert knows how to improvise!

C.J. Cherryh's
The Sword of Knowledge

The Sword of Knowledge Cuts Two Ways . . .

The Roman Empire. Imagine its fall. Now imagine that warring time with *cannon*—and a working system of magic. C.J. Cherryh did. In *The Sword of Knowledge*, we bring you The Fall, according to C.J. Cherryh.

A Dirge for Sabis, C.J. Cherryh & Leslie Fish
The Sabirn Empire is embattled by barbarian hordes. The key to their savior—forbidden knowledge. But will the Sabirn rulers countenance the development of these weapons, even to save themselves?
69824-9 * $3.95   _____

Wizard Spawn, C.J. Cherryh & Nancy Asire
Five centuries have passed and the Sabirn race lies supine beneath the boot of the Ancar. But rumors say that among the Sabirn are some who retain occult knowledge. The Ancar say this is justification for genocide. The Sabirn say genocide is justification for anything. . . .
69838-9 * $3.50   _____

Reap the Whirlwind, C.J. Cherryh & Mercedes Lackey
Another half milennium has passed, and new barbarians are on the rise to threaten the ruling tyrants. Once again, it will be a battle of barbarian vigor and The Sword of Knowledge!
69846-X * $3.95   _____

Other Baen Books by these authors:

The Paladin, C.J. Cherryh
65417-9 * $3.95   _____
Twilight's Kingdoms, Nancy Asire
65362-8 * $3.50   _____
*Carmen Miranda's Ghost is Haunting Space Station
Three* edited by Don Sakers, inspired by a song by
Leslie Fish
69864-8 * $3.95   _____
Knight of Ghosts and Shadows, Mercedes Lackey &
Ellen Guon
69885-0 * $3.95   _____

Anne McCaffrey
vs.
The Planet Pirates

SASSINAK: Sassinak was twelve when the raiders came. That made her just the right age: old enough to be used, young enough to be broken. But Sassinak turned out to be a little different from your typical slave girl. And finally, she escaped. But that was only the beginning for Sassinak. Now she's a fleet captain with a pirate-chasing ship of her own, and only one regret in life: not enough pirates.
BY ANNE MCCAFFREY AND ELIZABETH MOON
69863 * $5.99 _____

THE DEATH OF SLEEP: Lunzie Mespil was a Healer. All she wanted in life was a chance to make things better for others. But she was getting the feeling she was particularly marked by fate: every ship she served on ran into trouble— and every time she went out, she ended up in coldsleep. When she went to the Dinosaur Planet she thought the curse was lifted—but her adventures were only beginning. . . .
BY ANNE MCCAFFREY AND JODY LYNN NYE
69884-2 * $5.99 _____

GENERATION WARRIORS: Sassinak and Lunzie combine forces to beat the planet pirates once and for all. With Lunzie's contacts, Sassinak's crew, and Sassinak herself, it would take a galaxy-wide conspiracy to foil them. Unfortunately, that's just what the planet pirates are. . . .
BY ANNE MCCAFFREY AND ELIZABETH MOON
72041-4 * $4.95 _____